Do The Dead Dream?

An Anthology of the Weird and the Peculiar

Do the dead dream?

"A collection that folds upon itself like a Möbius strip. A twisted landscape of the humane, the weird, and the fantastic."

Mario Acevedo
Author, University of Doom

Do the dead dream?

"Stylistically edgy and willing to muck around in the darker corners of life, the stories in *Do The Dead Dream?* are both bold and gritty. Readers looking to be soothed and reassured about the human condition, seek elsewhere."

Mark Stevens
The Allison Coil Mystery Series

Do the dead dream?

"F. P. Dorchak's anthology—a collection of forty-five short stories—spans decades and showcases the author's wide-ranging talent. With tales that are at turns engaging, suspenseful, twisty and often slyly humorous, Dorchak focuses his penetrating gaze on those things we too often take for granted—and makes us laugh or shiver in the doing. Reading *Do the Dead Dream?* takes you across a threshold into a Kafkaesque world where anything can happen; if Rod Serling were still on Planet Earth, he would be the first to offer his voice for the audio version."

Barbara Nickless
The Sydney Parnell Mystery Series

Do the dead dream?

"So reminiscent of the *Twilight Zone!* Imagine a story between light and shadow, between science fiction and superstition, between what you know about horror, and what horrors one can only imagine. Gritty and beautifully crafted, *Do the Dead Dream?* is the sort of collection readers will enjoy story after story."

J.A. Kazimer
Author of CURSES!

Do the dead dream?

"Do The Dead Dream? is a masterpiece. F. P. Dorchak effortlessly weaves the real and surreal into twisting, epically personal stories. "Etched In Stone" and "Tail Gunner" challenge what we know as real and yet are completely human tales of love, loss, and camaraderie with incredible resonance. This is a collection of the highest order from a supremely talented author."

Kevin Ikenberry
The Protocol War Series

Do the dead dream?

"From the surreal to the all too real, F. P. Dorchak's stories delve into the realms of the mind, otherworldly beings, loves lost, and the fickle nature of death. With a little bit of everything, this collection of stories will haunt readers long after they've closed the book."

Shannon Lawrence
Short Story Author
Blogger, The Warrior Muse

Do the dead dream?

"F. P. Dorchak's short stories take a look at the world in an inside-out, rarely visited way. These are neither happily-ever-*after* tales nor ghost stories solely meant to creep you out. They are worlds that can be deliciously understated like dreams of dreams, as enigmatic as time warps, and as unexpected as falling in all directions at once. We meet werewolves and undead and people whose past lives bleed through. These tales are nostalgia-meets-a-future with nighttime borders that hint something is not quite right, each one putting the reader in a graying state between sleep and wakefulness."

Karen Albright Lin
WritersLaunchPad

Do the dead dream?

"F. P. Dorchak blurs the lines between reality and the paranormal with his vast collection of unnerving tales that are sure to keep you up past midnight."

Joshua Viola
Denver Post bestselling author

Do the dead dream?

"From a dangerously precocious little girl who befriends gargoyles to a conventional guy who discovers (first hand) an invasion of mind-blowing creatures, F. P. Dorchak offers up a collection of horrifying short stories in *Do The Dead Dream?*, which he delivers with an inimitable, unique voice. The reader accompanies Dorchak's characters' bizarre experiences that manifest as rapid-fire flashes of thought-pandemonium . . . as would naturally occur under such unnatural circumstances. Just when you think the path is headed in an obvious direction, Dorchak jerks the road out from under your beliefs to find yourself suddenly drawn along a most unexpected thoroughfare."

Jan C. J. Jones
Executive Producer/Writer
FOREST ROSE PRODUCTIONS, LLC
A Journey with Strange Bedfellows

Do the dead dream?

"You may think you've read it all, but F. P Dorchak's *"Do the Dead Dream?"* will test the limits of your imagination. Picture Stephen King as a mad scientist, mixing bits of *Night Gallery* with a generous helping of *Black Mirror*, a dash of *Altered States*, a pinch of metaphysics, and a healthy dose of surrealism. Dorchak takes you forward and backward in time, puts you in the cockpit of a plane, plunges you into the ocean, and ushers you into other realms you never expected. Buckle up for a unique and unforgettable ride."

Paul Gallagher
Writer/Editor
Blogger, Shadow & Substance

Also by F. P. Dorchak

Novels

Sleepwalkers (2001)
The Uninvited (2013)
ERO (2013)
Psychic (2014)
Voice (2015)

Short Stories

"Clowns" (2016)
"Broken Windows" (2017)

Anthologies

"Tail Gunner":
*The You Belong Collection, Writing and Illustrations from
Longmont Area Residents* (2012)

"Broken Windows":
*You Belong 2016, Words and Images from
Longmont Area Residents* (2016)

Do The Dead Dream? (2017)

**WAILING
LOON**

F. P. Dorchak

Do The Dead Dream?

AN ANTHOLOGY OF THE WEIRD AND THE PECULIAR

 WAILING LOON

COLORADO SPRINGS, COLORADO

Except for, and in addition to the following, all stories have previously been published on the author's website, 2015 – 2016:

"Fear," first appeared in Tyro Magazine #19, edited by Stan Gordon, copyright © 1989 by F. P. Dorchak

"Attention Span," first appeared in Tyro Magazine #26, edited by Stan Gordon, copyright © 1990 by F. P. Dorchak

"The Coming of Light," first appeared in Tyro Magazine #32/33, edited by Stan Gordon, copyright © 1991 by F. P. Dorchak

"Brains ("Mozky")," first appeared in Ikarie: Měsíčník science fiction, publisher Ivan Adamovič, copyright © 1992 by F. P. Dorchak

"St. Vincent," first appeared in Black Sheep #40, published by Madelon Rose Logue, copyright © 2001 by F. P. Dorchak

"Blondie's," first appeared in Black Sheep #45, published by Madelon Rose Logue, copyright © 2002 by F. P. Dorchak

"Etched in Stone," first appeared in The Waking Muse #1, copyright © 2002 by F. P. Dorchak

"The Death of Me," first appeared in Black Sheep #48, published by Madelon Rose Logue, copyright © 2002 by F. P. Dorchak

"Freefallin'," first appeared in Black Sheep #60, published by Madelon Rose Logue, copyright © 2004 by F. P. Dorchak

"The World's Greatest Writer," first appeared in Black Sheep #62, published by Madelon Rose Logue, copyright © 2005 by F. P. Dorchak

"Tick, Tick, Tick, Tock," first appeared in Black Sheep #64, published by Madelon Rose Logue, copyright © 2005 by F. P. Dorchak

"Etched in Stone," first appeared in Apollo's Lyre Ezine, edited by Bret Wright, copyright © 2005 by F. P. Dorchak

"Dark Was The Hour," first appeared in Apollo's Lyre Ezine, edited by Bret Wright, copyright © 2007 by F. P. Dorchak

"Tail Gunner," first appeared in Black Sheep #103, published by Madelon Rose Logue, copyright © 2011 by F. P. Dorchak

"Tail Gunner," reprinted in The You Belong Collection, Writings and Illustrations from Longmont Area Residents, edited by Steve Kenworthy, copyright © 2012 by F. P. Dorchak

"Broken Windows," first appeared in You Belong 2016, Words and Images from Longmont Area Residents, edited by Steve Kenworthy, copyright © 2016 by F. P. Dorchak

"Garden of the Gods," reprinted in Black Sheep #138, published by Madelon Rose Logue, copyright © 2017 by F. P. Dorchak

Always, for Laura

Foreword

I've known F. P. (Frank) Dorchak some 25 years, beginning when we studied together in a critique group. Frank has always been creative, serious, and diligent in his writing and open to learning techniques to expand his considerable natural talent. Even when I worked with Frank in those early years, he was intrigued by *the weird*.

Frank asks questions most of us never consider. *Do the Dead Dream?* He offers a variety of examples of what the dead might dream. He mingles dreams with reality in ways readers may be uncertain which is which—until reflecting back after his book is set aside for the evening. Backstory plays a large role in some of his tales. I suppose the dead wouldn't dream a lot about the future.

As a writing instructor, I teach standard techniques to help aspiring writers polish basic skills. Frank favors the non-standard in creating what he wants readers to experience. Some of his style isn't what I'd use in writing techno thrillers or mysteries, but Frank knows his audience and genre better than I do. He has a talent for including vivid details that maintain a pace where other writers might fail. In some cases, Frank relies on stream-of-consciousness to propel his stories toward conclusions that aren't yet obvious. But then again, he writes about the non-standard and things that aren't yet obvious to you and me.

Frank's fans will find many stories to enjoy in this Anthology of the Weird and the Peculiar, short fiction he created over nearly 40 years. Frank is living proof that even a very nice guy can write very weird stories.

Jimmie H. Butler
Founder, Pikes Peak Writers Conference
Common Problems of Beginning Writers
A Certain Brotherhood
Red Lightning-Black Thunder
The Iskra Incident

From The Editor

Do the dead dream?

I don't know . . . but if they *read*, they should read this collection of short stories by F. P. Dorchak. And if they do dream, reading some of these stories may give them nightmares!

Whether he's taking you deep sea diving to your death, parachute jumping to find your lost love, to the house you grew up in to reclaim your broken soul, or on a walk that never ends, this author *really* takes you there. When a red hand beckons from beyond, a red envelope is slipped under the door, or a chain letter starts a terrifying chain of events, you will identify with the excruciating angst of these characters . . . some of whom will stay with you long after you've put this book away (under a bunch of blankets at the bottom of a chest so the scary little clowns can't get at you).

But later you'll dig it out because you want to re-read the stories that affected you deeply, with passages like this:

"Laughter, the warmest most pervasive and all-encompassing kind filled me, and as it did I felt it radiate outward into all of existence . . . at that moment, I'm sure, all of creation everywhere must have, for that instant, agreed with itself. At that one moment, I am sure there was absolutely no strife and everything agreed with everything, everywhere."

Joyce Combs
Editor

Preface

I apologize (okay, not really . . .) for this long opening (I always tend to "go long"), but I figured this book is so massive to begin with—over 167,000 words—that a couple of extra pages of Front Matter ain't gonna hurt anything. But given the breadth and scope of this effort (covering 39 years of my writing life—but I've actually been writing since I was six years old), I really need to talk about what brought me here, so I hope you'll forgive me for getting all "Stephen King" on you, as I sit here in an Adirondack camp on Lake Titus, in *waaay* upstate New York, completing my thoughts on this massive anthology of the Weird and the Peculiar.

And speaking of "anthologies": the term has been practically employed as a collection of stories by different writers . . . but if you research for a definitive definition and use of the term (and Jimmie Butler and I did go round and round on this), you will also find that sometimes "by a single writer" and "by a raft of writers" are in the very same definition, as it is in the Random House Dictionary of the English Language, Second Edition, unabridged: "*1. a book or other collection of selected writings by various authors, usually in the same literary form, of the same period, or the same subject . . . 2. a collection of selected writings by one author.*" If you dig even deeper, you will discover that the origin of the term "anthology" is literally defined as "a gathering or collection of flowers": *Antholog'ical. [Gr. anthos, a flower, legein, to gather.]* So, there you have it . . . "anthology" means a gathering of flowers and we've morphed it into a collection of *somethings.* You will find "anthologies" out there from single authors, and there's even *The Beatles Anthology* (*"the story of The Beatles by The Beatles"*), so I'm in good company, *yeah, yeah, yeah.*

Now, while I respect the passion some exhibit on this subject, the subtitle of this body of work, which Jimmie Butler and I developed together, *is* about the Weird and the Peculiar, and I do like to mess with perceptions . . . so, without apology, I offer you: *DO THE DEAD DREAM? AN ANTHOLOGY OF THE WEIRD AND THE PECULIAR.*

There are always so many to thank for any endeavor . . . and the creation of a book is no different! Thanks to Joyce Combs for her skilled editorial wizardry and friendship! Joyce . . . I can't thank you enough! Joyce is a fierce proponent of my writing and stories. She *gets* them, and for that I am eternally grateful, if not humbled. Thanks to

Lon Kirschner for his incredible creepy cover art and friendship! He always blows me out of the water with what his extraordinarily talented creative mind brings to life . . . uh, back from the *dead?!* I love to see others' interpretations of my work, and Lon, damn it, he *never* disappoints! Thanks to Pam Headrick for her formatting sorcery (because, really, it *is* sorcery)! She is ever so wonderful to work with! So patient, so kind! Without each of my core team, this book could never have been possible—and it almost wasn't.

To my family—thank you for your support and encouragement!

Laura, my wonderful wife, you and your love sustain me and are very much a part of my writing and its processes!

A hearty thank you to the *Writer's Digest* correspondence course, "Writing To Sell Fiction," and my late writing instructor, James Kisner. You are remembered.

Thank you to my late friend and fellow author, M. E. (Moe) Morris. I still think of both you and [the late] Virginia.

To the Rocky Mountain Fiction Writers' (RMFW) critique groups of the late 80s and early 90s—*thank* you for taking me under your collective wings! You were (and still are!) a great bunch of people and writers and showed me so damned much!

John Stith and the late Edward Bryant, Jr. Thank you both for keeping it *real*.

And there are two more individuals I need to specifically call out in some detail:

I'd met Jimmie Butler, Colonel, USAF (ret.), sometime around 1992, when he'd moved to Colorado. He'd started a writing group in Colorado Springs, Colorado, as well as the Pikes Peak Writers Conference (PPWC). Jimmie is a graduate of the Air Force Academy and a decorated Air Force pilot who flew 240 missions as a Forward Air Controller in O-1s and O-2s during the Vietnam War. He also flew C-141s and was Chief of Staff of the U. S. Space Division. Now he's an author, speaker, writing instructor, and photographer. He writes techno thrillers and mysteries.

Why do I mention a guy who doesn't write in my genre?

For nearly all of the 25 years that PPWC has been around, I'd helped out in one capacity or the other, as well as attended Jimmie's critique group in its infancy. It's through Jimmie and PPWC (and, obviously, RMFW) that I'd learned most of what I've come to know about writing and the publishing world. It was through PPWC that I'd come to meet and even gotten to know—at a "handshake level"—industry professionals: editors, agents, marketers, promoters, authors, producers, screenwriters, artists. Jimmie and the PPWC have had *the* most profound and impactful effect upon my writing career. But Jimmie Butler had done far more: he'd also imparted a wealth of literary knowledge and identity upon our Colorado Springs community. The Denver area has had RMFW and its slew of brand names, but from what *I* know, Colorado Springs had had no real literary identity until Jimmie came to town. Yes, I know, there are brand names from here, but people generally—and arguably—didn't associate Colorado Springs with *writing*, I feel, until Jimmie Butler created the PPWC. Of all the people I've met in the publishing world, Jimmie Butler has had the most profoundly influential impact upon my life as an author, and I can never repay him enough for this. Thank you, Jimmie, for all you've done—not only for me, but for countless other authors out there in the world with whom you've also come into contact, with your novels and your instruction. You were responsible for the influx of other successful professionals in *all* of the different aspects of writing and publishing. In my humble opinion, you've reshaped the Colorado literary landscape, whether or not you admit to it.

My oldest story in this anthology of the Weird and the Peculiar is from 1978. I'd written it at the age of seventeen for my fifth-period Saranac Lake Central High School (SLCHS) English class, in Saranac Lake, New York. It's called "Crypt of Vampyres." I mention "Crypt" because Jeff Spence was my English teacher for that class. Mr. Spence (it's hard to call him anything else, even after all these years) was (as I remember him) a tall, curly haired and affable guy, who'd always been quick with a smile and a laugh—and sharp of wit. Always joked around. Mr. Spence positively gushed over "Crypt" as he'd read it to our entire class that April day. I can still see and hear him doing so . . . emphasizing certain turns-of-phrase and words here and there . . . pointing out cool imagery—I was positively stunned and thought about it much over these near-forty years.

Here was *a professional English teacher* absolutely taken by something *I'd* written.

He was beside himself—even questioning the class's non-responsiveness to things he'd found noteworthy. That had been the first time I'd ever experienced that kind of unbridled enthusiasm for anything I'd ever written, and I often think back to that magical April 6, 1978 day.

Yes . . . that was 39 years ago. Man, looking back over your life is *weird.*

All I knew was that that had been gracious and cool of him to so express his excitement to the class . . . to me . . . in the fashion that he had. I'd always wanted to tell him that—and about how good of a teacher he'd been and what an impact he'd had on me—and I'd finally gotten that chance in July of 2017, when, through online networking, I'd found him (well, someone I'd contacted had, but you know what I mean)! It felt so weird (my favorite word) as we'd messaged each other . . . like I'd straddled time . . . part of me going back to that 1978 era and talking to good ol' Mr. Spence again . . . his shit-eating grin always on the verge of cracking up . . . while present-day me was observing this interaction "back" in the future of 2017. After I'd told him how he'd had an impact on me, he'd thanked me for reminding him of the importance of the work that teachers do.

In*deed*.

Teachers have an incredible responsibility placed upon their shoulders, and I think that, testing and graduations notwithstanding, seeing the fruits of their labors are largely delayed . . . sometimes for years—*sometimes forever*—unless a student seeks them out later in life. I'm sure they wonder how we turn out. And for people like me, I wonder how *they'd* turned out.

Now I know.

But another weird thing about all this is that ever since high school I've held this desire locked away inside me to contact Mr. Spence and tell him all this—and now that I've done it, well, damn it, but it's so *bizarro*, man! It's like that song that talks about how life is different when you've realized and lived out all your goals. Well, I certainly haven't done that, but it's pertinent here in that one goal I've had for 39 years has finally been realized. And with that realization comes a deep sense of satisfaction. I let a teacher know how he'd impacted my life . . . and that felt *good*.

Mr. Spence was (and I'm sure still *is* . . .) a good man who did great things as a teacher, as do all teachers. And as did my other SLCHS English teacher, Mrs. Carolyn Dougall. I wasn't a fan of diagraming sentences and all that "grammar stuff," but Mrs. Dougall, you were also a fun teacher and taught me the fundamentals of English I still use—well, and *abuse*—in my writing efforts to this day.

"Crypt of Vampyres" is heavily rewritten, but as I did so, I intentionally kept a measure-of-error in it to keep the original tone and atmosphere of the *writing* of the original story (as I also did with other stories). It really is funny the techniques I'd employed—or tried to employ—in "Crypt" . . . and how far I'd come in my writing life (such as it is) since . . . no real commercial success, but much personal satisfaction and some happy fans. "Crypt" foreshadowed what the rest of my writing would try to do. How I'd play with mood . . . and tone . . .

experiment with other aspects of writing, like sentence structure. I'm not saying I'm some Stephen King . . . or that I'm even remotely wildly successful . . . I'm just one other writer out there in a seemingly endless sea of writers . . . expressing an aspect of a much larger *gestalt* of myself that happens to *be* a writer . . . but I've followed my writing dream, have been able to write my entire life, and actually created a body of work that *I* enjoy and am pleased with. So, here it is . . . for good or ill. Take a look. Maybe you'll find something that strikes your fancy . . . and if so, then perhaps (as they say) I've done my job.

Why so large a tome? Simply stated, because I wanted all my work up to now to be located in a single repository. And, yes, there were cost considerations, since I am independently published, but the decision was largely based on a literary "ease of warehousing." I will write more short stories, but I wanted the initial body of my work easily accessible, comprehensive, and undivided.

Over the years there have been those who've read and commented on these stories, helped edit, but their names and identities can't be included for one reason of the other—have been lost in the Mists of Time. To any I have missed—*thank you*. I *am* eternally grateful. Writing isn't nearly as solitary as it's cracked up to be.

As much as possible, I have updated these works to maintain relevancy. Beneath each story's title is its original creation (copyright) date. Some of these stories have changed a little . . . some . . . a lot . . . from when I first released them, let alone their online release in 2015 - 2016. As I'd stated earlier, they'd almost been lost forever. I can't believe how many of these I'd started and *then just filed away*. But, it has been a fun ride these past couple of years . . . and this, too, has also long been a dream of mine.

Way back in my twenties my dad had once asked me, after having read one of my horror stories (I think it might have been "Attention Span"), why I liked to write this [horror] stuff. He had been an upstate New York Forest Ranger at the time, and I can only imagine that he had seen plenty of death and gore in all the searches he'd been on—not to mention was perhaps concerned that *some-son-of-his* had been writing weird-and-violent shit (and *reading* it; he'd once smashed my paperback copy of *The Exorcist* on a bedpost of mine). At the time I hadn't had a good answer for him. I mean, for whatever reason(s) and from wherever these crazy ideas incarnate and insist themselves upon this reality (for make no mistake about it, they *do* insist themselves) . . . they fester and breed and fabricate until they are hopefully authored. And if they are not—

(why do I write all this stuff, Dad?)
They haunt me.

F. P . Dorchak
Lake Titus, New York
August 13, 2017

A Teacher's Preface

What a joy it is for any teacher to have his student contact him after 39 years to tell him how his encouragement in English 11 inspired a life-long avocation as a writer! F. P. (Frank) Dorchak reminded me that on April 6, 1978, I had read his story "Crypt of Vampyres" aloud to the class, praising his use of imagery that effectively showed, rather than told, his story. He just emailed some of his more recent work to me, which is notable in its use of atmospheric detail, alternating internal and external action, clever twists on familiar expressions, and a wonderful ambiguity about what is real and what is imagined by his characters. Certainly, artistic creation is its own reward, but I wish Frank every success with the release of his upcoming collection of short stories, *Do The Dead Dream?*

Jeff Spence
Former English Teacher (retired)
Saranac Lake Central High School, Saranac Lake, NY

Do the dead dream?
They do ... oh, yes, my friend, they do ....

The Wreck
2000

There was nothing but the comforting sound of our breathing—and the bubbles it made as the air exited our regulators and entered the 100-foot column of crystal-clear water above us, shooting for the surface like scattering rats. I watched our bubbles as they left us . . . and smiled as blue-striped grunts, silvery permit, and creole wrasse playfully darted among them.

This was paradise, baby, pure and simple.

Visibility was at least a hundred feet in these waters off Bimini. We'd just begun paying out our guideline and were preparing to enter the Bimini wreck *Her Majesty*, when I'd had the oddest feeling compelling me to look up and off to our right. Carl, my friend and dive buddy, was tying off our guideline to a heavily used post just outside *Her Majesty*, which still held bits and pieces of spent guidelines past, when I noticed this new shadowy structure shimmering in the distance. This had *not* been there when we first came down. At first glance it looked just like any other piece of distant coral reef set against the crystal blue of Bahamian waters—or perhaps another wreck—but there was something more to this shadow . . . something unnerving. We hadn't spotted it on our previous dive, and there were not supposed to be any other wrecks manifested in these waters. I directed Carl to it, who turned and did a double take. We both looked at it for a few moments . . . perplexed . . . then he looked back to me and shook his head and hands before him, indicating "no." Tapping his slate, he reinforced the need to press on with our planned dive. We'd check it out later. Then he looked back to the odd structure, again to me, and shrugged his shoulders and hands in an "I dunno" gesture.

We entered *Her Majesty* . . . .

But let me start from the beginning. My life had been like any other basic, hum-drum existence . . . at least as hum-drum as anyone's life could be at twenty-two. Nothing really stood out from my life that ever pointed to where I'd end up—or where I'd been. I was your basic kid, in your basic home, living your basic life: growing up, school, girls, jobs, and finding life quietly unfulfilling. Looking for excitement, I *craved* it. There was something I was meant to do . . . I just knew it . . . but hadn't yet found, though I remained ever confident it was out there. I'd skydived, Bungee jumped, hang glided, but nothing so filled my existence and soul as sailing and diving. Being out around water and onboard *ships* . . . and when I first discovered I could breathe underwater (with scuba gear, of course)—it opened up whole new *worlds* to me! Such wondrous life was hidden beneath the waves! I simply loved the water and was utterly at one with it. Found I could hold my breath for a solid five minutes within it. The possibility of drowning never crossed my mind—indeed, I thought, what a beautiful way to go, being totally filled with and at one with the sea!

I wasted no time in signing on with dive operations along Florida's east coast, mostly hanging around Miami. Within the world of the open ocean, I found I was particularly drawn toward wreck diving and took in every wreck possible, ranging from the Atlantic's graveyard off North Carolina, down through the Bahamas and the Caribbean, and ranged as far as Truk Island, the Mediterranean, and northern Scotland—anywhere and everywhere I could get to and think of, and always—*always*—the thrill of another wreck excited me . . . until I began to notice a disturbing trend, something that quite upset me. Once down there, inside or around whatever wreck I was enjoying . . . well, there was no other way to describe it . . . I still felt something *missing*. Something was lacking . . . anticlimactic . . . and I could never put my finger on it. What the hell? What had happened to all my initial excitement?

So I soldiered (well, *sailored* . . .) on, like everybody does in life.

I took in all manner of wrecks, no matter how contradictorily excited and hollow I ended up feeling. If I was doing what I was meant to do . . . *why was I constantly unfulfilled?*

Eventually, I ended up on Andros Island in the Bahamas, and it was there I felt the strongest magic, felt closest to whatever called me . . . *drove* me. I was only there a couple of months before hopping over to Bimini, where I took up with yet another dive operation, one that specialized in wrecks. It was also here where I'd found myself a hundred feet down and a quarter mile off Bimini, ready to penetrate the wreck of *Her Majesty* while spotting this new, odd structure, no doubt also encrusted with colorful coral and sponges and all manner of Atlantic life swarming around us.

It was magical, there was no other word for it.

But what *was* it?

The more glances I stole back toward that shadowy structure, the more confused I grew. It had to be a wreck. The more I looked at it, the more it looked like some kind of angled skiff sticking up out of the sand. But was it my point of view or the structure of what we were looking at that was so deceiving? There really wasn't much to go on from our distance and position, and it actually looked more like a lone section of reef—but if you looked at it—how do I say this?—really *looked* at it with the intention of decrypting what it was you were looking at . . . *then* you began to find, either by trick of the water, distance, or angles and your mind . . . an emerging organization. A definitive construction of some odd, obtuse kind. Its perspective messed with your mind, I tell you—*it was like the shape of the vessel formed before your very eyes.*

It was absolutely maddening.

Was it hiding behind coral growth, or was *it* coral growth?

It was like looking at those puzzles that spelled out words, but at first glance were nothing more than carefully laid out patterns of deceiving narrow strips.

I simply had to have a closer look . . . .

Early Bahamian winters can mean mid-eighties, which is hot for the islands, and today was just such a day on board the *Wreck Mistress*, Carl's boat. Skies were growing low and overcast, winds balmy, and it actually started to interfere with our initial hundred-foot viz. The day had quite the surreal effect to it, going from bright, balmy, and sunny . . . to cloudy, moody, and a difficult-to-describe "duality." Like I was sharing this day, this moment in time with . . . something else. And the brewing storm only added to it, though still hours out and slow moving. It was far enough away so as to not be a problem, but it was definitely headed our way.

Her Majesty was your basic, two-hundred-and-seventy-foot wreck, upright on a sandy ocean bottom, with about a twenty-degree list and covered in a century's worth of coral growth. Like most wrecks out here, it'd gotten caught in a storm and sunk, all hands lost, and lies just yards from the Gulf Stream drop-off—which was great for the mixture of shallow reef life and big-boy pelagics, like amberjack, wahoo, and permit. *Her Majesty* had been a Miami rum-runner back in the days when that'd been a problem, but, as interesting and tragic as that may be, I'd lost all interest in her once I'd spied this newer find. The funny thing was—as if pre-ordained—once we'd gotten only about twenty feet into *Her Majesty*, a loose piece of ship came crumbling down before us, leaving us dead in the water and totally blinded by stirred-up silt. You don't know vertigo or zero viz until you've experienced stirred-up silt inside the claustrophobic confines of a wreck. Anyway, we paused until the debris cleared enough to reassess our situation, but any further exploration had been cut off by the collapsed debris, which looked like actual chunks of the decaying ship's structure. Our plan cut off at the knees, I had to admit I was anything but disappointed! We aborted the dive.

Or, should I say *exited*, since we didn't exactly head back to the surface. Carl being the first one in was the last out, which put me first in line out the hatch, and after exiting I simply couldn't take my eyes off that obtuse, jagged piece of indeterminate shadow a hundred feet out. But, I had to wait for Carl, it was the polite and procedural thing to do. As he rolled up our guideline, I hovered, staring at the object of my growing obsession. I checked my gauges and found I had a good twenty-nine-hundred psi left in my tanks, not counting my bailout bottle. I looked to Carl, who was shaking his head and hands before him "no."

No.

Such a stickler. To rules.

With that much air left, why *not* try something else? The passage of my bubbles, the underwater ballet of wrasse, jacks, and grunts—and I even saw one helluva *huge* Nassau grouper eerily float by—how can you not take the opportunity, especially with a nearly full supply of air? As my exhaled bubbles danced and burbled about my face, I realized . . . in that one highly defined moment . . . that this was *the* turning point in my life. I know all about your "plan your dive and dive your plan," but give me a break! *This* was exciting—didn't he *feel* it?

Didn't it wrap itself around his insides like it did mine?

Come back to dive another day my *ass.*

It was here . . . *I* was here . . . and air was plenty. No brainer in my book. But Carl, true to form, gave thumbs up for the surface. Like the good buddy, I responded with an "ok" and agreed. He began his ascent . . .

And I unhesitatingly headed toward the beckoning shadow, Carl not even a dim consideration.

I don't know what came over me . . . I mean, I'd *mentally* committed to resurfacing, even prepared to resurface by grabbing my inflator/deflator hose to dump air for our ascent . . . but when I actually began to put body in motion and kick off, it was like I was a sliver of mindless metal drawn to one *helluva* commanding magnet. I had gone perhaps ten feet before Carl noticed I wasn't beside him, and he'd scurried back down and grabbed me behind my head, at the first stage on my tank, jerking me to a stop.

What are you doing? he signaled.

I don't know, I signaled back.

Up, he gestured forcefully.

OK, I returned, and this time he kept direct eye contact with me. He began his ascent, and I—again—continued on my course toward the mysterious wreck. This time Carl hadn't finned an inch before he again jerked the ascend signal into my face. If gestures could kill, this one murdered. Then he pulled out his slate and scribbled *what's up?!* and *are you narced?* on it, underlining "narced" twice. I again gave him the "I don't know," then pointed to the narced question and shook my head "no." You could see his exasperation as he looked between me and the new wreck, checking both his air and mine. Then he paused and again brought up his slate. On the back of it we did a trick we'd designed a while ago to check if anyone in our group had ever gotten nitrogen narcosis. Topside Carl had randomly written down the numbers one through six, and down here we were to point them out to whomever brought up the question, as quickly as possible, in ascending order. I rattled mine off in record time. Carl looked back to the new wreck, then back to his slate, and scribbled *Just a quick pass, then UP. Five minutes.* He underlined "UP" and "five" more than several times, tapping his pencil point into the slate for emphasis. Carl's a good man. A good diver.

I again signaled "OK," and off we went. I didn't know what had come over me, but I felt this was the right thing to do. And as we both proceeded, I had a sudden flash of mental imagery . . . *stars* . . . billions of them. The image was powerful but fleeting, and though the image departed, the feeling didn't. The feeling that I somehow *belonged* with those stars . . . .

We arrived at the "reef" . . . the *object* . . . and I was overcome by emotion . . . strong, *powerful* waves of the stuff that actually brought tears to my eyes. It was as if all my senses had taken complete leave of me . . . all of my dive training and experience had abandoned me. Carl, I noticed, was responsibly taking notes and sketching out the wreck. Man, that's why I dive with the guy. But, I was concerned with other matters, like experiencing the most passionate need to touch, to *contact* whatever this was—and whatever it was awakened some weird kind of arcane recognition within me that was hard to explain and far from *complete*. I felt like an amnesiac . . . *spellbound*.

We explored the wreck, and I noted how the odd, complicated lines didn't match anything I'd come to know as a ship, boat, or skiff. It simply didn't fit any rational design I'd come to associate with ocean-going vessels. This thing was completely alien, and as we continued alongside I noticed it had even become difficult to discern what was wreck and what was reef. What was visible appeared to be about fifty to seventy-five feet in length, but its physical configuration, once again, didn't appear to be anything *sea*-going, unless what we were looking at was damaged, perhaps banged up during some ancient storm or topside battle. Which brought up another point . . . the material of this thing also didn't look like anything familiar . . . it wasn't wood and it wasn't metal. To be honest, it actually looked more like some weird kind of a semi-translucent substance similar to those silly little balls I used to play with as a kid . . . the ones with all the

(*stars*)

glitter in them. And what's more, the material actually reflected its environment back at you like a gigantic ornamental gazing ball (which would help explain the difficulty we had in focusing on it), but not in a bright, shiny way—more like in a *movie*, I guess would be a better description.

A movie?

Like a cloaking device, if you wanted to get all *Star Trek* about it. I wondered what it would appear like from above. If my guess was correct, it probably wasn't visible at all, because it simply reflected the environment back at you. That would explain why there wasn't anything on any map. And it didn't look at all recent, but instead looked like it had been resting here for the better part of an *eternity*.

I could no longer contain myself. I reached out and touched the thing, and not at all to my surprise found myself jolted with yet another surge of emotion *shooting through me like liquid electricity!* It was like sticking your finger into an electrical outlet multiplied a million times over, and it literally stopped me dead in the water. I was emotionally and spiritually stunned as it continued to kick wildly throughout me. Maybe stunned is the wrong word (though its intensity is correct)—I was

Contacted.

I felt as if all this incredible emotion had been downloaded into me—or released from *within* me—I don't know which. All I do know is that all I ever was, all of whomever I thought I was, was touched . . . as if by the very finger of God. That is the only way I can even come close to explaining what happened. From that moment on I had inexplicably changed . . . was no longer the man I thought I was. I had become something so much more, and I actually felt stopped up with all this emotional information—and I do mean emotional—for *intellectually* I was no better off than before and would even go so far as to say I was *worse*. Any so-called answers I found by physical contact and direct observation of this wreck only served up more questions. But that hollow, unfulfilled feeling that had been constantly plaguing me had instantly evaporated. I stopped and brought my hands to my head, eyes closed. Coming here, touching this . . . this . . . *thing* . . . had opened up such deep and powerful emotional channels within me that I felt I was going to explode—at a *molecular* level. My entire body tingled and shook, and I couldn't believe this . . . but I was actually *crying*.

Kind of annoying when you're wearing a face mask.

It was at that point that Carl again grabbed my tanks and yanked me up off the sea floor. I was limp in his grasp as we ascended, and he grabbed my inflator/deflator hose venting my air, then shoved it into my hands, forcefully directing me to look at him. As we rose, I felt the wreck's effect on me begin to dissipate . . . not leave, but just . . . slip away . . . and I honestly felt it wasn't so much a proximity issue as it was more of a, if you could believe this . . . *respectful consideration*.

None of this was making any sense—good Lord, *what was going on?*

As you can imagine, once we surfaced all hell broke loose.

"What the *hell'd* you think you were *doing?*" Carl yelled, as we bobbed in rougher-than-expected water, waves that were much worse than before our dive. I also noticed that the skies had grown darker, too, a weird steel-blue I'd never seen before mixing into a deep, dark *hurtful*-looking black farther away. Carl was beside himself, wildly cursing up a sailor's stream at me. Once on board, I'd barely begun to unhook and slip out of my BC, our buoyancy control device vest that contains our tanks and other gear, when he again lit back into me. The storm that wasn't supposed to hit us was building in intensity, and our boat was tussled about somewhat more than when we'd first anchored. Winter weather, I guess. Lonnie, our Divemaster, and the rest of the crew of the *Wreck Mistress,* initially all smiles as we surfaced and boarded, were understandably confused and politely stepped back, letting us clear our own gear.

"Do you mind telling me which part of 'five minutes' you didn't understand?"

I was numb. Though the hold of that specter-from-below's grip on me had somewhat—and I mean *somewhat,* for it was definitely still with me—lessened, I still heard its whispers. And there were more images

. . . of high seas and dark skies . . . stars, more and more fricking *stars* . . . and I looked to our darkening skies and jostling seas before I calmly answered Carl, feeling more at peace with myself than I'd ever been.

"I don't know," I said calmly, though confused. I felt like a Buddhist monk meditating on a mountaintop.

"What? That's *it?* That's all you have to say for yourself? Were you narced? Nitrogen get ya?"

I shook my head. "I don't think so. It wasn't narcosis. I . . . I don't know what it was, Carl—really, I don't—I'm sorry—"

"Okay," Lonnie asked, finally assisting us with our gear and separating Carl and me, "anyone care to explain what happened down there?"

"Well, Junior, here," Carl began, "decided to go on a sightseeing tour after *Her Majesty* turned sour on us—we had a collapse—but instead of aborting, he spotted this other wreck and just decided to go have a look-see. So we spent five minutes checking it out—or *I* did. Time's up, and I keep trying to get his attention, and he's just ignoring me, until he sank to the bottom in a near catatonic state."

Everyone reached for support as a particularly rough swell assaulted the *Mistress*.

"What other wreck?" Tanya asked. "There's no other wreck down there."

"Oh, there is now," Carl said, barely containing his rage. "I don't know why I'm so pissed off—gee, maybe it's from almost getting *killed* down there—"

"Wait-wait-wait," Lonnie said, raising a hand, "*what* happened?"

Carl related everything. I guess in my haste to check out the other wreck I'd been somewhat ignorant as to just how close Carl had been to getting hit by whatever it was that'd collapsed into our path down there in the first wreck. He had every right to abort and surface.

"I'm sorry," I said to Carl, actually embarrassed, "I-I didn't realize how close you were. I just didn't—"

"You're damned *right* you *didn't. Didn't* gets people killed!"

Overly dramatic or not, he was right. Lonnie pulled Carl aside.

"Okay, Carl—why don't you come with me and calm down a bit, huh?" Lonnie pulled Carl starboard, and I dumped my head into my hands. Tanya came over.

"You okay?"

I looked up to her. "*I didn't know*," I said. "I really didn't *know*."

Tanya lowered a sun-bronzed hand to me. "It's okay, honey, it's understandable. We all get excited. We all have one wreck where we get stupid . . . this is yours. He'll get over it . . . but, you have to tell me—what did you guys find down there?"

I got up and went to Carl's BC, removing the slate from its clips.

"I don't really know, but Carl sketched out some notes. I was just way too engrossed in the thing to write anything down. Here's what he did."

I handed her the slate and sat back down, shaking my head. It was a weird, angular sketch jutting out from ocean bottom (several lines crossed out and restarted), notes jotted all over it. If I hadn't known any better, I still would have thought it part of the reef. When I looked up, Carl and Lonnie stood before me.

"I'm sorry I got so heated over this," Carl said. "You didn't know. You got excited—that's all." Carl extended his hand. I looked at it—and him—and stood up, shaking it. That seemed to make everything better, but the sea, I noticed, grew more uneasy. As we completed removing our gear, Carl finally asked, "Okay . . . so, what happened down there . . . at that other wreck?"

I took a moment before replying.

"To be totally honest, Carl, I haven't the faintest idea." I got up and began dipping my equipment in the clean tank. "It was like nothing in my life up to that point ever mattered. Once I spotted that wreck—and where the hell had it come from, anyway?—once I spotted it, it was like I was being sucked into a vortex—a whirlpool of some kind. I'm not kidding. Each and every time I acknowledged to you that I'd be following, my mind and body had every intention of doing so . . . but, when I actually put myself into motion it was like I had no control! There was no choice in the matter. There was never any question of what my *body* was going to do—and when you agreed to take a look, well, it was the most joyous moment in my entire life. Like revisiting a lost love. Have you ever been so overcome by emotion while diving on any of these things? Has there ever been a wreck that just so captivated you—emotionally—that you felt so . . . *overcome?*"

Carl looked at me, shaking his head. "No, I can't say as I have—I mean, I'm awed, sure, fascinated even—but I can't say I was ever so overcome by a find as to become emotional."

"Well," I continued, "I guess I'm different, because I was, and on such an incredible level. It was creepy, totally creepy—but *awesome*. I have to go back. Have to see this thing on full tanks."

Carl looked down to the deck and nodded. "Okay," he said, pensively, "weather says we have two . . . maybe three hours, but we have to do it like every other dive. Agreed?"

Of course I agreed.

"We plan it, we dive the plan. We chart it out, look for any entry points—if there are any."

Again, I agreed. And when he said those words, there it was again. I thought the feelings had faded with distance, but they hadn't. I mean, we were only really a stone's throw above it—what "distance"? I felt the same emotions again welling up within me, my soul, and I would have leapt over the side that instant if I hadn't known any better, or Carl had said we were heading home. Decompression sickness, killer storm—they all meant nothing. Getting back to that ship *did*, and just knowing that we would be diving on it again was all I needed to restrain myself. After all, had I immediately jumped right back in, they certainly would have proclaimed me crazy, aborted any further diving, and headed back to Bimini. I wasn't going to let that happen. So, I waited out our surface interval, and we planned our next dive.

The dive was planned, lunch eaten, and I was like a kid at Christmas! We decided Carl and I would be the first down to do the initial survey. Then Lonnie and Tanya would follow to continue where we left off, weather permitting. Carl and I would also scout for entries.

I couldn't get my gear on fast enough.

Just before I entered the water—and I was the first to splash—thoughts of Atlantis entered my mind. After all, we were in the Bermuda Triangle. Not far from the Stones of Atlantis, in fact. It all fit. There be mysteries in these waters.

Carl and I descended down our line to *Her Majesty*, still there, of course, and turned to take a bearing. It was still there, and oh, how it sent my pulse racing! Of all the wrecks I'd ever dove, this one drove me mad with anticipation! I just had to get inside her! I swear, I felt I was going insane—and I cared not one bit! It took all I could muster to restrain myself—I didn't want to be landward bound—and performed like the perfect buddy, swimming side-by-side with Carl. It took forever to arrive.

And then . . . we were *there*.

When Carl wasn't looking, I stole a glance at him, but he seemed totally unaffected by this wreck, its *presence*. There was more to this find than what we could or couldn't see. Why was I the only one who felt it? I've heard others feel they've lived other lives, and I guess, to be totally honest, I've always felt I've lived other lives, as well, but it wasn't until this wreck that I really *believed* it. *Felt* it. Somehow I was connected to this thing, and no one else felt it but me. I had to know, to find out . . . I had to get inside it and it couldn't wait; as much as I promised myself and my friends, I just couldn't wait.

Carl motioned for me to follow, and, following our previously agreed-to plan, he was to monitor time and depth, while I sketched out the wreck. As if I was going to actually sketch it, I pulled up my slate and pencil and put the two together. But I didn't need this. I knew what I needed to do, and I suddenly knew where to find the entrance.

I skimmed along the side of the ship, Carl watching me. My attention was fixed upon it. It was constructed of the oddest material I'd ever seen—and seemed to shimmer "in and out" until we got right up on it and it became more "solid"—a translucent, sparkling substance that continued to reflect the sea and surrounds. It was excellent camouflage, and I doubted if anyone would see it, even if anchored directly over it. But still, something tugged at my soul. There was something here and it *needed* me—not Carl, Tanya, or Lonnie—*me*.

The wreck was meant for me and no one else. I finally understood this.

I rounded the farthest-most section of the wreck . . . then suddenly dove down to it . . . and there it was, hidden among the shadows and encrusted orange-cup coral. It wasn't visible, but I knew it was there. As soon as I got down to where sand met wreck, I reached my hand to the ship—and it passed through what should have been outer hull.

Before I knew it, the rest of me followed right on through.

My body, my *soul*, had a life of its own! I could hear my cells sing—actually *rejoice*—all nerve endings tingling in excitement!

Then Carl snagged me.

But I'd already *penetrated*, and it stole my breath away . . . it had been the most exhilarating experience I'd ever known. For the instant I'd been *in* that wreck, I'd lost all care about Carl, didn't care about depth or time or air supply, didn't care if I ever again surfaced. This could have been my living room, my bed, someplace where I was so comfortable and at peace. Topside watching a sunset. I felt so at home and at one with myself. I hadn't really been able to discern anything useful about the internal structure of the craft, though, because I couldn't really see anything. It was dark inside. *But it all felt strangely familiar.* Like I'd done this before. I wasn't discovering anything new here . . . I was *re*discovering. Well, at least until Carl yanked me out. And there was one other thing—

I'd *seen* something inside.

Movement.

Well, of course, that was it. The dive was history, and I'd only brought it upon myself.

Again.

Carl immediately aborted, dragging me up to our fifteen-foot safety stop where the surge was noticeably stronger than during our descent. Carl draped me over the hanging PVC pipe, anchored to our bobbing boat above, and never took his eyes off me. I never resisted. I was still overcome with the feeling that no matter what happened from this point on, I had come home and *would* dive again. I would get inside. Nothing could stop me. No longer was the feeling one of urgency, but of love and longing. Of course, back on deck, I again had to deal with the wrath of Carl, and this time I had no excuses. I was caught, pure and simple, and I was gutted and gilled.

"*Goddammit*," Carl exploded, "what the hell's the matter with you, boy! You know perfectly well you just don't frigging jump into something like that! Geez, we just *talked* about this!"

He was right. I couldn't argue with him. He was the skipper, the *Mistress* his barge. But what he didn't know was that though he might be skipper up here, down there . . . *that* was mine . . . *that* belonged to me, and no one—*no one*—was keeping me from it.

"Tanya!" Carl barked, "Check his equipment—his tanks. Make sure his air isn't contaminated. In fact, Lonnie, grab me that oh-two," he directed, pointing to the green cylinder at Lonnie's feet. He was taking no chances, putting me on pure oxygen just in case I might be going DCS. I couldn't argue with him—possible decompression sickness—I would've done the same in his fins. "Lie down," he directed, and when Lonnie came over with the oxygen, he placed it over my nose and mouth. I gave in and lay back, holding the cylinder. A little oxygen never hurt anybody.

As I lie there, everyone monitoring me like I was bent, I heard them talk. I also felt the boat rocking more and more as we tossed about in the growing swells and silently watched as the skies grew darker still. That storm wasn't turning, it was heading straight for us. Seemed to have picked up speed. We'd have to head back to land soon, and by all rights, should have already.

"Look," Carl began, "I don't know what's going on with you, but we're going to treat you as if you got narced and bent, and we're making for port. Advisories and radar indicate the storm's turned, headed straight for us. We don't have any choice—"

Carl was going to say something else, but even his seasoned sea legs buckled beneath him, and he had to grasp the rail to regain his balance.

Carl continued. "We've mapped the wreck . . . its location anyway . . . and can come back. Be better prepared."

The sea again threw another wallop at us, this time our equipment rattled and slid around us, some of it falling on deck. Lonnie and Tanya scrambled about, collecting it. The winds were definitely picking up. Tanya shouted out from somewhere astern, "Carl—we gotta get outta here!" Carl paused, looking up and mumbling something about how this storm couldn't *possibly* have gotten here this quick, then shouted back to her to fire up the engines and hoist anchor. My heart—like Atlantis—sank! Carl looked back to me, and I know he saw it in my eyes.

"Look . . . I promise we'll come back, and you can be *sure* we'll continue this conversation, but right now we have our asses in a sling, so we're *out*."

He looked at me a moment longer.

Did he see it? Did he see my answer?

Carl turned his back to me, and I gripped the railing harder. I sat up. The seas were rough, rain now, in sheets, pouring out of swollen skies as if to implore us—*me*—to stay, and, as if on cue, there it came sliding toward me. I wouldn't have believed it, had someone just told me about it, but I was there, staring at it. A BC strapped with two tanks and my bailout bottle slid to my feet, mask and snorkel caught in the regulator and hoses . . . fins nearby. From my position and to my utter amazement, I could see on the dive computer that both tanks were fully loaded. I couldn't have been more shocked. And to add to this? It was all *my* equipment—my vest, my tank, and my mask and fins.

I was electrified.

There was no thinking involved . . . I had given that up long ago.

I was running on emotion, pure, hot, and sweet. I was a sliver of steel, and I yielded to the pull of my undersea magnet. I tossed the oh-two away and was in the BC, fins, and weight belt before I realized it, and when I turned, there was Carl. I'm not sure if he'd actually taken a swing at me, or if he'd just reached out for me, but the boat bucked, and he missed. On the return rock we both piled into each other and he grabbed on, shouting into my ears, "Are you fucking *nuts*? You're gonna kill yourself! What in hell are you *doing*?"

I pushed him away, thankful Lonnie and Tanya were busy elsewhere on the boat. "I have to do this!" I shouted back. Wind and rain lashed my face like whips.

"You'll fucking *die*, don't you goddamned *care*?"

At that point I did the cockiest thing I'd ever done and just . . . shrugged. That's all. I just shrugged. Then I smiled . . . from his point of view probably the most wicked and yes, *crazy* smile he'd ever seen. "*I don't care!*" I shouted back, both shocked and accepting of my reply, which seemed not to come from me, but from some deeper, all-knowing part *within* me. Carl froze and at that moment I felt more distant from him than I'd ever felt from anyone. It was like we no longer knew each other, had just passed each other by on the open seas. I remembered all the other wrecks we'd dove, the beers we'd had, the islands we'd explored, but none of that mattered *at that moment*.

I was a man out of time, out of *context*.

I suddenly felt as if I were in the wrong company.

All Carl could do was watch me hurtle myself off his boat and into the maelstrom of water and torrential downpour.

Drowning? *Ha!* I *laughed* at the possibility!

What I was doing was *right*—the most right thing I'd ever done. It wasn't just about feeling pulled—I *wanted* to go. I felt at home, here, in these waters, and even for me in my present state of mind, what I'm sure sounded quite maniacal, I yelled *"bring it on!"* laughing into the torrent.

The *Mistress* rose and fell before me, and at times I was lifted high above its decks. I saw Carl, barely clinging to the rails, aghast. Watching me. I could see my death in his eyes and how much he wanted to jump in after me—but I also saw that he knew it would do me no good. And to my horror, I noticed that he held my mask and snorkel. It didn't matter . . . with or without them I was going back. To my surprise he stared at me a moment longer . . . then threw them out to me. My hand shot up into the rain-whipped sky and—amazingly—caught them.

They flew directly to my hand.

I couldn't believe this! I wasn't meant to depart this place. I was *meant* to go back down below. As Tanya kicked in the engines and turned back toward Bimini, the *Mistress* began to motor away, and the last I saw of Carl were his lips mouthing words I could no longer make out.

I'm sure he was wishing me luck.

All this flashed through my mind in an instant as I now bobbed . . . alone . . . a quarter mile out to sea in the middle of an angry storm, watching my lifeline beeline it for the safety of a mere spit of land. A small part of me remembered what it was like to be sane, to be together and bored, all on the safety of solid ground or a rolling deck, and I felt a part of myself begin to cry pathetically—but a deeper part of me silenced that whimpering slob. I had cast my lot . . . there was no turning back (not that I even wanted to). I put on my mask, clearing it with only mild difficulty, even in this storm, deflated my BC, and slipped beneath the angry sea . . . .

No sooner beneath the surge, I forgot all about any storm or how dead I already was. Never had to worry about decompression sickness ever again, I chuckled to my sick, sick self. In no time I was amid the permit, wrasse, and the wreck . . . and I touched her. We were alone now, finally. Just the two of us. It was as if we'd been lovers, long separated and I was mad for reunion. I couldn't get there quick enough, and once there, finned inside the entrance-that-wasn't-an-entrance . . . .

It was dark inside, but I had my dive lights with me and switched one on. I shined it about and checked my air. I had just shy of three-thousand pounds. Nearly full tanks. At this depth, not counting my excitement, I probably had about a good fifteen-to-twenty minutes of air. Fifteen minutes is a lifetime to a dead man.

Looking around I noticed there was little—no, *no*—debris, inside. No silt. In fact, I'd seen not one fish in here, either, though I had seen some kind of movement on my last foray. Apprehensive and excited, I directed my light ahead, half-expecting to see a head pop out, but all I saw was an empty, narrow corridor leading straight ahead on its slanted journey downward. *Damn* it, but there was something vaguely familiar about this place.

I followed the corridor.

Guiding myself through the interior, I passed several open compartments, all positioned at different levels . . . more like cubby holes, really. Some only went in a hair's breadth, many went in inches, and a few were tiny, narrow flues that disappeared away into inky, fluid darkness. Parts of walls appeared solid, like the entrance, but allowed my hand to pass through. I continued on. Finding a corner, I took it, still descending. The wreck was at an angle, digging deep into the sand, so my journey now took on an absurd, surreal tone. I had several minimal bouts of vertigo while descending along the oddly angled corridors and had to use my bubbles as an "up" reference. This craft was *enormous*. As I continued who knew how far in and down (I wasn't counting kick cycles and certainly had no guideline), I began to wonder just how large this thing really was. It couldn't be as large as I was experiencing, but here it was, here *I* was—still going down. I'd passed more compartments . . . but felt no urge to stop—until now. I entered one on my right, by previous standards large, but only, perhaps, eight-by-ten-by-eight. As soon as I entered the room, my entrance disappeared and panic overtook me.

I was trapped!

Good God, my weaker shrieking self chimed back in, *what the hell had I done?* One hundred feet or more above me raged a howling storm, I had only about ten minutes of air left—if I was lucky—and my only salvation, the *Mistress*, was hurriedly making for land!

What had I done?

I really *had* to be crazy! Ten minutes of air, and I was sucking it in faster thanks to water pressure and my sudden panic.

I tried to slow down my breathing, but the panic monster plowed right on into me. As much as I knew I had to relax, I simply couldn't. I was dying, and I'd totally done it to myself. Me. No one else. All my actions had finally caught up with me! I had no place else to go, and no time to do it. I simply had to make the best of my remaining existence.

Huddling my arms across my chest, I closed my eyes and tried to think of the most calming scenes imaginable . . . grassy spring glades . . . babbling brooks . . . being back in my comfortable bed, covered in cool sheets and a comforter (and how it was all still there, now . . . the sheets, pillow, and all—but forever without me) . . . being in the arms of old loves . . . but the image that surprisingly had the most effect and finally 100% calmed me down . . . the image that actually *slowed my breathing* . . . was this damned wreck itself. *That* was what got me to relax and center myself.

I'd simply had a moment of human weakness . . . but I was better now.

I had a mission to accomplish.

Opening my eyes, I looked straight ahead and saw it. Another opening . . . shimmering, translucent . . . directly before me. Not comprehending, but wasting no time, I passed through it.

Continuing on down the passageway, I once more grabbed my light, still lanyarded to my wrist, and directed it ahead. I hadn't gone two kicks when something shot past the distant end of my beam. I jerked to a stop, heart jumping.

That weren't no fish!

I had no idea what it was, but all I caught was a shadow. I swam up to where I saw the *something* swim past and took the turn. What my light fell upon made my jaw drop. *How could this be?* In total awe, I looked in upon a vast, cavernous interior, still canted at its crazy angle, the end of which my light beam could not discern. Even down here visibility remained crystal clear, but I could see no end.

It hurt my *mind.*

I hurriedly swam inside. How could what I entered be so damned *immense?* This was impossible.

I didn't want to look at my air supply, but ended up doing so, and found that I must have smashed my console against something during my panic attack, because it no longer worked. Great. Oh, well.

So, I pushed on farther—I had to go farther!

I could only imagine how deep I was, wondering when the poisonous effect of compressed oxygen in my air supply was going to get me—when I laughed. I hadn't enough life left for that to be a problem, and if oxygen toxicity got me first, then *c'est la vie!* Anytime now . . . anytime . . . and my current breath would be my last. Images of training flashed through my mind, of the time one of my instructors had demonstrated what it felt like when your tank ran out of air. He'd turned off my first-stage junction and I'd inhaled.

The air simply . . . *stopped.*

Just like that, matter-of-factly, like it was no big deal.

The purpose of this, my instructor had calmly informed me, was to see that there was never any immediate need to panic. If you're a good diver you always have an emergency air source—a bailout or pony bottle—and you have plenty of precious seconds to swap them.

Again, to a dead man, extra seconds are a lifetime.

So I'd inhaled, and, indeed, realized that after taking that last breath, I had plenty of time to make the old swapparoo. I had, in fact, discovered an ability that few could master: the ability to hold my breath for a solid five minutes. Depending on many factors, of which physical activity and state of mind were paramount, I found I could add as much as twenty or so seconds to that number, but come thirty-five seconds, and I was in the panic mode, realizing sooner or later, I was gonna be inhaling whatever was in front of my airway with insane ferocity. There was actually a point, I'd found, around those thirty-to-thirty-five seconds, where I'd again *exhaled*, and it seemed to actually stave off that inevitable Final Inhale. That was all there'd be left at that time. And no school would ever train this, but you later eventually find out that you also have a breath or two of air inside your inflated BC. A few more seconds. So, I figured I had about five-to-six minutes of reprieve once my tanks ran out.

Crazy how things like this run through your mind when you're insane. And then I was trying to do the Zen thing, too, where you focus on exactly what you're doing *at the moment* in the belief that you can actually *expand* that moment . . . expand *Time.* And that's when I came upon it.

The body.

It was just lying there, on its back, barefoot, loose robes gently floating about it, and it didn't slide. I mean, we're still at this surreal angle, but the body didn't move. It stayed on the floor where it was as if it were level. Anyway, it seemed long, this body, which would make the creature tall, and a "creature" it was: its face was gaunt, yet peaceful, its body long and slim. It was definitely humanoid in appearance, but it was definitely *not* human. And, strangely, the creature didn't scare me. I think I'd gone quite beyond that. I was a dead man, and it was just a matter of technicality when I would actually inhale H-2-O. I still had precious minutes of exploration left and I *was* going to exploit it to its fullest.

I floated to a stop above the body, and where I should have been terrified, I was totally at ease . . . yes . . . and calm. This was what I was meant to do. I was *meant* to find this. I was *meant* to be here . . . in the middle of this fantastic cavernous enclosure, an untold hundred-plus feet down . . . in the strangest craft anyone had ever seen. I was floating over the strangest creature I had ever laid eyes upon—and I wasn't the least bit afraid—

And neither was I afraid when it opened its eyes to display black, star-filled sockets.

I never gasped. I remained completely calm. Instead, I just stared back at him/her/it as he/she/it stared back at me, and I gave the final suck on my current tanks' load of air. The creature brought up its hands from its sides and interlocked its long, slender fingers, resting them on its belly, as if curiously observing me. I cocked my head to one side in utter fascination of this strange being and held that last breath. Even in my present, near-death state, filled with my last breath of air (I swore I could actually *feel* the oxygen dissipating throughout my body), I was utterly captivated by this gaunt "lengthy" creature covered in flowing robes, with an incredibly weird-assed alien face never before imagined, who stared back at me with starry, compassionate eyes. Yes, they were compassionate, perhaps not so much in the physically expected way, but *psychically.* The eyes were as black as space itself . . . but inside that blackness, that deep and dark space, was the light of a trillion fires . . . scrolling and flying about, as if I were flying *into* them—

DO NOT BE AFRAID.

He/She/It said mentally.

I exhaled, gained a second or two, and switched to my pony.

The creature remained prone on the bottom, where it was, at least physically—but mentally *it was inside me.* Its voice was the most permeating experience I'd ever known. The most comforting. When it spoke, it filled my cells with its words and meaning—more than just words, it was pure, unadulterated *meaning.* This being's *essence.*

But I'm very afraid, I responded mentally.

THEN WHY ARE YOU HERE?

I had no choice—

THERE IS ALWAYS CHOICE. YOU CAME OF YOUR OWN VOLITION.

Then it was a choice where I had no say in the matter, I replied.

Before I could go any further, I was flooded with staggering imagery. I was skip breathing, not taking full breaths, every breath, and I could feel that panic monster again starting to rise up within. I had to again beat that bastard down. Why, now, while doing what I was meant to do, was this frightened part of me resurfacing? Because I was drowning. Even while staring Death in the face, while sharing its very breath, shouldn't I be *glorious*? At one? Embrace the inevitable? But instead of making the best of my time left on earth, I was using it for fear and panic, and that, to me, at that time, was unfathomable.

What would you do if you had only five minutes left to your life? Five *breaths*?

And it was then that I was besieged by the images . . . images I had been waiting for my entire life . . . images that filled all the empty compartments in my existence like a few cubic feet of this sea would soon be doing to my insides.

As I stared into the swirling stars of this creature's eyes—no, not just *eyes*, but his/hers/its very *soul*—I was catapulted back *eons* . . . past such lost civilizations as Atlantis, Mu, or Lemuria . . . no, I was pulled back *further*—I was pulled to a civilization Humankind had no concept of—*could* have no concept of—and not just in terms of time or physical distance, but of *idea* and *concept*. It was the equivalent of discovering a civilization's remains that were buried beneath the *continent* you lived on—how could you ever discover such a thing? With Continental Drift, whatever might have existed so far down in the earth was now forever covered over by miles of, now, to you, bedrock. Scoured and dragged across a layer of earth so far down and unapproachable as to be unthinkable. Or melted into the magma beneath it. To be able to get to such a discovery, one would have to be able to step outside convention—outside of *life*—to pick up the earth and slowly . . . carefully . . . peel it apart. And that is what I felt I now experienced. Not just of this planet on which I was dying, but of *reality*.

This creature was peeling apart reality for me.

This thing took me back to an *age before there* were *ages*.

And I don't mean before the piddly concerns we humans have, concerning whether or not there was or wasn't some kind of primordial soup, I'm talking before the existence of *anything*. Before existence *itself*. Before whatever it was that gave meaning to the creation of the universe—for to have a universe, you had to have something for it to *be* in . . . contained in . . . give it *definition*.

What are you? I asked.

A smile caressed my soul.

CREATOR.

God?

Laughter, the warmest most pervasive and all-encompassing kind filled me, and as it did I felt it radiate outward into all of existence . . . at that moment, I'm sure, all of creation everywhere must have, for that instant, agreed with itself. At that one moment, I am sure there was absolutely no strife and everything agreed with everything, *everywhere*.

NO . . . WE ARE NOT GOD AS YOU UNDERSTAND THE CONCEPT. WE ARE CREATORS. WE CREATE. IN YOUR TERMS, WE ARE THE NEXT BEST THING TO GOD. WHAT YOU SEE BEFORE YOU IS BUT A TINY PORTION OF THE TINIEST SLIVER OF THE TINIEST CONSIDERATION OF US. THIS FORM BEFORE YOU IS LIKE THE TINIEST PORTION OF A SNEEZE—YET AS IMPORTANT AS YOUR CONCEPT OF GOD.

I sensed it was trying to put me at ease. But still, the images continued to fill, *engorge* me. I honestly didn't know if I could physically or psychologically handle all of what was being thrown at me. What this creature was . . . where he/she/it came from . . . was so unimaginably, *inconceivably* distant in the realms of *things* that I felt my mind begin to separate from my being.

This creature had something to do with the creation of *Existence* itself.

And if this was what *this* creature felt like, how could I ever hope to experience God? How could any of us? The creature sang when it— *they?*—spoke . . . notes and meaning that were so unfamiliar to human life . . . yet so *integral* to it . . . notes and tones that were between the spaces of all meaning and thought and *worlds* . . . .

And it was then I was jerked back to my present moment, *my* reality, my Zen and the art of drowning (for now, I truly saw there really *was* an art to dying). If I could just get past the fear, the panic, the overwhelming sensation of that first inhalation of salty fluid where salty fluid wasn't meant to go, I would see the "art" involved. The fluid that gave us sustenance and life was now also bringing about my death (and just what *is* death, anyway?). As centered and controlled as my mind was, this was new to my body, which seemed to suddenly take on a consciousness of its own—and brought with it more images . . . of a race of beings younger than the Creators. A race of beings that were just and purely a *body* consciousness . . . a blueprint, if you will, for all of our human definition. *Our* term "life" was far too limiting. These other creatures existed so that *we* could—*our race*—mimic and learn. This embryonic species was to show all following life forms how to walk and talk and breathe—and *be*—but not just us . . . countless *other* races and intelligences that also occupied other spaces and realities . . . .

I looked down to my convulsing body like a detached observer, as I (again) took a last breath from my pony. I pushed back that panicked-me and brought up my inflator/deflator valve to my mouth. I inhaled that absolutely last vestige of air I would ever inhale and felt the BC deflate around me. I sank to the floor alongside the Creator, or whatever he/she/it was, and also didn't slide. He/She/It continued to watch me. Be there with me. At least, in my case, I wouldn't drown alone, and I noticed, happily, that he/she/it was actually *holding my hand* . . . and its touch was . . . metaphysical. I saw such a look of concern and compassion on its face for me that I cried underwater for the second and last time in my life. This being cared for me in a way that was difficult to comprehend. Death was minutes away.

DEATH SO FRIGHTENS YOU, it said, again, mentally. WE ARE SADDENED BY THIS. IT WAS NEVER MEANT TO BE, AND IT SO PAINS US TO SEE YOU IN SUCH IMAGINARY AGONY. IT WILL NOT LAST.

But it was hard for my body to listen to me, let alone the creature's words, though my mind was fine with the drowning and all. It was my body that was used to the air . . . that *needed* the air . . . not my mind, not my soul, and with its impending loss, behaved as it now did—begging for it. *Pleading* for it. Making those insane promises if I could give it just five more minutes. I was not some Zen master who could control the functions of my body, though I understood its needs. I knew that my body would jerk and spasm and in all probability thrash until its life was ended, put out of its misery. Mentally, I was prepared for this, so I responded back to my starry-eyed companion that I was ready—as ready as I could ever be—and after my five minutes ran out (who's counting at this point?) steeled myself for the inevitable.

Closing my eyes, I spit out my regulator.

As I did so—for I wanted it to come quick and fast—I again completely exhaled and noticed that seemingly contradictory response giving me a reprieve of still a precious few more seconds. I paused until I could pause no longer.

Then I inhaled.

Hard and deep.

If you're gonna do something, go all out, right?

The rush of water into my mouth was startling, to say the least.

We are used to great intakes of water into our mouths and down into our throats . . . but what we are *not* used to is this water rushing past our glottis and into our *lungs. That* is something we are taught, from day one, is wrong and very bad, and there is little argument there. As I knelt there, holding hands with this incredibly loving and benign creature, I again cocked my head in fascination, but this time not at the being before me, but at myself. Curiously, I found—after the initial body jerk—not dissimilar to plunging your face into a bucket of ice water, it really wasn't all that bad. I swallowed and some water made its way into my stomach. The salt water was upsetting, sure, but I knew it wouldn't last forever. So, I thought, what the hell, and swallowed some more. My being was now totally filled with water . . . and I was amazed at how I was as totally at one with the sea as anyone *could* be. As many had been before me. I chuckled—yes, actually chuckled. All this life-long build-up of fear and panic in our lives about death is for naught! As I enjoyed the actual feeling of water totally filling my being (my stomach didn't seem to bother me anymore)—not just being a part of my cells and blood, but also a part of my lungs and stomach and sinuses—I realized it really wasn't all that bad. The Creator holding my hand smiled.

HAVE I SPOKEN THE TRUTH?

You have! I mentally replied.

I was observing how my body began to shut down . . . slowly, quite gracefully, actually . . . as the lack of oxygen—or at least my body's particular way at getting to it—closed up shop, when a curious thought entered my mind: *I hoped that Carl wouldn't let any guilt he may have felt for my staying behind eat at him.* He had nothing to do with my decision to jump ship. It was . . . all me . . .

. . . groggy . . . it was like going to sleep . . . the shutting off of my physical mechanisms . . . the drowning . . . and I felt my hand go limp in the creature's hand and gradually float away from the creature . . . but its smile . . . its deep . . . starry . . . com . . . pa . . . ssionate eyes . . . those . . . were the last things . . . my physical eyes . . . ever saw . . . and . . . I was more . . . grateful . . . than I could . . . ever . . . relate . . . .

But where my life was supposed to end came a new beginning!

I found I was still . . . *conscious.*

I wasn't breathing, not in the conventional human-accepted sense of the concept, yet I was *alive.* And beside me remained this creature. We were no longer on the submerged sea floor of an unknown shipwreck . . . but were standing on the *deck* of it, adrift in a strange and wonderful ocean . . . an ocean I just seemed to know that was, again, that term—*blueprint*—for *all* oceans. My new body, if you could indeed call it "new," was afire with sensation I had never before felt— and was that true? Had I never before felt this, or—

I had an epiphany: *I was this creature!*

Or, more precisely, I was somehow a part of—one and the *same* with a portion of—this creature.

How can this be? I asked.

YOU ARE A PART OF US. WE CREATE—THIS IS WHAT WE DO. WE CREATED YOU, SPIN-OFFS OF US TO GO OUT AND EXPLORE IDEAS AND CONCEPTS. THIS IS NOT TO SAY THAT ALL OF YOUR RACE ARE PART OF US, IN THOSE TERMS, THEY AREN'T—ONLY BUT A HANDFUL, AGAIN, IN YOUR TERMS. WE CREATED THE *CONCEPT* OF CONCEPTS, BUT WE ALSO HAD TO CREATE THE *EXPERIENCE* OF A CONCEPT . . . ITSELF A CONCEPT.

I'm a concept?

EVERYTHING IS A CONCEPT. EVERYTHING IS AN EXPERIENCE.

The starry-eyed Creator and I stood side by side on the deck of this most oddly shaped, inconceivably designed ship. There were unseen dimensions to this vessel just as important as its physical properties.

WE CREATE THINGS, AND WE CREATED THE LIFE YOUR RACE LIVES, WHICH IS ONE PROBABILITY WITHIN COUNTLESS PROBABILITIES. WE HAD A CONCEPT—A THOUGHT—OF WONDERING WHAT IT WOULD BE LIKE TO LIVE SUCH AN EXISTENCE, AND AS WE THOUGHT IT, IT WAS. YOU WERE CREATED AS AN EXTENSION OF US TO EXPLORE WHAT WE CREATED. WE CREATED THE EXISTENCE AND THE NEED TO *EXPERIENCE* THAT EXISTENCE. THE CONTRADICTORY EXPERIENCES OF FEAR AND NO-FEAR. LIFE AND NO LIFE—*YOUR* LIMITED CONCEPT, AS WELL AS OTHER CONCEPTS OF DEATH.

It made sense. What good was existence if there was no experience? How could it *exist?*

THIS BECAME THE BLUEPRINT TO THAT EXISTENCE AND AN ENRICHING EXPERIENCE ON OUR PART TO EXPERIENCE WHAT WE CREATED. CREATING THE EXPERIENCE AND EXPERIENCING IT ARE ONE AND THE SAME. THERE ARE UNLIMITED VERSIONS OF YOU—US—

EXPLORING ALL THE POSSIBLE PROBABILITIES WE CREATED. AS EACH FINALLY BECOMES SELF-AWARE OF THEIR EXPERIENCE, EACH RETURNS AND IS REASSIMILATED WITHIN THE WHOLE. YET THERE NEVER WAS ANY SEPARATION TO BEGIN WITH. THERE IS NO CONTRADICTION IN WHAT WE HAVE SAID.

What was that wreck?

IT IS A PSYCHOLOGICAL-PHYSICAL CONSTRUCT WE USED AS AN EXTENSION OF OUR SELVES. THE WRECK IS MERELY A PROP, A TOY, FOR IT STILL EXISTS WITHIN AND WITHOUT TIME AS YOU KNOW IT, AND IS A PHYSICALLY SYMBOLIC TRANSITIONAL CONCEPT NEEDED TO RETURN EACH OF YOU TO US. IT IS FADING OUT OF YOUR TIME AS WE CONVERSE. WE ARE TOO GREAT AN ENERGY TO BE SO CONTAINED IN ANY ONE REALITY. ASPECTS OF *OUR* EXISTENCE EXTEND THROUGHOUT *ALL* EXISTENCES. YOU ARE A PART OF US. SIMPLY? YOU RETURNED TO US.

But there is nothing inside the ship.

TO YOU. NOW. THERE ARE WORLDS AND TRANSITIONS AND PORTALS THROUGHOUT REALITIES. WHAT YOU SAW WAS THE LIMITED PHYSICAL CONSTRUCT—TRANSLATIONS—OF THESE ENERGIES. YOU WILL KNOW SOON.

I saw that we were now surrounded by powerful waves of towering crests and abysmal troughs. Suddenly, we—this creature, thought-vehicle, and myself—were moving through the most incredible seas I had ever imagined—*and I was exhilarated!* We were unaffected by the maelstrom, yet at one with it. *Excited by it!*

OUR ENERGY CREATES THIS EXPERIENCE. HERE, THE RULES ARE DIFFERENT. WE CREATE THE RULES. THE BLUEPRINTS FOR THE RULES. THE BLUEPRINTS FOR *ALL* BLUEPRINTS.

Instantly, I was no longer separate from the creature that so lovingly stood by me (if I ever was; I still felt it holding my hand as a part of me continued to hover in fascination about the drowned body of my extension into the physical world—but I also experIENCED ALL THE OTHER PORTIONS OF MY THEN-LIFE AS I LIVED AND BREATHED AND . . . CONTINUED TO DIVE WRECKS IN THAT OTHER REALITY . . .). NOW *I* WAS THE CREATOR—MY EXPERIENCE HAD BECOME TOTALLY ASSIMILATED BACK TO WHERE I HAD ALWAYS BEEN. WE

LOOKED INTO MY OWN STAR-FILLED EYES AT THE EXPERIENCE WE CREATED. IT WAS NIGHT NOW, AND WE EXPERIENCED THE WARM, BALMY BREEZES OF A TIME SO INCONCEIVABLY VAST AND DISTANT IT ANNIHILATED THAT OLD PART OF ME. WE CREATED THEM. WE STOOD ON THE DECK OF THIS THOUGHT-VEHICLE, SAILING ACROSS THIS UNIMAGINABLY DISTANT TIME THAT IS NEITHER PAST NOR FUTURE . . . CREATING AND EXPERIENCING THE SEA AND SALT THAT KISSED OUR FACE AND MATTED OUR HAIR AS WE STARED UP INTO THE STARRY NIGHT WE ALSO CREATED. WE CREATED SO MUCH SEA, BECAUSE WE *LOVE* THE SEA. ITS DYNAMICS, ITS BEING. AND WE HAD NEVER FELT SO AT ONE WITH ANYTHING AS WE SAILED UPON IT. OUR ROBES GENTLY FLAPPED WITH OUR PASSAGE BENEATH THE STARS. OUR FACE KISSED THE BREEZES AND WINDS THAT KISSED OUR FACE. WE WERE IN A TIME SO DISTANT IT DEFIED ANY CONCEPT OF TIME, YET WAS INTIMATELY INTEGRAL TO IT. WE, A RACE OF BEINGS THAT ARE THE CLOSEST THING TO ALL THAT IS, OF WHICH WE ARE ALSO A PART. WE SMILED. AS DISTANT AS ALL THINGS MIGHT APPEAR, THEY ARE ALL RELATED. WE CREATED IT SO.

AND AS WE SAILED ON INTO OUR CREATED CONCEPT OF NIGHT, WE LOOKED FORWARD TO MOVING ON TO CREATE OTHER EXPERIENCES AND CONCEPTS AND REALITIES FOR OTHER RACES AND EXISTENCES, AND WONDERED AND LOOKED FORWARD TO WHAT NEW AND EXCITING EXPERIENCES WE WOULD *YET* CREATE. OUR THOUGHT-VEHICLE CHANGED SHAPE TO KEEP UP WITH OUR NEW CONCEPTS, AND AS WE STARED OUT OUR STARRY EYES FOR THE LAST TIME BEFORE WE TOOK ON OTHER FORMS, ONE THING CROSSED OUR MINDS:

BRING IT ON.

Walkers

Severen's feet mindlessly shuffled on with bland repetition as he opened sandied eyes. The sky was clear and there was a chill in the air as early morning reds and oranges splashed across the horizon. The terrain was dusty and desolate.

Severen lifted his head and stretched.

He'd dreamed of being confined to something called a "chair" . . . with wheels on it . . . unable to use his legs. He remembered it'd been a good dream.

"Another day," he said, and rubbed his eyes, cracking open his mouth into a wide, morning yawn. Severen looked around and saw Techen, immediately to his left, who also began to stir.

"Mor-ning, Tech," Severen greeted, mouth full of sand. He spit out the silica granules.

"Yeah, right."

Severen smiled back and shook dust from his hair, then looked around to the faces immediately behind him, several rows back. Most were still asleep. Then there were the faces behind those, and still more behind *those* . . . the unfathomable mass of Walkers who filled in all the way to the rear horizon. And all of them walked . . . all of them trudged aimlessly across desiccated terrain. They were a people of many ages and varieties, and the sound of their incessant plodding unmercifully assaulted Severen's morning grogginess, bringing him back to a reality he'd much prefer to have escaped. It was an ancient march. A tiresome one. At its best, it was

" . . . time to send one of us to investigate. Agreed?" It was Strutter, an Old Walker, who had finally come out and said it. "With that having been said, we must send one of us." His voice was weary with age, but he was the wisest of the Walkers. All of the Council nodded, including Severen.

"We're sorry to drop this upon you, Severen, my friend, but it is the will of the Council that you should go. You are the healthiest of us to withstand the rigors of the journey."

Severen flinched, but remained strong—Council-bound—and accepting of the challenge. Somehow, he had come to expect this, despite the fact that he knew of two others who were supposedly younger than him. Smoothing out his Council uniform, he straightened up and addressed Strutter.

"I agree and I accept."

"Good. We wish you our best."

There was something about Strutter's look that sent a chill through Severen.

Those not of the Council, but closest to them, turned to each other and began to spread the word, and with a bow of his head, and eyes closed, Severen immediately slowed his pace and began the rearward journey. He shifted his shoulders and twisted his body, as he allowed the peopled interior to swallow him up. It seemed

Colder back here. Emotionally colder.

He had never been back more than a half-a-generation or so before, and had labored long and hard to get to his present position on the Forward Council. People in the interior were less friendly, less open (*how well he remembered that*), and now he had to go back in—*deeper*—to investigate rumored trouble at the rear.

The Rear.

He'd heard of only one other walker who'd gone as far back as one generation, and now he was to go *all the way back*.

To the end.

As far as he could physically reach—and to make matters worse, he was to come *all the way back*.

If possible.

It was a quest that bred mixed feelings among the Council, a quest that Severen felt severely hindered by, for further progression on his part, at least for the time of the journey, anyway, but he was duty-bound and the rumors had to be laid to rest. The killings (if there truly were any killings) had to be investigated . . . and stopped.

Feet on autopilot and still facing to the front of the March, Severen retreated deeper into the interior. Uncountable bodies, both familiar and unfamiliar, brushed and flowed past.

If there really were any killings going on, it would probably do the horde well, he thought. Everyone knew there were far too many Walkers, and that, no matter how heretical the thought, they really could stand to use a thinning.

Facts were facts.

As Severen continued backward, he noticed something no one had ever mentioned. This feeling of going backward was almost an *erotic*, stimulating affair . . . and he wondered why it was so outlawed to the common masses. He noticed that going back just two or three rows had no real effect, but once you got the momentum going and traveled through at least a quarter of a generation, the sensation suddenly overcame you. It was a heady, whole-body phenomenon that was very much like sex. Everybody, except the aging and dying, went forward, and he had not known anyone who had gone this far rearward before—except in childhood tales, of course.

(forward)

But it was a good feeling.

Severen also noticed how some began to regard him with suspicion—

Or fear.

Many turned to those beside them and whispered, all the while keeping a watchful eye upon him. He couldn't hear them all, but occasionally did catch something like: *It is not often one from the Council travels rearward. They must surely imagine something dire.* Or: *What has become of us that one of them dares invade our privacy?* But, overall, Severen found the people most accommodating, actually somewhat more talkative than he'd expected. He would have quite an enlightening report to pass on—if he ever made it back—or passed it on to a Communicator.

Although he had probably been doing it for the past few rows, Severen became aware that he'd begun to slow down. He'd come across a tightly knit group at one point and found that he'd grown increasingly bogged down. Twisting about, Severen glanced behind. He saw that the jam-up seemed to go on for quite some distance. He faced forward. *Just enjoy the ride, Sevvy,* he told himself. He looked around to the people beside him and attempted conversation, but as usual, only ended up in passing people by. Until he spotted a particularly quiet and hulking figure of curious intensity, off to his left. Temporarily delaying his rearward passage, Severen redirected himself laterally toward the man. People moved, respectfully, out of his way.

"Good day, citizen!" Severen hailed, "perhaps you can assist me?

My name is Severen, of the Forward Council."

The man wheezed once, then gave him a quick, non-interested glance. "Yeah, so?"

"I've been sent by the Council to investigate goings-on at the rear. There have been recent rumors surfacing—"

"Surfacing? Where've you been, mate? Them's rumors been around fer *generations*."

"Excuse me?"

"I means, yer frigging behind the times, mate—an why would the Council send back one-ah its own? Why not someone more expendable?"

Severen bit his tongue. He needed to regain control of this conversation.

"Okay, so we're a bit behind the times, can you assist me or not?"

"What do you want?"

"Information."

"What's in it fer me?"

"A better position in the March—"

"Oh, sure, an where would *that* get someone like me? It's not like we're getting anywhere with all this drudgery."

"I can see about making you a Communicator."

"Oh, a Communicator, huh?"

"Yes. It'd be low level to start, but it'd be a beginning."

"Well, I can't tell you much, y'see, I'ze only *heard* the rumors, like you, but there's somethin nasty going on back there. I only heard a one guy who made it back, and he went mad. Was sent back to the rear. You ain't gonna like what you find—if it don't find you first."

"Please, elucidate."

The man looked back disapprovingly at the Councilman's choice of words.

"It's *dark* back there . . . people . . . *disappear* . . . an . . . an there's somethin' else."

"What else?"

"Don't know. The man went 'n got all unscrewed before he could tell—but he was about to say *somethin'*, I could see it in his eyes. It was like he couldn't quite bring himself to say it."

"That all you got?"

"Told you it weren't much."

"What was his name, this fellow?"

"Chim, or Jorg—no, Chjort, that was it. *Chjort*."

"Thank you. Want the position?"

"Whatever."

Severen allowed the crowd to advance past, as he continued rearward.

"Sev'ren!" the man yelled back.

"What?"

"Take it easy, mate. It turned Chjort nutty. Killed the others."

Killed others?

(*expendable?*)

"Thank

You never really knew just how large the whole damn thing was from the front. Never really knew until you got inside it. All you saw were rows upon rows of bodies, and bodies going back as far as the eye could see. *Way* back. But as Severen ventured in, he got a true feeling for just how large this exodus was, more so than any of the Communicators (those who ran messages within assigned districts and kept the masses informed), the Forward Council, or any other mythical hero he'd ever heard about. Communicators came close to getting a truer feel for the size of the March, but they never ventured beyond their own boundaries. Each generation had several districts, but the number depended on how large a generation was. Lately, generations had been growing.

Council members . . . they really knew nothing.

Anybody could be a Council member, though there had to be a *proving* to see whether that person was truly worthy of the position. Everyone wanted to be up front, to make laws and institute changes, but not many were willing to work for the privilege. To pay the price. To see something other than the backs of their contemporaries. That was what had initially driven Severen. That, and the love of a woman, or, more to the point, the *scorn* of one.

Severen had fallen in love with a woman named Thea. She had been strong, and the most beautiful woman he'd ever laid eyes on. He'd first seen her when she was only two hops over from him, magically having appeared out of nowhere. They'd flirted, and when Severen finally made his move, he found her more than interested. They were soon marching side by side. Copulating. Inseparable. Then he began to tell her of his ambition, that he wanted to start a family of his own and become one of the Forward Council. That was where things had begun to deteriorate. It seemed she had no ambition to go to the front, a place where you couldn't hide.

Hide.

She'd had something to hide. She hadn't liked being put up for display. She'd liked where she was, free to drift about . . . to see others.

And Thea had no intention of starting a family. She'd liked being able to see whom she wanted, and do what she willed. Severen had been nothing more than a passing encounter for her. Sure, she'd liked him . . . even the sex and good times they'd had together . . . but that was all. Severen had awoken one morning to find her gone. Just as he'd found her . . . he'd lost her.

He never did find out what it was she had to hide, but figured she was probably trafficking in the powerful sleep drug, Utopa, the most common offense in the March. The drug gave the power to dream while awake, for as long as three days, after which subjects usually became hooked and zombie-like. Some, those of stronger constitution, lasted longer and became junkies, but most withered away and died. Either way, all were eventually sent back to the rear. In the end, Severen's break with Thea had been for the best. Associating with pushers wasn't conducive to a Council position.

Severen found himself again eavesdropping.

" . . . Celila and Trax were doing pretty well until Celila's Communicatorship," a pair of Walkers discussed.

"Took her away, didn't they?"

"Yep—but they're still seeing each other, wouldn't'cha know it. It's been a hard road since she's the youngest Communicator and gets all the rotten assignments—she's gone nearly all the time."

The other gave a knowing nod and wrinkled his face disapprovingly. Severen remembered that name. Celila. She was new. Swift. She was also a good Mediator for the Council, which wasn't good for her man, since she'd most probably get promoted and see even less of him. It wouldn't be until her next promotion, a supervisory position, that she'd have any time for a relationship—and who'd want to wait that long?

Severen angled off into a different direction, and looked up to the sky. It had darkened noticeably since he'd last checked. He realized he was now into the very heart of the March, sand almost completely obscuring the sky. Don't even talk about the noise. And it was also decidedly colder . . . not just emotionally, but physically . . . and he didn't like that. It should have gotten warmer, from all that body heat. But it

Wasn't life a bitch? It seemed that all one had to look forward to was to live long enough to get to the front lines. Then what? Severen had gotten there, and where had it gotten *him?* He was back to where he'd started—hell, he was *farther* back than where he'd started. He'd actually *regressed* . . . .

And he'd just blindly accepted this task. How easy it had been to plod along aimlessly in life and be the yes-man.

(easy)

This whole thing was entirely overrated. What was he supposed to do once he found what he was looking for? The gruff-one had mentioned that *others had been killed.*

What others, and *why; what* had killed *whom?*

Severen had no knowledge of anyone else being sent that far back, let alone being killed off.

But what if others *had* been sent back?

Was there something the Forward Council wasn't telling him? What was that look in Strutter's face all about?

Was he even supposed to make it back?

That last thought rocked him like an earthquake.

Maybe he was an offering.

An offering.

"No, no—that can't be. The Council isn't like that. They're *Lawgivers. Elders.*"

So why choose him?

The only ones on the Council who had any real power were the old ones. *The ones who'd been around a while.* So where did that leave the younger members? If the elders didn't die, then the younger went nowhere.

(except on journeys like this)

But he knew of no one—

Then it hit him.

There *was* something about a journey!

He remembered . . . as a child . . . that his parents had told him about a Council member they'd met who'd gone back on a similar trek. Severen didn't remember the purpose of the trek, but did remember the look on his parents' faces when they talked about it. They were *scared.*

Why?

Because little Sevvy had already made up his mind that he *was going to join the Council when he grew up.*

Millions of tiny switches clicked on and off inside his head.

Spark.

And there were always bogeyman stories from childhood about what went on back there . . . *way* back there. Stories of the dead coming to life and ripping the aged from their generations, never to be seen again. Of screams and howls in the dead of night. Maybe there was more to the legends and myths than people cared to believe.

Spark.

Spark.

Or tell.

Contact.

A conspiracy within the Council!

Severen was suddenly slammed into.

It wasn't the normal hiking-through-the-lands-trip-and-tap—no, this was a full-on grind that lifted him up off one foot and had him tottering for a moment as he skipped across the terrain, trying to regain his balance. When he did regain his footing, he whipped around hard to see the face in the crowd that must have started the upset. It was a face that sent a chill up his spine. It was an evil, twisted face that didn't look real . . . but continued to hold his gaze.

Severen maneuvered out of the face's path to see if it would follow. It did.

No sooner had he repositioned himself, than the face again followed him . . . but had also gained in row. Severen looked around. Found that the generation of people around him suddenly seemed to have aged a great deal. Many were white-haired and bent over . . . more shuffle than walk to their strides. Many had only half-opened eyes, or failing eyesight.

This meant the dead were even closer than he'd imagined. Maybe a *lot* closer.

Severen maneuvered toward a stout individual and there held his position. The old man looked to him.

Why do you come to me? his gaze begged, *I am old and not long for the March. Go away.*

I am sorry, old man, but I have no choice, Severen's eyes replied, *I am on a mission. From the Forward Council.*

So you would have me killed for the Council?

Before Severen could make his facial reply, the stalking face was upon the old man. Severen had been so hypnotized by the ancient one's gaze that he'd forgotten to keep track of his pursuer. He looked on in horror as he saw its face—and what was left of its body. It was dead and stank of carrion. Powerful, clawed arms raked out from underneath powerful, shredded shoulders . . . arms that hopped and grappled from shoulder to shoulder and supported a smoldering torso. It tore asunder those it touched. It was a torso that supported a head and shoulders—*and nothing more. There was nothing below its gaping and dangling chest cavity.*

Severen watched as the old man was torn apart by the corpse; he backed away with weak, flaccid knees . . . and noticed that those alongside the old man had also moved away . . . silently and without question.

As if this was accepted routine.

"*No!*" Severen shouted.

But still his feet took him away.

"*No!*" he shouted, but still his gaze was upon the old man.

"*No!*" he shouted, but still the corpse crawled and rent. Rent the ancient one to pieces . . . .

"*NO!*"

Severen watched as the old man's eyes were separated from their sockets . . . .

His words had no effect on the killing. No effect on the dismemberment that went on (as he watched). Words that could not stop the direction his feet were taking him.

Away.

Severen saw the old man crumple soundlessly, wordlessly, to the ground.

Accepting.

Why do you come to me, the ancient man had pleaded.

Because I am on a mission, he had replied.

A *mission*.

He was on a mission to find out what was going on at the rear. Well, he'd just found out—and now he was running away.

This is the real *reason I was sent back. I'm no investigator—I'm a* sacrifice.

Looking to a cripple beside him, Severen saw the walking stick he possessed and grabbed it without thinking. The cripple looked at him and smiled, then allowed himself to fall to the ground—and was quickly trodden asunder by those that flowed over from behind. Severen was shocked to discover he felt no emotion one way or the other. Turning, he looked back for the clawed corpse and hefted his newly acquired weapon. He was lucky, the wood felt solid and sturdy. It was dense and would wield well.

Severen backed up and readied the staff, glanced behind himself several times, but still could not see his attacker. It was getting darker. Colder. Out of the corner of his eyes he thought he saw something and turned slowly, not sure there was really anything there. Yes, three positions over . . . a face glared back at him with a mouth full of teeth and decayed flesh.

Grinned hideously.

Severen followed that smile down to its neck, then down to its chest.

Down to its waist.

There was now more body to this corpse than when Severen had first encountered it!

Severen looked to the newly acquired legs . . . legs that had not originally belonged to that creature. Legs, he recognized, that had belonged to the ancient

(*why do you come to me?*)

man with the penetrating gaze.

The creature had stolen the ancient one's body.

The very thought made Severen's stomach heave, and, indeed, he nearly did. He tried not to imagine the horrors the ancient man had been put through to give up those legs.

The monster approached, and the crowd widened.

Good, Severen thought, *more room to swing this thing.*

"*Come on!*"

The corpse lunged awkwardly, but Severen managed to hold his ground as he lifted the staff in a backward arc and quickly snapped it forward. It connected, and the corpse took the full force of it in its waist, easily splitting in two. The top half flew forward and the bottom half crumpled to the dirt. Severen then watched as the creature latched onto another walker. Not allowing it time to gain another claw hold, Severen again rushed it. He rose his weapon high over his head and brought it crashing down onto the center of the corpse's cranium, splitting it open. It emitted a rancor that made Severen gag. The thing writhed in pain, but uttered no sound, and the walker it was attached to hardly seemed cognizant of the attack. Severen finished off the creature by hammering it free with the staff, and it went tumbling to the ground—and to the rear of the March.

Great, that's the last place I wanted this thing to go, he thought.

The March then folded back in around Severen as if nothing had happened, and as he wiped the sweat and fear from his brow, one of the walkers adjacent to him turned and smiled. Severen regarded him blankly.

Then vomited.

What was going on back here?

Severen no longer knew just how far back he'd gone, and it didn't really matter, he guessed, because things weren't right. He could no longer see the sky, and it was almost always dark, now. And there were times he had actually thought he'd heard screams—and laughter, hideous, hideous, laughter—from the rear. Every time he would look back, fear would grip him and give him a good throttling. He didn't want to go back there. It was a No Man's Land. A festering graveyard.

Nothing good was back there . . . .

He had given up on the quest long ago—blew it all off. His sojourn had now become more of a matter of *principle*. Of what was *right*. He recalled how it had bothered him to accept the quest . . . at why *he* should have been chosen . . . but found he didn't feel this way about this new revelation. Some things just felt right, even if they were wrong . . . .

But who would know of his intent?

There were no longer any Communicators this far from the Council, so information of his whereabouts wouldn't exactly be known, and to the masses he would just be remembered as the "one from the Front" performing his duty in the defense of his people. He would fade away into the annals of history as just another soul lost to the rear.

Or sacrificed.

His blood boiled.

He had his pride and *no one* was going to sacrifice *him*.

As unfortunate as his present situation was, he had to make the best of it. He was too far back to just turn around (so to speak) and return home. If not for the Council, then he had to do this for the others. His fellow walkers.

But, by the gods, the more he thought about it, the more it made sense! Send the *young!* The *virile!* Those who could better challenge the Old Ones. Send them to the rear to appease whatever was there—*just keep it from coming forward.* Keep it away from the front . . . *from the Forward Council.*

Severen looked to the staff. To those around him. If they weren't dead, they were very near. Their shuffling was pained and slow, their bodies decayed. It wouldn't be long now.

He was scared as hell.

Severen's pace had slowed quite a bit, either from fear or uncertainty, but slowed down it had.

The air now had a distinctly different feel to it, and it stunk. Rotted flesh. Nervously he glanced behind himself (as he tore off a piece of fabric from his uniform and tied it around his mouth and nose), but could no longer see beyond two or three rows. It was as dark as night and there was a thick haze, one that he'd walked right into.

As if he had any choice.

Rotted, moldy flesh, he thought, *so many particulates in the air.*

His mind began to drift back to the conspiracy. As right as he knew he was, he tried to coax some sense out of the activities that had led him to his present situation. Of course the Elders wouldn't have taken on this journey themselves, they probably wouldn't have survived it, and sure he wasn't the youngest—not by far—so why had *he* been picked above all others?

Maybe because you'd risen from within *the March, Sevvy, old boy.*

Of course.

He hadn't been born into the Forward Council, like the others. Strutter had *always* been there, had been there even before Severen's parents had grown, and Techen—Techen was born into it, he knew that. But what about Quix? Se-Er? Yes, they, too, all claimed birthright. In fact, Severen now saw, he couldn't think of one of the Forward Council who *wasn't* of direct bloodline (except Strutter, but he was *the* Elder, *the* Rule-Maker), so why would the two younger members be any different?

They wouldn't be—unless another insider was being cultivated as he had been . . . .

This wasn't exactly the feeling he needed just now.

An unexpected rocking from the row directly behind him caught him off-guard and sent him into an adjacent walker, as he tripped across a particularly deep rut. The man he'd hit crumpled to the dirt and had, in fact, actually disintegrated.

"Oh, no—*no* . . . I can't be *there* yet!"

Another walker near to him opened a hardened, white eye and winked weakly.

"Y-yer not . . . there yet . . . ," he said.

But you'll wish ya were!

The words put Severen temporarily at ease. If one was dead, then others were sure to follow, and soon. The graveyard

(*answers*)

was not far away.

Destiny.

Ah, the hell with it.

Spinning around on his heels and actually facing *toward* the rear, Severen hefted his staff before him and pitched himself *forward*.

Into the pitch blackness of the unknown.

It wasn't long before he'd found that all those surrounding him were, indeed, dead.

None moved out of his path as he approached, so he came to wielding his staff and smashing them out of his way. Their bodies crumbled into dust as did the first. Or as near as he could tell, in this darkness, to which his eyes had grown exceedingly well accustomed.

He also saw that the ranks had thinned out considerably, and this bothered him.

What was *beyond*? *Was* there a beyond?

Would he fall off some edge that rolled up after the March's passage?

Old wives tales told to disobedient children.

Yet tales that still scratched at his troubled, adult psyche.

Movement. There had been movement up ahead.

Severen felt the fear again seize him, but fought it off and cocked his head. There was a figure that ran behind the few bodies that still shuffled past. He squinted, but the figure had darted back into the darkness. It was an upright figure, to be sure, like him—but *quick*. All this time, he thought he'd been alone. The fear returned.

There's nothing good back here.

He tightened his grip on his staff.

What had he gotten himself into?

He continued forward and heard noise . . . this time from behind him.

Then the noise moved somewhere to his left.

Then back again behind him.

Spinning around, Severen brought up the staff just in time to deflect the brunt of an attack. A dark figure had bounced off him and run back into the dark, but not before leaving tears in his clothes and stinging gouges in his flesh. Severen thought of the similarities between this attack and the earlier one—but that this one had legs.

Severen spun around several more times, making sure that the thing was gone. At least temporarily. His temples throbbed with his quickened pulse, and his chest heaved with shortened breaths. Adrenaline surged through him. There was more movement . . . more of them.

Terrific.

"Who's there! By the power of the Forw—"

A black thing lunged, and this time Severen wasn't as lucky, his staff slammed up hard into his forehead. Warmth spread down and over his eyes. At the same time, something ripped deeply into his right arm and there was another splash of warmth upon his face. Blinding pain quickly followed . . . then the thing was off him.

By the time Severen managed to reopen his eyes, another was upon him.

Pain or no pain he cocked back the staff, and, twisting around with it, slammed it hard into what he surmised was the torso of the creature. It took all the spring out of the thing's attack and Severen watched it crumple into a heap. Quickly recovering, Severen barely had time to react to another one, so he ducked . . . only netting a gash to his forehead . . . and followed the shape around. He brought his weapon down square on the thing's back and there was a more-than-satisfying crunch. The thing didn't get back up. Severen backed away, whirled his stick about him, and peered into the darkness for more.

But none came.

The ache of his body grew more painful as the shock wore off, and his gait turned into more of a labored shuffle. He'd managed to stem the flow of blood from his wounds, but the pain that racked his body had to be more than just from cuts and bruises.

Infection.

Infection that spread rapidly. If Severen didn't miss his guess, he probably wouldn't make it til sunrise, if there *was* a sunrise anymore . . . .

Severen dreamed as he dozed. Dreamed of a dark and thick blackness . . . a blackness from which nothing returned. He saw eyes . . . two large . . . all-seeing orbs that emerged from the darkness, only to return back to it. And he saw claws . . . lots and lots of claws . . . that all tore and ripped into him. Ripped him into big, chunky pieces—

He awoke with a start. Couldn't believe he had

(*been allowed to survive*)

dozed. He was alone. Except for the occasioned walking dead he passed. He no longer swung at them.

Severen had never really given much thought to what was actually at the rear, the *ultimate* rear. To what it might actually look like. He just wished he wasn't there, now. On the surface, he tried to convince himself that he didn't care to know, but deep down he did feel a sense of duty. A yearning for more.

Must know.

Must.

Bring back information . . . crush the conspiracy . . . .

Back—back to *whom?*

The people.

The Council could no longer be trusted. They were all suspect. All in on it. Had been since the dawn of eternity. All those sent back in the legends and myths had been sent back as fodder for some evil god. Sent to keep whatever was there from coming forward and destroying the rest of the March.

Was sure of it.

Dead sure.

Never had there been any mention of the dead coming back to life from the graveyard. Never. Had always been left as a black void of nothingness. A place not spoken of during the light of day, barely even whispered of during nightfall.

It was a lair.

But a lair to what?

What evil force made its home there, and to where did its power extend?

Severen checked his arm's dressing. It was a mass of dried blood and torn material . . . and there was a gangrenous pus that festered around the wound. Severen touched it with the end of his staff and it burst, splattering onto his face a smelly spore-like substance that got inside his mouth and nose. He didn't bother to check his other wounds. He felt the infection as it ate away at him. He didn't need any further confirmation.

Severen lifted his throbbing head.

"What . . . *are* you?" he coughed out into the darkness.

Two blazing red eyes opened their lids from the darkness before him.

"What do you want from me. From *us?*"

The eyes floated. He was sure they were amused with him.

Gathering all his effort, Severen hefted his staff and swung it out before him. The eyes remained untouched . . . were now filled with a mass of scrolling stars.

Not much farther to go. Care. No longer cared. Never make it back . . . .

Eyes.

Disappeared.

Severen plodded forward toward the rear, using his staff as a crutch. Had lost all feeling in his left side. Numb on his right. Vision grew cloudy . . . .

DO. YOU. KNOW. WHO. I. AM?

Came the voice.

DO. YOU. KNOW. WHO. I . . . AM?

It was a voice. Inside his head. This was it. Had finally gone delirious. Alone; seeing ghosts. Hearing voices. What difference did it make if he answered? Was dying anyway . . . .

No, I do not know . . . who you are . . . but I'm sure this . . . poison . . . has invented something good . . . for me.

I AM . . . THE . . . UNNAMED.

Severen looked into the blackness and laughed.

Well, aren't you *a grand delusion!*

I . . . AM . . . ALL.

Pleeeased to meet you . . . .

Silence.

Severen felt the uneasiness that accompanied that silence. Felt, for the first time since his last attack, that maybe, maybe he wasn't all that alone . . . maybe it wasn't *delirium* he was talking to . . . .

YOU HAVE COME . . . FOR ME . . . YOU ARE TO BE MY . . . COMMUNION.

PREPARE YOURSELF.

"Who *are* you?"

I AM ALL.

" . . . said that, but . . . what *are* you?"

No immediate response.

I AM . . . THAT WHICH KEEPS THE MARCH . . . FORWARD.

That which keeps the March forward. Severen shook his head. "Don't . . . understand."

IT IS NOT YOUR PLACE . . . TO UNDERSTAND.

PREPARE YOURSELF.

That which keeps the March forward. Could it be possible that the March was *evoked* by this thing? *Controlled* by it? That the March was nothing without it? But the March had been going on since time immemorial . . . .

Forever.

I AM BEYOND THAT.

Eternal.

Severen's head hurt. He stumbled. *I'm going to die, I'm* really *going to die . . . .*

Severen placed the staff out before him for support, bore the majority of his weight on it . . . but only managed to continue forward in short . . . shuffling . . . movements. Movements that brought immense pain. Severen jerked; felt something burrow into his brain. His *mind . . . .*

ENOUGH . . . TIME.

A gigantic claw shot out from the darkness, and with it, a deafening clap of thunder. It smashed through Severen's stick and grasped him mid-body, lifting him up off the ground. Severen went limp and expelled a loud *huh!* as his staff fell in pieces about him. He had a sudden flashback of helplessness as a child . . . unable to keep a dying grandparent from disappearing into the rear of the March . . . and felt like that child again. But there was also an unexpected ease with who he was . . . what he had *become.*

He felt small and puny . . . yet *complete.* He retreated inward.

There was warmth there.

The two large, red eyes again formed in the darkness before him and Severen was pulled in. Severen looked directly into the eyes and spoke:

Go on . . . I'm prepared . . . .

Severen floated. Drifted within nothingness. There he found the thing he had come for. The quest. The reason. It was fear, plain and simple. Fear from the Walkers as they had built it up over their generations; over eons.

FEAR.

From turning back. Fear . . . from looking behind—forward. Fear that they were being followed . . . devoured from that which was behind them. Darkness. And it had caught them. Exacted its toll. Its price for existence.

PAY HOMAGE TO THAT WHICH CONTROLS THEE . . . .

The Girl Who Chased Gargoyles
1992

I knew her long ago . . . in a past so present . . . a bright, wispy sprite of a girl. She loved to climb things. She also loved her bubbles. Blew them everywhere. It was those bubbles that had set me free.

But that was so long ago. In a past so bright. And I miss her.

And now I will tell you her story.

Angela was her name. She was so bright and cheerful that I didn't think there was a thing in the world that could ever bother her. She had long, silken hair and a smile as dazzling as the sun.

The sun. A sun that had grown dark with the death of her parents.

But that's for later.

For now, she skipped and sang everywhere she went. And (as I have said before) she loved to climb. Trees. Rocks. Buildings. Anything. There wasn't an obstacle she would not tackle and this so frightened her parents, for there was nothing they could do. She was a most willful child, and a very sure-footed one—the most sure-footed I have ever seen—there was no fear in her, only wonder and amazement. To her, *everything* was beautiful. *Everything* was *fun*. There was no such thing as evil.

She was indeed the purest of souls.

One day, while walking through town with her parents, Angela had spotted a building that had immediately captured her fancy. It was an old, abandoned remain and her father, a construction worker, had told her that it was a building scheduled for destruction. This brought a momentary frown to Angela's face.

"Why?" she asked.

"Because, Angela, to all things there must come an end."

Angela thought about this.

"Why must all things die?"

"Well, I think it's God's way of telling us that we must live life to its fullest."

"Well," said Angela, "that's what *I'm* going to do."

That's the way she was. Nonplussed. Practical (in an idealistic kind of way) and direct-to-the-point. Death didn't seem to bother her like it did other kids her age. In fact nothing seemed to bother her quite like it did the other kids. She was always the one to explain things to her friends, always the one to comfort them when they lost their favorite marble to an opponent in a game. She was always there when she was really needed and had such a love of life and all that it encompassed.

One day she came back to the doomed building, and, as do all kids (for she was, after all, but a child) found her way into it. Blowing her little bubbles, she made her way up the creaking steps with their curved banisters, through the hazy interior and up to the very top.

Where she found the monsters.

But to her they weren't *monsters* . . . they were their own form of life no matter how ugly, and, eventually, they were her companions . . . her . . . friends. She would come to talk with them. Have fun, for though she was so bright and sweet she still had no real friends her age, at least any who could understand her. Some people are just born more aware. Her own parents barely (if they ever really did) understood her. Angela was always off dreaming somewhere—and we all know how dreamers are treated.

So, as often as she could, Angela would journey into this building and climb the dusty, creaky stairs to the top. There she would come out on its ledges and sit among the stone creatures of the sky, the leader of which called itself "Pandor." She hadn't known the word "gargoyle" until the monsters themselves had told her. Or so she told people . . . and that made her situation in life very difficult.

"*Gargoyles*, you say? On top of *what* building? Do your parents know about this, young lady?"

And all she would do was vigorously nod her head up and down, her smile so bright and innocent, and say, "Yes, yes they *do!*" Then she would skip off in some random fashion and leave behind a stunned and indignant lady, poised on the sidewalk, her eyes the size of silver platters. She did not yet know how to keep things to herself, but I suppose that was just a product of her love of life and her desire to share it with others.

It did get her into trouble. Her and her parents.

It had been a day like any other as she skipped homeward, singing to herself, but once she walked through the front door of her home, she felt the change. Slowly she followed the sounds of voices and stalked toward the kitchen. Peeked around a corner. There she saw her mother and father talking with a strange lady she had never seen before. A lady who seemed to ask her parents an awful lot of questions. She was so very official looking, like her teachers at school, only more so.

Do you give her enough food, clothing, and other care?

Is she bathed regularly?

These are her grades, but do you ever discuss them with her?

Do you get involved with her life, play, and fantasies?

Why is it that you let her climb around condemned buildings . . .

Who was this lady, and why was she asking all these questions?

So Angela left her house and went to seek out her friends . . . the monsters. It was the monsters that had told her . . . as she blew her bubbles for them . . . that this lady was going to try to take her away. That this lady was not to be trusted.

Maybe you should not tell people about everything you do, Angela. Like when you climb up here to play with us.

"Why?" she asked, "why would anyone want to do such a thing? What have *I* done? I haven't hurt anybody."

Because that woman is an evil person, Angela, prone to sticking her nose into the affairs of others. But do not worry about it, we will not let her take you away from us. We love you.

And we will take care of this lady.

So Angela shrugged her shoulders and continued to blow her bubbles, and the monsters continued to talk with her.

And that was just the way Angela was.

When she had arrived home later that day, Angela found her parents waiting for her. They looked *very* troubled.

"Angela, honey, we have to talk with you," they had said. They were such model parents. "There was this lady over to see us earlier, a very important lady, who was very concerned that we were not being good enough parents to you. Do you feel we are not being good parents?"

Angela looked from father to mother, then back again. "No, Daddy, I don't think so. Why—do *you?*"

That question, even given their daughter's already sagacious level of development, came as a cold slap in the face to the both of them. However, having grown somewhat accustomed to her often poignant points of view, they replied back to her.

"No—no, honey, your father and I love you very, *very* much and we work very hard so that you can have the best of all possible things in life."

"We try to always be there for you," her father cut in, "but this lady," he paused to look to his wife (who squeezed his hand very tightly, Angela noticed), "well, she can be very persuasive to the wrong kinds of people. She can take you away from us without much say on our parts. She tells us," he again paused, "she tells us that there are those out there who are concerned that we are not providing you with proper care. That we let you climb around condemned buildings and—"

"And talk to *monsters*," her mother cut in.

"Is this true—are you really climbing around condemned buildings? Tell us this isn't true, Angela, it's very dangerous to do things like that. You could get hurt. You could fall and *die*."

Both parents looked at Angela very hard.

Angela remained undaunted. She knew what her parents wanted to hear. *I would never get hurt*, she thought, *they would save me, my children, they love me and would never let anything or anyone, harm me—and* you *too. But she knew what they wanted to hear, and what she had to say.

"No."

And that was just the way she was.

And we will take care of this lady.

It was the next day; an article in the paper. Social worker murdered in apartment parking lot. As gruesome as the details were (parts of her body have not yet been found), her parents breathed a sigh of relief. Granted their file would surely remain in the records even though the case worker was dead, but hopefully no one would ever come back a calling.

That day Angela made her way back to her children and asked them about it.

Yes, we did it. We told you we'd take care of you. Your parents. If something were ever to happen to your parents, something would happen to you, and we won't have that. We love you, Angela.

"And I love you. But is that right, what you did, to make someone die?"

Is it right to take away from someone that which is loved by them?

"Hmm. I guess not."

Wouldn't that instead make such a person who would do such, evil and dangerous?

"Why, yes, I guess it would."

Then we have done good, ridding you and your family of such evil, have we not?

"You have. Thank you."

Then blow more bubbles for us, Angela, we love your bubbles.

And Angela blew more bubbles.

Because that's just the way . . . .

The next day Angela was at the library and looked up what gargoyles were. First she found they were waterspouts, but she knew that couldn't be right, for water spouts couldn't talk. Then she found the *other* descriptions . . . .

"Pandor . . . do you know God?"

Pandor remained quiet for a moment before answering.

"Why do you ask, child?"

Well, the other day our class went to the library looking up mythological creatures 'n stuff—I know what that means—and I saw a picture of you, I mean what *looked* like you. I asked Mrs. Gartle if I could do extra credit and look up gargoyles, and she said yes. It said you were . . . *tal-is-mans* . . . used to terrify the devil and forced to serve God."

Pandor stared back unblinkingly.

"But the worse part was that it showed a picture of you eating people. Like me."

Pandor stared.

"Is it true? Do you eat people? Do you know God?"

Pandor shifted its dense stone frame, sending a dull shudder throughout the stone battlements and up through Angela's diminutive frame.

"We are . . . what we *are*. Manifestations. Surrogates. We are the horror that men fear. Gods. We are evil incarnate. Inchoate—"

"—I do not understand—"

"—no one does, child—"

"—*teach* me—"

"—but it is *you* who are teaching *us*."

"Do you eat—"

"Yes. We eat that which is your kind."

"Why."

"Because it is necessary. Nothing more."

"Will you eat me?"

"It is not necessary."

"Will it ever be?"

"No."

"How do you know?"

"We know."

"Do you know God."

"God knows us."

"Is that good?"

"It is nothing. It simply *is*."

"*Do* you *know God?*"

Pandor turned away.

"Okay, so you don't want to answer that. Fine, be childish. Then answer this—do you know your true purpose? The books said your exact function is unknown."

Pandor smiled, the first time Angela had ever seen him do so. The crack that opened across its face like an earthquake sent a shiver down Angela's back. It looked *painful*.

"We are . . . *what we are*. Child. Do not look too deeply—*you may never come back*."

Angela retreated backward and lost her balance, tripping over a loose piece of rubble. As her arms flailed out behind her she closed her eyes in preparation of meeting concrete . . . when stone hands reached out and gently grasped her. Angela looked up to see the carved face of another gargoyle.

"And we do not want *that*, either. *You must watch your step, child*," Pandor said, thickly.

"Thank you. But there is so much I do not know, and I don't know if I like that."

"There are many things even those such as ourselves do not know. Yet we still are. We *exist*. The same applies to you, my child. You still are. You *exist*. We are here for you. We do not want evil to befall you."

Angela gave Pandor a sharp look.

"Does that make *me* God?" she whispered delicately.

"I only smile but once a lifetime, child."

But Angela would not let it die. She became fascinated with the topic of God. Fascinated that her companions seemed to treat her as one. It was a topic that she had never really considered before.

God.

All powerful.

All knowing.

What is *God?*

Angela thought about how she seemed to know so much, so much more than anyone else her age, let alone the adults.

Am I God?

Have I enslaved the gargoyles to be my *talismans?*

Could it be true?

They do protect me—

Answer my questions—respond only to me—

But how can this be?

I am but a little girl.

               —a little girl who knows too much—

Angela slept and dreamt of her monsters, but it was a dream filled with dread. It threatened her. She saw herself atop the building, like she had been when she had first found them. All silent and still they were, poised on the precipices of their battlements; lurched forward . . . but going nowhere. Then she came out to the edges and began to blow her bubbles. Stood next to the one that she had come to call Pandor. It looked so *scary*, she remembered. So *real.*

She let loose her bubbles and a particularly large one drifted past the Pandor-gargoyle face. Angela looked back down into her bubble bottle, ready to blow another one when she heard a loud thundering sound and felt a burst of wind pummel her.

She looked up to find she was standing alone on the battlement.

Where once had stood a statue, now there stood nothing but still crumbling mortar. She gasped, turned to run, but instead came face to face with the very monster that had only moments before been motionless beside her.

Angela dropped her bubbles and went rigid.

Tried to scream but nothing came out.

Her eyes traveled down the length of the monster's form and to its massively taloned claws. Noticed how the creature actually hovered, however heavily, inches above the battlement, its wings beating the air.

As Angela took steps backwards, away from the gargoyle and towards the building's edge, she felt claws wrap around her. To her horror, she saw other gargoyles were also breaking free. She looked back to the first one and saw it bring out its hand from behind its back. In a cruelly twisted claw, rested a bubble.

I offer this back to you, child.

Dream-Angela reached out and took it.

But that was where any similarities from her past ended. No sooner had dream-Angela grasped for the bubble, when it suddenly burst open and spewed blood all over her. Angela looked around to see the faces of other gargoyles. They all leered. Hissed. The first gargoyle stepped aside, and behind him sat a box. It was a dark, subtly vibrating box, Angela thought, but didn't vibrate *physically*.

No matter how much she didn't want to go, she came closer to the black, black box. She had to see. The box was blacker than black, and slowly it opened. Angela heard whispers . . . layers upon layers of multitudes of far-off and indistinct voices. Something tugged at her mind. Voices that rose in a crescendo as the top of the box continued to open.

Something called her name. Reached into her soul.

It was then that the dead light began to pour out from the opening—

Angela awoke.

And found herself standing alongside her bed, bent over and soaked in sweat.

The next day found Angela dreamier than usual, aloof even.

While at school people would find her sitting in class, or out in the play yard just staring off into space. Several times classmates had come running up to her to see if she was okay and she would just ask them *Are you God? Do* you *know God?*

When one of the children mentioned this to Mrs. Gartle, Mrs. Gartle simply had to investigate.

"Angela, honey, are you all right?"

Angela continued to stare off into the clouds.

"Angela, it's me, Mrs. Gartle, can you hear me?"

"I hear."

"What's the matter?"

"Why nothing, Mrs. Gartle. I am contemplating."

"Really, child, you simply must get more to the point. And where do you get all these big words, anyway? Come with me."

"But I don't have to."

Mrs. Gartle froze and choked out a half-choked, *"E-excuse me?"*

"But I don't *have* to go with you, Mrs. Gartle, it is not *immutable—*"

"You will do as you're told this instant, young lady! Just because you think you're smarter than the rest of your peers doesn't mean you're smarter than me. You will listen to your elders!"

Mrs. Gartle grabbed Angela by her arm and dragged her back into the school building. That night Angela's parents received a phone call from Mrs. Gartle. About the disrespect she had displayed toward her and the students. Mrs. Gartle was curious if Angela had been behaving this way at home, and why, and when Angela's surprised parents replied that she hadn't, but that they'd certainly deal with it. Mrs. Gartle took them at their word and hung up. It wasn't so easy for Angela, however, who found herself answering before her parents and then performing an extra regiment of chores before going to an early bed.

But in bed, one can dream, and in the dream, Angela met a white light. A light that asked her

Do you question God?

I question everything.

Why?

It seems to be my being. It is what I am.

It is?

Is it so wrong to question?

It is not.

Why do I question?

It is as you have said.

What I am?

You learn quickly.

What is my purpose? Am I God?

You are intensified. You are . . . more than you are.

I don't understand.

The white light laughed. *Be careful. Do not ungrace yourself, little one.*

I don't understand.

Angela awoke. Felt different.

Empowered.

For Angela had decided she was God.

Angela sat in front of Border Elementary School when Mrs. Gartle, the principal, and another student, came out the front doors. Heavy storm clouds and gusty winds were rolling in, but there was as yet no rain.

"There she is," the terrified little girl had said, pointing, her finger trembling mightily. "She's right over there."

"Okay, thank you, Susan. You may return to your class, now." Susan turned and hurriedly left. The principal and Mrs. Gartle looked to each other. It was the principal who spoke first.

"Angela—Angela would you come over here please?"

Angela looked up from the thing that occupied her attention and stared detachedly at the two.

"Would you come *here*, please?"

"Okay." Angela got up and walked over, still clutching her object.

"What would you like?" she asked.

"We would like to know what you're telling the other children," the principal said.

"That's easy."

"Well, what is it, then?"

"That I'm God."

Mrs. Gartle brought a trembling hand to her mouth and squealed, but principal Phillips remained quiet, if somewhat annoyed at Mrs. Gartle's inappropriate reaction. Angela looked up to the two, proud of her newly realized discovery.

"Is that all?" Angela asked.

"No. No, that's not all—Angela, why do you believe such a thing?"

"This-this is *blasphemy!*" Gartle exclaimed, but the principal motioned for her to remain quiet.

"Why do you think this, Angela? We're very curious."

"Because . . . well, because of the way things *are.*"

"We don't understand. Can you be more specific?"

"Well, I can't really tell anyone, you understand, I did once and that person died."

At this point Mrs. Gartle, brought her other hand to her mouth and rushed away from the two of them, back into the building. The two could still hear her as she cried out about blasphemy, damned souls, and something about the sweet baby Jesus. Mr. Phillips turned away and suddenly found himself sweating.

"Angela, now you know this isn't true. Did you think you had this person killed?"

"Well, not me. Others. But I told you—I can't *tell* you. You might die."

"Angela, would you show me what you're playing with?"

Angela brought her hand up to Mr. Phillips. "Here."

Mr. Phillips grabbed her wrists and felt his legs go weak. "*What did you do with that frog?*"

The frog hung limp in Angela's tiny, pink hand, it's tiny pink tongue squeezed out of its mouth.

"I killed it. I was just trying to make it come back to life."

"Angela, I think you'd better come with me—would you do that, please?"

"I don't really want to."

"Would you do it as a favor to us mortals?"

Angela thought for a second. "Okay. But only for a minute."

"Thank you."

Angela sat in the office. She had lost track of just how long. Her feet didn't quite reach to the floor, so she contented herself by dangling them against the frame of the chair. She wasn't happy with Mr. Phillips. He had made her give him her frog and had thrown it away. It was only in the trash a few feet away from her, but Angela was still mad. Because she had been made to sit in the principal's office and not move, she couldn't bring the frog back to life. It was such a waste.

But she was God.

Nobody made God do *anything.*

Angela looked at the principal and Mrs. Gartle, both of whom stood outside the office and talked rather loudly. Angela knew they had called her parents.

She was God.

But what she really wanted right now was to bring that little frog back to life, otherwise, she wouldn't have squeezed the life out of it.

Angela hopped off the chair and went to the plastic waste basket. She saw how the dead frog lay belly up on wads of crumpled paper and she looked back out into the outer office. Then she reached down into the trash and grabbed it.

Possession.

Eyes closed, she cradled it against her chest and began to hum.

Live!

Live!

—she thought—

Come back to me, little frog—come back!

"Angela! Put that frog back into the trash!"

Startled, Angela dropped the frog back in the garbage.

Principal Phillips.

They wouldn't do this to me if they knew . . . .

Disheartened, Angela quietly went back to her seat and sat down.

Phillips closed the door behind him and thoughtfully went to his chair, leaving Mrs. Gartle somewhere outside. He leaned forward in his seat and clasped his hands together on the desk before him.

Oh, great, now he's going to act real grown-up on me, Angela thought. *I hate it when they act this way.*

"Angela . . . I've called your parents. They're on their way. What do you think of that?"

"I don't like what you're doing and neither do my friends," she said, her forehead angrily scrunched up.

"Let's talk about these friends of yours, shall we? Just who are they?"

"I'm not supposed to tell."

"Because I could be killed, is that right?"

"Yes."

"And they've killed before."

"Yes."

"I don't suppose you could tell me who they killed, could you? I mean, it's done, isn't it, so no harm could come of your telling me, now, could there?"

Angela paused. *This is a trap, I know it. I feel it.*

"Why should I tell you? I don't trust you."

"Because I want to know more about you—"

Just then the door opened and in came another woman. "Hello," she said. She was about the age of Angela's mother and about as pretty. She carried a little black notebook.

"Now, Angela, this is Mrs. Beale, she's a friend of mine and is also interested in helping us."

"Hello, Angela. I hear you have a dead frog you're trying to bring back."

"Yes."

"Now, Angela," Mr. Phillips continued, "Would this person who was killed be Mrs. VanWygyn?"

"I don't know a Missus VanWeegin."

"Okay. How about the lady the city had sent over to see your parents. Could she have been the one killed?"

Angela froze.

How did he know? He's not God.

The frog. Live, little frog, live!

I'm God.

"How did you know?"

Mr. Phillips looked to Mrs. Beale. "We know a lot."

"But I know more. You're in trouble and I don't like you. You took my frog away from me—I wouldn't have killed it without bringing it back to life! You're also keeping me in here! You probably also sent that mean woman to my family, too! I don't like you at all! I hate *all* of you!"

Angela was now standing on her feet and shouting. Her face ballooned into a puffy red and she felt decidedly different. Not happy like she used to be.

We will let no one harm you, Angela.

We love you, Angela.

We are your friends.

"Live, frog—*live!*" Angela cried aloud, rushing to the garbage, but Mr. Phillips got to the trash before she could. Even though she was faster, Mr. Phillips was closer. He snatched away the trash can and placed it on the floor behind him.

Angela fumed.

"You're all alike! You all want to rule us kids! You never let us do what we want! You think you know it all, but you *don't!* I do! My *friends* do, and we'll kill *all* of you!"

(we will take care of them, Angela)

(go)

"I no longer want to stay here! *Let me go!*"

"Angela, please sit down," principal Phillips said. Nurse Beale got up and nervously came towards Angela.

"Angela, we can help you, if only you'll let us—"

"I won't let you do *anything* to me! I'm *God!* I have made *life.*"

Nurse Beale looked back to the principal. "What do you mean—"

A sound came from the trash can.

"*Come forth!*" Angela commanded.

Mr. Phillips and Nurse Beale looked to each other.

The trash can moved.

Outside thunder and rain suddenly and furiously unleashed from the skies.

"You . . . are doomed! *Both* of you! I warned you but you wouldn't listen! I tried to tell you, but now it's too late. *Too late!*"

The trash can jiggled.

Mr. Phillips shot back in his chair. Lightning flashed outside the window behind him. Angela began to laugh. It was not a very nice laugh.

"It's too late," Angela said in a low, dark tone.

The frog leaped out of the trash can and onto principal Phillips' desk.

We've come for you, Angela—

A powerful concussion catapulted Phillips forward and over his desk while Nurse Beale was knocked up against the wall. Rain and storm now blew in through the destroyed window behind Phillips' desk. When next he looked up, principal Phillips found Angela laughing, her face rain-swept and swollen. Nurse Beale was shaking her head back and forth, a nasty cut across her forehead bleeding all over her. On the window ledge, and occupying the entire opening, sat a stone nightmare, its massive wings unfolded behind it. Water fell from its features like a newborn hell spawn and its mouth was a grotesque caricature of pain. Phillips looked at its fangs and claws. Looked into its cold stone eyes.

"*We have come, Angela,*" the monster said.

"I warned you about this—I *warned* you!" Angela said to Principal

Phillips and Nurse Beale, "Now you must die!" Angela cried. "I am God and you have transgressed!"

The gargoyle looked to Angela.

"You must *pay!*" she said.

The gargoyle continued to stare at her.

"Take me away, Pandor, and do what must be done."

The gargoyle continued to stare at Angela, then the principal. Lightening flashed close by and the smell of ozone filled the room.

"*Kill them!*" Angela shrieked.

Principal Phillips stood up—a leg kinked and he barely caught himself—his clothing torn and his body bruised. He knew there were broken bones somewhere. "Angela, what are you doing? You are *not* God—but you have the devil at your command! Stop while you still can! We can help!"

The gargoyle looked to the man. Lightning and thunder again struck, this time shattering the remaining office window.

"*Kill,*" Angela again commanded.

The gargoyle hopped inside the room and snatched Angela off the floor. Principal Phillips made a move towards the two but the gargoyle backhanded him with such force that before the rest of his body had collapsed, Principal Phillips' head had flown off and hit the wall next to Nurse Beale—who promptly collapsed into unconsciousness.

Angela and Pandor flew out into the angry purple sky.

Why do you act this way, Angela?
Because it is what I am.
Is it?
Yes.
You have changed. You compromise what is.
I am God. I *am* what is.
You have become evil.
No. It is *you* that is evil. God *is*
Dead.
No.
No.
Nooo.

Angela, you have corrupted yourself.
I do not understand. I made the frog come back to life.
No. That was not you.
Was it *you?*
It was what I am.

Answer me directly! I tire of these games!

I am only a product of the force which drives me. I am not what controls me. You said so yourself—I am a tool.

I see. So it was God.

So you say.

Enough!

Angela, we cannot serve you any longer. You no longer suit the purpose which suits us.

Angela held back a rising choke in her throat. She looked back at the stolid stone face which she had come to call a friend. But Pandor had become more than just a friend.

Rain still pounded out of the skies and assaulted the two of them, and thunder and lightning continued to crack open the heavens. She watched as the rain ran down the gargoyle's features. In Angela's mind it made Pandor look like he wept.

"How can you choose your own purpose—I *control* you! You said so!"

I did not. You merely used the magic which you are—had—and set us free. I never said you were our purpose, *I merely said we loved you and would have nothing harm you—*

The conversation was broken off by the sound of sirens in the streets.

They have come for you, Angela. We cannot save you from yourself.

"I don't . . . I don't *need* you. I am—"

A bolt of lightning hit the battlement nearby and sent a huge section of the building toppling into the streets below. One of the gargoyles tumbled over with it. Angela watched in disbelief as the monster made no attempt to recover itself and return to the battlements.

You have done this, Pandor continued. *You have reopened the box . . .*

Box. What box?

The box . . .

Listen to my name, young Angela, what is its true *ring?*

Angela searched her mind. All this time she knew it had sounded eerily familiar. Now it finally dawned on her.

Pandor.

Pan-dor-*a.*

Box.

"That was nothing more than a myth," Angela angrily replied.

No, it is much more than that, young one. I am what some myths referred to as the First Woman. The releaser of all that is evil to humanity through my insistence of opening the box. I have been made to pay for that transgression by becoming an instrument of humanity. The form does not matter. Only the idea. The substance of what is.

"I do not believe. You are here to serve *me*."

Pandora remained silent.

Another bolt of lightning struck another precipice, but on the other side of the battlement. Though she couldn't actually see it, in her mind Angela saw another gargoyle tumble over.

You have destroyed what was. Now you must reap what is to come. Form does not matter, little one.

"Angela! Angela Pedernasy! Can you hear us?"

It was the police. Angela looked over the side but choose to ignore them.

"Pandora, have I done wrong?"

Pandora held her gaze. *What is done, is done. There is no guilt assigned. There is only the present.*

"But—b-but I don't think I *understand!* I'm . . . I'm losing something here. I . . . I feel funny. What is happening to me? To all of this?"

Pandora looked to the sounds that came from below.

"*Angela Pedernasy, your parents are here. They have something they want to say.*" There was momentary silence as the loudspeaker was passed from one set of hands to another.

"*Angela, honey, this is your mother.*"

Angela stiffened.

"*Angela, please talk to us, we want so much to understand. We want to help!*"

"They cannot help, can they," Angela said flatly.

Pandora shook its head side to side.

They cannot.

"*Angela—we know we have probably not been the best of parents, but we tried. We're here for you and want to help. Please, honey, talk to us!*"

Then another bolt from the sky again hit the building, with yet another section of it toppling street ward. As it fell, Angela felt clammy. Something felt awfully wrong.

Then there were the screams. Explosions.

Her parents.

Mommmmmyy—

"*Daaadddyy!*"

Angela rushed to the building's edge. Saw the rubble below. The smoke. Emergency personnel were clambering around the broken bodies and destroyed vehicles in the destruction below.

"*Mommmy—Daaaddy!* What have I done! I've killed you! *I've killed my parents!*"

Pandora came to Angela. Lightning strikes were now continuous, chipping away at the building and sending both rubble and gargoyle alike to the streets below. Those in the falling debris' path fled.

"I am not worthy to live! I have killed the very parents who have given me life!

"Pandor, I wish to remember you the way things were. I have made a big mistake. I may have been wise for my years, but not for my humanity. I have destroyed my parents and I have destroyed you. There is no cause for me to live anymore."

Another bolt of lightning struck and this one took Pandora with it. Angela watched as the gargoyle seemed to topple in an exaggeratedly slow fashion over the side. It kept its eyes on Angela as it fell.

The form is not all, my child. The idea is.

Pandora's eyes seemed to grow and fill her mind.

"*Pandor!*"

Gone.

Angela stood alone. The building quaked all around her.

Oh, my God, what have I done?" Angela said . . .

And threw herself over the side.

Because that was just the way she was.

The form is not all
my child.
The idea
Is.

And thus is the story of a brilliant moment of humanity. Of a silken-haired girl, called Angela. She was a special one to me and still is, for she still lives, but on a different level now. And I, Pandora, also live.

For it is not the form that matters.

But the idea.

And she was the girl who chased gargoyles.

Etched In Stone
1991

Smoke drifted in patches across the battlefield, periodically exposing smashed and deserted artillery and the mutilated and destroyed remains of both blue and gray. Muted, distant groaning filtered from everywhere, seemed to rise up from the bruised and battered earth itself. The air, thick and black, continued to carry within it the energy of atrocities stilled only moments before.

"*Helppp . . . meee . . . .*"

A soldier. Twisted about a sweaty and bloodied head. Coughed painfully, blood issuing from parched and cracked lips . . . dirt and gunpowder coating the inside of his mouth. He knew the battle had only just ended, yet something remained unsettled . . . more . . . there was more to *follow—*

Movement. Up ahead, through the smoke. The soldier squinted, waiting. Again coughed. Slowly, shadowy figures pressed closer, the clink and clatter of weaponry cutting through the unholy execration. The soldier's uneasiness grew.

What color were they?

Sweat—or was it blood?—stung his eyes. Squinting hurt. He couldn't make them out. The humidity, the *stink* . . . .

What color were their uniforms?

The detail continued their sweep across the field, bending over and poking at things.

Bodies.

The soldier couldn't make out their color, but felt their uneasiness. Something was wrong. The moment felt . . . *altered—*

"'Theyah's anotha, sah!" one of the detail alerted.

The wounded infantryman craned his neck toward the voice—just in time to see uniformed arms raise a musket . . . on the end of which was a bloodied and slightly bent bayonet. The prone infantryman watched in exhausted hopelessness as the blade screamed down from the sky and slid neatly into his side—

Paul Donner awoke in excruciating pain, clutching his side, sweat soaking both pillows and sheets. He tried to get up, but instead only managed an awkward and contorted roll out of bed, onto the floor. The sound—the *grind*—of the bayonet twisting in the dirt beneath him . . . *within* him . . . still echoed painfully. He again tried to get up, but only collapsed back to the floor, gasping for air. Abruptly, the pain subsided and Paul pushed himself up from the floor to sit against the bed, fumbling for his wound.

But, there was no wound . . . only pain . . . and the pain wasn't real.

Nothing. There was *nothing.*

Paul got to his knees . . . then his feet . . . then immediately began tossing about bed sheets and pillows.

Again, nothing. No dirt. No blood. No blade.

"What the *hell?*"

Paul staggered into the bathroom, switched on the light and stood before the mirror, eyes closed.

Relax, he mentally chanted, *relax, relax, relax—it was only a* dream . . . .

Slowing his breathing, then chuckling, he opened his eyes to stare into the cold, unfeeling glare of a battle-weary Confederate, upraised musket and fixed bayonet coming at him. Paul yelped and dropped to the floor as the bloodied blade lunged out from the mirror. He grazed his head against the sink, but just lay there . . . curled up . . . listening to the distant notes of a bugle and clattering equipment.

He swore he inhaled the acrid odor of spent black powder . . . .

But no more jabs . . . and no one came for him.

No one crawled out of the mirror after him.

Cautiously, he felt his way back up the sink and again looked into the mirror.

Nothing. Nothing more than a perfect reflection of the crease of the ceiling and wall above him.

Donner's day went from rude to confusing. The more he stewed over the dream, the more obsessed he became. It had been about the Civil War, of that he was certain, but everything else was a haze. And he couldn't shake that soldier's image, the one lunging out at him from his mirror. There had been so much *hate* there . . . a face twisted and framed by enough scars, dirt, and rage to create nightmares for lifetimes. The soldier's eyes had been wide and insane as if he'd been to hell and back. The eyes of one who cared little for life—his enemy's or his own.

And there were so many questions, like which side this dream-him was on (he figured Federal, for no other reason than *he* was from New York). What was his rank (enlisted . . . maybe a corporal), and how old he was at the time of his dreamed death (early to mid-twenties)? Then he tried to actually get inside the head of the doomed soldier . . . .

Got to be able to separate fantasy from reality.

It took some time for him to break free of the gloom, but once it began to shake loose, he gave Becky a call. Becky Decker worked for a travel agency down the street in Old Town Alexandria, the place where Paul had first met her. He'd gone in there one day to ask for directions, one thing led to another, and before he knew it, he'd asked her to dinner. That had been nearly six months ago.

Or had it, Paul suddenly wondered. *Had it really been all those months ago or had I just made it all up?*

"Where the hell had that come from?" he asked himself. "I'm running myself into the ground—of *course* I'd asked her out six months ago—how *hadn't* I? She's my girlfriend. I'm on my way over to see her. If I hadn't met her, she wouldn't be there, now would she?"

He left the apartment.

The day was sunny, hot, and humid, the final days of August living up to its dog-days reputation. The approaching end of summer was nigh and Paul felt as if he were on a mission. Something was out there . . . beckoning him. All his life he'd felt he'd had a particular calling, but now he felt as if at a crossroads . . . as if whatever was meant for him was just around the corner. He didn't know what this urge was . . . but here he was catching up to thirty and still unfulfilled. He needed to settle down and get a grip on things—but what was he supposed to do? He knew there was something important out there for him—

Or headed for him.

Donner rounded a corner and passed an angry, recessed figure in an alleyway, a figure he never noticed, but who wore a tattered Civil War uniform and finished loading a large caliber, rifled musket. The soldier forced the rammer home into its slot beneath the musket's barrel, and, after Donner walked past, strode confidently out into the sunlight to brazenly take up position on the sidewalk behind him. The figure half-cocked the hammer, installed a new percussion cap, and leveled his weapon at Paul's back. Pulling back the hammer the rest of the way, the soldier fired.

An ear-jarring report split the air—just as a car backfired.

Donner found himself crouched low, poised like a tiger, senses heightened—an apparently instinctive move he found most disquieting. He straightened up. Smelled black powder.

"*What th*—"

Donner regained his composure and continued on . . . but felt watched . . . he looked behind him, but saw nothing out of the ordinary.

"It's going to be one of those days, ain't it."

Musket smoke evaporated.

"Hi, honey!" Becky said, getting up and out from behind her desk to greet Paul as he entered the office. "You okay?" She rose up on her toes and gave Paul a quick peck on the cheek. "After your call this morning I've been all worried about you!" Hands on his shoulders, she slid them down along his arms to his hands, interlinking her fingers with his. "How's your side?"

"Oh, fine. There's hardly any pain now, and I still didn't find any bruises, except from the fall."

Becky examined Paul's forehead, gently touching the wound. "My poor baby . . . ," she said.

"Yeah, it still hurts. Poor baby needs much lovin' to fix!"

"Hmm, sounds like a challenge—but I'm starved, let's eat first, then we can talk about what it takes to fix you, later."

"Tell me more," Becky asked, intently focused on Paul. The server retreated, taking their menus and orders with him. Paul shifted uncomfortably in his chair, feeling unaccountably awkward in the restaurant and not knowing why. They'd been here plenty of times before—

Hadn't they?

"Well, I only remember a portion of it. There was this Civil War battlefield. I was the wounded soldier I told you about, and I guess I was only momentarily unconscious, because when I came to my wounds still bled. The fighting had only just stopped and my ears were ringing—and there was this weird, anticipatory silence to everything . . . and everywhere around me men were either dead or dying.

"And the *stench*.

"I peered through the smoke and haze and saw soldiers approaching, but something wasn't right—about them or the whole feel to this dream, for that matter.

"Before I know it, I'm being gutted."

Paul shuddered. Took a sip of water.

"This is *fascinating*."

"Yeah, well, you didn't wake up with rusty iron twisting in your kidneys—"

"Oh, Mister Drama Queen." Becky swiped at him with a napkin.

"*Drama Queen?*"

"And what about that Rebel soldier in your bathroom?"

"It scared the hell out of me! I just have this terrifying nightmare, then I turn around and walk smack into this . . . this . . . "

"Ghost?"

"Yeah. I actually wet my pants—but if you tell anyone, I'll deny it."

Becky burst out laughing, drawing attention from surrounding tables, to which Paul turned and said, "It's okay, she's only *just* been released!"

Becky snatched a roll from the basket and threw it at him and squealed a high-pitched "*Paul!*" before continuing. "No way—you actually peed your *pants?*"

"And if you *ever*—"

"Don't worry, I'll only tell my mother!" she said, giggling. "Okay, okay, so you had this wild dream and saw this weirdo dream rebel—what other weirdisms have you experienced?"

"Well . . . nothing else—except that there was this odd smell of gun powder when a car backfired by me on the way over here. I nearly—"

"Peed your pants?"

Shaking his head, Paul buried his face into his muscled and callused hands.

Donner spent the rest of his day driving aimlessly around the Alexandria area lost in thought . . . and ended up in an area he'd come to call Cemetery Row, a gathering of a half dozen or so cemeteries grouped together in a small area. They had names like Bethel, Douglass, Saint Paul's Episcopal, Christ Church, and, way in the back, the Alexandria National Cemetery. He'd frequently found himself coming here, quietly strolling its grounds, over the past months. He'd found it quite by accident. He exited his truck.

Was restless.

Something was definitely out there . . . waiting for him? . . . seeking him out? . . . he couldn't deny it, but here he loved the quiet solitude that came from strolling its headstones and crypts, and all the tall, mature hardwoods drooping and rustling over well-kept grounds. It was the strangest feeling he'd had all day, thinking how right it felt to be among the dead and the decayed . . . almost a *yearning* . . . .

When Paul had returned to his truck, he buckled up, fired up the engine, and immediately felt light-headed. Grabbing the steering wheel, he steadied himself and squinted past the windshield. More pain hammered him . . . and a sudden fog rose up around his truck.

Again the thick odor of black powder . . . and that high-pitched ringing in his ears.

Tasted blood and dirt.

His heart raced, his throat constricted.

He felt as if someone or something was reaching into his very soul and trying to squeeze the life out of him—

Paul stared into the fog. At first he thought it was only his imagination, but the shadowy, indistinct images coalesced. Refused to abate.

Line upon line of men were charging a hill, the fighting thick and furious.

The scene then shifted to a wooded area and he saw large numbers of Confederate cavalry charging outnumbered, but colorfully dressed Federal units. One of these scarlet-pantsed men turned to Paul.

Looked directly at him.

His damaged face quickly filled Paul's world and from all around him came muffled whispers:

Etched in stone . . . .

Etched in stone . . . .

The words tore into him like hot lead. Then the giant, damaged face spoke.

"*Who are ye to desert us?*"

Paul snapped free of his trance and whacked his head against the headrest.

The fog dissipated.

Wiping sweat from his forehead (he swore he felt grit beneath his fingernails), it took him several moments to reorient . . . and he had to actually curtail the sudden urge to run—to get away—*away from* what?

Paul stomped on the accelerator and sped away from the quiet and the dead.

He couldn't get into his apartment fast enough. Slamming the door shut, Paul rushed to his couch and collapsed there.

That was too much.

It hadn't been a dream—he'd been wide awake and conscious this time.

What the hell was going on? Those images had definitely been Civil War . . . and what was the big deal with it all of a sudden? He'd always been fascinated about it, sure, but what did that have to do with the price of tobacco in Richmond? Everywhere he looked these past few days he ran into one weird occurrence after another—and from that war. How could dreams . . .

How could dreams turn into reality?

Confused but hungry, he headed for the kitchen. Threw together some leftovers. After he sat down at the table, he stared down at a plate of

Food.

Time to eat.

Time to find reality.

Paul reached down and picked up the fork . . . but it felt funny.

He speared it into his dinner . . . brought it up to his mouth . . . and saw that the utensil was no longer the four-pronged stainless-steel implement he'd taken out of the kitchen drawer, but a crude, two-pronged apparatus consisting of thick, rusted metal wires wrapped around each other. His plate was a beat up and worn tin platter, and his apartment—

His apartment was gone.

Paul sat before a cramped, nighttime campfire, soldiers angrily staring him down and mumbling a barely audible chant. Through the firelight Paul also saw that their faces were not just angry, but weary. Saw that he wore the same Federal Zouave uniform everyone around the fire wore. The red and blue of his uniform were no longer bright, but torn and faded, splotched with

(*blood*)

sweat stains and dirt.

"W-what's going on, here?" he asked.

No one answered. Just glared. Paul looked about the camp. All attention was focused on him . . . and he felt it like successive musket volleys.

Who are you to desert?

Fire!

Etched in stone.

Fire!

Back to bone.

Fire!

"*What the hell is going on?*"

Where had everything gone? His apartment—*Becky?*

The mumbling grew until a large burly sergeant with dirtied rockers astride dirtied stripes made his way toward him. The sergeant, tough-looking and angry, stepped into Paul's face, forcing him back with his mere presence. Paul smelled the chew on his breath, juices still wet on the man's handlebar mustache. Inches from his face, the sergeant spoke.

"What makes *yew* so spay-shal, soldier?"

Paul saw that the man's teeth were sporadic and rotting; winced at the repressed anger that flared from spiteful eyes . . . at the smell of battle still ripe upon him. This man . . . was his superior.

Superior?

"This is all wrong . . . all *wrong*," Paul said. "My life . . . I should be . . . *here*."

The realization was like another back-to-back volley.

"*I should be* here!"

Paul spun around, stumbled, then ran off into the woods. The men remained, watching . . . just watching . . .

. . . back to bone . . .

. . . etched in stone . . . .

Paul plunged headfirst through brush and trees, branches slapping thin, stinging welts across his body.

Events were falling into place, but he still didn't know why or how things had gotten so bizarre. How was he supposed to belong to the past when he was alive and kicking in the present? Was everything he'd been living a lie—a *dream?*

Had he had it all backwards?

Was the past his present—the present his *future?*

What was real?

But he knew . . . *knew* that that sergeant was his superior . . . that that camp *his* bivouac . . . and these stinging welts *painful.*

Paul raced blindly into the dark, leaving far behind the men at the campfire, their murmurs still rattling about in his head.

He leapt over a downed tree and landed confidently on the other side, but a large branch again snapped across his face, sending him painfully to the ground. Eyes watering, he remained on the ground, dazed. He had no idea where he was, yet continued to experience the crazy déjà vu. By touch, Paul examined his face and felt the long, raised welt that had risen . . . felt the tackiness of the blood that flowed out from it. He allowed the pain to refocus his thoughts as he traced a finger along the welt like an old lover revisited. Gaining some resolve, he crawled back over to the felled tree and listened.

Felt the dirt between his fingers and beneath his nails.

The firmness of the tree against his back.

Heard the crackling and popping sounds that were up ahead . . . the smell of burning wood.

Campfires. Muffled conversation.

What color were they?

Paul crawled toward the noise, the loose tatters of his uniform snagging on underbrush.

He pulled himself free and continued forward on belly and elbow. Found himself cradling the familiar heft of a Springfield rifle. It all felt . . . *perfect.*

This was where he belonged.

Shortly he came to a small rise and found more soldiers.

What color were they!

Paul cautiously watched. They were but a handful, and looked as if they were nearing completion of a task—when he suddenly lurched forward, overcome by a shortness of breath and a stab of pain that exploded from his side. Clutching at the pain he remembered the wound from his dream, and looked down.

"This can't be—"

Paul searched his tunic and ran his fingers along his side until he fingered the sucking gash that was an open hole from the well-thought-out design of a triangular-bladed bayonet.

"Yer bout to take yer rightful place, Yankee," came the voice from behind, and Paul jerked and grunted as the bayonet was again thrust into him, this time in a viciously twisting action . . . .

He bled heavily as he was taken into the Confederate camp. Wave upon wave of pain engulfed him . . . but he didn't die. Men led him through rows of graves, some open, some not, but all fresh.

And still he didn't die.

Peering through the feverish haze he saw the bodies of the dead and dying. They looked empty . . . familiar . . . .

"Ya're a blaspheme a nature, boy, n we aim ta see what's wrong'd put right, y'hear?"

"I-I don't understand—"

The soldiers snickered. Again, the anger . . . anger not directed at the war, but at him.

"What is it—what have I done to so offend you?"

The soldiers remained silent as they continued directing him toward the end of the dug-out plots. Paul welcomed the inhalation of dirt and decay. Workers nearby, in blue and gray, Zouave dress, put their shovels aside and scrambled up from the graves to stand beside their holes.

"There'ah," one directed, "etched in stone, Yank-ee."

Etched in stone

Etched in stone

Back to bone

Find yer home

The chanting filled his mind and soul.

The soldiers' hold on him lessened and he fell forward.

Paul wanted to ignore the truth . . . to return home . . . to be rid of the fiendish nightmare that had tormented him night and day—*but where was home?*

What was a dream and what was reality?

A young Confederate, not sixteen years of age, bent toward him. His face was young, but his eyes bespoke of a truer age.

"This *is* home, sah."

Home.

This is home, sah.

This is . . . .

Paul rolled over, fork clutched savagely in hand.

He opened his eyes and stared at it.

It was four-pronged. Stainless steel.

And he was on his apartment's floor.

He shot to his feet and flung it away. Dinner was all over the floor.

Things were beginning to make sense . . . blackened, dark sense, perhaps, but sense nonetheless. Trembling, he rushed to the phone and dialed Becky. Her phone rang twice.

"Becky?"

"Yes? Paul?"

"What are you doing tomorrow?"

"Just working, why?"

"Take the day off. Cancel. Call in sick—"

"Paul . . . what's the matter, are you all right?"

"No, I'm not . . . but tomorrow I will be. We're taking a short trip. Somewhere that'll end these nightmares. I'll pick you up at seven."

He hung up.

"Okay—"

Paul picked Becky up at six-fifty-eight the next morning, August 30th. He said nothing after she got into the truck.

"Are you going to tell me what this is all about?" she asked.

"We're goin' to Manassas."

"Manassas?"

"That's where the answers lie, Becky, that's where they all lie."

Shivers ran down her spine.

In less than an hour, the two arrived at Manassas Battlefield, Virginia. Fog hugged the ground and trees lined the road and fields like specters-in-waiting. The drive had been a silent one, the tension thick, and Becky had chosen not to say much. She figured Paul would talk soon enough for the both of them.

And she was scared.

"Have you been here before?" she asked, sheepishly.

"Once. Long, long ago." Paul's eyes took on a faraway glaze.

"Paul . . . you're scaring me."

"Scaring you? Yes, I suppose I am—I'm sorry, really I am, you have to believe me. Come, let's stop here and get you a map." They pulled into the Visitor's Center, but found it closed.

"I didn't think it'd be open yet," Becky said nervously, and got out of the truck. She looked through the locked glass doors of the building, cupping her hands around her eyes against the glass.

Paul got out of the truck and went to the trash. "No matter. Here," he said, and picked out a loose flyer from the trash. "You won't need anything other than this. Let's go."

Becky and Paul drove along the deserted, winding road, Becky followed his travels on the map, and read from it as they drove. They stopped at the tiny parking lot alongside a singular stone building.

"Shall we go for a walk?" he asked.

"Sure," Becky said.

But the hair on the back of her neck prickled. She felt unstable and unsure. Getting out of the truck they both walked up to the stone building and immediately Paul reached out a shaky hand to touch the building, as she read from the flyer.

"The brochure says this building was used as a hospital," Becky said, "that it's one of the oldest structures around."

"Yep, there was a lot of dead and wounded that went through here."

Becky looked up to him, then back to the paper. His voice was different, but he was correct. Ignoring the increased thickness to his voice, she pointed to the hill behind it. "Up there an attack had formed . . . ."

Paul stared off in a different direction.

"Paul? Are you listening to me?"

Paul continued to stare off into the distance. Becky came up to him and poked him in the side. Paul jolted and shot her a startled look.

"*Paul—are you listening to me?*"

"You know . . . it's so weird coming back," he said. "Everything feels so . . . not *set*."

"Is this part of what's been going on?"

"Yes. It's very . . . disturbing. I feel as if I've been here before."

"But you said you had."

"I . . . have. But not in this lifetime."

Becky backed away. "Paul, now you're really scaring me. I don't like this at all."

"And you think I *do?*" he asked, wheeling around to face her. "You have no *idea* what hell we went through!"

There was that something different in his eyes again, something different about him. She felt like she was looking into the eyes of another . . . someone older . . . soulfully weary. In his features were an accumulation of years that absolutely terrified her, like Time was screaming past in hyper drive right before her eyes.

Becky smelled dirt and decay.

Felt dirty herself.

"Let's go over there," Paul said. "There's a sunken, unfinished railroad and more battle lines . . . the Deep Cut," he said, pointing. Becky looked down to her sheet and saw that he was again correct. They got back into the truck.

Becky said, "Here the railroad crosses, and back there—"

"Back there is where we started defending our lines," Paul said, finishing.

"What's this 'we' stuff?"

Paul turned to her.

A bugle echoed in the distance.

"You hear that?" Becky asked.

Paul nodded, maintaining eye contact.

"Sounds like a reenactment. This doesn't say anything about reenactments," she said, checking the brochure. "Wanna check it out?"

"That's what we're here for."

Swinging the truck back onto the main road, they dipped through the gently sloping hills and troughs of the valley. The fog refused to lift, in fact grew worse, as did the humidity. Paul took the truck off on a side road and brought it to a stop. He got out and Becky followed. She watched him stare out over another field, at the end of which was a tall, narrow monument surrounded by several cannon.

"Well, this is it," Paul said, flatly, "this is where it all ended."

Becky looked down to her sheet of paper. "But that's not what the brochu—"

"I'm not talking about the brochure, Becky, I'm talking about *me*. Back behind those trees—they'ah," he said, pointing, "we were set up, camped. We were a small force . . . barely a company . . . suffered heavy losses . . ."

Becky looked at him, her paper hanging uselessly in her grasp.

Etched in stone

Etched in stone for all time . . . .

" . . . the Confederates were beatin' the tar out of us. I was wounded pretty bad, as were most in my unit—"

"Stop it! Paul, stop it right now! You're scaring me! This is nonsense, you hear me? *Nonsense!* You're here, with me . . . *now. In the present.*"

"Are you so sure?" he asked. Again he faced the fields. "I was with the 5th New York. Volunteers. Duryée's Zouaves. You kin check it out fer yourself. I was . . . I don't know . . . I was somehow caught up in a strange warp between life and death . . . I don't really know, it's all beyond my ken . . . but I remember being called into my commander's tent that night, being asked to go on a mission. A secret scouting mission. I was to meet an agent somewhere—but I never made it. I was captured by a wandering Johnny patrol. I didn't know they was that close, jee-zum."

Jeezum?

Jeezum crow.

"Anyhow, I was put under guard by the Rebs until battle broke out. I managed to kill my guard—who would've kilt me anyhow, seein's he wanted to fight, and had my unit got closer he wouldna wasted his time w'me. I woulda done the same . . . so I kilt him.

"You know, while I was thinkin' bout what to do, I sees this Reb. He's a standin' there, not six feet from me reloadin' his musket. He had the cartridge between his fingers—the end bitten off and the paper still 'tween his teeth—when I sees a hole rip right through his chest and out his back, bringin' him to a complete standstill. He just stood there, like he was gonna finish loadin' that musket. Then he just fell backards, real serene-like, fell back to the ground with blood gushin' up from his chest. So I takes his weapon and hightailed it out of there.

"Somehow I made it back to my unit . . . and into battle . . . and I was wounded, wounded real bad—like my dream told me. We were cut down by a perfect hail of bullets. Successive horrendous musket volleys we'd never seen before. I'd never seen anything like it, rippin' apart our haversacks from our bodies, burstin' our canteens, and explodin' our rifles to pieces as we held them . . . we was cut to ribbons where we stood, and all within an *instant*. I seen comrades struck from that murderous rain with better'n half-a-dozen rounds before hittin' the ground. It was wholesale *slaughter* . . . ."

Donner paused, eyes closed for a moment, before continuing. Becky just stood there, openmouthed and dumbfounded.

"The battle had just ended when I come to—

(*what color were they?*)

"and them Johnnies, they was goin' through the bodies, checkin' ta see if we was dead'r not, and if not, makin' it so. Well, I wasn't, and they stuck me."

Tears erupted from Becky's eyes like waterfalls.

"This isn't true—you're making it up!" Becky pleaded, "it's some kind of cruel joke—*tell* me!" she cried, reaching out and shaking him. "*Tell* me!"

"I don't know what happened, I really don't. Somehow I . . . I must've been missed. Ya know, there was lots of us out there on the field that day, Death could've easily missed me—and I thinks that's what's resented by all those it got.

"They want me back, Becky.

"The dead want to set things right. There's even a grave with ma name on it."

"Stop it—*I don't want to hear anymore!*"

In the distance the bugling grew louder . . . closer.

"No! *I refuse to believe this!*"

"Look," Paul said, pointing out into the fields, "there they are. See'm? Comin' . . . comin' for *me*, honey."

Out in the fields, Becky saw line upon line of men, Federals and Confederates, some carrying the standards for their units. All around them were the sounds of gear clinking and readying, the sounds of bugles, the rustle of men trampling through woods and fields alike.

"Paul—"

Becky looked at him, but Paul now wore the tattered and bloodstained uniform of a Duryée Zouave, the rank of corporal wrapped across his sleeves. His face was drawn and weary, his skin tracked with the spoils of battle. But the face . . . the face was still *Paul*. Becky looked to his side and gasped when she saw the small tear and blood stain that spoke of the bayonet wound she knew to be there.

"This can't be real—*can't* be!" she cried, her face red and swollen.

Paul came to her. She again smelled the black powder . . . the sweat and blood he wore like a red badge of courage. "Why you—why *us?*

Can't they take someone *else?*"

"They *is* no one else, Becky. Only *me*. I been tryin' ta tell ye. I'm the only survivor—the only ghost left ta put ta rest. Ma stone be waitin' fer me, Becky. Come."

Paul led her toward the small cemetery that stood on a rise a short distance away. The two ignored all other plots and walked through to the one at the rear, off by itself. She shivered in his arms. A marker rested by the plot . . . his name freshly carved into it. Becky let out a scream, but Paul delicately silenced her, bringing her into his arms.

"This is it. Ma home. Ma restin' place."

"Please, don't go, Paul, I *love* you . . . *please* . . . ."

"I cain't, it's just the way it is. I have no control over't, never did. I don't know if I lived all I did, or just dreamt it. I know I never quite felt right in anythin' I did. Maybe cause I was missed by the Reaper my livin' just messed things up real bad and I'm the result. I cain't ainswer't."

The advancing soldiers were now close enough to make out features. Federal and Confederate alike . . . side by side . . . they leveled their bayoneted muskets before them.

Etched in stone
Etched in stone
Take your place among the bone.

"I—I hafta go," Paul said, suddenly doubling over in pain. Becky backed away in horror, as she saw a ghost soldier

(what color were they?)

yank his bayonet from Paul's body. Intense rage and hatred filled the soldier's face as he ripped free his iron spike.

"*Paul!*"

"It's . . . okay. They don't undahstand—heck, I don't neither. It's just ma time ta go, as it was meant to be a cent'ry and a half afor. Know that I loved ya, my dear, sweet Becky. Yer the one thing I never had in my life then—"

Paul again gasped, his whole body jerking from yet another ghostly impalement, this time from a fellow Zouave. Paul doubled over, crumpling to the ground onto all fours, and looked up to Becky. Sweat poured from his brow. Becky knelt beside him, supporting him.

"They want me ta stop dallyin', ma sweet. I been away long 'nough and they want me back. *I have ta go.*"

Paul stopped enough only to cough up blood. He brought himself shakily to his feet, Becky still by his side.

"G'bye, Becky. Put a flower on ma grave, would ya, darlin'? I'll always be dreamin' a ya."

Tears rained down his face.

Becky clawed after him, but Paul Donner, Corporal, 5th New York Volunteer Infantry, hobbled towards his grave. More ghostly soldiers appeared and disappeared . . . successively impaling him on his march toward his marker. Finally standing before his plot, Corporal Donner turned to face Becky one last time, while another soldier came before him and raised his bayoneted rifle ready to strike—but hesitated.

Rather than spear him, the ghost brought its weapon upright against his side, snapped to attention, and saluted. Corporal Donner saluted back.

Etched in stone
Back with bone
Home is home
And bone is bone.

Becky looked away and wept, and when she looked back . . .

He was gone.

As was the rest of the war.

Becky remained where she was, map clenched tightly against her heaving chest. The fog continued to cling and the humidity rose . . . .

The warm, early morning breeze kissed Becky's hair as she placed daffodils upon the grave, beside the remains of the other flowers she'd already lain there. She stepped away from the plot and looked out over the damp fields, wiping away a tear. She could hardly believe what had happened here a century and a half ago. What had happened here a *week* ago. But the words on the marker didn't lie, though they could barely be made out after 155 years. She knew what they read and she wept. She knew he hadn't been a dream.

How could he?

She was with child.

Corporal Paul Donner
5th N.Y. Volunteer Infantry
August 30, 1862

Blue Diamond Exit, Mile Marker 15
1989

"It's up just ahead—see that Chevron sign?—it's *that* exit!" blurted an excited Annie Jackson, pressed forward in her seatbelt as she eyed through the sweltering July Nevada night for their exit. "I see it, I see it," Neal, her husband, said. The soft orange glow of the dash bounced off their faces.

Their beat-up pickup rattled south along Las Vegas's section of I-15, its windows rolled down, air-conditioning broken. They had been driving for about half an hour. Neal looked to the green-and-white reflective sign that boasted "*Blue Diamond Road, Exit 33.*"

They exited off I-15 headed west, onto Blue Diamond Road, also known as Nevada 160. Drove past shopping centers and housing developments, before finally hitting total darkness. Neal thought about the stark contrast of where they were not twenty minutes ago to where they were now. About the harsh traffic and lights of Las Vegas left behind. About their present wild goose chase. There was very little civilization out here. It was a decidedly eerie darkness. A place with no "Strip," no casinos, no shopping centers. Just the Blue Diamond gypsum mine somewhere up ahead.

And darkness.

He looked over to his wife. She was now turned away from him, looking out her window, lost in thought to the stars. Her hair buffeted in the wind. There was magic in the air . . . at least for one of them . . . and there was still some fifteen more miles yet to go.

There had been a time when he had actually been crazy about her hair, her skin, her— At one time he'd been crazy about a lot of things.

Annie pulled her attention back in the cab and looked to him. Neal returned a thin smile. He *really* wasn't into this. It was all horse-shit. But not to Annie—no, she *knew*. She was told she was being groomed for an elevated position within the group.

The Group.

Neal had met "The Group" all right. Had gone to one of their meetings after they had blown into town and canvassed the desert with their flyers. Was totally turned off by its entirely charismatic approach. Their leader, Ed Horton (whom Neal had quickly come to call "Mr. Ed,") was made out to be some kind of demigod because of his "privileged knowledge" about aliens and UFO's.

UFO's indeed.

And just how far was Annie intending to go with all this, anyway? And groomed for *what* position?

Well, it wouldn't be long before they'd both find out. Mile marker 15, the supposed site of a previous visitation and subsequent abduction, was where they were all about to meet. The rest of her group. Marker 15 was scheduled for another visitation tonight. News crews had been deployed.

Everyone knew this because they were told it was so.

By Mr. Ed.

Aliens. Not the kind in need of history lessons, green cards, and five years residency, nope, not those kind.

Aliens from the *stars*.

The kind that (in theory) come swooping down from the sky in nifty little space ships; the kind the government repeatedly discloses aren't there—wherever "there" is—and the kind that are also reportedly locked up in some sort of secret-secret cloak-and-dagger government installation at Langley, Virginia or Groom Lake, Nevada, dealing in a mutually parasitic give-and-take with certain high-government officials.

Those kind.

At least this was what Mr. Ed would have everyone believe. And his sources were reliable. Very, *very* reliable.

"*Really?*" Neal had gotten very adept at vocalizing.

And Ed's sources?

They ranged from "other people" to the National Inquirer. He also counted himself as a source. He'd *seen* things, he'd tell his followers. Highly-Top-Secret-and-extremely-classified-things.

Really?

"Did you ever think that it could all be a clever form of disinformation by the government—for whatever the reason?" Neal had once tried arguing. It wasn't that Neal wasn't a believer in extraterrestrial phenomena, but the whole extraterrestrial thing had become so trashed by the media and weirdos that it was hard to believe *anything* without first seeing and touching some kind of *evidence*. And when you have to get your information from people who get orgasms at the tiniest flicker of light in the night sky, well, the credibility factor does far more than just *dip* . . . .

As they drove onward the temperature began its upward climb, and Annie instinctively went for the window handle. Her rolling down of the window was quickly brought to a halt when she realized it was already rolled down as far as it would go. All this punishment because Neal hadn't felt the need to buy a replacement air-conditioner for his damned pickup.

It was too expensive, he said.

It was winter, he said, which had now turned into summer, he ignored.

They were locals, they could get by without it, he said.

Well, it would be better to live with a little less money than to die of heat exhaustion—or pay alimony in a nasty divorce settlement—*she* said.

Annie cast him a brief, unnoticed scowl. She then redirected her attention back out the window to the rearview. It was dark ahead of them. Very dark. And dark behind them. Very dark, indeed. They had, for all practical purposes, left behind the comforts of civilization for the harsh realities of the Nevada desert, and this was to be their last sign of civilization on their trip west.

And Annie was *beyond* excited.

Neal switched to high-beams. He looked to the dark shapes rising and falling to either side of them with great trepidation. It had all started three months ago.

Annie had glimpsed an op-ed piece in the *Vegas Visitor*, a publication given to her by a friend of a friend. It talked about "*Space Intelligence—see it for yourself and YOU be the judge!*" All that in one header. There was to be a seminar held at the Las Vegas Hilton. They'd both been amazed that a hotel of such caliber would even consider hosting such a function, but, doubt it or not, it was there, and she'd begged and begged to go there, so they had. It had been their first encounter with the man Neal had come to unaffectionately refer to as "Mr. Ed."

Ed Horton was a narrowly built six-plus-footer, with a back bent over in a slight hunch. His countenance was not one of "*Hi, I'm here! Pay attention to me!*" but more of "*I'm here—and who gives a shit?*" The weirdest thing about the man was that his face didn't quite match the picture of him Neal's mind had painted. His face was more like an entirely separate entity, a backdrop to thick eyebrows and watery eyes, with a head covered in a wild silvery mane. And he'd always seemed to have his hands cupped before him, giving you the impression his hands weren't exactly . . . appealing? But it was when he opened his mouth that the horse-feathers really flew, and his hidden charisma would suddenly crackle and sparkle and make itself known. He had a voice that was deep, dark, and

Hypnotic.

And it came from a mouth full of teeth. Menacing teeth, however his smile tried to belie that observation.

When he spoke his eyes took on a new light, and they focused on everyone. There was no place to hide. If he saw you waver, he'd hook your eyes and bring you in deeper. He did stuff like:

" . . . *you're open-minded, aren't you? You believe in certain things you can't see, don't you?*" They'd all nod openly to themselves.

"Faith," Ed would verbally underscore, "*faith.*"

A couple of UFO-hallelujahs ejaculated from the audience.

He would then take up a new stance on stage and turn away—only to swing back around and zero in on a particular skeptic he had spotted earlier, his focus laser like.

"There are *trillions* of other planets and star systems out there. *Trillions!*" Mr. Ed had said to Neal-in-the-audience, "Just by the Law of Averages alone—*just by basic statistics!*—how can you discount the existence of other planets out there with *intelligences* on them?"

Then he'd gesticulated to his right eye and continued to Neal alone, "can you look me straight in the eye and tell me that you believe we are the *only* life forms in this almighty cosmos?"

He'd stopped. Waited for Neal's reply.

The *reply.*

Neal had felt the heat and weight of everyone else's stare and chuckled to himself —but oh, no, Mr. Ed wouldn't let Neal off that easy. He just stood there, *staring* at him until Neal reluctantly replied in the negative, knowing full well the hopelessness of the situation. Ed had then dropped his hands with grand fanfare and a huge sigh of relief, pleased with both the win and the manipulation. Everyone else in the room followed suit, nodded knowingly, silently (re!)affirming to themselves that he *did* have a point.

And Neal wanted to punch the man in the throat.

The entire scene had been reminiscent of a religious sermon—but that hadn't stopped Ed. No, sir, Ed goes on. And *on.* All the Eds of the world do. The group always gets smaller, but there still would be a gathering of the few who wanted to "learn more." To become of the "in-crowd."

One of the Chosen.

Annie was the topic that time around, and she had gradually become Ed's *right-hand gal* topic (Neal had another definition for Ed's "*right-hand gal*" . . .). Ed's eyes always lit up around her. Saw the flaming potential she possessed.

Annie had come to the seminar on a whim, for want of nothing better to do. She had been bored. But from where first had come boredom, now grew a cause, a movement—something outside her marriage she could attach herself to. Something she really wanted to believe in and become a part of. And she had also found in Ed a person who seemed to have the inside track on esoterica. After all, he didn't seem to be benefitting from any ulterior motives . . . he was a fairly well-to-do man to begin with. Ed said he'd heard of extraterrestrial visitations years ago and had decided to do a little of his own investigations. What he'd found was that he couldn't discount *all* of it, he'd said. That he'd become converted to the cause. His Mentor, it had been rumored, had been abducted somewhere in New Mexico—least that's what ol Ed had alluded to, never actually having come right out and *said* so . . . .

He always just kinda smiled and wandered away, hands cupped before himself . . . .

Neal and Annie came to an intersection in the straight, flat road to Blue Diamond. The crossroad went off to their right and quickly dumped out of sight. It was down there that there was supposed to be a Vegas camera crew. Ready to catch any aliens who would just happen to land and strike a pose for the cameras.

They went straight.

"Annie, what if these aliens of yours don't show? What are you going to do then? What are you going to say?" Neal asked.

Annie looked at him.

"Ed says it would just mean that they weren't ready."

Annie smiled triumphantly, but the glow from the dash gave her face more of a maniacal look to it.

"Annie—will you listen to yourself? That's a cop out and you *know* it! You were told that they would land *tonight*—no ifs, ands, *or* buts—*tonight.*"

Annie continued to smile, directing it out the window. She shook her head slowly, like one of the converted.

"Ed said there would be times like this. That there would be those who would try to shake our beliefs. Derail us."

"Oh, fuck 'our beliefs.' You're out there, Annie, *waaay* the fuck out there. I really don't like this at *all*."

"If there are too many people there with negative vibes—"

"—oh right, I'd forgotten about *that* part—"

"—the aliens won't land."

"Oh right: '*Bad vibes, Zandor, no land!*' Get real, Annie, why should that deter them from making an appearance? They're so advanced with their space ships and all—"

"Neal! You just don't understand, do you? It *hurts* them! Literally *hurts* them, Neal, like loud noises hurt *us!* Bad vibrations and negative thoughts can actually *kill* them!"

Annie glared across the cab at Neal. He gave her one last incredulous glance before he returned his attention back to the road.

Neal thought, *There's a whole fucking* planet *full of bad vibes, how can they even come anywhere near this place without their delicate little minds exploding?*

"Annie, I wish you could see yourself, I really do. That's such a lame argument and you know it. If it was that important for aliens to land and make themselves known, don't you think they'd do it *anyway*—or at least create some sort of advanced alien-kung-fu shielding device to protect their precious little heads?"

Annie had long since ignored his words and instead studied the stars above, the hot wind tossing her hair in and out of the cab.

Fuck this shit.

Neal's lights suddenly danced off reflectors up ahead. He slowed the truck down a bit, dropping a gear. Off to the side of the road he spotted the mile-marker post. *Fifteen.* He saw a van and several cars pulled over to the right of the road. Off the road a little farther to the right, some twenty feet out, was another car. Its reflectors also danced before his lights. Neal pulled his Ford to a stop just behind the van. Looking to the rear to make sure no one was coming up on them, he turned the truck around and faced it back in the direction they'd just come from (*just in case*, he thought . . .).

Once out of the truck, they noticed there were several people milling around beside the van, where a campfire was going, apparently making a regular party out of the evening. Neal glanced back up the road in the direction they would have continued had they not stopped, and saw that there were other groups. These seemed, maybe only because of the distance, generally quieter, thereby attracting less attention. The group directly in front of them actually seemed to be showing off.

It was when he turned to Annie that he noticed just how utterly dark it was out here—not even a moon. It always seemed darker in places where one was unfamiliar. He looked off to the northeast, where the twinkling lights of Vegas lie. A dark shape absorbed some of its brilliance. A mountain.

"Well, at least it's a beautiful night to stargaze," he mumbled absentmindedly, looking up into the night sky.

Annie looked at him through the darkness.

Neal remembered the times they had gone out stargazing, just the two of them. Remembered the love they had shared beneath the stars. He longed for how things had been. For the love they had so believed in, and had so *shared*—

Ed's name was uttered out in the darkness.

"*Ed Horton?*" Annie queried back out into the darkness. She hurried off in the direction of the conversation. Neal remained. Watched the sky. It was so *black*. It brought him back to his days as a kid when he would brave the cold night air and early morning (or late-night) hours for a glimpse of Andromeda . . . the Magellanic Clouds . . .

That seemed oh *so* long ago.

Presently all he could see were all sorts of lights as they floated across the sky. Red and blue, or just plain white. He knew aircraft when he saw them, but sometimes he saw extremely faint lights that buzzed across the constellations. Satellites. A sure test of good eyesight *they* were. He also knew that by not looking directly at things in the night sky you could sometimes see them better. He didn't really know why that was, just that it worked. Something about peripheral vision and rods and cones.

Neal looked back toward that van. They were such a boisterous group of partiers. And there were only about five of them. One thing he could tell right off was that they all smoked cigarettes. All of them. And judging by their conversation he also figured one wasn't quite eighteen, one was the "matriarch," easily in her mid-thirties, and the other three were somewhere in their twenties. The teenager was a girl. The other three consisted of one guy and two girls.

Suddenly Neal noticed something that filled him with an unaccountable and acute sense of dread. Situated between himself and the group sat a lone individual. It was like driving directly into the sun and finding that the vehicle directly in front of you had suddenly stopped and you were in the process of smacking into it.

This man, this vehicle directly in front of him, said nothing. Kept to himself.

If anything was obvious about this man, it was that that he wasn't with the van's group. He sat in what Neal thought to be a lawn chair (it squeaked and appeared to have that characteristically unsteady wobble), and stared straight ahead, or so appeared his silhouette.

"Neal?"

Annie's voice.

"Yes—what is it?"

Annie's shadow quickly came back into view. Though he couldn't physically make it out yet, he knew she had that annoying sparkle in her eyes; that telling tone in her voice. She always got this way before and after one of her meetings.

God, this whole business *smelled*.

He kept thinking: should have brought the Glock; should have brought the *Glock* . . . .

"What is it, honey?" Neal again asked.

"Those people over there said that Ed said the aliens would come up over that mountain there," she said, pointing north, toward the low hills.

"Fine." Great, he was losing her big-time and he couldn't do a damn thing about it.

"God, honey, I can't wait! It's going to be *sooo* neat! Just think of it, aliens—*landing*—and we'll be the first to see them! God, I hope Channel 5 picks them up!" Annie rubbed her arms and scanned the horizon. The best Neal could muster was an eyeball roll. He got back into the truck.

Driver's side window still down, Neal listened in on the group at the van. They talked about all-things-alien. Ed's name came up. Again. And again. *Mr.* Ed, Neal thought, and laughed to himself. *Yup, Mr. Ed, straight from the horse's ass, yuck, yuck, yuck.*

"What's so funny?" Annie asked, coming up closer alongside the pickup.

"Oh, nothing. Just chuckling to myself."

Annie looked back up to the stars.

The group at the van grew more talkative. Quite animated, in fact.

"*Should we take out the crystals and have Martha do her thing?*" one asked.

"*Sure!*" resounded another. It sounded like the teenager. Votes in, a flashlight switched on. Neal could just make out the shapes that moved about, some larger than others. The silent individual between them continued his-or-her muted vigil. It was almost as if Neal could have walked right on through him and not have spotted him, let alone disturb him. He was like a ghost—only *partially* there.

Martha was seated in her own chair, acting modest about her crystal talents, Neal mused—but he knew she was just playing the audience.

"C'mon, Martha," another challenged, "show us what you can do!"

Martha moved. She must have been a huge hunk of a woman, three-hundred pounds easy, Neal thought, by the size of her silhouette against the campfire.

"Okay, I'll do it. Bill—you got the crystals?"

A flashlight moved toward the van.

"Sure—just a minute! They're in a box back here." Bill fetched like an obedient puppy. "What do you do with them, Martha?" asked the teenager.

Neal watched the light from the flashlight dance into the chunk of darkness that was the van. He saw its beam periodically come into view through the windows as Bill presumably rummaged about inside. Neal also saw that the lone figure in the chair between them shifted a bit. His chair again squeaked.

So he *can* move.

"So, I run them over the length of a person's body and it rejuvenates them," Martha said, pulling Neal's attention back to the group. "The crystals give off a spark, and you can feel new, renewed energy flowing through you."

"*Really?*"

The girl's use of the word made Neal sick.

"Here they are, Martha," Bill said, and brought out the box. The group huddled around it.

Neal strained for a futile look. Martha, Neal assumed, since he really couldn't see, brought out a crystal from the container.

"Okay, who's first?" Martha asked.

Bill answered first. Neal imagined frowns forming on the girls' faces. What a wiener.

"How about Tina," someone else was heard to say, "she's never had it done to her before." Martha turned toward the shadow that had to be Tina.

"Tina? How about it?"

Neal could only assume Tina looked to the others, and Bill's enthusiasm instantly deflated.

"Well . . . sure—why not?"

Martha got up (not so gracefully) and went over to the girl.

"Okay, Tina, just turn your back to me and relax. Now breathe deeply."

Tina did as instructed.

Neal watched the silhouetted matriarch move the crystal up and around Tina's silhouette. There were distinct *clicking* sounds, accompanied by little sparks of blue light that periodically popped out from the crystal. Neal straightened up in his seat and again strained for a better view.

How the hell did she do that?

"That stuff really works, you know."

Annie's voice had startled him. He'd forgotten all about her standing there in the dark.

"How does it spark?" Neal asked.

"It's the properties of the crystal. I know you don't believe in it, but it works. You can see for yourself," she said, pointing.

Neal sat back in his seat and felt a bit silly at having been caught. "Yeah, sure."

It had now been a good hour and a half and still there were no sightings. No silver spaceships; no little green men or women. Nothing. But the crowd had not dwindled, in fact it had even gained some as time went on, and there had even been one mildly amusing incident that had transpired.

Some people who had been driving by (to *where*, God only knew, at this hour) stopped alongside the van to ask what was going on. All night long that group had been espousing, rather loudly and proudly, how important this alien landing was going to be—never even questioning that there might not even *be* one. As this car stops to ask what was going on, the questioner never even got the politeness of an acknowledgement. Just silence. Rude . . . unanswered . . . silence.

Fucking hypocrites, Neal mused, don't even have enough conviction in their own cause to tell others about it.

He laughed out loud.

The man in the folding chair continued to just *sit*.

As much as Neal enjoyed the outdoors, this was getting to be much too bogus for him to take any longer. Getting out of the truck, he went in search of Annie, who'd wandered off after the crystal display, and happened to be only a few feet away on a nearby rise.

"Just how long are we supposed to wait out here, anyway?" he asked, coming up alongside.

"I guess 'til midnight," she said hesitantly. "Maybe there's stuff going on at the other location—you know, where the camera crew is?"

Neal rolled his eyes skyward, subtlety shook his head, and returned to the truck. The things he did for—

Love?

Again finding himself alone and in the darkness (which he actually found comforting), he looked back to the van. Shifting position, he leaned against the truck's hood and better positioned himself to eavesdrop. He listened as the group seriously considered if the planes flying overhead were actually flying saucers or not. Bill—the *man* of the group—was the one the others turned to for their answers. The "expert."

"They're out there, outta gas, and with no road map," Neal said, as he got back into the truck.

A gentle breeze drifted through Neal's truck. It actually felt as if it had cooled off some. On the breeze rode the scent of the Nevada desert and cigarette smoke. He decided to get out and stretch his legs some. As he did, he listened to the sound his feet made as they crunched on hard desert soil. It all seemed *too* real, like the whole scene was out of a film noir (Ted Turner's colorized and rotting soul notwithstanding).

Looking up, he crammed his hands deep into his jeans pockets. There was, he spotted, an extremely faint light bugging across the stars. He sighed, knowing full well it wasn't an alien spacecraft but a good ole earth-orbiting satellite.

Okay, he was getting bored.

Then he decided—why not, why not just go over and meet this mysterious person who never moved, breathed, or talked—and introduce himself. Maybe strike up a conversation. It would at least pass some time.

He made his way over to Annie, who stood in front of the pickup.

"Annie, I'm going to go over to say 'hi' to that dude over there."

Annie looked toward the silhouette.

"Okay. But be careful, honey. I'll be watching you, okay?"

Neal smiled. "Sure." He wandered over, but still focused most of his attention to the stars . . . and the crunch the desert made beneath him.

"Hi. My name's Neal. How're you doing?"

The figure moved, but only slightly. Looked up to him.

"Pleased to meet you. Name's Angus. How're you doing tonight?"

The man sported an odd, thick foreign accent. And not a Scottish one, either. Neal casually squatted down alongside the silhouette's chair, looking off into the darkness.

"Oh, I'm fine I guess. I'm here with my wife," he said, directing back behind him. Angus cast a casual glance toward Annie. "I'm more here for her than this UFO business."

The man settled back heavily into his chair. It squeaked.

"You're pretty quiet—you with anyone? Ever heard of Ed Horton?"

"Yes . . . I'm here with a few others. They're around somewhere. And yes, I know Ed."

A sudden commotion ran out from among the van's group. Neal and the man both looked over. Neal guessed the guy he was talking to was in his mid-to-late thirties. Strapping. His voice exuded a definite presence of *power*.

In fact a rather uncomfortable sense thereof.

"Hey, Bill, will ya' look at that?" one of the van groupies asked. It was Martha. He also noticed how she actually got up and out of her chair. "What *is* that? Is it *them*, Bill, is it?" Of course everyone else in the area heard them, and they all looked toward the low mountains to the north. Neal also saw the light there, seemingly perched atop the low peak. He also saw another light that quickly came in from the west to meet it.

"Those can't be airplanes, can they, Bill?"

There was a moment of silence before Bill passed his judgement.

"Nope. They're not airplanes."

A man of decision.

"I thought not!" quickly agreed another. In no time people began getting out of their vehicles, and somewhere Neal knew that Annie was also moving in to join them. In no time groups of people all trudged noisily past Neal and his silent partner, Angus, and over to the vehicle to the right of them.

"Bill—I think it's them! I really think it's *them*, Bill!" Martha excitedly exclaimed. Her little gathering following faithfully behind her like a procession of ducks, as they better repositioned themselves to view the lights. They met up with the other group, of which Neal was sure Annie was one. The light in the west still moved toward the stationary one over the hill.

"There're really here! It's *them!*" Tina cried, her shrill voice once again causing Neal to want to hurl.

"Oh, God, I'm getting goosebumps!" Martha cried, "this is it, really *it!*"

Neal, now back to his feet, couldn't hold it in any longer and burst out laughing.

Angus turned to regard him.

"They're getting orgasms over goddamned *helicopters!*" Neal said, blurting it out loudly. "They're goddamned *helicopters!*"

Now Neal heard Angus making a noise.

He was chuckling.

Neal still couldn't quite make out Angus's face, but it seemed (if this could be true) that his face was *thick*.

Neal and Angus looked at each other through the darkness and both laughed loud and heartily. Angus's laugh seemed deeply guttural, almost primitive, and this caused Neal to cringe and break out in a cold sweat. He wasn't sure if his mind was playing tricks on him in the darkness, or if, in fact, Angus was really deformed in some way—which could explain why he choose to keep to himself. Neal just got the idea that Angus's mouth was somehow malformed.

The easterly moving chopper finally met up with the stationary one, and together they continued their journey southeast. Neal laughed harder and found he couldn't stop. He was utterly dumbfounded that there were still people as gullible as these jokers appeared to be.

"Fucking *helicopters!*" Neal again said, far louder than intended.

It was at this point that someone in the crowd picked up on it (heard him?)—and it sounded like, of all people, Martha. Her view had suddenly changed.

"I . . . I-I think they're helicopters, Bill. God, I really do think so. Yep, helicopters, all right . . . as I figured . . . ."

The hub-bub abruptly came to an end. There was a lot of mumbling and tail tucking, and the crowd quickly dispersed. Just like that. Neal and Angus continued laughing as the group quickly ambled on past, several of the disgruntled and darkened faces turning to them as they passed.

"Angus, I can't believe there are people out there that are *that* stupid!"

"Oh, but I can, Neal. Ed and I deal with them all the time."

"You do?"

"Sure. These people believe that they're here to witness a grand alien visitation. Look at them—pathetic, hopeless little creatures."

Angus again chuckled, and this time there was no mistaking it. It was thick with spite.

Evil.

Neal looked at him.

"You mean," Neal said, "this isn't . . . *none* of it?"

"Nope. At least not in the manner they're expecting."

Neal's knees went rubbery.

"H-how do you kn-know this?"

Angus again chuckled, and this one was worse than before.

"*Because I made it all up.*"

Angus's subsequent laughter thundered above their conversation and carried over to the van group. To those surrounding them. It was an unabashedly *wicked* laugh.

Neal's eyes froze on Angus's dark form.

There was no mistaking it now. Angus's face *was* messed up . . . *changing*—was still in the process of that change—whatever *that* meant. It didn't make any sense.

"In a way, Neal, I feel sorry for you," Angus said. "You're not gullible and stupid like they are." Angus forced thick words out of an extended mouth. It was like his tongue was impeding his speech.

And in the next instant, Neal felt an unimaginably powerful force strike him. It clobbered him like a flying slab of concrete to the head.

Neal collapsed hard . . . and that was all he knew.

"What's going on here?" someone asked out of the darkness.

Flashlights clicked on everywhere. Annie turned and quickly retreated back to the truck. She'd *heard* something. Felt an indescribable sinking in the pit of her stomach. She'd just managed to dodge out of the path of some rushing *thing* . . . and tracked it as went toward the group she'd just left.

"Neal? *Neal?*"

No answer.

The crowd behind her was suddenly hit by a flurry of fangs and claws that ripped into their weak and atrophied flesh. Shrieks cut the air into ribbons and the group split apart. No matter where anyone ran they all seemed to blunder into more of the same. Hitting the mêlée blind, like running smack into a brick wall in the dark. The attacks came from everywhere. It was so very dark. The pack liked it that way.

Annie continued to call out for Neal. Never saw him on the ground, only ten feet away, bleeding and unconscious.

The shrieks increased, found no refuge from the continually growing feeding frenzy. Annie heard other groups up the road going through the same butchery. She even saw several of the van group as they tried to rush into their van. One large lady collapsed before she could get to it. Closely behind her Annie saw two huge forms. One of them wasted no time in falling upon her screaming and writhing form, while the other continued on into the van and violently rocked it until its hunger was satisfied.

The crowd Annie had been with was in the midst of its own attack. She saw—*heard*—silhouettes ripped apart. She was in a nightmare. This couldn't be real. She felt something roll up and against her foot and looked down.

She really didn't want to see what she saw.

Gradually the sounds of struggles had died, and the only sounds that remained were those of quiet tearing and mastication. Squinting, Annie thought she saw several human forms as they ran off into the night, but everywhere she looked she found no Neal . . . and found herself underneath their pickup. Slowly . . . carefully . . . she came to a crouching position alongside their truck.

The un-air-conditioned one.

She would never complain about that again.

Annie slowly backed up to the driver's side. For some odd reason, she had been spared. She didn't even attempt to second-guess why. She was given a way out, and by God, she was going to take it.

But what about Neal? Where was he?

Inching her way into the cab of the truck, Annie ducked low, whispering Neal's name. Tears streamed down her face as she started the vehicle, and the sudden turn-on startled her. The jerk told her the vehicle was already in gear. Dirt and gravel spat out from the tires as the truck dug out a deep channel on her horrified exit.

Several of the spitting stones hit Neal's still unconscious frame.

A hairy head popped up from within the vehicle off to the truck's left, but went back down and continued on with its business. Several of the other werewolves also looked up and over to Angus as Annie made her getaway.

Angus staved them off.

She could go. They had plenty for tonight and there would be plenty of time for her later. There was always time. As for her man—he'd let him live. He liked the guy. Might have other plans for him.

Annie never once hit her brakes as she sped back toward I-15.

Neal lay in the dirt, blood pooling against his back as it sluiced out from the van. All around him lay chunks of the slaughter. The breeze was still warm, but now it carried with it a sickening aroma.

And the silence was deafening . . . hollow echoes of screams and agony still a thick memory in the air.

No more crystals.

No more stargazers.

No more cigarettes.

No more pack.

Neal's eyes opened . . . they strained and tried to come around in their sockets. Focus.

Pain. Lots of it.

His nose twitched. He felt his face pressed into the dirt. Was afraid to move. Felt as if an 18-wheeler rested atop him. As he tried to move, he experienced yet another wonderful splash of pain and fell back into the dark void of unconsciousness . . . .

In the still-night-sky above came a point of light. It was faint at first, but quickly grew in presence.

The light descended and hovered momentarily, scanning the terrain. Silently and swiftly the circular craft maneuvered over Neal's body and another light immediately emerged from beneath its belly. It locked onto Neal's form. As this light faded, so did Neal. The craft hummed and hovered above the desert a moment longer before it shot back up into the stars

And disappeared.

The Red Envelope
2003

Naked and sweaty, Harry Black stumbled through the overturned bourbon and vodka bottles littering his scant, alcohol-reeking apartment bedroom on the way to the closet. Images always the images: his wife . . . their three kids . . . Daddy's law firm . . . being fired from his stock analyst position . . . his anything-but-gradual descent into hell at the hands of his own personal weapon of choice: bourbon. And bourbon's Russian cousin, vodka. And throw in a little hanky-panky for good measure.

Disoriented and disillusioned, Harry switched on the closet light and reached up to the top shelf, pulling down the cloth-wrapped parcel he'd stashed there only days ago.

Or was it last month?

All time blurred when you were at one with the bottle. Didn't frigging matter. *Before Now.*

Tears running down his face, he hugged his little package tightly into his chest and collapsed against the wall and floor. He sat there, legs sprawled out before him like a naked rag doll, and stared blankly at the bed and its rumpled sheets. The spent bottles. The "lady" with whom he'd shared those sheets earlier was long gone, but his guilt was not. Harry unwrapped his little parcel and openly wept. A .38 Special. For those special moments you just couldn't trust to any other method. It was loaded; he'd seen to that during one of his of-late infrequent in-betweeners, when he hadn't yet made it back to the booze, which he never should have left in the first place. Figured he'd have to have it all primed and ready to go, so as not to make any mistakes. Fumbling around for ammo, you know, when he was, well, as wasted as he currently was wasn't going to help matters.

Without further ado, he cocked the hammer and stuck the barrel into his mouth.

Was this what it was like giving guys blow jobs?

And why were they called "blow" jobs when it was really sucking?

Was the origin of the term really about sucking on a bullet?

Oh, yeah, he was about to give himself one helluva *a blow j—*

He spied a partially drained bourbon bottle at his feet.

Well, now, can't have that can we? One more for the road, old boy? One more certainly wasn't gonna hurt anything, now was it?

Harry removed the barrel from his lips and reached for the bottle.

Damn, what a waste that would have been!

Smacking his lips at the taste of oiled gunmetal (he'd bought it from a place that actually took care of that which it sold), he drained the last of the rust-colored fluid in one well-practiced swoop . . . looked to the bottle . . . then tossed it away. It skimmed maddeningly across the floor and under the bed, until it came to a clunking stop somewhere outside his field of view. Squeezing his hot, swollen eyes shut and wincing from the pure goodness of the devil's-own burn down his throat and into his belly, Harry again licked his lips and returned the barrel to where it should be—when a loud, pounding commotion at his apartment door interrupted. He jumped, jerking the gun from his mouth.

Never one to be deterred from his chosen path, Harry reinserted the barrel and repositioned his bourbon-kissed lips about it.

The knocking returned, however, and louder, and Harry swore the person was in the room with him. Again, jerking the gun from his mouth and feeling a different pain in his belly this time, Harry shouted out in a half-whine, half-plea for mercy, and to please *go the hell away.*

Didn't his visitor understand his need to rid himself from himself?

Of putting himself out of his—and everyone else's—misery?

Of solving the whole "suck" or "blow" job quandary?

The knocking ceased.

Sobbing now, hand and revolver limp on the floor beside him, Harry slurred a whispered "thank you," and again brought the gun back to his mouth . . . but no sooner had he re-inserted the barrel when he heard—*felt*—another knock he *swore* was inside his head. This time, Harry shot stupidly to his feet, dropping the weapon. He threw his hands to his ears as the knocking continued—loud, powerful, and unabated . . . *inside his head.*

"Go *away!*" he yelled, wavering stupidly on his feet.

When it didn't, he stumbled, bouncing off walls and door jambs, and with some difficulty angrily navigated his way into a living room he'd never expected to again set foot in. The hammering at the door (and inside his oh-so-throbbing head) continued in a steady stream of pound-pound-*POUND*.

POUND!

POUND-POUND!

He reached for the door (twice—it seemed to keep moving), hastily fumbled with the lock, then threw it open.

"What the *f*—"

He stood naked and uncertain before a deserted hallway.

Angrily he glared at the apartment across the way with its scent of cooked cabbage thick in the air (or whatever it was that aggravated his already sickened stomach). Scratching matted hair and steadying himself against the door frame, he poked his head out and around the apartment door, blinking and squinting down the length of the hallway.

No one.

Not a goddamned soul.

He waddled out into the hallway, felt a squirt of urine leak out onto a leg, and continued to squint down the length of hallway. Admittedly, his vision wasn't at its best in his present state, but he could still make out that he was the only one out here. Alone, naked, and drunk. He turned to re-enter his apartment . . . and stopped. There, on the floor before him, and just inside the door, lay a red envelope.

Addressed to him.

Harry Black Jr.—without the comma, just like he wrote it.

Harry clumsily stumbled back into his apartment, then turned back around and teetered to a stop just before the envelope. He blinked. No illusion. There it was . . . brilliant—almost *radiant*—and very, *very* red. He'd never seen anything so deeply, so thoroughly *red* before. It almost hurt to look at it for any length of time. But with his entire world spinning before him . . . surprisingly, this did not. It remained solid—stable. Unmoving. And it had his name on it in splendid, flowing gold calligraphy—which actually seemed to float above the somewhat translucent envelope paper.

Like you could reach into the envelope, the paper, and get

(*blown*)

sucked into it.

Harry stooped over to pick it up and grew momentarily faint, took a tumble, even. He collapsed to his hands and knees, hands thrown out to either side of the letter, face directly over it.

Read me.

Harry Black Jr., it read simply in its floating calligraphy . . . no comma before the suffix. No address, no apartment number—just his *name*. Regaining his balance, such as it was, he picked up the letter and got back to his feet. Stumbling around, he made one last check out into the hallway, red envelope in hand. Nothing. Closed the door.

Harry couldn't take his eyes off the envelope as he carried it into the bedroom; like a fish chasing a shiny lure he held it before him, and when he looked up, the first thing his gaze fell upon was the gun. There, on the floor by the closet. Ready and waiting, purpose yet unfulfilled. He picked it up.

Blow me, Harry, I love how your lips feel wrapped around my barrel . . . we have work yet to be done here . . . .

Don't desert me now, we work well together, you and me . . . don't spoil a good thing . . .

Suck me, Harry, suck me!

But as Harry stood there . . . letter in hand . . . staring at the gun with heavy, alcohol-fueled eyes . . . another thought also entered his mind, as insistent as his beckoning gun, the knocks had been drowning out all other thoughts:

Open me!

Ooo-pen meee!

Harry lifted the letter and ran an unsteady finger underneath the envelope's flap. It was almost as if it'd opened itself. He was expecting a paper cut—*wanting* a paper cut.

Inspected his finger.

Nothing.

Inside the gold-lined parcel lay nestled a sheet of high-quality stationery, also red. Very red. He removed it. The paper was thick and heavy, with perfect, sharp creases as if ironed. He unfolded it and read the singular line:

What is your passion?

That was it. In raised print. That was all it said, in beautiful, gold, calligraphy set into the center of the sheet.

What is your passion?

Harry flicked the letter away, tears heavy in his eyes, his face a grimace of pain. With a lump in his throat, he grumbled and said, "*Here's my goddamned passion,*" pressed the barrel of the gun into his right temple, and pulled the trigger.

Nothing.

He pulled it again.

Still nothing.

"God*dammit!*"

Looking to the revolver, shaking it, Harry saw it was, indeed, fully loaded, and crazily began to click off the trigger several more times, aiming the revolver at his head, his cheeks, and various other parts of his anatomy—but still . . . nothing.

"*Fuck-fuck*-fuck!"

In a fit of disgust (and almost losing his balance), he pitched the revolver across the room, where it slammed into the wall . . . and discharged . . . just as a loud set of emergency vehicles went honking and squawking outside and below his apartment. Mewling pathetically, and never one to give up, Harry dove after the revolver for yet another try—but stepped on one of the many empty bottles littering his apartment and—

Harry's eyes fluttered open.

The floor roiled and bucked under him like an earthquake and he couldn't focus, let alone open his eyes.

He'd had a bad, bad dream. This was no earthquake—he'd tripped and fallen on the CN tracks, in Waukegan. Waukegan, Illinois. He'd done this once before . . . it had been his inaugural bender. Yeah, that was it—no earthquake, just a rampaging locomotive thundering through his two-sizes-too-small skull.

He opened his eyes.

Red.

Envelope.

Closed his eyes and groaned.

Fuck.

Opened his eyes again and saw that damned red, red envelope . . . propped up on the floor before him by its oh-so-crisp extended flap, so he could clearly read his name on the front. He couldn't—didn't—move and just stared at it . . . wincing in waves of pain. His floating name glistened in the rising morning sun, some two feet away from his face.

Harry Black Jr.!

What is your passion?

Read me!

Get up off the floor and read me!

Great, now it was actually *talking* to him.

But Harry wasn't stupid, or naïve, just hungover. He knew everyone had their own inner dialog, their own inner voice running rampant inside their heads . . . some were just a little more active, like Harry's had always been, that's all. Letters didn't *talk* to anyone. They conveyed messages . . . scribbled there by their writers.

Do you feel better? his little voice inquired. *A bit hungover, perhaps? Good*

. . . now, read *me!*

Slowly, Harry pushed himself upright and sat up against the wall, and the world spun in direct proportion to the square of his movement. His head protested from the knot he'd received from his little tumble. Still naked (and now chilled) he saw the gun . . . the spent bottles—his spent *life*—all before him.

Shivered uncontrollably.

Good God, had he *really?*

Had he really just tried to take his own life?

What'd happened to him, for chrissakes?

Lifting a trembling hand to his head, he felt as if he was about to . . . and did.

Into his lap.

Well, his voice chided, *isn't this just how you imagined it all those years ago as a kid growing up in Waukegan? Successful and well-to-do? Well, whoop-de-do, congratulations, my boy!*

Dehydrated, weak, and now reeking of sickly sweet alcohol-vomit, Harry stiffly picked himself up off the floor and stumbled into the bathroom, where he caught a cold, hard look at himself in the mirror.

Yeah, this is it, sport! It don't get any better than this, do *it?*

Harry turned away in disgust. Leaned against a wall. Wiped away vomit from his chin and used an upraised arm against which to rest his forehead as he turned to the wall. Closed his eyes and tried to blank out all thoughts. Tried to wish it all away. When he'd next open his eyes, he told himself—confidently—it would all be gone . . . and he'd be back with his wife and children . . . the way it *used* to be . . . in his dreams.

One . . . two . . . *three* . . . .

He opened his eyes. Looked down to his pelvis. Vomit. Still there. Nakedness . . . still there. Dismal failure of a life . . . *still there.*

Harry backed away from the wall and turned on the shower, as if recovering from suicide attempts was what he'd done every day, then slowly, carefully crawled into the bottom of the tub and rolled onto his back. Pushed the shower lever with a foot, increasing the water temperature, and let the hot, soothing water wash over him. The closest thing he had to a confessional. Showers always seemed to make things better. Must be a water-womb thing. He just wished he could sleep here, warm water splashing over him, forever and *ever* . . . .

You're a long way from Waukegan, Illinois, mister.

Remember Waukegan?

He lifted his head (yeah, it spun, but what the hell, he'd just tried to take himself out, so, what was a little pain and vertigo?) and looked out the stall. If he leaned forward a bit, he could just see into the bedroom and make out (big surprise!) that damned envelope. The red one that seemed to glow in the golden morning sunrise.

Waukegan . . . .

(*what's your passion, friend?*)

" . . . so, Son, have you decided what you want to be when you grow up?" an eleven-year-old Harry Black's father had asked him one beautiful summer's day, while he'd helped out at his father's law firm—when he should have been outside, swimming, playing explorer, or chasing dragonflies.

Harry blurted out his answer before he realized it, an answer he'd been thinking about for a long time, by boy's standards anyway, an answer that had been burning inside him *forever.*

"I wanna be a *saint!*"

Not only had Harry's father stopped dead in his tracks, but so had everyone else within earshot in the office of Black, Hegelsson, and Millot. After all, when one's father, a respected and successful lawyer, asked what it was you wanted to be upon growing up, the expected response was lawyer, stockbroker, or financier extraordinaire. *President,* even.

Not some fucking *saint.*

Hell, they didn't even know if the "s" was capitalized or not.

But the Harry Senior response had been what was expected, had Harry Junior been a little older and known about awkward moments in public places with respected community leaders: laughter, quickly followed by one of the usual, tension-easing expressions parents use, such as *Well, don't those darned kids say the* darnedest *things?* Or *That's no kid of mine, heh, heh!* Or *Agnes! Did you lose our son in the supermarket and bring home the neighbor's kid?*

As soon as possible, however, when everyone returned their attention to work, had come the not-so-well-known trademark Black-Senior-fatherly-glare that young Harry was far more familiar with—*in privato.* His father's *real* glare unmistakably said, "*How dare you embarrass me like that, you little shit . . . we are going to talk about this later, don't you mistake that, then I'm gonna kick your ass from here to Lake Superior . . . .*"

Ah, the wonder years.

Passion.

What had been his passion?

Where had it gone?

And what the hell kind of question was that, anyway, and from *where?* Some stupid-ass piece of junk mail slid underneath his door? A joke? Well, bad timing, pal.

Harry lay back down in the tub and allowed the warm water to spray over him. He pressed the shower lever more to the left with his toe, upping the heat more still.

Now all he wanted to do was to die.

Gruesome or quiet, it didn't matter, but he couldn't even pull off that simplest of tasks without screwing things up. Like his entire life . . . all fucked up.

After an untold amount of time trying to drown his sorrows in the shower, Harry toweled off and reentered the bedroom. It was no hallucination, after all, it was still there among the bottles and the .38. That damned letter. Scooping it up off the floor, Harry sat on the edge of his bed and looked at it with a somewhat bruised—if sobering—mind.

What an odd little piece of paper.

It didn't look like a chain letter . . . it was crisp and fresh—Hallmark quality—but who'd delivered it to him? His name was clearly written on the front of it—in golden, *floating* letters—but that was it, no address, just his name—and that brought up another matter: who'd been wailing on his door last night, interrupting his planned departure from this world?

Harry winced. Don't try to think too hard, yet, my friend, as sober as you may feel you're still in hangover mode.

Last night.

He looked around the room.

Spent bourbon and vodka bottles everywhere . . . not to mention, he thought, rubbing his head, that little bruised reminder on his scalp . . . and his revolver. It was all real, none of it made up. There it was, the gun, lying on the floor. Innocent as ever.

And he was thirsty. Very, very, *thirsty.*

His glanced down to the red sheet of paper in his hands.

What is *your passion?*

I'll tell you what my goddamned passion is. *Booze.* And lots of it. Firewater, my friend. Al Ke Hall.

But it hadn't always been that way, had it? that stupid, nagging, voice inside insisted. *It hadn't always been the bottle. You'd had other passions before. Cynthia. The kids. Before that . . . you'd actually* wanted *to be a saint, hadn't you? What'd happened, Harry, where had you taken such a wrong turn? Where had you* sinned?

I don't know what'd happened. All I know is that Daddy beat me down over the years, told me I'd not amount to anything if I didn't Get In Gear, and that no son of his was ever gonna be any kind of a deified bullshit saint. *Saints were* dead *people, for crying out loud, people who did great things with their lives, died or were murdered in hideous and gruesome ways* then *became canonized. You couldn't be a saint while living and you certainly couldn't make a living* while living as a saint—*not to mention marry and have kids, and by God, that's exactly what you'll be doing, so you better find yourself a more practical way of living, my boy!*

And are you even my *boy?*

Yeah, he'd actually said that last part.

That's exactly what'd happened. Life had gotten in the way, like it always did. What the hell good was it to grow up, anyway? It was far better to die while you still had dreams than to grow up and lose them all. Become contaminated by the ugly realities of Life. Life just *sucked.* Sucked out loud, and there ain't no way around it.

Harry again looked to the paper.

What is your passion?

But he'd had that passion, once, so very long ago, in another life, and that passion had been to help others. Pure and simple. To be the best possible person he could be. To be—in a word—a living, breathing, not-dead *saint.* Adult rules meant nothing to kids. He'd seen that show, *The Saint.* If Simon Templar could do it, then, by God, so could Harry Black!

It was then that Harry felt something he hadn't felt in a long, long time.

Affection.

Not anger and hatred, but a sadness and empathy for that little boy he used to be . . . and how sad it had been that he'd killed him . . . him and his dreams. He missed that boy . . . that young and naïve Harry Black Jr. (without the comma). God, had he so messed up his life that he was forever damned? It didn't have to be the official, religious sense of the word, but it suddenly hit home how he still wanted to do nothing but *help* others. And maybe that was why he'd married Cynthia. She— neither of them, actually—had been perfect in any sense of the word, but he'd seen something in her . . . something that'd touched him— once—something in her that had made him fall in *love* with her . . . .

Yes, deep down, Harry'd always wanted to be someone who went around the world helping others out. If they didn't have enough money, he'd give it to them. If they didn't have work, he'd find it for them. If they were lonely and destitute, he'd help them out, become their friend. A shoulder to cry on? He was there. But what had happened along the way? Daddy had had other plans for him and he'd been shipped off to college. Got his degree and had then been inserted into Daddy's law firm like some square peg into some square hole. So, in an effort to get out from under Daddy's colossal and almighty thumb, Harry'd found an investment firm to work for. If he couldn't be a saint, so the logic went, he could at least make lots of money and someday create a foundation of some kind, and *still* get part of his dream to come true . . . .

But more life had gotten in the way, hadn't it?

You see, there had been this Christmas party, and there had been this girl, see?, and they'd both gotten rather looped, Harry and this girl, and ended up in this broom closet. And . . . well . . . one thing'd led to the other . . . and before he'd known it, Harry Black had found himself engaged to Miss Cynthia Barlow, daughter to Troy Barlow, CEO and president of the firm that provided him with his rather lucrative remuneration. Three kids, several bank accounts and Christmas parties later, Harry found loving wife Cynthia in the broom closet yet again, but this time with another. Long story short, it wasn't long afterward that Harry had found his new best friend—the bottle.

(Better a bottle in front of me than an affair affronting me!)

That had been his bottle—*battle*—cry.

That had been his *life*.

And when he'd finally confronted Father-in-law with this information on his wunnerful daughter, what had been the reply?

Have his *own* goddamned affair.

No one divorced in this family, he decreed, be a man and take control of the situation! Suck

(blow)

it up. This is the Big Time, my *boy*, and you obviously hadn't been satisfying her up to now, so you better shape up, bring her back around, and get with the program—*or I will make your life extremely uncomfortable.*

Oh, he got with the program all right. Program Bourbon. Program Vodka. Program Tiffany. Program Veronica. You name it, you drink it, you fuck it. But it, eventually, all came back to that one little, nagging question, didn't it?

What is your passion?

He knew it; was surprised it was still there. Thought it'd been killed long ago with that little boy. Saints were supposed to go through trying times, weren't they? Lives full of despair and torment, only to (somehow) rise above it all in death and become, what—*anointed?*

And it was still his passion after all those years. He no-shit wanted that dream.

Harry looked to his letter, again, and just about had a heart attack. He shot to his feet, tossing it away. Where it had previously only had that one line on its crisp, stiff paper, it now read:

Do it.

In beautiful gold calligraphy.

Harry stared at it.

Do *it.*

He blinked. Rubbed his eyes. The words remained.

What the *hell?*

Cautiously, he walked over to the letter and its envelope. The letter was face up and twisted at an angle to him, its envelope beside it. Harry angled his head to read it without touching it. Repositioning himself . . . he kept his focus on the golden calligraphied words. Again rubbed his eyes.

Okay, what was going on, here?

Had he really blown a hole through his head and this was Hell?

He picked up the letter and held it out before him. Crisp, heavy paper. Picked up the envelope. Gold lined. Also heavy and crisp. Brand new stationery in a brilliant, vivid almost translucent red.

This couldn't be happening. Letters didn't change from one set of wording to another without someone *doing* it.

But he held the evidence in his hands, and where had been the words "*What is your passion?*" now were the words "*Do it.*" And what had he been thinking about when this happened?

Being a saint.

Helping people.

Do it, the words demanded.

Do it, don't fucking think *about it*, his dark, little voices cried.

Harry folded the letter up into its tri-fold and hastily stuffed it back into the envelope, then put it on the nightstand. Backed away. He stared at the bottles littering the bedroom floor. The gun . . . still there. Looked to the rumpled bed. Thought about last night and how he wasn't supposed to be alive this morning.

He wasn't supposed to be here, today, plain and simple.

The neighbor's cat was supposed to have found him, scratching at his apartment door because of his putrid stench. Or someone was supposed to have called 911, because of the gunshot . . . .

But none of that had happened, had it?

Except for that accidental discharge and *still* no 911.

Now, what the hell was he supposed to do?

Harry Black pulled the lapel of his jacket up around his neck. It was pleasantly brisk, if such words as "pleasantly" were to enter his mind. Late October, and he was supposed to be dead. It was almost as if he felt that other him *was* dead—up there in that apartment of his, right now—lying on the floor . . . his brains blown out across the room in one of those funnel-shaped gore and spatter patterns. It made him shiver. He'd come so close to actually *doing* it—and was that something he'd *normally* do? Was that something that was a part of the normal Harry Black Jr. psyche?

Was cheating on his wife?

Was looking the other way when his boss shaved off some numbers?

Was living in an apartment his wife knew nothing about (or did, but didn't care)?

Where had Honest H gone? What had happened to him that he had to accept a life so heinously less-virtuous and off-target than planned?

Right here, fired back the answer. *Right here, right* now.

Where had things taken such a wrong turn? Did it even matter? No matter how you may have been raised there eventually came a point in your life when you were considered an adult, which meant there came a time when *you*—and no one *but* you—were held responsible for *your* own actions. All of them. Sure, it'd been easy to blame his life on his parents. Or, once free of them, on his wife and her father. Bad business practices. But when it came right down to it, no one had twisted his arm to marry her, and no one had twisted his arm to go down the path he now found himself trekkin'.

A fine saint he'd make, indeed.

What is your passion?

Do it.

Well, if he was supposed to have killed himself, was there, now, anything more daunting?

If he (or the letter) had changed that part of his life—could he change other aspects?

If the worst had already been averted, what did that make everything else? Why not just walk away from it all? Start anew?

Do it.

And, just where to start?

He pulled out the envelope from his jacket pocket. The idea came to him in a flash.

Mrs. Barbara Crown.

That's where he'd start.

Harry stood before the post office mail box, thinking, *little did anyone know he wasn't supposed to be here.* That he was supposed to be lying in a pool of his own gore, back at his apartment, stinking up the place.

But one little red letter had turned his entire life around. Now, he was standing in the post office, poised to do good by someone.

Harry looked to the envelopes he held, ready to be mailed. In all of them were hefty sums of money to help each of those he had chosen to help. He had more money than he knew what to do with (well, not exactly, but it sounded good in his head), why not spread it around, like to Mrs. Barbara Crown and company? An old neighbor of his back in Waukegan. Make a day or two a little brighter. Barbara Crown used to let him hang out with her when he was a kid . . . watch TV . . . dog sit when she went on trips. He'd recently heard that she'd run into some tough times. He hoped this would help. Harry deposited the envelopes and turned to leave the post office, when he spotted an elderly gentleman having problems opening a mailbox. Smiling, Harry walked over.

"Excuse me, sir, but is there something I could help you with?"

"I'm having trouble opening this box. I can't seem to get the combination to work," the man said.

"Let me find someone to help you."

Harry went off to one of the windows, talked to one of the employees and in no time a helpful postal employee assisted the gentleman in gaining access to his mailbox.

Harry Black had spent the better part of the week reevaluating his life and cleaning up the mess he'd made of things the past ten years— though he kept the apartment. He cleaned out the bottles and got rid of the gun. He'd also filed the paperwork for that non-profit foundation he'd always wanted to start, listing his children as silent partners. Of course, he wasn't telling Cynthia any of this. Once he named his board, he quickly asked *them* to select the as-yet-unnamed head of the foundation. He would remain in the background.

But as Harry now sat in his apartment, sipping tea, and looking out over three a.m. New York, listening to the sirens off in the distance, he looked to his red letter on the table before him. Something about it felt different; felt . . . restless.

What is your passion?

Do it.

Where the hell had it come from? Who'd sent it to him? Was he being *watched?* Tracked? By whom? And there had been the unnerving business about who'd been knocking at his door. He knew he'd been drunk, but he remembered something distinctly disturbing about that intrusion. Not only persistent, but also like it had been not only at his apartment door, *but in his head.* How could that be? And the knocking didn't go away until he answered it. Then there had been no one in the hallway!

Had he imagined it all?

Gotten it all messed up in his drunken haze and suicidal tendencies and that letter had (in fact) been there all day?

Of course he had. It had all been in his head, the weirdness of it, anyway. The letter was obviously real because he had it, and it was anything but to be ignored. A vivid red envelope with his name floating on the front—in bright gold. He lifted the envelope up to the light and poked at it with a finger. Yup—his name actually appeared to float above the envelope just like a hologram.

This was clearly deliberate.

Inside, a red letter; written in gold . . . in the center of the sheet . . . the line *"What is your passion?"* that later changed to *"Do it."*

Or did it?

He opened it up. *"What is your passion?"* was still there. Where had the *"Do it,"* gone? Had it really ever been there, or had he just pleasantly gone momentarily insane? He ran his fingers over the raised lettering. They were real. How could words change themselves? They *can't*, that's how. He set the pair back on the table.

Okay, he had to have imagined the "Do it" part. But, it almost didn't matter, because the end result had been that it had saved him from personal annihilation and turned his life around. Given him the passion to start over . . . to say no to his current path . . . and forge ahead on a new one. He wished he could repay whoever'd sent it—

Harry's blood ran cold.

There again on the letter were the words: *"Do it."*

He shot to his feet.

"How? How do I *do* this?"

Do it.

Was all it said.

Go for a walk.

Those words entered his head, and he swore this thought was different. It didn't quite feel like it had come from him, it felt . . . alien. Maybe it was just his heightened sensitivity to what was going on, his current, estranged state of mind, but *this* voice felt separate from who he was.

Go for a walk, the voice in his head insisted.

A walk—in *this* neighborhood, at *this* time of night? He'd be asking for it, he thought back. This wasn't exactly rural, upstate New York— this was New York *City*. People didn't just go walking certain streets at night unless they were looking for—

Go for the walk.

What is your passion?

Do *it.*

Hey, you were going to kill yourself just the other day, the voice countered, *what difference does it make if something happens now? Where was that backbone you had a failed-suicide ago? One day you're all gung-ho to leave this world and the next you're afraid to go outside your apartment?*

Life is funny that way, ain't it?

Harry chuckled.

Point made.

If he'd been so ready to end it all, this should . . . this should just be a walk in the park, shouldn't it? Live and let live! Die and let die! We all have to die *sometime* of *something,* and all his time was borrowed, now, wasn't it? A life he wouldn't have had, had he never received that letter. A regular red letter day if there ever was one! There ain't ever gonna be any more overt acts of Divine Intervention the rest of your life, baby, so grab this one while you can!

Yeah, a lot of strange things had happened as a result of that letter. Go with it. *Do it.* Take that walk.

That letter. The red, red one. With the shiny, floating, gold calligraphy.

Harry threw on his jacket, stuffed the letter into a pocket and locked the door behind him. He felt curiously liberated . . . and sad. As he walked away, he turned and looked back to his apartment.

The closed door seemed so lonely.

Distant.

Two-dimensional.

It really was interesting how life turned out, wasn't it? He would not be where he presently stood had a certain outcome occurred over another. Would not be standing there in the hallway looking back at that door, right now, had things turned out just a wee bit differently.

Booze and bullets. Nothing good ever came from mixing those together. Ever.

Harry left the building.

He found himself walking up steps inside some other building, in an area of town with which he wasn't familiar. It wasn't a friendly, *How ya, doin, neighbor?* area, either. It'd happened before, this zombie-like state. And he remembered how once, while in high school, he'd been driving home, but had been so tired he'd never actually—*consciously*—remembered driving home. He'd done the whole twelve-mile trip on autopilot—and at night. And another time, while in college, the same thing. He'd been so preoccupied with an upcoming test, he'd actually walked smack into a light pole on a public street. So this was not without precedent . . . but this was the first time he'd found himself entering what looked like a crack house at two-twenty-two in the a.m., the smell of death and decay and *gunk* everywhere. He actually stopped partway up the stairs and thought about heading back, hell, *running* back. He did not feel at all good about being here. There were far too many shadows in this dark . . . foreboding den of iniquity . . . for it to be any kind of safe. The people he passed? Well, the polite description would be that they all appeared to be "societally challenged" . . . .

But . . . they left him alone.

Never . . . never in a million years . . . had he ever thought he'd be caught dead inside one of these places—yet here he was.

That's when he realized he held that envelope in his hand. He was holding it and it still had his name on it. Harry found himself again moving upward. Up, ever upward along the creaking, dark steps until he came to the landing he was meant to step off on. His legs and body

(*the letter*)

had a mind of their own.

Do it.

Yes, he knew the difference between this experience and what had happened before. There was no hiding it this time . . . it was the letter. As much as he tried to ignore the weirdness of all that had happened, there was no ignoring it now. Whatever this letter *was* . . . it was definitely on overdrive . . . on a mission . . . and he was its merry

(—*don't shoot the*—)

messenger boy. Harry felt its sudden and intense sense of urgency. Hey, it saved his life, maybe it was about to save another! Harry backed off the skepticism and allowed himself to just go with the little red package. It wasn't easy, but it was doable.

He'd been through worse, right?

At the landing, Harry turned right and went down into a darker part of the building. Wonderful. He could see shadows moving about down there, too, but, like a roller-coaster ride, he just told himself to go with it. The letter knew what it was doing, and had saved his life—and who knew how many countless others before him. He had to trust it.

As they made their way through the shadows, Harry watched—*felt*—those in the dark watching him.

But they all allowed him

(*them?*)

to pass.

He couldn't get out of there fast enough.

Harry now stood before a door at the far end of the hallway. Boy, had he gone through with his earlier intentions, he would never have known this hallway, either, at this time of night. How lucky fucky for him. There were definitely some experiences one could do without.

He stared at the door. Looked to the letter in his hand, still with his name on it, which seemed to . . . not so much *glow* in the streetlight-illuminated darkness of this narrow, rancid-smelling hallway, but . . . it was more like he could really see the depth of *redness* to it.

Okay, magic or not, this was très weird. But, still, there was that sense of urgency—*hurry!*—and he wasted no time in sliding it under the door, giving it that little extra shove to make sure it went all the way in. He could feel it riding on a cushion of air as he slid it under the door.

But that wasn't enough.

For some strange reason, he felt—was absolutely *consumed* with—the notion that he had to wail on that door to beat all *hell*.

(*And hurry it up, mister—Do it!*)

(*Hurry!*)

So he did.

But it wasn't any ordinary, familiar knock he'd felt exit his body; no, this one left goosebumps all over him as he did it.

The first time he knocked took him by surprise, because his hand just reached out and slammed against the door with a mind of its own, but as he tried to take control of it, the knock began to consume him, and he began to severely pound on the door . . . he was actually . . . reaching out . . . *into* the room trying to make (*oh, give me a break!*, he cried, mentally) . . . some kind of . . . extrasensory *contact* . . . with whoever was *in* there.

He paused. *Oh my God—this was for real!* his little voice again cried. He listened, holding his breath. He still couldn't hear much, but felt someone *was* in there . . . someone*s* . . . and he'd heard faint movement . . . .

Now, entirely certain he was possessed, he found himself pounding against that door as if his very life depended on it. With all his heart and soul he laid into the door and saw as it shook before him from a power he'd never known he'd had.

And he didn't stop.

His knuckles bled.

He rapped and *rapped*, pounded and *pounded*, and in his mind's eye he saw them, the two of them, in the midst of a life-and-death struggle, a man and a woman. He knew not what brought them to this brink of self-destruction only that he now clearly saw—*in his mind's eye*—the man pinning the woman to the floor, his hands closed tightly around her slender neck. He saw the woman frantically reaching about behind her for something, anything, and saw her hand grab onto a pair of scissors, as she was ready to—

He poured his heart and soul into his plea, the force of his knocking, and found himself as if in the room with the couple, knocking not on the apartment door, but *right behind them*—beside them, knocking with an intensity of the gods *inside their very heads*.

And with that, his sense of urgency immediately faded and his consciousness withdrew from the door, emotionally drained.

As his consciousness withdrew from the scene, backing out of the apartment, he saw the red envelope, there, on the floor on the other side of the door.

A new name was now written in floating gold calligraphy on the front of it.

He smiled.

His job was done.

Exhausted, Harry left the apartment and walked uncaringly past the dark shadows in the hallway. He made his way all the way back down to the dark streets below.

He'd done it, by God!

Saved the life of not just one person, but *three*, for as his consciousness withdrew from the apartment he'd also seen the child. Had seen that, somehow, those scissors had turned into a wooden play ball and that the woman had clubbed the man in the head with it, instead, knocking him out. But the thing that had really turned his stomach was that he'd also seen and felt *rage* . . . all this uncontrollable anger within the man and a history of violence. He couldn't bear to continue sampling the lives that had been taken over and controlled by such wickedness. The fact that the wife had bravely decided to take a stand and fight back was commendable, however things hadn't exactly gone in her favor . . . and more importantly their eight-month-old had been in the same room with them during their possibly to-the-death struggle . . . a no-win situation for all three—until he showed up . . . *they'd* showed up . . . him and that red envelope—and he'd begun pounding at their door with an intensity that was more than just Harry Black Jr . . . .

Outside, Harry found New York was still there . . . as cold and dark as ever . . . and he actually found that vaguely comforting.

He felt high, as if walking on air.

He'd saved *lives* this past week, when he'd originally meant to take one. Had he actually gone through with it, he wouldn't have known this building, this night, never would have heard the noises that were presently going on all around the city . . . the smell that was distinctly New York City. Wouldn't have helped that man in the post office, or set up that foundation he'd always wanted. Yes, life was funny! It didn't always go the way we thought it should, but did manage go the way it *needed* to go.

Harry turned a corner and came upon a Mercedes that was stopped in the middle of the street.

All feelings of elatedness vaporized.

Harry looked to both sides of the street . . . behind him . . . saw no one . . . yet felt something wasn't quite right. He cautiously approached the car and found a lady sitting in it, nervous and wide-eyed, clutching her cell phone. Armed with a smile, he approached, calling out to her.

"Ma'am! Do you need any help?"

Without rolling down her window, the lady projected her voice through the pane and said, "It just stopped! I was trying to take a shortcut home, but the engine just quit on me!"

Harry observed her hands nervously gripping the phone. He again checked out the streets. Still clear, yet his senses remained heightened.

"Okay . . . and you let it sit for a little while before trying to start it up, again?"

The woman nodded vigorously. "Yes . . . and I've called for help and a tow. They're on the way."

"Okay. Could you pop the hood? I could take a look."

The lady gritted her teeth in a hesitant grimace. "I'm sorry . . . I, well . . . look, I-I don't know that I should. I . . . ."

Harry sadly nodded in acknowledgment, looking down to the asphalt, and sighed. "You don't trust me, I understand," he said, looking back up to her and making positive and profound eye contact.

Something was very, very *wrong* . . . .

"Are you going to be okay?" he asked.

The lady again nodded. "I-I think so."

"Do you have 911 dialed into your cell?"

The lady nodded vigorously, showing him her phone.

"Well, okay, then."

Harry was torn. Should he leave or should he stay?

What would a saint do?

And who was safer here—her, in the locked car with a working cell phone—or him, outside unarmed? He doubted she was going to let him in with her . . . but what could he do by himself should someone decide to check her out, so to speak? Maybe he could walk up a little way and duck into a dark corner, and keep an eye on her, maybe that would be the mitigating action. But would telling her that help her feel any safer? She didn't know him from a hole in a wall, and for all practical purposes, he could be a rapist ax-murderer. For that matter she could be a decoy for all *he* knew. There just wasn't any way to win any more. The world was growing far too paranoid. Far too angry. Far too *fearful.*

Harry grimaced.

"Well, then . . . I'm just going to go—okay?"

At this, the woman's eyes grew wide. As Harry made a move to leave, the lady nervously rolled down her window an inch.

"Do you . . . do you *have* to?" Her tone had taken on a softer, gentler manner. "I-I'm sorry . . . I'd let you in, but—"

Harry suddenly smiled that *everything'll-be-all right smile*, and, indeed, he actually felt that way.

"Ma'am," he chuckled, "it's all right—I *understand.* Neither of us knows the other. If it makes you feel any better, I can just walk on over there," he said, pointing, "and duck in the shadows. I'll keep an eye on you, til your tow arrives, then leave. How's that?"

The woman studied him, then nodded.

He could see the conflict on her face and it pained him to see *her* in such philosophical torment.

"Well . . . okay, I guess," she said.

Harry again turned to leave, when the lady said, "I'm *so* sorry." Her eyes were beseeching, sorrowful.

She rolled up the window.

Harry smiled and continued on his way. He wondered what he would really do if the need arose, and scanned the street before him for something to use in defense. There was still unfinished business, here, he felt it, and no sooner had the thought crossed his mind, when he heard a loud, glassy concussion behind him. Spinning around, his heart sank. Two guys stood to either side of the Mercedes, one with a baseball bat, the other crouched with a gun, held out anxiously before him. They both looked to Harry when he popped out of the shadows. The lady was frantic inside the car, but he could see her on the phone.

911.

Harry didn't need to think about anything. Hell, he'd been ready to take his own life days ago, this was nothing—except that a fellow human was now in danger. Someone *beside* him.

God*damned* people!

Why was it we felt the need to harm each other?

Harry rushed back toward the lady.

The thing about life, a distant part of Harry thought back to on his hurried return, was that it *was* funny. A lot of the time

(. . . *baseball bat to the stomach* . . .)

we never know what will happen

(. . . *to the back of the head* . . .)

and why

(. . . *arms shattered* . . .)

only that there are times

(. . . *legs broken* . . .)

we simply must do

(. . . *bullet to the head* . . .)

certain things when called upon . . . .

Be careful what you wish for.

Blondie's

1995

Rain crashed down in severe, impenetrable sheets as if the anger of the gods was being visited upon me. It was deafening, thunderous. I punched through it, tears blinding me. A midsummer night's dream, I mused. Some dream, indeed. It'd been some time since I'd last been through Iowa, a lifetime ago for all practical purposes, but all I know is that whatever I did, whomever I was with, it all paled in comparison to her. I've never met anyone like her—before or since—and though we barely talked, had never really even *held* each other, I never stopped thinking about her.

This, of course, didn't sit well with my girlfriend at the time, but, as I said, that was a long time ago . . . .

Maybe the gods aren't angry . . . just sad. Like me.

I remember that midsummer's trip as if it were yesterday. I was with Grace. We'd been making a marathon drive back from her parents' home and it had been raining hard then, too. We'd taken two cars, because I'd met her directly from a business trip and we were driving back to North Dakota. It was somewhere between midnight and three in the morning when the rain slammed down so hard we could barely see, and since Grace was in the lead I followed her as she pulled off onto some obscure back road that wasn't on any map. We pulled off and found shelter beneath an overhang to an ancient gas station. We sat there for some time—I had gotten out of my car and gone to hers. It could have been a beautiful setting . . . could have been quite romantic . . . if it hadn't been for our fight just before leaving her folks. We'd been dating for about two years then and Grace had brought up the idea of marriage, but not just marriage—marriage and *children.*

Why do people always feel the need to bring more souls into the world?

I may be a bit unconventional—or unreasonable—but I feel that there are quite enough bodies already populating the planet, thank you. Anyway, don't get me wrong, I *loved* her . . . then. I wasn't so averse to taking her as my wife as I was against having kids. I was young, still a bit wild, and had no intention of being tied down to a family let alone *children.* Anyway, we'd left her folks under somewhat strained circumstances. She'd even snapped at me that maybe it was a sign we drove in separate vehicles. Things weren't going well and let's just say they didn't get any better.

So, I'm in her car, the downpour still mercilessly pounding the countryside, and we just sat there. The sound of the rain was curiously soothing for all its furor, even hypnotic. The night hung thickly over us like a heavy blanket—and the fact that it was three in the morning was even better. Have you ever been awake at that hour? I mean, really *awake* and *experienced* the fact that others—most really—were still tucked away snugly in their beds, dreaming? It's quite cozy, like living film noir. At any rate, Grace broke the silence first. She wanted to know what I wanted out of life. I told her I didn't know that I was just busy living it. Well, didn't I want to live it *with* someone? Of course I did, I told her, it's much more fulfilling and enjoyable when you can share things with one you love. Don't you love me? she asked, of course I do, then why won't you marry me—it's not about *marrying* you, Grace, it's about the *kids* part, *the kids' part?* what does that have to do with anything—everything, dammit, I can't explain it, but it's scary and there's too many people in the world and why are you trying to pressure me I thought we'd been through all this already . . . .

It wasn't long after that that Grace burst out of the car and into the downpour. I went after her, of course, to find her standing and sobbing out in the middle of the muddy road we'd just come on down. I tried to hold her, but she wouldn't have it. I felt my life ripped apart— after all, I *loved* her—I didn't want her to go, but something wasn't allowing me to accept her proposal. Then I looked to her and saw she was staring at the building we'd parked alongside. It was kind of funny, because I, too, got caught up in whatever was going on at that moment. We were parked between some of those old-time gas pumps and the building. Slowly, Grace began to walk away from me. Again I followed. Totally ignoring our vehicles we went to the building. Above the awning, or roof we'd parked under, was a sign we could barely make out through the downpour: "Blondie's" it said. Instantly intrigued, we forgot about our problems. Grace got to the door first. She reached out for the screen-door handle and pulled, then worked the inner doorknob, which opened into a darkened interior. A *dry*, darkened interior. We both just walked on in . . . .

It was the strangest experience I've ever had. There was an immediate calmness that befell us—and a deep, emotionally powerful . . . *something*. I don't know what it was, I just know that I immediately felt like crying. I looked to Grace, but she was already looking at me. I couldn't tell if those were tears in her eyes or remnants of the storm.

We just stood there . . . looking at each other.

This time it was my turn to make the first move. I flipped on a light switch. Partial lights flickered on. I broke away from Grace and began to take in the place. It was an old-time gas station-restaurant, like in those old forties movies I love so much. Even had that musty, nostalgic smell and creaking floorboards. I immediately fell in love with the place. But where was everyone? Sleeping? Then why was the door left unlocked? I mean, back-country Iowa or not, most businesses I knew didn't leave doors unlocked overnight.

"I'm gonna look for a bathroom," Grace mumbled and went off in search of one.

I walked about the room, listening to the rain not only pounding the building, but my soul . . . and found myself falling deeper and unaccountably *deeper* in love with the place. It really was quite quaint and I immediately wished we'd found this under different circumstances. Grace was in the restroom for some time, so I sat down at a table in one corner of the room where I felt particularly drawn to. There was a *Wurlitzer* . . . old, polished-but-quite-worn-out wooden tables, two of them . . . display cabinets that were now empty and could have at one time or another been home to candy, pies—whatever— but, what really piqued my interest was an old calendar tacked up on the adjacent wall. It was dated 1944—I remember that—and there was this picture of a woman on it, but over her picture was tacked an old black-and-white photograph. "Vargas Girl" had been scratched out beneath the calendar's picture, and beneath that was scrawled *"Blondie."* I smiled. Someone else was in love . . . at one point, anyway. Someone had stood where I now sat and had put up their wife's or girlfriend's picture over this Vargas Girl. I reached up and removed the black and white and looked at it. Though a bit faded, I was instantly shocked by the emotional intensity of this woman. She was quite attractive and was staring out across the boundaries of time . . . at *me* . . . pleading.

She wanted something, but what?

The longer I stared, the more I wanted to kiss her, to hold her. She seemed lonely . . . desperate. I placed the photograph on the table before me and folded my hands beneath my chin. I couldn't pull my eyes away from her and just . . . stared. Into her eyes. Large and dark. I wanted to feel what she was feeling at the time of this picture, feel her thoughts, her lips, her—

"What are you looking at?"

Grace had returned and to my utter amazement I had all but forgotten about her. Embarrassed, I pushed away the picture.

"Who's this?" Grace asked, picking it up. "She's pretty." She put the photograph back on the table. "Did you find anyone?"

"No. It seems a bit weird, but I think whoever owns this joint forgot to lock up. Lucky us."

"Yeah," was all she said, turning away.

Grace walked off toward the checkout counter, but I remained seated. I couldn't pull my eyes away from the beautiful face in this picture.

What had this woman's life turned out like?

Had she fought with her boyfriend? Her husband? Have children? I was caressing the edges of the picture when Grace called out to me.

"Nolan, could you come over here, please?"

Reluctantly, I got up and did as requested.

"What?"

"What should we do? It's still pouring outside, I'm cold, I'm hungry. No one's around—"

"—well, that's not exactly so," came a soft voice from behind us. Both of us turned to find a woman standing in a bathrobe, arms crossed, at the entrance Grace had used for the restroom. "You're welcome to wait out the storm, here, if you'd like," she said.

Grace and I looked to each other for a long moment. "Y-your door was open, and—" I began, when the woman again interrupted.

"Some of us tend to get complacent out here, especially us few remaining optimists. The offer still stands. I've got coffee brewing in the back."

Just then we smelled the rich, elevating aroma.

"I hope we didn't wake you," Grace added.

"Oh, no, it wasn't your fault. I haven't slept . . . well . . . in a long time . . . and when you used the bathroom the pipes . . . they have a life of their own. Why don't you both have a seat—or stand, as you prefer, I know you've probably been on the road all night."

The woman disappeared into the rear.

"Guess she lives here," I said, as I directed Grace back to the table.

"There's something weird about her," Grace said, sitting.

"I know, I felt it, too." Once again I reached for the photograph.

"She's very pretty, isn't she, the woman in the picture?"

Startled, I hesitated in my answer. I felt embarrassed, like I'd been caught in an affair. "Y-yes, she is. I keep wondering what her life must have been like—"

"Hard."

Two cups of coffee were placed before us.

"She was my grandmother," our mysterious woman said, continuing, "She and her husband started this place."

"Is that who tacked this up there?" I asked.

"Yes," she said, looking toward the calendar, "it's remained up there all these years—until you took it down."

"Oh—I'm-I'm so sorry!" I said.

"That's okay," she said, smiling warmly, which actually kind of unnerved me, "you didn't know. Sometimes change is good. Do you mind if I sit with you?"

"No, go right ahead, I mean, we barged in on *you*," Grace said.

I looked to our coffee and found that each already contained the cream and sugar we both took in them.

"Thank you for the coffee," I said.

The woman smiled.

It almost seemed like another me, then. Another life. As I now try to navigate through this downpour I recalled all the other times I'd been through here between Cedar Rapids and Grand Forks. I've been through countless rain storms, always searching for that one, unmapped road, and never have I found it. But I felt closer each time I came out in search of it . . . felt—*feel*—irresistibly drawn to it, like metal to a magnet. I've tried to explain this feeling over the years, but eventually just gave up. I tried to explain all my failed relationships and lonely nights . . . my failed employments . . . but in the end gave up, merely trying to cope. A pipe dream. That's all it was. A futile attempt to keep my life going in spite of all the failures I'd created: never staying at one job long enough to get on a first name basis; never staying in relationships long enough to consider marriage—and always wondering how Grace's life'd turned out. Always wondering if—maybe—*maybe* I should've taken her offer . . . .

But that magical night remained with me forever.

As that woman sat at the table with us, I felt something about her reach out to me—like her grandmother's photograph. Once or twice under the table, I felt her leg brush against mine. I said nothing, thinking it just one of those unseen beneath-the-table moments, but I felt her touch on several occasions and soon became extremely uncomfortable—not because of the contact, but because I *wanted* the contact—and found myself irresistibly attracted to her. This went beyond any purely *physical* attraction, because—and don't get me wrong, she was beautiful—but it went *deeper*. Like we knew each other on some level I couldn't explain—and didn't necessarily want to. I was enjoying this mysterious bond, but was also hoping Grace wasn't picking up on it. But within a short while, I found myself doing the unconscionable: I found myself *trying* to touch this woman *as I sat before my girlfriend*. I'd place a foot just so, a leg or hand in a certain position.

I couldn't believe what I was doing!

And all along this woman showed no hint of our hidden interplay, carrying on a perfectly normal conversation with my girlfriend and me. Then it happened. After all the coffee this woman had been serving us, Grace got up to again use the restroom. As soon as Grace had disappeared into the dark, the woman turned to me. She never said a word, but my excitement grew. I shook with anticipation . . . and, yes, embarrassment.

She smiled.

Gently took my hand.

Oh, her warm, soft skin . . . the feeling as we finally held hands out in the open was *indescribable!*

Gently and lovingly, she caressed my skin. I felt as if I'd known her forever. I pictured us making love—not a mere fling, but feral, passionate *love*.

I took in everything about her . . . her expressive yet not overly full lips . . . the wisps of loose hair about her quietly beautiful face . . . the depth and *loving* of her intense scrutiny. The softness of her touch . . . and of how profoundly her touch *moved* me.

I don't know how long we carried on like this, but gradually my uncomfortableness gave way to pure, uninhibited adoration. She lifted my hand to her beautiful lips and kissed and nipped at my fingertips; turned my hand over and kissed my wrist.

I nearly died!

I squeezed her hand . . . took it within both of mine and kissed hers . . . realizing that at any moment Grace would return. I tingled with bizarre excitement and reached for her face—*what was I* doing? We came in closer. I could feel her warm, moist breath upon my skin. She parted her lips to meet mine . . . her eyes hypnotic and yearning. I closed my eyes . . .

And our lips touched.

It was electric, like a spiritually arching jolt. We both locked in this unbelievably metaphysical kiss that lasted an eternity—when she broke away. I heard Grace's approach and hurriedly wiped my mouth, but the woman didn't.

Again, she smiled, demurely.

"Miss—oh, I guess we never got your name—the light burned out in the bathroom—"

"I'm sorry—I'll fix it immediately—"

"Oh, don't bother now, it's no big deal, it was only the dark, you know. I don't think I'll have to use it again, anyway. We should probably get going," Grace said, as she turned to look out the windows.

I suddenly realized that the rain had let up enough that it no longer battered the building like boulders. I looked to the woman beside me, who was already looking at me with searching, painful eyes . . . eyes that literally scared me, because I felt I'd seen them before. Her face had somehow changed as well . . . in a deeply terrifying way I couldn't explain. It was like she was beginning to emaciate . . . but it was an emaciation I found I was very much attracted to—

"Nolan—*what are you doing?*" came Grace's sudden, fierce outcry.

Immediately terrified, I looked to her.

"*Just what the hell do you think you're doing?*"

To my utter astonishment, I looked to the tabletop—and found myself clutching this mysterious woman's hands.

My blood chilled and I shot to my feet, quickly yanking back my hands.

Grace stared at the both of us. She said not one word, but inside I knew every thought that raced through her mind: *is this what he'd been doing while I was away—how could this be?, we'd never even met her before . . . maybe marriage wasn't such a good idea after all . . . .*

Still without a word, Grace turned.

That look of hurt that had been on her face tore my soul from my chest. As I reached out for her, Grace never turned around, but thrust an upraised hand before me like a pissed-off traffic cop. I was stopped by the force of her silent command and stared back at her. Grace quietly opened the door and went out into the night. I again made a move toward her when the woman grabbed me.

"*Please . . .* ," she begged, ever so delicately.

Images flew through my mind . . . us living happily together . . . us again making love—but they were more than mere images . . . they were as if I had actually *lived* them for one long, luxurious, moment.

I took the woman's hand into my own and gave her my own pleading look. *I didn't want to leave her* and I couldn't explain it.

What the hell was going on here? How could I do such a thing in front of my girlfriend—a woman I could have married? How could I feel such emotion for a woman I'd never before met?

Grace started her car. Gunned the engine.

"I . . . have to go—I don't *know* you. Don't you see? *I don't know you, yet want to stay with you.* Can you understand me? *I* can't. I have to go . . . with *her.*"

I broke free and rushed from the building out into the storm.

Grace had already left . . . her taillights disappearing into the darkness and rain. Quickly, I got into my car, brought it to life, and left the pumps. As I spun out into the rain and mud, I looked into my rearview and froze. The building that we had taken refuge in had melted from sight. I'm not saying that the rain had again become so thick that only yards from it it had been made to *appear* that way—no, what I'm saying is that as I looked into my rearview I *actually saw it melt into nothingness as the rain pelted it.*

GOOD-BYE.

And so I've thought about it all these years and still come up with the same questions. Had she been a ghost? Had it all been an hallucination? Had we ever met before?

No, I'd never seen that woman before in all of my life.

Every map, every person I'd ever talked to had no recollection of that road, or building. Of that woman. No folklore, no legends, no nothing.

So what'd happened?

Something had to have occurred, because Grace had seen her, too, had seen us holding hands, for chrissakes. Grace'd never stopped after she'd gotten into the car that night, except for gas, and when she had, I stopped, but she turned and gave me that same murderous glare and silent command. It was over. I didn't even try. We both knew this was the end. No longer had it been about kids, if it ever really had been. I let her go and watched as her taillights again left me for the darkness.

Forever.

Ever since then I've failed at everything. I got fired from every job, never had second dates, and after a while, not even firsts. Got evicted from apartments—had two cars totaled in accidents—increasing and ever-deepening bouts of depression, you name it. I finally admitted to myself what I needed to do. I had nothing holding me back anymore, so where was the harm? I'd gotten into my car, filled it up, and headed into rainy oblivion.

And here I am.

I've gotten pretty good, over the years, at driving in the nearly undriveable. Learned the Iowa backroads pretty well. But I'm tired. I need to find what was, all those years ago. If I can't, well, I don't know what I'll do.

So the rain pounds down upon my windshield . . . cursing me for all I've done . . . and not done. Bursts of thunder and lightning jar my senses. I take one more turn up ahead, and slide down a small hill into a dip. The rain seems angrier here, and I have to slow down still more. I look to the speedometer and see that my speed barely registers.

Why am I even driving?

Because I need her.

I'm exhausted. I peer ahead, looking for a place to pull over and uncover the sleeping pills . . . so many, many, of them . . . beneath my crumpled jacket on the front seat. I briefly look at them.

Enough of *everything* . . .

When I spot something up ahead.

I get closer and try to make it out—and what do I see?

An ancient gas station.

A roof covering gas pumps.

I break, and my car slides into a muddy and crooked stop before the pumps. I get out, deafened by the roar of the rain, pummeled and wincing from the force of the storm, and stand there . . . looking to the building.

I can't believe what I'm seeing!

And there's a light on.

Legs weak and shaky I approach the screen door. It's solid all right. Grasping the handle, I open it. Open the main door. I enter the room and see a shadowy figure slumped over one of the tables in that far corner. Her head hangs low.

I am without words as I approach, for I know it's *her*.

Sure, I've aged some, as I know she has, but what's right is *right*.

I get to the table and see an old black-and-white photograph still lying on the table where I'd last left it. I look to the woman who still sits in the same chair I'd left her in. I gently place a hand on her shoulder—cold at first—but soon feel her warmth. She lifts her head . . . and I come around and sit beside her.

"I've waited for you for so long," she softly whispers, in a wavering, tortured voice. Tears stream down her cheeks.

Heart in my throat, I look into her eyes and see the same woman

I'd seen all those years ago. *Exactly* the same. I'm not sure how I know this, or how much I believe it, but it makes sense. She isn't a ghost, at least not in the conventional sense—no . . . she's a *wish* . . . .

"*I'm* Blondie," she whispers, "*I'm* the woman—"

"I know. The photograph."

She smiles.

"It's hard to explain," she says, "but I've *always* loved you . . . just as you've always loved me. We're two people of the same hunger. Both of us wanted something neither had . . . but somehow reached out across time to find. There are other . . . lives . . . we all live, some in dreams, some not. When you looked into that photograph, you created all of this—"

"But how could I? We got here *before* I found the picture—"

"Desire has a way of warping time. I can't explain it myself, only know my want . . . as do you. However it happened we know the reality of the outcome. Can we live in more than one reality? I don't know. I only know that I didn't want to live in the one I had been in up until that picture. I had to leave. The moment you read my need . . . *desired* me . . . you took me out of that life and brought me into this one. That's all I know, all I care about. I'm no longer where I was."

"And me?"

Again, that warm, gentle smile.

"Your choice. You still have that choice—"

"No . . . I don't. There is no choice—can't you *see?* I've always been with you since that moment—everything else I've ever done, or tried to do, has left me. *Never had I anything since I left you.*"

She smiled again—*oh, how I so love and missed that smile!*—and we both knew.

Why try to know and explain everything? Why not just live in the moment and leave the explanations to Who or Whatever runs this crazy ride.

I reached out to Blondie and took her hand and immediately felt a lifetime younger—older?—who cared. We were together and I would never, ever again abandon her. We had both found what we so desperately sought—and it was just that—we both needed to *need* it . . . *desperately.*

The rain continued to pound relentlessly, but it wasn't angry, not in the least. And as our building and pumps melted away . . . along with my car and the remains of my previous life . . . I realized that there had never been any anger in the rain—only tears of joy.

Rainy Nights and Christmas Lights
1993

Rainy nights and Christmas lights. That's all I can think of. All I want to think of.

I only just stumbled into this . . . inn . . . moments ago, seeking relief from the bitter cold of an angry blizzard. It's dark, but I don't know the time. I have no watch. It's very desolate—not just for my own heart, but for the souls outside as well.

No one wanted to be out on a night like this, and God only knew how long I stumbled about out there dazed . . . disoriented. The weather, frigid and snowy for most of the day, had turned more brutal, forcing all life in from the streets. I, too, searched for a place to take me in, but nobody would have me . . . everyone hurrying home for their own families. Was I a leper? It was only this inn that took me, and I had to barter my soul just to gain entrance.

Her name is Laura, and I love her like no other. I love her more than life itself!

Sure, we had our differences like everyone else, but nothing— *nothing*—changed my deep unfaltering devotion for her. Not even the times she said she was leaving . . . .

But now I sit before a raging fireplace in a darkened room, utterly alone. It's cold, and the chill I feel burrows into my marrow. Just now I think I see a waiter or waitress behind me—but turning find no one.

I look about the room and see it is small by some standards, large by others . . . and has not quite a dozen tables, including those in the alcove to the far end. Each table has unlit candles and neatly placed silverware atop it. The shadows I see are disturbing and gnaw at me. It is all so vaguely familiar, this place, and I feel I should know it, but I

. . . I feel disoriented.

Deep memories stir . . . nothing surfaces.

I am just as helpless as when—

Death.

I love her, *oh dear God, how I love her!*

Why is it that I alone survive?

Why should *I* have this cursed privilege! What I would gladly give to have her back! Why did not both of us perish—it is so much better that way, you know, to be together in death than alone in life!

Oh, how I curse God and all that is life! I curse the devil for the torture! I curse everything, except—

Rainy nights and Christmas lights.

That's what she said, my Laura, the one with the beautiful hair and loving smile.

The one I was to marry . . . to begin a new life with. Suddenly I rush to the front door and pull it open.

The wind, the storm, she wails and batters me back!

I hear glass shatter as the door slams behind me into the wall. I know it is hideously cold, yet I don't feel it. All I feel is the pain in my heart.

Rainy nights and Christmas lights.

Christmas lights . . . .

There are Christmas lights strung across this building, and as I stand there I am suddenly hit with realization. I know where I am. Know exactly where I am. This is the inn my love and I frequented when . . . when we were *whole* . . . but, worse than that *it is the place where my beloved was so cruelly ripped away from me!*

I scream into the wind! To the innkeeper who admitted me! Here—*you have my soul, why not also take my heart?*—oh why even to be created, only to die? Why is life nothing but torment!

Why are we to love only to lose?

Again I look to the lights.

Still strangely they are lit. Out of place. I peer through the blinding, heavy snow, but see no others. No movement.

I am all there is.

There is nothing beyond the snow-covered flagstone steps I know are before me. Nothing exists beyond myself and this haunted inn. But the lights. I remember

Standing out on this porch one rainy summer night . . . my Laura wrapped around me . . . her breath warm against my neck. We gaze lovingly at each other stretching out the moment to eternity.

"Rainy nights," she bubbles.

"What?" I ask.

"Rainy nights . . . and Christmas lights!" she blurts triumphantly, radiantly.

I adore her smile and know, right there, why it is I love her.

"Rainy nights and Christmas lights," she says again, lyrically, still beaming.

"That is so beautiful!" I proclaim, and hug her tightly.

"*Hold me,*" she whispers sweetly into my ears, "*hold me and don't ever let me go.*"

I knew I'd marry her.

But the tears now freeze to my face and the wind rips me apart.

Take this too, Devil, take all there is I have left!

My voice is nearly gone, and I tear into my clothes to get at my heart—that eternally pumping and vile thing! Fingers unfeeling, I cut into my skin and bring forth blood, but it, too, freezes, and I realize I am truly—*truly*—doomed—*unable to even take my own life!*

I slump forward to the snowy porch and bury my hands and face.

Rainy nights.

And Christmas lights.

So I am resigned to the fate of this dispossessed inn. It seems fitting that I should be held here, a place my love and I so enjoyed. It is so fitting to be forced to relive those moments, those memories . . . the moment . . . of her death.

Her death.

We had finished dining, leaving the building for a stroll. Ever the adventurous soul, she had leapt upon the ledge of a stone wall that guarded the creek below. Those Christmas lights had hung above her. I remember how the water was still visible, unfrozen.

And . . . the *rocks.*

I had hoped she wouldn't fall and rushed to her—

"May I take your order, sir?"

Startled, I upset my coffee and send the porcelain cup flying across the room to shatter somewhere.

How had I come to holding a cup of coffee?

I look up and see, in the dark and standing entirely motionless, a waitress of ageless beauty. I could barely breathe, yet alone spare a word.

"W-what? Wh-who are you?"

"Your order, sir, do you care to order?"

She placed a menu before me. I stared at it for an eternity . . . then lifted my head to look out the windows. All I see is the storm, which has increased its intensity, if that be possible. I also notice that I have gripped the edges of my table in a mighty hold, knuckles most assuredly bone-white.

The fire crackles.

"I-I already ate," I said.

"As you wish," she says, most politely, and withdraws the menu.

"B-but I could use some more coffee," I continue. All she did was turn . . . and smile. I could have sworn she'd spoken, but I did not, for the life of me, see her lips move.

I'm sure you could, she said.

I know it was dark, and I know I am not in the most stable of minds, but I know what I experienced. She *spoke* . . . yet did not move her *lips*.

I blink. She is gone.

I need my woman and I need her now! Forever! I cannot and will not live this way!

The pain is unendurable!

How does one survive such agony?

How can others live through what I continue to grieve over? Nothing means anything to me anymore! As much as I don't want to dwell on my beloved's death, I feel compelled—it was our last few moments together . . . the last time we'd kissed, held each other . . . gazed into each other's eyes or felt the warmth of each other's touch.

I so desperately want to die and be among the dead with *her!*

I attempt yet again to get at my heart, my wrists, with knives . . . forks . . . broken glasses . . . but am strangely without strength or succor. Instead, I collapse upon my table and heave great tears into the wood . . . .

I remember my arms reaching out to her.

One moment she stood atop the wall . . . pirouetting beautifully and telling me how much she loved me and would never, ever leave me—and the next—the next I reach out for her and clutch only air . . . huge fists full of it . . . and watch helplessly as she tumbles over the side like newly falling snow . . . drifting down, down . . . ever downward . . .

(*Christmas lights . . .*)

in her grasp. I watch until I can bear it no longer . . . .

"Your coffee, sir."

I bolt upright. A busboy is pouring fresh coffee into a new cup. His back is to the fire, and he seems aglow. His smile is genuine, but he, like the shadows, scares me.

"Where—"

"Nowhere, sir," he says, and fades from view back into the shadows, his Cheshire smile the last to go. I look to the coffee poured, and it remains . . . small curls of ghostly white steam disappearing into the dark. I touch the cup and find it warm. Solid.

"I don't want *coffee!* I want *Laura!*"

I pound the table. Again.

And again.

I drift off.

Time has again passed, and as I have already told you, I know not how much, but it is still evil and blinding without, dark and foreboding within. I watch the spoils of snow as it batters against the windows of the alcove, and there are times I feel the building shudder, or think I do.

Maybe it is just me.

The fire is still alight, though I have yet to touch it.

Where did that gentleman who admitted me go off to?

The shadows close in upon me. Something is different.

Rainy nights and Christmas Lights.

She had grabbed Christmas lights . . . .

That's all I want back. I want that summer night again—*I want her back!* I will gladly mortgage my soul to have her! Anything, I just want that moment to remain, to never change. I want to spend that moment in eternity with my Laura. She is all I live for . . . all I want to *die* for

. . . .

Yet cannot die.

This I know for some bizarre reason, but I shall try one more time. I look to the fire and spy a poker. Going to it, I raise it and touch it to my chest; feel its dull accusation. Stoking my emotions, I raise the weapon with mighty intent—but alas, it misses its mark and strikes the wall above the hearth instead. I anchor the handle end against a wall, the point placed firmly over my heart . . . and ram myself forward . . . but I slide harmlessly off. I attempt yet one more blow, but I am again deflected, this time the poker pulled from my hands as if by some unseen force.

I pound my fists into the wall.

Laura! Why has this happened?

I want so much to die and join you—I no longer wish to bear this tragedy!

I collapse at my table and once more try to dream . . .

Of rainy nights and Christmas lights.

But I hear a door open.

Something *is* different . . . .

I hear footsteps and look up.

A figure is in the doorway. Stands still.

"*Who . . . are you?*" I ask. "I can take this no longer! Please, *take* me, I am yours!"

I cry, my blood long since cold, my sanity frayed. I hope the figure to be Death's messenger finally come for me.

"*I know,*" the figure says, and it is a soft, pleasant voice.

I rocket to my feet, chair spilling out behind me.

I know that voice!

"*Laura?*"

Unstable, I grip the table for support. Again, I ask, "Laura—i-is that . . . *you?*"

"Yes," she answers, moving out from the shadows. "I am here, my dear."

It *is* her, there is no mistake! As sure as I live, it is *her!*

"But—but you'd—"

She smiles ever so lovingly as she approaches.

"No, my love, it was not me who died. I had grabbed a string of the Christmas lights . . . and when you saved me from falling by diving for me . . . you yourself fell. Don't you remember?"

My throat is suddenly dry. I collapse to my knees.

"But—that would make you—"

"—dead? Yes, I am indeed."

Still she smiles, unaffected by her words.

My heart pounds, rises into my throat.

I choke.

I love her so much!

I touch her and find her as cold as I am.

"H-how?"

"Does it really matter?" she asks casually, "I am here."

Standing before me, she reaches down and I grasp her hand. She pulls me to my feet, and I notice she places an empty prescription bottle on the table.

I say nothing.

"*Tell me how much you love me,*" she says, drawing in close to me.

I see the concern on her face . . . feel the tears on mine and cry, "*I love you with all my heart and soul and will always—ever—be there for you!*"

"And I, you, my darling. I love you more than life itself!"
And so I know.

We sit at our table . . . together at last . . . and gaze into the fire. Our hands are tight and true, our hearts one. The blizzard still rages, but I no longer care. As we look to each other, we are no longer cold.

What Dreams Are Made Of
1994

Wake up, Harry—time to go!
Words that were more than a distant echo . . . they were
(flashes of a face I can't make out)
pain.

I tossed about, caught up in blankets that refused release. It seemed an eternity before I finally broke free. It was so comfortable, the warmth of my bed. So unyielding.

Let's go, Harry—
The words again. Do I know the speaker? I feel I should. Where am I? What time is it?

Summer. That's right—*summer*. The first day of summer vacation. I'm home from my first year at Syracuse. Damn, but how those finals twisted your thinking around, getting you to believe there's nothing outside of school. *Nichts.* Professors'd have you believe there's only English Lit, Philosophy 101, German for Beginners, and any of a number of other courses you'd rather forget once the sun comes out and things begin to green up. I've got big plans, so I bulked up this year. Twenty-one credits. It nearly killed me.

(nearly k—)
Where am I?
I open my eyes and find it dark . . . feel . . . movement. We're in a car . . . but I just thought I was at home—the bed, the *blankets*—

It's raining, a constant, soaking rain. A comforting sound if you've ever just listened to it.

I'm so tired!
The voice stops calling me, but reminds me of a time when I was

a kid, about thirteen, I think. My dad and us had all piled into that red station wagon of ours at one in the morning. Our big vacation down into Pennsylvania. Amish country. We'd drive straight through, stopping only for potty breaks.

When we'd stopped at a gas station, it was dark and raining. Dad had stopped and Mom had asked the four of us if we'd needed to use the restrooms. My sister and I had, so we'd sprinted through the rain until we'd made shelter, done our business, then sprinted back. I thought how neat it had all looked, lights sprinkled across the damp, rain-pockmarked pavement. The fact that it had been maybe three in the morning and the rest of the world had still been snuggled away in bed had been so cool. Peaceful . . . *mystical.*

But now I'm traveling down an unknown road with my dad behind the wheel and Mom, no doubt (because I haven't actually gotten around to poking up my head from the back yet), sitting against him, eyes closed, drinking in the steady hum and rock of the station wagon, as was I . . . .

But I need to get my act together.

When did I get here?

I remember how we'd talked about taking a trip when I got back from college, all of us, but I also remember something else just beyond the memories. I wasn't coming straight back after school. I was going somewhere else first . . . a party. Yes, that's what it was. There had been this party someone I knew was throwing—or maybe not someone I *knew* . . . but there was this party I was to *go* to. Only then was I going to begin my trip north . . . hitchhiking . . . to my home at Dead Bog Lake. Despite its name, a beautiful, deep lake we lived directly across from, complete with boathouse and lakefront property. Situated deep in the Adirondack Park. Dark waters. My dad's a Forest Ranger. Mom works as an Administrative Assistant down at Land's End, a rich-folks' estate. But something doesn't feel right . . . isn't . . . *complete* . . . like I'm missing a crucial piece to some weird little puzzle . . . .

Have I remembered something wrong?

The car's slowing. We're coming to a stop. Potty break. Not for me; I don't have to go.

It's still raining.

We've been going for several hours now, and I lift my head. Dad's driving, his right arm around Mom, who's now fast asleep. He and Mom are all wet, as I notice, I am too. The car pleasantly smells of Borkum Riff pipe tobacco, the only brand my dad used. Smoking's supposed to be bad for you, but I love that smell, especially that brand.

Besides, he's my dad; he'll live forever.

"Almost there, Son," my dad calls back to me. His voice brings out such deep emotional tones from me. I wonder where the rest of us are: Michael, John—Theresa. Is it just me on this trip? I guess they all had other commitments. It's been awhile since I've seen my folks—about a year—my siblings, longer. Christmas vacation I had to spend at an apprenticeship downstate. I didn't mind—I knew I'd see everybody soon enough and this *was* school—my first year, as I've already mentioned. My first year as . . .

(*how could I have forgotten?*)

The car again slows. Mom's up. She turns around to look at me, strands of wet hair matted against her face. She looks hollow . . . as though she's been crying, but her voice betrays no such emotion. "*Hello, dear,*" she says. "*Did you have a good nap?*"

"Sure did, Ma," I say.

Her voice makes me feel warm. I'm happy to be home again. Feels like I haven't been this warm since forever. After all, don't know the next time we'll be together. Like I've said before, I've got big plans for yours truly . . . .

"Well," continues Mom, turning back to the front, "we're here."

"That's right," Dad says.

God, I love that tobacco. Cancer or no cancer it's a comfortable smell. Brings back warm, cathartic memories: fireplaces, Dad-talks and walks. Fishing. Lord, how it's so easy to get wrapped up in

(*blankets*)

studies. School. Fucking finals just throw your life all to hell. But that's past. We're on vacation now. Just the three

(*where* are *the others?*)

of us.

We unload the wagon. Still, it's raining. Heavily clouded—like we're going to get squashed between heaven and earth—

It's a beautiful day.

No one else was around. That's fine, we're not here to see others. It's funny that there was only this one old guy at the KOA entrance. Something was off about him. No one anywhere else. The man had no teeth, it looked like, but a big fat grin. Pulpy face. "Thirty bucks," he'd said, more like grunted. Dad gave him the cash and we found a spot.

"Hey, young man," my dad shouts over the top of the car as I reach over to unload. "You sit your butt down. This is *your* vacation. Let your mother and I do the work. You've done quite enough already!"

For some unnerving reason, I don't quite know how to take that, but okay, I say, and pick out a stump. I almost fall down. My feet are tangled up in that damned blanket again. Christ. But the blanket reminds me of the time we went down to Gettysburg, Pee-Aee. We'd stopped along the road one sunny day at a rather large rest area, on a rise. Mom had pulled out a blanket—probably this very same one— and spread it out over the grass. We sat under a large shade tree. Dad had gone to the soda machine and spent his change getting all six of us sodas.

Dr Pepper. I love Dr Pepper.

Ah, vacations. I wonder how many more I'll get to go on before I've become part of The Working Class. Before—if and when—I ever have a family of my own.

Now there's a thought.

The tent's all set up and the rain pummels us harder. Dad started a fire that managed to keep itself going despite the downpour, and Mom was busy cooking fish we'd caught after making camp. I love the smell of campfire trout.

"You couldn't have picked a finer day, dear," Mom said, beaming to Dad. Thunder rumbled its throaty growl across a fractured, purple sky.

"Yep, well, I try to get the good Lord to bend an Almighty ear every now and then," Dad said.

They laugh, and Mom curiously eyes Dad. I didn't for some reason; something nags at me. It had to do with that party, I think. Timelines. I'm not really sure and that bugs me. What went on at that party? *Where* was it? Did I even make it? *Why is everything so damned hazy?*

I need to sort things out.

"Mom . . . Dad . . . I need to take a walk."

They look at me like I'd slashed my wrists or something.

"Honey," Mom says, her voice quivering, "how about we go with you? I mean . . . how often do we get to see you, you know? You're away in college . . . will probably take another apprenticeship—who knows?"

I reconsider. She has a point. Anyway, I guess I really wouldn't mind the company . . . but I shiver.

"Okay," I say.

Mom and Dad are back to smiles.

"It's a beautiful evening for a stroll, anyway!" my dad says, large drops of water still smacking down from an angry sky.

We walk.

Mom and Dad are in front of me some. I hold back. They're like lovers rediscovering romance. That's cool. I don't have a girlfriend. A couple girls I boinked back in school, but that's about it. But one . . . one really got to me. She had this red hair and cute freckles. I met her while working the information booth at the student union. Her name was Anna, and she was also new, looking for some information about movies and stuff. One thing led to another and we ended up doing the nasty. She had the largest, deepest brown eyes. So understanding and open. God, how I suddenly miss them. I could've loved her. I can't wait to get back to her. But summer came, and she went home to the Catskills and I headed north to the Adirondacks.

North.

To that party.

I'd hitchhiked. Didn't tell my folks. They wouldn't have approved. Shit, my dad's a Forest Ranger, next best thing to a cop up here; a gun, cuffs, and everything. Ranger of the woods. They didn't always carry 'em, the guns and handcuffs. I can remember when he told me how scary—my word, not his . . . I don't remember what he used—it was to him that they were told they had to. Was a big change for The Department. That and all those damned *Coll-edge* Boys. They're taking over the place, he'd complained. Don't know a damned thing about the woods, but sure are makin' policy.

So I get this ride north. Actually more than one, it's a bit of a ride by the speed limit—which is about all you can do with all those damned troopers out there. They just keep spilling out of the State Police Academy. Thicker'n gnats on a hot summer's evening, Dad says. Fuckers—

That's when I fall. Now, I mean, following my folks. I tripped over a log

(*what's so important about the . . .*)

I wasn't paying attention to.

Mom and Dad hear me tumble and turn to me in wide-eyed horror. Rush to my side.

"*You okay, Son?*" Dad asks, hastily checking me over. Mom's examining my face, wrists, and ankles. She used to be a nurse.

"You look okay. How do you feel?" she asks.

I start laughing. "I'm fine, Mom! I just wasn't watching where I was going, that's all."

"Well you should know better than that, young man, or there won't *be* a next time," Dad said. His face was set. Puffed and angered.

"Now, Lloyd, there's no need to get all out of sorts. It was a simple mistake. You can't fault him for lack of judgment. He's young—still learning."

"Just think what *could've* happened!"

"But nothing did . . . *here*," Mom said. She brought a trembling hand to his face, trying to calm him down.

"Dad—I'm all right, really. Remember that time I put my hand through that door window—the facial cuts looked worse than they actually w—"

"These aren't facial cuts, dammit."

"Okay, okay," I say, "I'll be more careful, all right?" I pick myself up and wipe off the mud. Pick watermilfoil and pondweed from my pants and shirt. After all, it's still raining, though more of a drizzle now. Mom pulls Dad away. I see the fire in his eyes. Why all the fuss? All I did was trip. Over a

(familiar?)

log.

Sheesh.

We complete our walk and return to camp. Water has already started to build up around it. It's late now, so we hit the sack, but I don't sleep well. I feel this constriction around my neck . . . but each time I reach to loosen it, there's nothing there. I lie on my stomach to look out our tent, into the night, and wonder what's out there. I listen to that soul-comforting pitter-patter of rain and watch the drops splash in the water about the tent. Don't touch the sides of the tent, my Dad used to say, it'll kill the waterproofing. I don't. It's so quiet. So peaceful. The smell of wet things and rain. I feel at home. How strange, I've never been here before—or have I? Doesn't really matter does it? I mean, vacation is vacation, whether or not you've been there before. I like it here. We're by ourselves.

What more could you ask for?

I must have finally dozed off last night, because I'm the last to get up. The rain has let up some, and is now only a misty drizzle, but water is everywhere . . . like an enormous wading pool. I pushed myself up out of it and exit the tent. There are water lilies floating atop the water around us.

"Good morning, hon!" Mom says.

She's already getting a start on the day, clad in a swimsuit and reclining on a chaise lawn chair. She's holding a sun reflector under her chin. I notice how the water mists on the reflector under her neck and get that eerie feeling again.

"Good morning, Son," Dad says.

He's cooking up fish and bacon, but it smells funny. The day feels thick and I feel sluggish. Just a little weak. I look down to my feet before I walk any farther and see that damned blanket again wrapped around my ankles. I caught it this time so I don't fall. Dad ought to like that.

"What would you like to do today, honey?" Mom asks.

"Gee, I really haven't given it much thought, Mom."

"Well, you better start giving it some thought, mister, or your vacation'll be over before you know it. *Do you want that?*" Dad asks.

Do you really *want that?*

Suddenly I'm no longer hungry. All I want is a Dr Pepper.

"There's one in the cooler, dear," Mom says.

I get it. It's in a tall green bottle. An old, filthy one with dirt encrusted under the cap's lip.

"I didn't know they made these bottles anymore," I say.

Mom looks up at me, kind of queerly, and says, "Oh, they don't." She says it just like I should have known better.

Sitting down on a large

(*logs*)

log by the campfire, I watch Dad.

"Be careful not to fall over that thing," he says, looking over a shoulder to me as he shuttled the fire.

"Oh, Lloyd, take it easy on the boy," Mom says.

Dad mumbles something under his breath. He's only toying with the fish now.

"Dad . . . uh . . . are you going to eat that?" I ask.

"No, at least I hadn't planned on it."

"What's that with it? Bacon?"

"No."

"What is it?"

"It's . . . it's seaweed, okay? *Pond*weed."

(*pondweed*)

"It adds . . . flavor . . . to the fish. Something I learned in the Navy."

Oh. I nod. Some things are better left alone.

After not eating breakfast, we go off for our hike into the rain-soaked woods. Mom and Dad, instead of being close to each other, this time are very much apart. Carrying on a discussion that they try not to let me in on, but I still catch in pieces.

" . . . but it's a *vacation*, dear," she says in hushed tones. "Who cares?" Dad says, "it's only going to end—then we'll all have to go back home. Go back to the way things are." "So?" Mom says, "what's

the difference? What's done is done. We'll have next year." "Sure,"
Dad says, but then I lose track of what they're saying and remember
another trip we'd taken. A canoe trip. Just Dad and us kids. Fish Creek
I think? We'd canoed out to a small island and set up camp. All the
essentials taken care of, we set out swimming around the island. Well,
more like snorkeling. Dad was right there in the water with us. It was
a dark, sandy shore. Smooth, silky, water.

(*feels so familiar*)

It felt great. We just drifted. Became one with the water.

(*why do I feel so uncomfortable?*)

Later that day we hung out in the tent and the sky began to howl
rain down upon us in *sheets*. We were situated under trees, but the force
of the rain was incredible. It shook our tent, sent little tributaries of
water inside the fabric along the seams. Water rushed down on all sides
of our shuddering shelter and we got scared. Dad asked us if we wanted
to stay. We chickened out. The rain let up and we broke camp and
hightailed it back to the truck across rough open water before it again
unleashed upon us.

Rain.

(*rain rain go away come again another*)

Party.

Water.

I shake with a sudden, tremendous awareness.

I remember my hitchhike now.

I remember two men—and a woman. A van. A ragged, rusty-
looking thing that seemed to have milfoil

(*pondweed*)

hanging from it. Had I known it was so ragged looking I wouldn't
have stuck out my thumb, but that day was getting dark and I was
almost home. Hell, I thought, one more try. They'd stopped, and the
guy in the back slid open the side door. There was a strange look to his
eyes. I felt

(*like I do now*)

uncomfortable. But I was already there, know what I mean? No
turning back. Tough guy . . . can handle myself. That's when I hear this
female behind him telling him to either let me in or to close the fucking
door. I get in. Mistake number one. I smell incense. I've always hated
the smell of the stuff. She's in the back, in a dark corner, and when she
sees me comes out of the shadows. She liked me. Thought I was cute.
As we drive, I tell them about this party I'd gone to. They tell me about
another.

Where? I ask.

Dead Bog, they tell me.

Really? You from there?

From around there, they say. Wanna come?

I-I don't know, I stammer. I really should just get home.

You nervous? the girl asks.

She's pretty fine looking under those haggard eyes and ratty hair and clothes. I notice what looks like an old, deteriorated cameo choker of some kind wrapped tightly around her throat. Her breasts float out from under her blouse as she leans over to me. I swallow hard. I mean *hard*.

No, I reply.

Well, good, we wouldn't want that, now, would we? she says.

Just then the guy in the back with us whispers into her ear. She smiles, one of her hands caressing a nipple. I look away. I definitely feel like I got myself into something I shouldn't have. Hey, I say, you can let me off anywhere you want, you know. I wouldn't want to be a bother. It's not much farther, and—

The girl comes over and

(*wraps* . . .)

puts an arm around me. Nestles her body right up against mine. We have something we'd really like to show you, she says, her face inches from mine. At first I swear she's cold, a friggin' *damp* cold, but that quickly passed as I saw more dark nipple. Lips a whisper away from mine, her breath smelled of something I couldn't quite put a finger on, but was, it turned out, alarmingly arousing. Her eyes were deep dark slits of seduction.

No bother, Harry, they say, we're your friends. Don't you like us?

Ah, sure, I say. Sure.

We can be pretty friendly, she says.

Sure.

I want her.

There's something incredibly erotic about the way she moves.

Breathes.

Now just relax, and we'll all have a good time at this party. I'm just going to change, she says. No *prob*-lem, I say, but before I realize it, she's stripping down right before me, keeping her eyes on me. She lifts a finger to her lips . . . lips I suddenly feel very much like eating . . . biting right out of her fucking mouth. I watch as her lips part and she places the finger between them, hooking her lower teeth. I become her finger and feel her lips wrap around me. Watch and feel their moisture as she sucks, closes her eyes. I want her so bad it hurts . . . but remember the guy who's in back with us.

I think back to my family and wonder how I got into this mess. I feel hopelessly distanced from my life. My mom and dad, brothers and sister. None of this feels right. None of it. But I'm aroused, *painfully* aroused, and need more. She's naked, now, openly flirting with me. I know the guy's watching, but I can't help myself. Her body is smooth and available and I want her in the most evil of ways and I no longer care if he's there. I need those lips. For real. Those breasts. I want whatever it is she has, and I'll pay whatever price she demands.

She leans back. Rocks her knees open and closed, breasts falling comfortably to their places. Stares at me. Unblinkingly holds my contemplation. Runs her finger about her body. In and out of places. Her scent is heady.

I think of Mom.

Would she approve of what I'm about to do?

Would Dad take me outside and slap me on the back and say, "*Way to go, stud!*"?

You sure you don't want some? the girl teases. She doesn't have to read my mind. I no longer mind the incense. Before I know it, she's leaned forward and is brushing her finger under my lips. Around them. I shut my eyes, drugged by her touch.

Fuck, I'd *kill* for her.

Gently she presses her finger between my lips and wedges it in . . . plays with my tongue . . . again forming that hook. I'm so intoxicated with her I can't see straight. I grab hold of her and try to force myself upon her—but she holds me back. Slowly, she says, laughing, but I don't want slowly.

I seem to have lost consciousness as my heart pounds up into my throat. I feel like I'm suffocating and suddenly find the girl atop me, hair flying wildly about her, almost floating. She moans; gyrates. Claws at me. Then she explodes . . . and I explode with her . . . .

I am jolted back to my walk.

Dad and Mom sit on a stump holding hands and looking at me. *Really* looking at me. I feel guilty, like they know my thoughts. Had I really done that? Had I *really*—and do they *know?*

They get up and walk away.

I feel like shit.

God, it's all coming back to me. Those people. That van. That party; a party I should never have gone to. I stand up shakily. I don't feel right. I raise a hand to my face and wipe away strands of bladderwort and water that runs down it. I trace my face and neck and flinch. There's a painful, ringed area around my throat. I can't see it, of course, but I feel it. That girl . . . raped me. Those people . . . seduced me. They—

Aren't human. Something about them was . . . is . . . will always be . . . *wrong.*

I look around for my parents, but they've already headed back for camp; Dad with his head down, Mom casting me a backward glance. She pulls Dad into her and cradles his head against her.

What's wrong? I wonder. *What did I do?*

I sit there for some time before heading back. The rain's stronger and colder. Severe. Like little knives raining down from the sky. The water's up to my knees now, and I slosh through it and the water lilies. My sneakers, my jeans are swollen and heavy. Water is everywhere, rising higher. My feet get stuck in muck. It's like a shallow lake with bushes and trees sticking out from it. *Me.* But I need to remember more. That girl . . . whatever she was . . . *is* . . . continued to attack me—

Or had I attacked her?

Oh, how delirious I was with her! Her scent! I could smell her passion like a beast in heat. Even now, when I remember how her body moved, I feel an instant need to have her. Seek her out and take her as no man has ever taken anyone before. I want her—*and* the pain.

She taunts.

Finally we had gotten to Dead Bog Lake and their party; down through a windy, shaded road. I felt strangely nostalgic as we passed my house, lights on in the kitchen. I saw a shadow at one of the windows and felt sad, like I'd never see them again . . . yet I had *her.*

That's all I really needed.

We drove to the outskirts of town, well, actually a township—okay a hamlet, if you must know—until just before the outlet. There's a strong, fishy smell to the air. We pull into a driveway and there's all sorts of vehicles, all kinds of people. And all the vehicles look as did the one I came in. Decayed and rusted. Matted in damp vegetation. As we stop, the others, The Three, as I came to call them, pile out of the van, and I'm left sitting in it alone, staring out into the mass of people, bonfire, and booze. The party feels odd. Smells corrupt. I try to get a good look at some of the people, but it's difficult. It's dark now, and the voices seem a jumble. Where is that girl—I don't even know her name.

How had things gotten so out of control?

I stumble out of the van and lean against it for a moment. I could just keep walking . . . right on up that road . . . to home . . . with the golden kitchen lights and my parents waiting up for me. They think I'm still on the road.

Again the guilt.

Home was so close, yet this woman and her seduction far closer. I hear my name and spot her. She's waving to me. This isn't right, isn't right at all. Things are feeling more and more absurd . . . more remote as moments pass. I feel a sudden urgency to run—to just get the hell out of there and as quickly as fucking possible. I feel a dark mass stalking me from the shadows. Huge, looming, and thirsty. Everywhere. Burrowing into my deepest, most recessed and cobwebbed of places, and find it difficult to breathe. Thunder cracks out along the darkened sky . . . deep, drawn-out rumblings that seem to go on forever . . . .

Mistake number two: I follow after this girl.

She is just as naked as when I last saw her. She moves her hips in wicked, sinful ways further igniting my lust. A man grabs her and they disappear from view. I rage! I must have her, my body screams, and I lunge after her. *I will kill that man. I will rip apart his body!*

But I'd lost them. My head spins.

I need her. I MUST HAVE HER!

I stumble about. Cannot see clearly. A red haze blinds me and grips my senses. All I can picture is her body wrapped around that man.

Hear

Their crazed desire.

I lash out, wanting to give her nothing but pure pain.

Little deaths, I laugh, I'll give her *plenty.*

I push through the crowd, bellowing my passion and anger. I hit shapes that were supposed to be people, but feel funny and soft. Bloated. I didn't care. I'm insane for her. My name is sung above the rising storm, above the din and clatter of the party, and I follow it down to the lake shore. To where I spot her, indeed wrapped around that man, their bodies rocking in the sand. Her screams are the only sounds I hear. My head splits open with jealous furor! I shake with anticipation of tasting blood. *His* blood. I will slowly rend that man's flesh from his bones.

When a sudden thought strikes me cold: *what would my parents think? God—what do I* care?

But as I continue forward, I begin to slow. My head hangs heavy for my conscience is strong.

What have I become? What in God's name have I become?

I look up and find her alone. Gyrating like Mata Hari. Teasing. Again. I try to look away, but cannot. I try to walk back to the road, the one behind me and a million miles away. But I . . . can't . . . .

Sorry, Mom.

Dad.

I shake the memory from my mind. I'm back at camp with my mother and father, aghast of my recollections. I can barely believe them. The water is chest level, now, and Mom and Dad are standing by the station wagon staring at me. I go to them. Maybe I don't need to know everything. Maybe I can still enjoy what's left of our vacation. I mean, how often do we get together? What's done is done, right?

"Mom; Dad," I begin, but they just stare at me. I don't finish what's on my mind. Something is lost between us. They look worn out and wasted. The water continues to rise; the downpour steady and forceful.

"It's a good day, isn't it?" Mom finally says to Dad. Her words are flat. Two-dimensional. Dad merely nods. "Remember more," he says to me. "Go on." Then he hands me a plate of whole, raw fish on a bed of pondweed.

I scrunch my brow together. "Why?"

"Because you're going to anyway."

"What's happening?"

"Everything. Let's go inside, dear," Dad says to Mom, and they disappear beneath the water and enter their tent. I'm left alone.

I remember it all, all right, and I'm angry. They tricked me, just like everyone else at that party. Like they tricked—

I want to go home, I tell that devil-woman back at the party.

You're not going anywhere, she hisses back.

You can't keep me here, I say, and begin to leave—but she grabs me. I'm spun around and no longer is she the seductress I knew, but a bloated, distended horror. I can't even tell if it was a male or female corpse I stared into the empty eye sockets of.

We're not done with you yet, he/she/it seethes.

I see things crawl beneath her skin. Dark algae pour out of her mouth. I scream. The others are upon me. I reach up to push them off, but my hands sink into bloated and stinking flesh. I am forced to the wet, muddy ground. Hands are all over me, tearing off my clothes . . . she—*it*—straddles atop me. I want to die. *Please, God, just* die.

What's the matter, she gurgles, *you no longer want to kill for me?*

I freeze. She brings her algae-gunked lips and teeth and tongue down to mine—I cannot take this! *Kill me!* KILL *me! What* are *you?*

They laugh. *We cannot tell you,* they say, laughing, *but we'd really like to* show *you—*

Out from behind my vision, a large water-soaked log is dragged. A noose is roughly fastened around my neck and attached to the log.

We can't wait to have you join our little family—

I no longer want to think. I sit at the camp, the water now over my head. I'm still holding the plate of fish Dad had given me. I no longer fear the water, for now I know it's coming back to claim me. Mom and Dad are out of their tent, plowing through the water like nothing's going on.

"Hello, dear," Mom says. "Would you like some dessert? Fish?"

I jump to my feet and toss away the plate in anger, which doesn't go far underwater. My mother looks to me, saddened.

"Well, I guess that's it, then," she says, she sighs and goes back to my dad, who seems to be crying, but I can't tell because of all the water. We're a part of it now.

I feel heavy.

I try to go after my parents as they return to the milfoil-and-pondweed covered van, but find I can't. There's a log tied to my neck. It's heavy and I have many rope burns. I try to loosen it, but it's impossible. All I can do is watch as my parents pack up and leave.

Didn't we arrive in a station wagon?

I sit back down, log lashed to my throat, and watch them disappear into the murky, underwater distance. Then I see others. Three others. I grow cold. Shiver. I know them. As they get closer, they beckon. They are The Three. Reclaiming me. I get up to follow them and find I am not at the campground, but Dead Bog Lake. To where I've always been. It was a dream. All of it. A vacation from the bottom of its dark and cursed waters. Or was it real? Actually happened? Had I one last visit with my parents? I won't know until the next time it doesn't happen. I awaken to my place among the fish and the milfoil. Where my feet are eternally tangled

(*no blanket*)

in lakebed muck and pondweed,

(*no more tripping and falling*)

where the log keeps me.

Where my old, dirt-filled Dr Pepper bottle lies directly before my own dead and glassy eyes.

(*no more coolers*)

And now I know things. About this lake. About my new family and my new life.

The girl and the guy in the back of the van drowned in 1807. A canoeing accident. The driver of the van drowned in 1973. Drunk, he'd driven off an embankment into the lake. And the old man at the KOA? He'd killed someone back in '51. Robbed a man for thirty bucks, only to be tracked down and killed by the kin, then thrown into the dark, slippery waters.

That party had been bait . . . as were The Three. As I will be so used. Bait for the lake to reel in more. Set its hooks. A lake with a dark, unspeakable hunger.

And once the taste of meat is acquired, it's a hard thing to shake.

Dark Was The Hour

2004

A slight chill radiated inward from the window as Frank Bishop stared out through his accusatory reflection into the snowy night. He rocked back and forth as the train gently cradled him through the high Colorado mountain passages with its comforting ratcheting sounds and motion. He inhaled the scent of leather and polished wood—nostalgia.

Fallujah sucked was the nicest way he could put it. And the fact that he'd left parts of himself back there didn't help matters.

"Ticket, please?" the conductor asked.

Frank jumped, shooting a hand to his side.

Of course he no longer carried his Beretta nine mil and of course this man wasn't a threat.

He gave the conductor his ticket.

"Thank you, sir," the conductor said. "Next stop, Idaho *Springs!*"

The conductor smiled an odd little smile Frank found unnerving and left. Frank closed his eyes, allowing the lulling metallic *Ta-tun–Ta-tun, Ta-tun–Ta-tun* of the train to

Fallujah.

A name he hoped he'd never—ever—have to speak or hear again.

But he still heard the

Explosions. All around him. His ears rung . . . his eyes swam . . . and his head pounded from the slight concussion. Lieutenant Bishop popped his helmeted head back up over the battered cinder block wall. Small-arms fire came quick and well-directed. He ducked back down.

"Sir! We really need to—"

"I *know!*" Bishop shouted back to the platoon sergeant. He wiped sweat from his eyes with bruised and battered hands caked in dried blood and powder burns. The cacophony and smell of rocket-propelled grenades, spent mortar rounds, and death filled the air.

The Fog of War.

"I'll head off to the left—*there*," the lieutenant said, pointing, "and you guys nail 'em with everything we—"

"Sir, you know you're—"

"What do you want me to do? Leave him there? You can see him as well as I can! I'm *not* leaving him behind."

The Marine sergeant passed on the word to the rest of the platoon.

Bishop took a deep breath, looked to his men, then

ran his hands through his hair. It'd been awhile since he'd been on this train. The last time had been when he'd been nine—was that right? His folks had taken them all on a Christmas ride between home—Idaho Springs—and Denver. Just before the car crash that had claimed them.

Had he made that up—or was that the concussion talking? His head still felt fuzzy. All that shelling . . . all that . . . .

God, it felt so good to do *nothing*. To just sit back and relax. Look out at the dark, snow-covered landscape like some Hitchcock movie. His dad had really loved Hitch.

A reflection in the window passed quickly behind him, and

Bishop spun around, his still smoking and spent M-16A4 useless at his feet. Nine mil already in hand, he pulled his KA-BAR combat knife up before him, and—in one swiftly efficient movement—took out the hostile who'd lunged for him. Another was close behind, but Bishop dispatched him just as efficiently. Breathing heavily, he quickly secured the room, sheathed the knife, and grabbed the dying marine's wrist. He looked at the wrist.

Something was wrong.

No time to think about it, he turned to leave when a tremendous flash of heat and noise and something *ungodly* kicked him in the very seat of his soul and launched him bodily into a wall. He was

crying. Something wasn't right.

Why was he crying?

He was going home . . . home for good. He was no use to the Corps any more. Had served his country. Had his decorations, which he couldn't look at without considering the lives lost—and saved. He was going home to his parents and girl. Their black lab, Boomer. Going to make a new life, if that was at all possible these days.

But what about those left behind?

Who was gonna keep an eye on *them?* Keep *them* safe? His buddies. Hector—how was Hector? Had he made it? Hector Gonzalez

laid down a searing blast of cover fire around the lieutenant's position. The lieutenant was still in there. Gonzalez had no choice. He couldn't leave him. Additional hostiles were quickly overrunning their position.

Gonzalez hand-signaled the platoon to cover him.

Gear rattling, Gonzalez tucked in around the wall then made his way through the rubble. When he got to an open twenty yards he immediately broke into an all-out sprint. The platoon kept up his cover fire. Gonzalez sprinted across the space and slammed his body against a wall. Just up ahead was Bishop. He wasn't leaving him, not after all he'd done at his own expense. No way. He'd stayed behind to allow the rest of them exit . . . when the blast had come. Gonzalez cursed himself for allowing the lieutenant to order them off like that. All he could think of was

"I'm not supposed to be here, am I?" Bishop asked the conductor.

"Of course you are, Son," the conductor reassured. "You're going home. For Christmas. The best one ever."

"But . . . "

The conductor smiled, and

Gonzalez had made it to the lieutenant. He was a mess. All he could tell for certain was that he was missing . . . *parts*. It hadn't yet registered just what, in all the still-settling smoke and rubble, but he wasn't . . . *whole* . . . .

"*Christmas* . . . ," the lieutenant whispered, "*Jea-nna* . . . ." His face was thrashed and bloodied.

"*Lieutenant?*" Gonzalez asked, but there was no more.

Gonzalez grabbed the lieutenant's

(*something was wrong* . . .)

wrist and quickly pulled him from the rubble as more fire opened up on their position. He turned to leave but lost his hold. He tried to re-grip the lieutenant's wrist, but only grabbed

Air.

Gone.

The lieutenant was

Gone.

Gonzalez spun around.

No body, no lieutenant. Only acrid ordnance stink and rubble.

"But he was just—*he*"

stood in the well of the exit stoop as the train came to its screeching halt.

"Have a great Christmas, Lieutenant!" the conductor encouraged, smiling. He saluted Bishop.

Bishop turned and looked up to the conductor. Bishop was bloodied and covered in dirt and grime and war in his desert cammies and gear. He still held his nine mil in one hand, soiled KA-BAR in the other. He looked to the nine mil. Outside.

It snowed heavily.

He cast a momentary, dour smile back up to the conductor, then carefully placed his weapons at the conductor's feet. He stared at the instruments of personal destruction one last time . . . rubbed a wrist and worked his jaw . . . a larger smile crossed his face. He uttered a single chuckle.

He looked back out into the dark, snowy Colorado winter before him.

It was always darkest before the light.

Bishop inhaled deeply of the cold, sweet aromatic pine of the evergreen woodlands mixed in with train exhaust. Saw Christmas lights through the heavy snowfall he swore he could now actually *hear*—heard Christmas music?—when a hand reached in to him from outside the train.

"Welcome home, Son," his father said.

Bishop again inhaled deeply, smiled . . . and stepped off the train.

Tick, Tick, Tick, Tock

2004

"Table for two?" the hostess asked somberly, escorting Tom and Lea Colbert to a booth in the very rear of the restaurant. It was a late mid-July afternoon and the air-conditioned interior felt like a life-or-death oasis. The couple nodded thanks, taking their seats as the hostess deposited menus, then quickly returned to the front of the restaurant.

"Is it even worth it?" Lea asked her husband.

"How would you rather go? Out in that heat?"

Lea said nothing, mechanically opening her menu. "I don't think I could even eat anything. Look. Look around. Is anyone else eating?"

Tom opened his menu and took in the restaurant without making it obvious. She was right. Everyone either sulked, stared blankly into oblivion, or quietly sobbed. There wasn't much dinner conversation. Several lone individuals, cowboys and cowgirls, simply sat and stared straight ahead into the western-motifed walls. The waitresses (they didn't seem to call them "servers" out this way) all congregated at the front of the restaurant around the white lattice-work behind the counter, where a hand-burned sign proclaimed "*$Cashier$.*" Off to the right of that were the restrooms, defined by cute graphics and words burned into pine board that said "*Cowboys*" and "*Cowgals.*" Tom's gaze fell across to the dinner special written up on a whiteboard. *Meatloaf Special*, it said, *mashed potatoes, veggie, dinner roll, and a salad. $5.50.* Clay Walker played quietly in the background from overhead speakers. There were pictures of many famous and not-so-famous cowfolk across every wall, ranches and horses, as well as a stencil that traveled the entire perimeter of the room with pictures of cowboy boots, spurs, horses, and that same old, bleached-and-weather-beaten steer skull.

Behind his wife, Tom saw quite the elderly couple not talking, partially eaten food sitting on the table between them. Bibles were open before the both of them and each clenched the other's hands. Inside this small, hole-in-the-wall western diner off the beaten path, all the curtains were drawn shut. It was as if nothing existed outside this tiny diorama.

"I'm just not hungry," Lea said, closing her menu and carefully laying it on the table before her. She leaned over it and buried her face in her hands.

"Well, I'm hungry and meatloaf sounds good. If we're gonna die, I might as well do it on a full stomach."

"How can you *eat?*" Lea lowered her tone to an intense whisper. *"How can you eat at a time like this?"*

Tom calmly set down his menu.

"I don't know, honey . . . all I know is my stomach's growling and I feel shaky. What difference does it make if I die starving or well fed? If the cook's cooking, I'm ordering."

Tom saw tears emerge from his wife's eyes. He reached across to her, but she continued crying, her shoulders shuddering.

"Honey . . . *honey,*" he said, "there's nothing we can *do* . . . we just have to live our last day like any other. What else *can* we do?"

"I know," Lea blurted, suddenly realizing the other patrons were eyeing her, including the group of cowboys and cowgirls at the large table up front. The small family to her right. They all stared . . . knowingly . . . at her.

"I'm sorry. You're right." Lea pulled some napkins from the holder and dabbed her eyes. "You're right. There's nothing we can do about it except what we're doing." She cleared her throat. Blew her nose.

"Hi, folks," the waitress said, showing up at their table with glasses of water in each hand. "Are you all right?" the waitress asked Lea.

Lea nodded, composing herself.

"Yes. About as fine as anyone can be right now, I guess. Thanks for asking."

The waitress smiled warmly and pulled the pencil from her beehived hair. "All we can do is what we can do," she said, reaching out to Lea with the hand holding the pencil and resting it for a moment on her shoulder before retracting it. "Now, what can I get you folks to drink?"

"Ummm . . . I'll have iced tea," Lea said.

"Same," Tom added.

"We have a meatloaf special today. And I must say it's really good—but I'm supposed to tell you that there's green peppers in it."

The waitress smoothed away loose strands of hair behind her ears. Her hand trembled just a little. Barely at all. She was a pretty woman in her forties, with a slim cowgirl's figure pleasantly packed into her Wranglers. Lea started to tear up again when Velma (read her name tag) reached out to her. "Honey . . . it's okay. When the Lord's ready for us, we just have to answer His call."

Lea recomposed herself, again wiping her eyes. She smiled blithely.

"Just get us two of your dinner specials, okay?" Tom said. Velma jotted that down and departed.

"How does *she* know there's a God? We've all had them, haven't we? The same dreams? Over and over again. Night after night. It's been on TV, books have been written about it. Psychologists have analyzed it the world over, but nothing—*not one thing*—has been done *about* it. It's *today*, and there's not a damned thing *anyone* can do!"

"Hon, please try to keep you voice dow—"

"Why? Tell me *why*, Tom? What's the point? We're all gonna die—the dreams *told* us so. The strong ones, *they* took their *own* lives—but look at us. We couldn't even do that—"

"Honey, *please*," Tom said. "Everyone else is going through the same thing. There's no need to get everyone all stirred up. We have to go sometime, don't we? What difference does it make if we go in our sleep, by old age—or in some apocalyptic *Götterdämmerung?* We've done the best we could with our lives, we've atoned . . . each of us in our own ways . . . there's nothing more we can *do*. We've all made our peace, and we've had two years to do it. Every one of us. The world over."

But here Tom began to tear up. He continued, whispering. "We have to be *strong*, dammit. For the others."

"But what *difference* does it make?" Lea again exploded, and this time she shot to her feet. "We *all* made the jokes at first, didn't we?" she said, looking to her captive audience. Even those who'd been quietly sobbing stopped and looked up.

"*All* of us . . . we thought, 'oh, something must be in the water,' or something similarly *stupid*. We *joked* about it. Then . . . then we sought religious and philosophical help, because that's what we do in times of stress, even if we aren't practicing about it."

Lea looked everybody in the eye, including Velma and the other waitresses . . . the cook, who poked his head out from the grill.

"We all made amends with everyone, tried to make up for all the little and not-so-little wrongs we'd done. Helped out those in need of any help. Did our best to be perfect little Humans—but it didn't seem to make any difference, did it? We still had those goddamned dreams—

those nightmares—*every* night, didn't we? *Don't* we? And today's the day . . . the day we all pay the Piper. And how can all of you just *sit there* like this? Like stupid . . . pathetic . . . little mice caught in a trap?"

"*What else are we going to do?*" asked the wife from the small family to her right, huddled together like frightened puppies. Her eyes pleaded, searching for an answer, anything . . . but Lea had none. She just stared back.

"*Mommy* . . . ," the woman's daughter pleaded, "I'm scared."

"Please, ma'am . . . *please,*" the mom then pleaded.

Tom got up and went to Lea. He put his arm around her and brought her back to her chair. He sat her back down, and she again began to quietly weep. Tom took up a chair beside her and grasped her hands . . . .

Tom and Lea just stared at their food. Two meatloaf specials on the table before them now cold. Iced teas also untouched, but leaking condensation down the length of their glasses onto the checkered tablecloth.

"Tom . . . how do we know this isn't a dream . . . a *lucid* one?"

Tom took his time answering, noticing that the late afternoon was quickly turning into early evening. The light outside the windows had changed . . . became darker, more . . . solemn.

There just wasn't enough time.

"I guess we don't, do we? That's what some of the experts were saying. That we could all just be dreaming this, and we'd all wake up to find our world the same as it ever was. Sane, rational, still there . . . what we remember."

"I've had some pretty real dreams before," Lea said. "Before all this, I mean. Where I couldn't tell the dream from reality? People thought I was crazy—"

"Not anymore," Tom said, snorting.

"No, not anymore, huh. Well, we've lived a good life, haven't we? You and me?"

Tom smiled and reached out to her. Twenty-three years of married love and emotion immediately welled up inside him. "Yes, we have, my love. The best life we could ever live. We always did our best, even before . . . all this."

"Yes, we did."

"We just have to look at it as . . . time to go."

The two sat silently for a moment, squeezing each other's hands before Lea continued.

"But, Tom, I know I've asked this before . . . but, *really,* what if this *is* all a dream? I mean it. This is all a dream and we're gonna wake up, you and me. Say this is *my* dream and in your sleep, you're not even dreaming about this—but *I* am—and we'll both wake up tomorrow, and you'll not remember your dream, but I'll remember *mine*—this dream—and tell you all about it, and nothing'll be wrong. Nothing. Everything will be as it normally is, I mean, like we're *used* to?"

"Honey, that's been said before, you know that—"

"Yes, but if it *is* my dream, then it's all just *me*, don't you get it? Or *you*. Don't you see? This is my dream, and when I wake up, none of this will matter . . . it will all have just been in my head. No one else's— the world isn't going to explode or whatever it is that's supposed to happen, because it's all in *my* head and *no one else's.*"

Tom stopped.

Yes, she had brought this up before. As had others. And, yes, books had been published on this premise more than once over the past two years.

But . . . *what if she was right?*

What if it *was* all a dream, her dream—or *his* dream? What if all this—the *dream* of the dream—was all . . . a *dream?* A lucid one, where he (or she) was just wide awake and aware and that just made it all the more frightening? And Lea just *thought* it was her dream, because that's how dreams work . . . that's the weirdness of them . . . *he's* dreaming, it's *his* point of view, and she's just a part of his dream . . . just like sometimes he's in hers. But if he was (also?) dreaming it, was it really *Lea's* dream—or his? How could he be aware in Lea's dream? It had to be his dream, not Lea's. And further, if he was aware he was dreaming and the dream was so intense and scary—and he knew this— why not change it?

"You know . . . you're right. We don't really know, do we? It could all be a dream of a nasty dream, and if it is, we can change it, because we're *aware* of it."

Tom stood up. Took in the restaurant. Everyone stared at him. He stared back.

Country music continued to play over the speakers. Somebody he didn't recognize.

The sky was now totally dark outside (wasn't it just twilight?). The curtains closed. This was their own little microcosm and it *did* feel different. Something was suddenly different about the whole affair. Not just the place, but also what *supported* this place . . . *life itself* . . . was the only way he could describe it. And he was conscious that everyone was still staring at him as if he was going to save the world—which he was, because it *was* his dream. Lea had said it was hers, but she was just saying that because she was in *his* dream, and that's how dreams worked. You never really knew—until you did. Then everything just fell into place.

"Okay . . . okay everybody . . . ," Tom announced, arms upraised as he walked away from Lea and their table and into the center of the restaurant. "She's right. She's right—*can't you feel it?* You're all in a dream, my dream—*all* of you."

The cook and waitresses stopped talking and—holding hands—came out from behind the lattice-work.

"*Think* about it. How could this be anything else? Nothing like this ever happens in real life—it's all boring and drab. Dull. *Practical.* Sometimes even downright brutal—but always, *always* the prime directive has been that nothing like this *ever* happens.

"Only in science fiction and fantasy.

"Books and movies.

"This is all dream world stuff.

"Armageddon? The end of the world? The world *never* ends . . . sure, it gets nasty, wars come and go . . . but it never *ends*. It only did once, if you believe in the Bible, but wasn't there also something about a promise that God would never do that again? So, if it's all true . . . my wife's correct—this is all a dream, but it's *my* dream, and not hers . . . and you're all in that dream. So, if this *is* the case—"

"Sir, this has all been talked about before," a cowboy said, pushing back his wide-brimmed hat. "And what about Reve—"

"Of *course* it's all been said before—because it's *my* dream! But that's exactly what I'm trying to say! There's no real time in dreams, everyone knows that—years can end up being mere *minutes*. Listen to what I'm saying! If this is all in my head and it's not reality then why do we have to live with it—right? We can *change* it. Each and every one of us—"

"But, if it's your dream, then why do we have to do anything?" another asked.

"Don't you see? Everyone knows dream logic never makes any sense—except in dreams—so *go* with it. This is my dream, so I'm telling all of you to go along with it! We're not all going to die, *because I'm not going to allow that to happen.*

"I'm saying, right here, right now that this is *my* dream and I'm taking control.

"I'm saying we *live. All* of us. And that we'll wake up in the morning, refreshed and ready to meet the day in all its beauty and splendor!" He spun around, arms upraised higher. "A day like any other day! Like we're used to! If it isn't a dream, then we all die with smiles on our faces, but if it *is* . . . if it is, then we change a bad outcome for a *good* one."

Everyone continued to stare at him.

"Come on, people! What do we have to lose? *Take control!*"

The quietness was slowly replaced with handfuls of intimate conversations. Tom watched as people hugged and kissed each other, but more importantly, he saw renewed *hope*. People, finally, had hope again, where they hadn't had any for two years.

He smiled, returning to his wife.

"Why isn't this *my* dream?" she asked.

"That's the beauty of it, hon—it *is*. But it's also *mine*. Whether it's yours, mine, or the cook's, it's still *everyone's* dream. The *dream* is dreaming *as well as the dreamer!* Credit doesn't matter. *We're* the only thing that matters—the *now!*" He took hold of both her hands and kissed them. "*Dream* with me, honey. We can do this!"

Everyone closed their eyes and many mumbled their desires over and over and over . . . but all concentrated with their hearts and souls . . . *upon lives they wanted to live.*

To live.

A better life. For all.

Beautiful homes with beautiful yards and beautiful pets and beautiful kids.

Beautiful birds. Singing.

Beautiful trees whispering in balmy summer breezes.

No wars, peace everywhere . . . love and plenty for *all* . . . .

And Clay Walker and the other singers continued to belt out their tunes overhead. People dreamed about the way it used to be, only better . . . simpler problems with simpler solutions. Simpler *times* . . . .

Outside flashed a brilliant, silent explosion that was gone the instant it ignited . . . and with it, all the world that had been known and loved. All of it . . . down to the last atom.

All the people . . . all the animals . . . all the dirt and trees. All the insects and birds. All the hate and love. All the oceans, the mountains, the stars . . .

Everything.

And, except for everyone in this one diner, reality . . . all of *existence* . . . simply ceased to b

The Coming of Light
1991

Barrett Bartholomew James awoke, groggily.

In fact, he wasn't at all sure he was actually quite yet awake, but more in that in-between state between sleep and wakefulness. There was something entirely odd about the way things felt. *Very* odd . . . like he was not all there . . . his more valuable pieces missing. He felt (in point of fact) like he was entirely someone else in *his* body.

As he lay there, trying to figure out who was in his body—and whether or not he was actually awake—Barrett focused on the room. It gave him the feeling of being wrapped within the arms of a jealous lover. He felt as if he were being smothered . . . and very much *wanting* to be smothered. Spying frost on the windows—and noticing the fire in the hearth—he figured it was cold and wintry outside. He then directed his attention to the bed he was in and found himself drowning within a sea of billowy comforters. Rocking his head back, he floated upon huge, down-filled pillows . . . and there was a tingling in his ears that loudly resonated in his head.

The fire cracked loudly and belched out a rather large glowing fragment onto the hardwood patch of floor. The ember blazed momentarily brighter before dying.

Should have had a screen there, he thought.

Slowly Barrett came to the only realization that made any sense: that he was, in fact (most assuredly), *himself* . . . and that himself *was* (in fact) the very awake Barrett Bartholomew James.

Throwing off the comforters, he swung out of bed and sat upright. He sat clad, neck to toe, in an archaic, almost comical pair of pajamas. With a chuckle he playfully fingered the material as he got to his feet and headed over to the heavily curtained window. His feet swished through thickly piled carpet that covered the entire floor except for the hardwood spot before the fireplace.

Wiping an opening on the clouded windowpane, he peered out . . . and was greeted by the most pleasant illumination of gas streetlights . . . in a small but bustling snow-covered town square below. He was on the second floor.

"Where the hell am I?"

Padding back across the room, he went to the mantel piece above the fireplace.

Pictures and trinkets, none of which he recognized, pictures that ranged from the ancient to the current. There were families, and there were singular moments. There were—

The bedroom door squeaked open.

"Oh, my! I'm sorry! You're awake!"

It was a pleasant voice from an attractive and unassuming lady in her mid-thirties. She held an armful of clothing. He froze. Was caught in jammies by a woman he didn't know . . . in a house he recognized not.

"Who are you?" he asked. "What is this place?"

"I'm Julie, Mr. James, I run the boarding house you're in."

"You know me?"

"Well, indirectly. I was told there would be someone new tonight."

"You were told? What's going on?"

"Oh, it's nothing, really—now let me give you your clothes and let you get ready for the evening. There's dinner downstairs."

Barrett watched her glide across the floor to his bed, deposit a set of cleaned and pressed garments that looked largely woolen, then return back to the door. He noticed mukluks had already been placed beneath his bed.

"You'll find a full set of undergarments in the bureau over by the window," Julie said, pointing. Barrett followed her direction, trying to keep up what little decency he felt he had left. It was tough doing so in garments that had a bomber's hatch on the seat. "If there's anything else I can do . . . please . . . don't hesitate to call, Mr. James—"

"Please—'*Barrett*.'"

Julie smiled. It was a charming smile and Barrett felt his insides glow with unexpected warmth. Things didn't feel right—they felt *good*—just not *right*.

"Okay . . . *Barrett*," she said demurely, a thin smile forming across elegant lips. Turning just before closing the door, she again addressed him. "Mr. Jame—*Barrett*—we're all very pleased to have you join our community."

"Thank you."

"*I'm* pleased to have you—"

Julie quickly closed and latched the door behind her as she left.

"God, if I didn't know better, I'd think she had a thing for me . . . now, where's the damned bathroom?"

Treading down firm but creaking stairs, Barrett made his way to the dining room. While in the quaint, antiquated shower things had begun to surface, though not much, but it was better than nothing. He remembered being a businessman (of some kind) from "The City." New York City. He remembered being on vacation upstate, but that was about it. He didn't know if he had a wife or a family—though he assumed so since he was wearing a ring, and a very meaty one at that. He just didn't know.

Walking through the softly lit house, he smelled the aroma of cooking. Found the heat of another fireplace. And plants were everywhere, even covering one unused piano he spotted in a room he passed by.

Making his way through drapery adorned doorways, his weight caused the hardwood floorboards to squeak. In no time he found the source of the aroma . . . also finding the dinner table cleaned by the previous users with but a single food-filled place setting awaiting his presence.

"Oh, there you are! Please, sit down and eat, Mr. Barrett!" Julie said smiling, arriving at the doorway. "I hope you don't mind that the others have already come and gone, but what with the Coming of Light, it seems there's never quite enough time. Always much too much to do, and no one seems to want to wait for anyone anymore, don't you know!"

"'Coming of Light'?"

"Oh, nothing to worry about just yet. You'll see it all in good time."

Barrett felt his head twinge . . . like a mild headache . . . but it was quickly gone.

"W-what others?"

"Well, as I said, I run a boarding house. It is a most rewarding job, and I really do enjoy helping others relocate—"

"Relocate?"

"I'm so sorry, I know it's a lot all at once, but please try to bear with me. Look," she said, extending a hand and leading him to the table, "why don't you first sit down and get some warm food inside—you haven't eaten in who knows how long—then we can go out for a walk. It'll invigorate and aerate and there're still quite a few hours left before—well, you'll just love it! We'll have plenty of time to talk then. Come!" Holding back a smile, Barrett allowed himself to be led. Her company really did grow on him.

As he made his way to the table, images flashed through his head, but nothing solid enough for a mental lock. He was as a babe lost in the woods. Wincing a few more times, which Julie didn't seem to notice, he looked—really *looked*—at Julie. It was more than her company he liked—he found her to be quite fetching, especially dressed in her checkered apron and floor length skirt (why such formal attire for everyday wear?), and though he didn't know her all that well, it was easy to see the openness and warmth her manner radiated.

But it was her eyes . . . large and warm . . . which really grabbed him. *He was totally captivated by her.*

By her *spell*.

"Well, Julie, I must say—you certainly do have a convincing way about you."

Julie blushed, bringing a lovely and delicately crafted hand to her mouth.

This was all too much—it was like a damned fairy tale. Nothing's *this* perfect.

"You'll be sure to explain this 'Coming of Light' during our walk?" Barrett took his seat at the table.

Julie's blushing quickly gave way to a look of mixed emotions she quickly changed back to a smile.

"Oh, it's nothing, really," she said, "it's just where the Nightfun ends and the Light comes."

"You mean 'dawn,'" he casually muttered, still somewhat preoccupied with the flashing images inside his head. He dug hungrily into the plate of food before him. "You really are a charming woman, Julie—from your mannerisms right down to how you express common everyday things."

"Thank you, Barrett." Again, the down-turned head, the expected blush.

"'Nightfun,' huh."

" . . . and over there is Pastor's Church. Isn't it simply the most beautiful building you've ever seen?" Julie asked, pointing a charmingly mittened hand.

"It is!" Barrett exclaimed, bringing the collar of his overcoat in more around him.

It was *all* beautiful, every bit of it.

And it was *snowing!*

It was all *too* beautiful . . . too perfectly quaint and hometownish . . . and Barrett again felt that strange *something* shudder throughout him—he felt it about the buildings, the people, the town's atmosphere.

And it all felt disquietingly *familiar* . . . as though he'd actually been here before . . . when he damn well knew he hadn't. It was a tight little microcosm, an entire universe built around the confines of glistening snow and homey neighborliness. A picture-book life and times the way all life should be. Several people passed by especially close, waving and hailing.

"Hello, Julie; Barrett! Wonderful weather we're having, ayuh!" some positively friendly New Englanders greeted. And most New Englanders he knew were not outwardly friendly unless they knew you. Grew up with you. Lived in the same town with you. Julie waved back, returning the greeting.

"Julie . . . how did they know my name?"

Hands tight to the front of her jacket, Julie looked up at him with her large brown, hypnotic eyes. Something fluttered deep within him.

"Everyone knows you, Barrett. It's a small town. Everybody knows *everybody.*"

Barrett found it harder to resist. She was a powerful magnet, and he but an iron filing. What was it about this place . . . about *her?* He felt . . . pleasantly uncomfortable . . . .

"Huh? What? I'm sorry, I seem to have forgotten my . . . question." Barrett flushed. This is *not* like me, he thought, *not like me at all!*

But what is *me?*

I don't—or never used to, anyway—get butterflies in my stomach over a woman. I'm married, sure. Or used to be, or still am, or—I don't even know anymore!

"God help me!" Barrett blurted, hitting out at a light post with a gloved fist. Frightened, Julie jumped back several steps. Passing pedestrians gave startled looks, but quickly turned them into empathetic smiles and continued on. Eyes full of concern, Julie came back to him.

"Barrett? What's wrong? Is it something I—"

"No—I-I don't know—but that's the whole problem, Julie! Just where *am* I, and what am I doing here? *How* did I *get* here?"

Julie came up from behind and brought her hands up to Barrett's shoulders. She felt them suddenly relax, and it brought an immediate smile to her face. Barrett spun around and took her face into his gloved hands. His resistance was quickly faltering.

"Where have I come from, what is this place, and who *are* you to have this power over me?"

Julie didn't attempt an answer, but Barrett quickly lost interest in the questions and brought her face in closer. "Nobody has ever wielded such control over me. I haven't felt like this in, well, in God knows how long."

"Is it so wrong to feel so good? To feel the way you've always *wanted* to feel—the way we're all *meant* to feel? Why analyze everything? Why not just *be? Live?*"

"I guess nothing's wrong with it, but . . . ."

Barrett felt her warmth through his gloves. Felt the warmth of her soul penetrating deeper, ever deeper into his soul and trying to bring out . . . *something* . . . *exploit* it. . . .

Her lips parted slightly.

Barrett spiraled helplessly into her.

CLANG-CLANG!

CLANG-CLANG!

It was the church bell.

"Oh! Come on! This is going to be *so* much fun!" Julie said, pulling away and flailing outstretched arms.

"Why? What's up?" Barrett asked, looking around.

Julie reached out for him, but then broke away, taking playful steps toward the convergence of townspeople still farther up.

"Come on—it's the skating competition! On Glass Pond! You're going to just love it!"

Barrett regarded her with loving consideration, watching her skip off. She was so childlike, so full of energy and desire. He started off after her when something else caught his attention. It was a sparkle, a flash of some kind. Julie's back to him, he diverted off towards the flash, to an area where the streetlights and the starless darkness beyond met. Beyond the haze. He was mere feet from the border when Julie turned, her face immediately draining of all color.

Something wasn't right over there, just up ahead of him. There was an icy tingling playing up and down his spine as he continued forward.

Felt old aches.

Movement became restricted, labored . . . .

"*NO!*"

It was Julie. She'd stopped dead in her tracks, her mouth a large "O" from her scream and the look of pure dread on her face. Bent forward, her hands were tucked forcefully down between her legs. She repeated her command. Barrett didn't just stop, he grinded to a halt, his mind's eye envisioning a mile's worth of burned rubber left on an open stretch of road.

"Barrett, no—*please don't!*"

Barrett turned, frightened more by the unexpected terror in her voice than the actual situation itself.

"What's the matter? I only wanted to see what was over there."

Seeing that he stopped, Julie ran for him, arms quickly wrapping him in a powerful hold.

Barrett again felt the butterflies.

"Julie," he began, initially amused, "I didn't know you cared!"

Julie hung on like a dying woman, her face buried into his shoulders.

"What's wrong?" he asked. "I was only—my God, you're *crying!* Whatever I did, I'm sorry, I won't do it again!"

"I'm sorry, it's not you, Barrett, but that . . . that *area* . . . it's off limits. It's The Place of Endings . . . and nobody ever returns who ventures there. I've lost . . . others have been lost there."

"'The Place of Endings?' Julie, you have to tell me what's going on here—no more cute little euphemisms—I need to know what's happening. I *have* to know."

"I can't, I—it was . . . a loved one. It was *horrible*. Later, please, Barrett, I really can't go on." She reburied her face into his shoulder, her face melting the snow on his overcoat.

"Julie, I like you very much, but I have to know—"

"—please, Barrett, I really . . . like . . . you, too, but the memories . . . are painful. Later I'll tell you everything—I will—but for now let's just enjoy ourselves. *Please?*" Julie's crystal tears were of such purity that they felt like cold knives of despair ripping through him. He was helpless . . . he . . . was *hers*.

"Okay. But after this skating competition of yours, we talk. Okay?"

She nodded, a pained smile on her face.

Glass Pond looked exactly like its name—shiny, smooth, and unmarked. Barrett was amazed at how reflective and clean the surface was and why there were hardly any marks made by the hordes of skaters flying across it. But possessed by an ever widening grin across his face, he found himself casually responding to everyone who passed them by. And he did this by name—first *and* last names. He found that their names magically popped into his head, and when he unconsciously began using them, they proved themselves correct. The townspeople were visibly pleased.

"Are you enjoying yourself more, Barrett?" asked one elderly couple.

"Why yes, I am, Mr. and Mrs. Greetallski. I really am! I'm finding this to be the friendliest town I've ever visited! And the Christmas spirit surely cannot be beat!"

"Well, we're all very proud to have someone as prominent as yourself taking up residence here," Mr. Greetallski said.

"And you certainly do add very nicely to the I!" Mrs. Greetallski chimed in, her rosy cheeks and frosty nose bursting with fervent holiday cheer. She winked. "He's a great catch, Julie. Be sure to hold on to him and don't let him get away!" Mrs. Greetallski said to Julie, as she leaned into her. Julie flushed with another blush.

"I could get very used to living here, you know," Barrett said, once the Greetallskis had left.

"I could get very used to you living here," Julie said, looking up to him as she came in closer.

Barrett brushed away a few nothings from her face. More people came by, some running and throwing snowballs (one or two of which landed at their feet), and Barrett watched as they passed, their chanting ringing in his ears long after they'd gone:

> *Get ready for the Light*
> *The Coming of the Light!*
> *One hour, one hour to go!*
> *Get ready for the Light*
> *The Coming of the Lightft t*
> *There is no Dawn, only Bright*
> *One hour to go—ho ho* ho!

Julie watched his reactions with a pounding heart.

"What *is* this—"

"—Coming of Light?"

"Yes! Why is it such a big thing to have the sun rise? Hell, it's not even near dawn now! Look," he said, pointing over to the other side of the Apothecary. "It's dark, pitch dark. Except for the street light glare, there's not even a *hint* of a rising sun!"

Julie continued to eye him . . . that look of a confused and caring face. Barrett looked back up into the gas-lit sky. Snow had been falling steadily and heavily ever since they'd stepped out into the street, but there was hardly any accumulation—in spite of the fact that there was already a fair amount on the ground. Everything looked perfect.

Planned almost.

Julie came up beside him. Barrett found that he really didn't care about who he was, or what this whole coming-of-light problem was. All he wanted now was to make his lips touch hers . . . to taste the firm slipperiness of her tongue and inhale the delicate scent of her breath, her *skin* . . . .

"The Coming is at 6:05 in the morning . . . ," she began, again coming in closer, their arms touching.

"Six-oh-five? Exactly?"

"Exactly. There is no dawn, only bright—only *light.*"

They turned to each other.

Face to face, he now felt her breath; felt a tingling, felt her shiver. *He* shivered.

" . . . only . . . *bright* . . . ."

A particularly large snowflake landed between their mouths, perched for but the birth of a second before melting. Barrett felt a wellspring of emotion that had been coiled up within the both of them; felt the explosion that now took them away—

Lips upon lips.

Teeth upon teeth.

Tongue . . . .

Passers-by smiled. He would fit in very nicely here, yes, indeed he would.

"*I love you* . . . ," Julie said, whispering.

"I . . . *I love you,* too, *Julie,*" Barrett also said, whispering intently.

"Barrett, I couldn't bear it should you ever leave! There is no one else here made for me!"

Barrett squeezed his shut his eyes. Opened them. A lump formed in his throat.

"I won't. I feel I can't . . . but I *won't.* I won't even *try.*"

"You could; you almost did. Could you remain here forever . . . living and doing the same beautifully boring life over and over? Again and again? With *me?*"

"I could."

"You'd never leave?"

"Never."

Then he looked down and noticed the wedding ring on her finger.

"You're my wife, aren't you?"

"Yes, my husband."

"But . . . but how? You had no ring when we first met—in fact, you called me 'Mr. James.' This is all too much, I'm not sure I can—"

"But you *will,* my husband, you *will!* Your love is all, your love is *enough.* It is all that matters—*nothing else does.*

"It is time we talk. Come, let's walk."

Julie led him away from Glass Pond and took him down a different street, passing Mrs. Goodall's Mercantile & Dry Goods (Mrs. Goodall waving vigorously through the window as they passed). A warm fire visible in the store's background. They then passed the New England Bank, a small tree nursery that was up on a hill (next to a water tower that boldly displayed "*Something* Towne" around its reservoir—Barrett couldn't see the first word, wrapped around the far side of the tank), a toy shop, village market, and more. Then they stopped. People were taking on more urgency in their steps, several still chanting about the Coming of Light—

at six-oh-five
there is no dawn, only bright . . . .
Only fifteen minutes to go!

"I still don't understand this no-dawn part. Every place has a dawn, honey."

"Not every place."

"And you mentioned '6:05' like it happens the same time every day."

"There is only light and dark, my husband. *Look*."

The two turned, and Barrett followed Julie's mittened hand. He followed it to a simple white-painted wood building with an unobtrusive sign hanging above a window.

Barrett James & Company, Realtors.

"Th-that's *me!*"

Julie raised a gloved hand to his mouth before he could continue further, her eyes burning into him.

"Come, we have only a little more to go. Brace yourself, my love, for what is to come next. Your love for us—this town and me—will bear you through. *Trust* us."

The two rounded a corner, and he found "*Julie James Boarding House & Hostel.*" The place from which they'd left. In a lower front window rested a real-estate flyer bearing Barrett's name. Together they walked up the wooden stairs . . . and into the warmth and glowing that was their home . . . .

A light switch flipped on.

The light illuminated a small novelty workshop. The owner, a bearded and slightly stooped man, entered, aimlessly throwing the morning paper down on a counter. Shedding his coat, he foraged about for several minutes, looking for something in particular. Going over to the cash register, he took out a receipt box, one that had "*Paid*" written on the front in small, crooked letters and fished through it. Finding the object of his search, he took it out, giving it a sad glance and a forlorn shake of the head before placing it on the table next to the paper. He looked at one of his clocks.

Six-oh-six.

Casting another grieved look at the paper and the bill, he went back out the door.

The front page story, only part of which was visible under the tossed bill, read:

> "Maverick Wall Street stockbroker Barrett B. James died last night in a car crash in the upper Catskills. Mr. James was pronounced dead at the scene.
>
> He and his family had been visiting relatives and friends for the holidays. Local authorities claimed no one was at fault in the accident. It had been weather induced; heavy snowfall had unleashed in blinding force on already existing icy conditions. The James family could not be reached for comment. Mr. James had ventured out on his own and had been enroute from a shopping trip . . . ."

Alongside the paper sat the bill of sale. "Barrett James, *PAID*, one complete Snow Towne village. AMEX Gold card; to be delivered."

Not five feet from that table sat a lower display, on which sat Snow Towne. In its center was Glass Pond. Along the edge was Pastor's Church. The tree nursery under the shadow of the water tower with the village's name painted across it. Somewhere, between Glass Pond and Pastor's Church, rested the porcelain buildings of *Barrett James & Company, Realtors*, and *Julie James Boarding House & Hostel*.

All through the village the lights were down, and everyone lay snug in their porcelain beds, dreaming, and waiting for the next cycle of the Coming of Light . . . .

The World's Greatest Writer
2005

"Well, have you ever actually *met* him?" the doe-eyed initiate asked.

"Uh, nooo, not *actually*," the immaculately dressed writer-in-white responded, "I've been told he's rather a bit of a hermit, you might say." The writer-in-white nervously fingered his cane and white hat meticulously positioned (posed) before him.

The young writer nodded thoughtfully, then added, "Okay. So, then, have you ever actually *read* any of his work?"

At this the writer-in-white's ego further deflated, upon which he grew visibly agitated. "Um, no, my dear, I haven't yet had the opportunity. *No* one has—"

"Then how do you *know* he's such a great writer?" pressed the young one, who held the older writer's gaze firmly, her manuscript cradled loosely in her arms between them. The young one had not meant to pin the learned author to the wall, but was merely genuinely curious. "How can you say so much about him when you haven't even read his work—or met him?" She furrowed her brow, patiently awaiting an esoteric, scholarly response.

"I know it's hard to believe, my dear, but it's his *reputation*, you see. Did you know he doesn't even use a computer? He uses a mechanical typewriter! The gentleman is simply . . . *extraordinary*. Exceptional. Have you ever personally met *God*? The *Pope*? No . . . you know of each through faith, through *reputation*. But that's what this reception is all about, my dear young one! He's coming out, as it were! Don't let your youth and impetuousness get the best of you! You are yet young— *learn!* Tonight, here, it is said that he will debut the opening pages to his Great American Novel! I mean, *can you fathom this opportunity before you?* The miraculous, *metaphysical* encounter we are all about to be granted? We are going to be the first to experience his words, his energy, his *soul*. His raw, unfiltered emotional fervor before they are all unleashed upon our common, illiterate public—we . . . *we* are the *privileged few*. Savor this moment, my dear writer, for you clearly do not comprehend the enormity of greatness which you are about to witness. Mark my words: this . . . will *never* happen again. In *any* lifetime. My God, how I wish I were in your shoes, a lifetime ago, to start over my profession at a much higher place, indeed!"

And with that, the writer-in-white spun away on his heels from the neophyte in search of others with which to intelligently converse. The neophyte watched as the writer-in-white discretely dabbed his eyes with a dainty, white handkerchief then quickly spirited it away back inside a lapel compartment.

Hugging her manuscript tightly into her chest, the young writer slouched off into a corner to ponder the learned man's words when another group of writers, editors, or agents made their way toward her no-longer-empty corner, though not inviting her into their conversation. After all, they did not know her and were too far along in their awe and adoration of I. M. N.. Authier III, the unmatched, unparalleled, unequaled literary (and spiritual) prodigy to humanity who had emerged out of nowhere.

Well, Canada, to be precise.

Our young, impressionable writer overheard the entire story, as one of the group informed another on the miraculousness of what the writer-in-white had just tried to impart upon her. This time, she heard . . . the *rest* . . . of the story:

There was not one person who could claim to have actually read a piece of Mssr. Authier's work. Not even his agent. Mssr. Authier's agent's claim to fame was the divine opportunity of which she had been a part: the reception of his skillfully executed proposal package. So masterfully woven was it—and in less than one page—on the whitest and most defect-free twenty-pound paper, with the cleanest, crispest TNR type that she immediately fell upon herself in a fit of hot, emotional blithering . . . which had so cleansed her being that her feline allergies had been summarily obliterated. Immediately, she'd called her estranged mother and apologized for everything cruel she'd ever done—or would ever do—including anything in all her future (or past) lives. Once she read her mother the letter, her mother likewise returned the compliment. The agent then immediately withdrew a sizeable portion of her investments and donated it to Readers Without Books and her top-two choices of battered parents' shelters. Instead of staying home and reading through the rest of her slush pile, she flew out into the night to the nearest homeless shelter and spent the rest of the night assisting those who begged money for a living.

This, off the power of the Mssr. Authier III's epiphanic proposal package (and on *one page* no less!). Well, after she called Penguin Random House (also known as "PRH" to some . . . or not . . .) and read his poignant, moving letter to everyone up the Food Chain, including the CEO, the CEO himself called Mssr. Authier and offered him a most lucrative contract on the spot. He'd been very convincing. The CEO informed the esteemed Mssr. Authier III in no uncertain terms that if he didn't take his offer, he was going to resign and take a bullet to the brain that very night. That it was his and his work *alone* that would make or break PRH—nay, the entire publishing industry, sir!—and that it was his moral and spiritual imperative to *not let publishing fail.*

Reluctantly, Mssr. Authier accepted.

PRH immediately put into motion a hundred-million-copy print run, foreign, movie, and audio and video rights, as well as an emotionally blistering promotional campaign that rivaled D-Day's 1944 invasion. Allowed Mssr. Authier's input on the cover. PRH also acquired rights to and sold a television series and coloring books for adults and children (grades one through four) to be included in the curriculum of all U.S. public schools. Europe was next.

A-preeminent-film-director-who-asked-that-his-name-be-kept-out-of-the-media was awakened twenty-five minutes later and sealed an undisclosed multi-million dollar deal via The UPS Store's faxes, securing Mssr. Authier's signature. The exact fax machine used by Mssr. Authier had since been removed from service and bronzed.

An online powerhouse took 110.3 million advance orders.

Mssr. Authier's agent offered him her hand in marriage.

Talk show hosts asked Mssr. Authier for *his* advice on secret, deeply personal matters that had troubled them all for years. And this brought out a major talk-show host of many years to disclose (yet another) comeback to do one, really final (this time) show with Mssr. Authier as the only guest.

A major rock band that had (among other letters) an "M" in its name had penned a ballad in his honor.

So, as this new group of writers continued to chatter on about Mssr. Authier's proposed deification, the neophyte found herself so emotionally overwhelmed, especially when certain lines from his proposal letter were refrained (now immortalized by the world and passed around like a veritable Internet Trojan and blowing up

YouTube) that she found her soul uncontrollably expanding toward supernova detonation. And when she heard the title of Mssr. Authier's proposed novel, she positively lost it and ran bawling for the ladies room, where she pulled out her meager manuscript and stared at it in weary, disillusioned judgment.

WWJD?

WWIMNAD?

She grabbed her manuscript in both hands, her heart heavy with all the wasted time and effort she'd poured into this piece of no-name tripe, and viciously and maliciously began rendering it into tiny, jagged, tear-stained shreds amid spastic grunts and shrieks of soulless despair, tossed it into a pile in the middle of the ladies-room floor, and set it on fire.

The young neophyte then—amid the now-activated sprinklers, billowing smoke, and floating ashes of her snuffed manuscript—pulled out a pair of scissors and the razor she always carried (because she was, by trade, a hairstylist) and immediately set about shaving her head and carving Mssr. Authier's initials into her scalp.

As the clock ticked closer to Mssr. Authier's scheduled appearance, the entire Radio City Music Hall buzzed over his other ideas for other books. How could he possibly have created a series out of this concept, they asked? Surely his first book would drain everything a reader had to offer? Could a person emotionally *survive* the first book? Could the *editor*? Surely PRH would bring in a *team* of editors . . . in relay fashion . . . to take over when the previous ones simply could go no further. Counselors would also have to be brought in, so the buzz went, with fat severance packages to take care of these forever-spent editors who would be of no use to anyone else or themselves, ever again. Yes, Penguin Random House would have to take care of them—indeed, it would be *their* moral obligation to do so, in bringing this genius to the world, and many in this room were willing to so give up their lives to be on that editorial task force, emotional sanity be damned! Every lawyer in the country began to point out that PRH would also be liable to the public for their emotional sanity, as well, once the book hit the shelves, so a non-profit foundation had been set up.

And what of the cover artist? The jacket copy writer? Marketing and promotion? Accounting?

Was *the-preeminent-film-director-who-asked-that-his-name-be-kept-out-of-the-media* even up to task?

There was talk from this person's camp that after just storyboarding the film this would be his last project. Anything after this one would be parochially anti-climactic. Useless. With this film, he would have said everything he could ever possibly have to say in this lifetime or any other.

(Unfortunately, Mssr. The preeminent-film-director-who-asked-that-his-name-be-kept-out-of-the-media had to decline invitation to the reception, because he had been so passionately ravaged from production efforts that he had to abruptly seek psychological counseling. Mssr. Authier sent his well wishes.)

PRH, taking the lead, had strategically pre-positioned counselors throughout the music hall—counselors who had, however reluctantly, because they understood the need to do so, shield themselves from Mssr. Authier's words with the most advanced ear-protection technology available. Nothing was left to chance!

Then it happened, and for just a moment the entirety of Radio City Music Hall fell silent, as if each person collectively inhaled for the first time since their arrival. The words

"He's here!"

shot from a watcher posted at the entrance and immediately twenty-three women collapsed and forty-five men spilled martinis on themselves.

In no time, Mssr. I. M. N. Authier III's motorcade pulled up before the music hall and security flooded the gathering. When Mssr. Authier III finally graced the gathering (amid floods of marriage proposals from both genders), it was as if God Himself had descended from Heaven. Mssr. Authier, dressed in a comfortable tweed sports jacket with tastefully adorned elbow patches, sporting his rimless glasses and a calm, soothing smile, arrived and was the epitome of graciousness—but was also quite embarrassed. Not only had he no idea his name had already been submitted for both saint- and knighthood, but he also had no idea as to the scale of what he'd spun into motion with the delivery of his (one-page!) proposal.

Yet he remained ever gracious as he shook hands and took a genuine interest in all whom he greeted—asking how their children and relatives were doing, did they have jobs, and if not, *please*, do give him a call, and he'd see what he could do about it, and would they promise him that they would get enough sleep before going back to work on the morrow?

Then one, without warning, wildfire-swift whisper erupted throughout the reception:

Where was the manuscript?

Had he come without his *words?!*

Were they all to be so callously *jilted?*

Teased so hotly, only to be summarily slapped without so much as a kiss or a hug? Good God, what had happened? Was it . . . *Writer's Block?*

The crowd again held its collective breath.

He somberly approached the podium, his smile evaporated.

Removing a handkerchief, Mssr. Authier paused, wiped tears from his eyes, then grasped both sides of the podium, damp hanky still clutched in one trembling hand. His voice wavered and cracked as he addressed the world (it was simulcast) in his wonderfully accented, melodic French-Canadian dialect.

"Ladies and gentlemen . . . friends. I tried . . . to keep from . . . how you say?—breaking down—before all of you here, tonight, but find . . . at the last possible moment . . . that, *mon Dieu!* I am unable to keep from doing so!"

Here he paused, again wiping tears from his hot, swollen face with his damp hanky.

"My friends! Let me share with you what had happened to me last night as I flew into Kennedy *aéroport* . . . ."

And with that, Mssr. Authier III launched into the most heartrending speech anyone in that room (or their progeny)—the world—had ever, or would ever, participate in. For two-and-one-half hours Mssr. Authier held the room in rapt captivation. Penguin Random House, foreseeing this, had trucked in boxes of Kleenex (®) brand facial tissues—unfortunately for Mssr. Authier's attendees (and further adding to their emotional turmoil), his likeness was on the sides of each box, promoting his yet-to-be-written novel. People gave up their writing careers following his speech, devoting their lives to the Peace Corps or Green Peace. Half of the counselors working the reception took early retirement (including those wearing the most-advanced-technology ear protection devices; though they couldn't hear a single utterance, they didn't have to . . . each experienced the emotion that had taken complete hold of the audience that magical evening) and entered therapy themselves. Those with outstanding traffic warrants turned themselves in the next day and insisted upon a minimum of one year of community service for evading the law in paying those fines. So overcome with exhaustion was Mssr. Authier himself at the conclusion of addressing his audience that he had to be assisted from the stage (his knees buckled twice) and escorted directly to his awaiting motorcade, where a saline IV drip awaited. Mssr. Authier was submitted for a Nobel and Pulitzer for his oration.

Mssr. Authier later reluctantly agreed to a special interview with a media icon (whose initials are real close to "AV"), whom he also brought to tears (at one point the entire 20/20 staff and operators behind the camera were blubbering unabashedly together on national TV, and it was the first time an entire five minutes of weeping was nationally televised without commercial interruption), where the following was made public:

Mssr. Authier had made the decision, since sending out his (one-page!) query and making his music hall debut that he would *not* write the proposed book in question. As an aside, said media icon (apologizing in advance for having to bring this to his attention this way) informed Mssr. Authier that his agent, having been scorned by his lack of amorous advances gave up agenting and had left for India to devote her life to the poor and destitute, vowing a life of celibacy. Following another crying spat, Mssr. Authier used this as an example and was further quoted as saying that after having witnessed the effects of his words upon the world . . . he had no choice.

The only moral and ethical thing to do was to *not* pen the novel.

The world was simply not ready for it. *He* was not ready for it.

The world (he cited tearfully) could not handle his words, and he could not handle the world after having seen the impact his letter and presence had had.

Media icon AV begged him to reconsider. Literally begged. But no matter how heartrending, how needed, how emotionally brutal and true his proposed work, he maintained he could not in all good conscience do it. It wouldn't be fair to humanity.

Mssr. Authier also decided to return all his advance monies (that he'd kept untouched in a separate, numbered account) despite Penguin Random House's vehement objections. He deserved every penny, PRH countered (with several of their A-list authors having offered up their own advances and royalties so PRH could make the author advance). Mssr. Authier said thank you and donated all that had been given him to world hunger organizations.

And, finally, Mssr. Authier vowed to never, *ever* propose to pen another book . . . ever again.

At this point AV lost all composure and decorum and pleaded with him to reconsider, as did her producers and camera people.

But he held firm and declined, laying a hand to her shoulder.

Following the interview, Mssr. Authier quickly disappeared into seclusion, never to be heard from again.

The preeminent-film-director-who-asked-that-his-name-be-kept-out-of-the-media's film adaptation of his proposed novel that had never been written created box-office records that, to this day, have never been broken. This Famous Person, as promised (and recovering nicely in extended therapy), quietly retired . . . donating all proceeds from the film to the International Red Cross.

Drive-Ins
1994

If you look close—real close—you can almost see them . . . .

Thirteen-year-old Randy Thornton pedaled his purple BMX bike up over the ridge, slivers of morning sunlight stabbing into his eyes from the other side of the rise. He brought the bike around and skidded to a quick stop. Surveyed the lot in front of him. White posts. Everywhere. Rows upon rows of nothing but white posts.

And a screen.

Randy got off his bike and walked with it among the posts. Looked up to the huge white screen that loomed above like a watchful giant.

Silver screen they call it. Silver—*like for monsters n stuff.*

There were lots of stains and rips in it, but Randy thought sure a movie would still work. He continued on, walking his bike beside him, and soon noticed what looked like a lump of rags in the center of the sea of posts. He moved in closer; saw how the bunched-up rags were actually a hunched-over man sitting in the dirt. A man who mumbled. Randy ditched the bike and came up to the guy.

"Mister? Mister, are you all right?" Randy stopped several feet from the man, who smelled like rotting food and days' old urine. "Mister, *are you all right?*"

Randy reached out. Touched him. The lump of rags shuddered, but felt light as a bird . . . like one push would send him off flying.

But fly he didn't.

Randy reached down and tilted the head back, then stumbled backward in horror.

He turned to run, but instead ran smack into a white post and got most of the air knocked out of him. He collapsed to the ground, painfully gasping for air. Looked back toward the man's still-upturned face.

All he saw was the gaping, black hole where a *face* used to be . . . .

Grandpa Jonathan sat back in his rocker, the old wooden legs creaking almost as bad as his bones. Jonathan inhaled deeply from his pipe and eyed Randy intently. Randy sat before him, at his feet on the front porch steps, awaiting his reply.

"Well," Jonathan said slowly, drawing out another puff, "that certainly is a mighty tall tale you're tellin' me—"

"It's *true*, Granpa, it *is*—and I never went back there again! *Never!*"

"So what do you suppose you saw?"

Randy scrunched his face into a tight little knot. "I—I don't know. It was like . . . like something from a *horror* movie."

Grandpa Jonathan's rocker creaked louder, and he chuckled to himself.

"Well, Son, I don't pretend to know what it was you saw, but I'll tell you somethin that'll knock your socks clean off." Jonathan leaned forward and put his face right into Randy's. "*If you dare.*"

"I-if I *dare?* What do you mean? Is it a *story?*"

Grandpa Jonathan smiled, took another long drag from his pipe, and leaned back. He looked out beyond his porch front with a mischievous gleam in his eye, towards the town of Twin Falls, Indiana. It was late afternoon and twilight was fast approaching.

Götterdämmerung. Twilight of the Gods.

Or whatever forces that be.

"You know, when I was younger, I used to run a small theater up over t'Marion, and as I look back on things, I think it was my most favorite job of all time."

"Why was that, Granpa?"

"Because, Son, I was promotin' *imagination*. The ability to drift off for a period a time and pretend you were somewhere else. *Someone* else. To let the worries of the day disappear for a spell. The fifties were a great time, Randy. It was probably the most naive time in all of history. It was before Watergate, Vietnam—the Kennedy assassinations—"

"What?"

"They were times when the people of this country believed what they were told, lock, stock, and barrel—*without* question. Well, or they acted that way, anyway. They believed anything their governments told 'em, or their neighbors. Or their movie screens. No one doubted anything."

"So what's wrong with that?"

Grandpa Jonathan looked down into the still innocent eyes of his thirteen-year-old grandson. Smiled. Patted him on the head.

"Grandson, even though you should pay attention to your elders— your daddy, your mother—even your old fart of a grandfather—even though you should heed us all now, there will come a time when you'll begin to make your own way in the world. Start thinkin' your *own* thoughts. You'll wonder: why *should* I do somethin' this way or that. Why *can't* I do it my own way. Isn't there a better way to do things? You'll get married, have kids—"

"*Eeewww!* Never! I'm *never* going to get married! And I'm never going to leave you, Granpa!"

Grandpa Jonathan's face opened into a wider grin, and he laughed mightily.

"That's a good boy, Randy, a *good* boy!" He again patted Randy on the head. "But all this is nothin' to fret over just yet. You have so many things yet to explore. There's still so much wonder to this world, and you're only just discoverin' it.

"Now, Randy, I tell ya this, and hear my words, Son—*don't ever let that sense of wonder leave ya. Never.* Cause when it's gone, it's a mighty hard thing to get back, if ya ever can. There're a lot of wonderful and strange things out there, and as bad as some things might seem to get, there's always somethin better . . . just waitin' to be discovered. Waitin' for *you*, Randy, my boy! Life is what you *make* it . . . not what you have to put up with.

"Anyway, I digress—"

"What's that mean?"

"I strayed. When you get old, that tends to happen occasionally. It ain't nothin' to worry about cause it's just God's way a tellin' ya to take stock of your life. Make peace. Anyhow, there I go again. I was talkin' about theaters—"

"Yeah!"

"Movie theaters were great, but what I really wanted to get into were *drive-ins*."

"Drive-ins? Wow. Hey, you mean like—like the one I was at?"

"Just like, though they were still workin' and not nearly so nasty. At least not at first. I heard about these drive-ins and decided to get into em. They were new to me, in the business sense, even though they'd been around for some twenty years by then. There was money to be made. Besides, I just plain liked em. It's kinda hard to tell ya just why, but it was almost like they were an entire subculture—that's like another way of life within the life you're already livin'." He stopped and looked to Randy to see if what he'd said had sunk in.

"I don't quite understand, Granpa, but that's okay."

Jonathan smiled, and looked up . . . noticed that the sky had grown substantially darker. Twilight was indeed edging its way in, and he wanted to finish his story before it had gone completely dark.

"Drive-ins were hangouts, like Fremont Park in town, especially on the weekends. Guys would take their gals with em and make out, hardly ever really watchin' what was up on the

(*silver*)

"screens. Younger folks would come in droves and make a party of it—some gettin' up to some major mischief, like lettin' the air out of tires or tyin' cars up to each other. Sure, they caused folks some trouble, but it was a *fun* trouble, *fun* times. All us grownups would outwardly sneer and chastise em, but inwardly we wished we had done that stuff; that we were as carefree as they were. It was such an *innocent* time . . . ."

Jonathan's eyes glassed over as he looked out over the town behind Randy. Abruptly he came to, and continued.

"Well, one day, back round fifty-two, I believe, we had this tremendous wind storm. No rain, mind you, maybe even a little thunder, I can't quite remember, but I do recollect the *wind*. It damn near blew things halfway around to the other side of the world, we said. Blew the roofs right off half a dozen houses, it did—"

"Wow!"

"—and even toppled over some folks's cars. The Sheriff—Clyde Toupe, I believe his name was—was out that night, even against his own better judgment, he later said, and his department's car was blown clean over and right on down the street!"

"No way! Was he in it?"

"No, he said he had gotten out to check on somethin', and when he got back it wasn't there. Fightin' against the gale and holdin' on for dear life, he looks down the street and finds it, sittin' there on its hood, all smashed up and useless. It was spinnin' like a toy top—well, maybe I made up that last part!" he said, winking to Randy.

"Anyway, folks round them parts said it was the work of devil— or God, dependin' on how guilty they were feelin' at the moment. The non-guilty, they were sayin' it was God's way a tellin' us that we were gettin' too complacent—too used to the way things were. That we needed to take more stock in what was goin' on *around* us and not to be so concerned with just ourselves. Get our heads out of the sand. Others said it was the devil comin' to punish us for our transgressions—our evil-doin's.

"Well, in any case, the town set about the huge task of cleanin' up. Sheriff Toupe—I'm pretty sure that's what his name was—got a brand-spankin' new car. Huh—I remember how the kids were havin' a field day with no law bein' able to run em down for a week or two before Clyde got his new vehicle . . . well, he did have his own truck to use, but without a siren and official paint job, it just wasn't the same! And the neighbors, they'd helped each other out with repairs and losses and things. It was like small-town Marion had gone through a war, or somethin'."

"What happened to your theater, Granpa?"

"Eh, I was gettin' to that. Well, my theater house, the one in town, wasn't damaged much at all, 'cept for the marquee—the lights—but my drive-in, that was quite another story. It had rips down the screen and debris from the storm strung out all over the place. Many of the speaker posts were damaged. Speaker boxes had been ripped right from their posts. It took quite a while for repairs to be made, but repaired they were, and at great expense. But the strangest thing I found that day was this guy sittin' in the middle of my lot."

Randy stiffened.

"Just like yours, though he still had his face when I found him. But he was missin' somethin' *else*. Somethin' much more important. He was missin' his *mind.*"

Grandpa Jonathan paused again. Randy looked down to the porch where Grandpa's rocker met the floor.

"Granpa—"

"You don't get it, do ya, Son."

He shook his head.

"Well, neither did I. I mean, how does a man lose his *mind* . . . in a drive-in theater? Sure, we played them grade-B horror flicks back then, but nothin' *that* bad.

"Anyway, I helped him up and took him into my office. All the time, he's a mumblin' and a droolin', and, boy, did he stink!"

Randy giggled.

"I tried to talk with him, but he just wouldn't—or couldn't—come round. Since I didn't know much about those kinds of things, I called the Sheriff. I figured he'd know what to do with him. So I called him and told him that I had the mayor in my office, and that he wasn't quite right . . . .

"In the end, nothin' I could do to fix the theatre could keep it goin'. It took me several months to fix the tears in the screen, the damaged posts, and the projector. Everythin'. And then really weird stuff started happenin'."

"What kind of weird stuff, Granpa?"

"Well, stuff like the projector always goin' out on me. Electrical fires in the speaker boxes. People runnin' over the posts. Fights. There was even one day when I remember the popcorn machine explodin' all over the place—but by that time it was far from funny. It was like that storm had been an evil wind, blowin' up from old Scratch himself. People started actin' funny, too, Randy. They weren't themselves. Some began to blame it on my drive-in. Why me, I don't know, but they said they didn't come away from my movies feelin' right. Feelin' *right?*

"So I had to close down. No one was comin' to my movies and I was no longer makin' any money. I eventually had to sell it to a development firm and they had the old theater bulldozed within a month. I still had my other theater in town, but it wasn't where my heart was. When that place was plowed under, a little part of me went with it.

"But that wasn't all. There was even *weirder* stuff just beginnin'."

Randy shifted position on the porch steps.

Jonathan took a small sip from a glass Randy hadn't noticed was nearby. Randy noticed how Grandpa Jonathan suddenly became more serious. His gaze had again drifted off beyond him, and it took a few shakes on his sleeves before Randy got his grandfather to return to the story.

And twilight had arrived.

"Well, Son, *your* story, you believe it, don't you?"

Randy nodded. "Of course, Granpa—it really happened."

"Well, that's what I'm afraid of. You see, so did mine. And I think there's some sort of . . . connection . . . between our two experiences, though for the life of me I can't imagine what. I guess there are some things in this world that just happens to folks, see, some things that have no rhyme or reason. No explanation. Now what I'm about to tell you from here on in, I haven't ever told *anybody*—"

"Not even *gramma?*"

Jonathan's eyes glazed over and he shook his head heavily.

"No, Son, not even grandma, and as much as it hurt me to keep secrets from her, I'm glad she never knew. I been carryin' this thing around inside a me for quite some time, now, not even sure *I* believed it. Sometimes when you keep things in they have a way of gettin' warped. Growin'. But I don't think this did. I *know* it happened, just like you know what happened to you, happened.

Randy nodded, keeping his eyes on his grandfather.

"It had been a few months after the old theater'd been torn down, about midsummer, I think, and I was drivin' by it one

(twilight)

"evenin'. I hadn't even been payin' attention when I drove past the lot, hadn't been payin' attention when I saw the old silver screen standin' there before the mass of little white posts lookin' like a graveyard—and I can see by the look on your scrunched-up face that you don't understand. And, again, neither did I, cause, as I said only moments ago, *that there drive-in'd been torn down, screen and all, some four to six months* prior *to this little drive by of mine.*

"It didn't end there. No sirree. Sure, I stopped then, even backed up to the field and took another look. But don't you know it, it was gone. Of course it'd never been there. It was just the same old empty field waitin' for some new development. There were no screen, no posts—no *nothin'*. But it had happened again, and again after that. It got so that I wouldn't drive by on that road anymore cause on almost every twilit evenin', I'd *see* it.

"Then one day, toward the end of summer, it had been a real scorcher, and I wasn't thinkin' straight. Nobody was. It was hotter than even old Eddie from down to the railroad could recall. Three folks from up to the old folks' home had died by the end of that summer from heat stroke. And, old habits dyin' hard, I found myself drivin' by that hellish place after it had grown dark. Man, even my soul was sweatin', and that ain't no lie!

"And there it was, boy, was it. That bedeviled drive-in was astandin' tall and proud. And it was *cold*. I remember that, cold as ice it were, and it chilled me right to my bones. And this time, it was worse. Worse than worse. *The damned theater was in full-on operation,* Randy. *Full-on—lights, movie, and* people!

"*No way!*" Randy said, inching closer to his grandfather.

"I stopped my car at the entrance—the old entrance exactly where it was before the place had been torn down—and parked. I was shakin' like a leaf in winter, but I got out and stood there. Riveted. There was a *movie* playin', Randy. Cars were parked. People were watchin' it, buyin' popcorn. And it wasn't a horror show, or anything like that. Nope. It wasn't anything close to a movie you'd expect to be playin' at a place like that, weirdness or not. No sir. The movie what was playin' was *Bambi*, for Jesus, Joe, and Mike! *Bambi*.

"Well, I was scared stiff. Couldn't move if I'd wanted to. But, boy, I had to. *Had* to. I had to see what was goin' on, even if the devil himself were in the projection booth. *I had to see.*

"So I entered the drive-in.

"I walked right up to the ticket booth and there was some young girl in there I'd never seen before, same girl whose face I still see in my nightmares. She just waves me on through, like she's been waitin' for me. And she smiles a smile that ain't quite right. It's still the same smile I see in those nightmares of mine. Somethin' about her face. Her *smile*. It was like her face was heavily blemished, you know, with zits 'n stuff, but worse. There was creepy crawly things that seemed to move about around inside them zits, her skin—but when you looked to them, focused on them, no movement. And when she smiled, heck, I don't know, but her mouth . . . it was only partially opened . . . but, I swore the inside of her mouth was *pure black*—like there was *nothin' inside*.

"So in I walk, and on played *Bambi*. Everywhere around me were cars, and folks doin' stuff. And none of it was right, either. There was a feelin' to everythin' that was cold and empty. I looked back to my car and saw it parked there by the roadside, but it didn't comfort me any. I felt like a prisoner, trapped behind bars, my life just outside and starin' back in on me, tauntin' me.

"*But I had to know.*

"I don't know how long I stayed there, but I gradually noticed somethin' that scared me even more. As I looked up to the screen and saw them little animated cartoon characters, I saw that even Bambi was queer.

"But why shouldn't it be? Nothin' in that place was right, so why should the movie be any different?

"Then it hit me and my legs ran out from under me like cooked spaghetti, and I collapsed. I looked up to the screen, I looked up and I saw that those animated characters weren't the animated animals I was used to, no—*they were people I knew from town*. All of 'em. Their faces caricatured up there on the screen, and by the Lord in heaven, it was them, right down to the crazy mayor!"

Randy jerked back, a cold blast washing over him.

"I lost it. I couldn't take it no longer. I screamed—I cried—I came unglued.

"I fell to the ground and slammed my fists into it, and when I opened my eyes . . .

"When I opened my eyes, it was gone. All of it. Every stinkin' piece. I was prone in the middle of this empty field bawlin' to myself and my car was parked not fifty feet away, engine runnin'. How I must've looked to any passersby!

"So I tried to get away, tried to get away as far as I could from Marion and this state, but somethin' held me prisoner. Held others, too. Made me forget my wants and desires. We were changin', it seemed, *distortin'*. Or maybe it was just me, lookin' at everyone else who was changin'. A Post Office or somethin' was later built up on that property, but it didn't matter. You see, when twilight came and you looked close—*real* close—you could almost see them. The people. The screen. *Everythin'*.

"So when you came in here and told me your story, hell, I had to tell mine, Randy, because I wonder if maybe, just maybe, this thing is the same thing that happened to *you*. Maybe it's comin' for me after all these years, after the ones it didn't get the first time, if that was the first time. Maybe it's just somethin' that happens to old theaters after they go away. I don't know. See, Randy, drive-ins have *magic*, and when someone takes away the buildin's and the screens—the speaker boxes—they can't take away the *magic*. It's somethin that lingers on . . . hangs in the air. Maybe it comes with the land . . . and hopefully it's a *good* magic. But I think every place is different. Did you know that at one time Twin Falls had six drive-ins in town?"

"Six? Really?"

"Sure. They done been torn down and built over, like the one I told you about, but they were there. In fact one of em's an apartment complex that you'll be passin' by as you go back into town—which, I might add, you better do if you don't want to get a whoopin'! Will ya look at the time! Randy-boy, you just let your old grandfather ramble on, now, didn't you!"

"It's okay, Granpa, I don't mind!"

"Sure, but the light is fadin' and you need some to make your way back. So git—tell your folks hello for me, and don't mind the ramblin's of an old coot! I'll call your folks to let em know you're on your way. I'm goin' to get my own woopin' from em for sure!"

"Oh, Granpa—"

"Now I mean it, so git—and, Randy—"

Grandpa Jonathan's face grew stern and took on a more concerned look.

"Be careful."

"I will, Granpa!"

Randy hopped up on his purple BMX, turned it around, and headed back towards town. He waved to his grandfather as he left, but the words still ran around in his head.

If you look close, real *close . . .*

You can almost see them . . .

Then Randy remembered the face he had seen at his drive-in. The black, nothing face that stared up at him and mumbled. Empty words from an empty face. Randy suddenly wondered why he had not asked

Grandpa if he could stay the night. It was Friday, there was no school tomorrow.

But he was already on his way home and Grandpa was calling his folks.

You could almost see them . . .

Randy pedaled straight home. His parents were waiting for him and immediately set to the task of scolding him for riding his bike so late—and didn't he know he could get killed? And what was your grandfather filling your head with this time? And don't you respect us? Do you want to die, is that it? Now go to your room, mister, and there'll be no supper for you tonight. But all this fell upon deaf ears, because Randy was too busy reliving everything his grandfather had told him. So, he gladly went to his room, gladly plopped down on his bed, and gladly tucked his arms up high behind his head.

Imagining.

Randy stared into the ceiling and wondered about what was real and what wasn't, and as he fell off into a troubled sleep he swore he heard the wind pick up. Swore he could hear it flipping over cars and knocking over buildings . . . .

The devil's wind.

Saturday mornings were great after the chores got done, but instead of going over to Todd Bearing's house afterwards (which was where he told his parents he was going to spend the night), Randy decided on other plans. He didn't feel right. His experience from the other day, as well as all that stuff his grandpa had told him, sat in his gut like a belly full of candy.

And there *had* been high winds last night.

It hadn't damaged things as much as in Grandpa Jonathan's story, but it had made a bit of a mess. Randy wanted to go back to that drive-in, to the one he knew . . . but was scared. What if that guy was still there—or another replaced him, even more worse than the first?

What if he went there . . . *and never came back?*

He knew what he had to do.

He had to go back. Had to *see.*

Had to.

Even if the devil himself was in the projection booth.

It was about an hour away from sunset, according to the Weather Channel, as he pedaled up the small (boy-it-didn't-*feel*-like-it) hill to where the abandoned drive-in was. He passed the sign that said it was to be replaced by an office complex of some kind.

An office complex.

What a bummer. Granpa said there used to be six of these things in town, and now there was only one. One drive-in. That sucked. He hoped there'd be plenty when he grew up so he could enjoy them. That subculture thing.

Armed with comic books and Mountain Dew, he braked his bike to a stop. There it was, just as he had left it. With one exception.

Nobody was sitting in the middle of it.

Randy walked his bike through the rows of upright posts, up towards the rear of the lot, and thought it did remind him more of a graveyard than a drive-in. He looked back over it. White posts, everywhere. Like gravestones. And that silver screen. Empty. Like one *huge* gravestone.

Grandpa and his stories.

He tried to imagine what this place was like during its heyday—cars packed in, music piped over the speakers, folks camped out in their cars . . . the back of their trucks . . . with pillows and blankets. Older kids necking. He had seen some of this from the one remaining drive-in in town, but not here. There was none of that here now.

Hello, Randy.

He thought back to the bum. The faceless one.

Chicken skin.

If you look close, Randy, really *close . . . .*

Shuddering, Randy turned away from the posts and took off his pack. He pulled out his comic books, can of Mountain Dew, and settled down on the ground.

And waited.

For what, he didn't really know. He just knew something was going to happen and he needed to see it. Maybe it was a movie. Maybe it was—

Randy's heart froze. At the opposite end of the theater grounds where he had entered the lot, he saw movement. He dropped his comic book and nearly spilled over his soda.

"Oh, no . . . ."

But it wasn't *that* man. That evil, *non-faced* thing that had mumbled out of a non-existent mouth . . . no, this was somebody different. Somebody *with* a face.

Quietly, Randy watched as the faced intruder came into the center of the lot and sat down—almost at the exact spot where Randy had last seen the other.

This new guy either hadn't seen him—or didn't care—because he

never looked away from the screen. The torn and ripped
(*silver*)
screen.

Then came another.

And another.

All with faces . . . all to stare at the huge gravestone before them.

Randy got up and backed away from the sudden rush of people, but only ended up running into two others who came in from behind. It was like the Night of The Living Dead, for crying out loud. Unperturbed, they all continued on down towards the center of the lot. Randy continued backing up and finally hit against the rickety perimeter theater fence behind him. He stood with his mouth open . . . and stared.

There must've been a *hundred* of them.

"No way. This can't be. I'm seeing things."

The sun had now set and began to cast its blood-red rays across the landscape. Rays that painted the screen, the rips and tears standing out even more, like poorly healed scar tissue. Red that flowed over the people and the white posts. All attention was focused on the
(*silver*)
now red
screen.

The pilgrimage had stopped, but not the red.

It was no longer merely a redness-of-twilight that simply colored things, but an integral part of the objects it touched.

The post.

The screen.

The bodies.

The very air.

Everything was aglow with vermilion. And it took on a life of its own. Randy could see the pulsation. It was in everything.

And still the masses waited . . . .

Randy knew by now that twilight must surely have ended, but in the deserted lot of the Peak View Drive-In, it had not. It had become its own little world. Twilight remained. Blood remained.

Had to see.

Randy pushed away from the fence and slowly made his way forward.

If you look close, real *close, Randy-boy, you can see—*

Randy entered the crowd.

Each individual's attention was anchored to the movie screen before them, their faces blank. Many mumbled, and a humming sound resonated just above them. As he looked around, Randy noticed something else. These people weren't bums or vagrants, at least not all of them. Many were dressed in fine clothes with shaven or make-upped faces. Some looked like they had just come from previous engagements. Randy reached out.

"Ma'am, are you

(*faceless*)

"all right?"

He touched the woman. She gave a little under his touch, but remained faced-forward. Blank. Red pulsated through her.

A sound came over the speakers and Randy jumped.

It was everywhere, echoing in deep throbbing notes that sounded more like the noise blood might make if its sound was amplified. Randy tested several others and got the same responses.

Nothing.

Just the sound of pumping blood.

Randy looked back to his

(*car*)

bike and found it gave him no comfort.

"I feel . . . I feel like I'm . . . *repeating* . . . something here . . . ."

Then his eyes landed on something so familiar that his insides went loose.

Grandfather Jonathan.

"*NO!*"

Randy sprinted across the crowd to Jonathan when the silver-red screen erupted into a blinding fury, knocking him off his feet. He careened into several posts. They were cold. *Burning* cold. The ground rumbled. Randy lifted his head and looked to the screen. It was a liquid red and pulsed in time with everything else. Vibrant colors danced across its canvas, like the 60's backdrops he'd seen on TV.

Randy looked back to his grandfather and saw he was still there. It was no illusion, no case of mistaken identity. Randy picked himself up and again lurched forward, knocking past others who merely righted themselves and returned their attention back to the screen. The rumbling in the ground nauseated Randy, vibrated parts of him he didn't realize he had.

"Granpa! Granpa!" he screamed, and reached out. He shook his grandfather's shoulders, but found the same reaction he'd gotten from everybody else.

"Granpa—*speak* to me! Come out of it, damn it!"

Randy came around to the front of him and blocked Jonathan's view of the screen. Randy found he had to step wide to keep his balance from the upheaving ground and saw how slowly it took Grandpa to focus on him. Jonathan turned away from the screen only enough to look up into Randy's face.

"Granpa—*speak to me!*"

Again Randy grabbed his grandfather's shoulders and shook him.

"They've . . . found me . . . Son," Jonathan said slowly, dreamily.

"*Who* found you?"

Jonathan spoke slowly, returning his forward focus.

"Don't know . . . *what* . . . they're called," he said, " . . . but . . . they fill . . . a void."

"Granpa—I don't understand—"

The vibration grew and Randy fell to his knees. Jonathan focused back on the screen.

"They come . . . at intervals . . . but not of *time* . . . ."

Randy saw reflections from the screen behind him change and turned to look at it.

The screen had changed.

It had somehow become *more*, and it hurt him to look at it. He felt his eyes trying to pop free from their sockets . . . felt his mind expand, almost painfully. The screen took on a three-dimensional depth. *More* dimensional. There was something within it—

Something was trying to get out.

"Granpa!"

" . . . it is a cycle . . . of *emotion*. Not time. Comes not . . . for everybody . . . but for those . . . ready . . . to . . . to accept it."

Randy looked around and saw that the people remained seated on the ground, but they took on a different look. Back at the screen, there were swirling colors . . . a kaleidoscope of images . . . some of which Randy found hard to focus on or make out. He turned back to Jonathan.

"Granpa, I don't want to lose you!" he shouted, "I *love* you!"

Jonathan turned back to him.

"Is . . . too late, Son." He turned back to the screen. "It . . . transfers . . . to others. Continues its journey . . . through others. Fills . . . the void . . . that exists *within* . . . ."

Grandpa Jonathan had faded out. His face appeared different, like those around him. At first Randy thought it was just the light, but it was more.

Then something clicked inside Randy's head: *transferred?*

Was *he* the one being transferred *to?*

The screen went dead. The pulsating had now become more of a subtle thrumming.

COME, RANDY

Randy spun around, almost pulling a neck muscle. It was a voice—he'd heard it—a deep, resonating voice that came from behind him.

From the screen.

"Who's there?"

No response.

"Who's there—why are you *doing* this?"

The screen remained dead.

Then it went white, like before a movie is brought up onto its surface. Randy watched. Watched as the people around him reacted to the blank screen. Watched as some cried and some laughed, while others had still other reactions . . . .

Randy looked to the person sitting next to his grandfather and saw a wide-eyed look that scared him. The person's eyes were screaming from their sockets, but no scream came from her mouth. As Randy looked closer, he saw a thin red line trickle out from her eyes, mixing with her tears. Randy turned away.

Another laughed hysterically, like a crazily stuck record.

Another had a more passionate, heady expression.

Then he turned back to his grandfather—

Whose face was fading.

Randy came closer and again grabbed Jonathan's shoulders. His face quickly began to fade from view. Taking another glance behind him, Randy saw that the screen was no longer white, but black.

Full of stars.

Cold, empty, *traveling* stars.

Randy shivered. Turned back to his grandfather. Grandpa Jonathan's face now had that same blackness—

And the stars.

The entire lot was in darkness.

"*Granpa! Don't go!*"

Jonathan's face swirled . . . folded in and out of itself.

Flipped, spiraled, and split.

Randy felt his eyes again pull out from their sockets, his mind again having difficulty focusing . . . understanding. He felt groggy. Found he had to brace himself away from his grandfather for fear of *falling into him.*

"*Granpa, no—don't go—I don't want you to die!*"

We all have to die sometime, Randy, it's a fact of life. This is how I choose to go.

Randy backed away.

"Why are you doing this?" Randy asked, "why did you drag me into all this?"

Because you are a part of me, a part of us all
We need to continue
To be remembered
To die
It is this emotion which is needed to
Continue
This bond

"You're not my grandfather!"

NO

Randy watched as his grandfather's face further dissolved and finally melted away.

Inward. Outward. Around itself.

Watched as his face became like the man's face he had seen that morning a thousand-million years ago. Watched as the face he had kissed and so loved over his thirteen years slowly and quietly disappeared.

Black and starry.

Gone.

If you look real *close* . . . .

Randy felt his grandfather depart . . . disappear. Watched as he hunched forward like the faceless one he had encountered. Watched as he felt the presence that had once been Jonathan Thornton quietly expel like a gentle, worn sigh . . . .

Randy didn't bother to lift his head. He knew what he'd find.

Randy felt unexpectedly emotionless as he backed away from the shell of his grandfather and returned to his bike. He looked to the others, but saw there weren't as many of them as there had been before. He watched as some faded away before his eyes . . . one by one . . . like stars snuffed out by a rising sun . . . while others . . . like candles in the wind . . . were simply *just not there anymore*. He looked back to his grandfather just as he, too, was gently snuffed away . . .

Randy picked up his bike and brought it around. The lot was nearly empty now. The sun was rising, and he was exhausted. He went towards the outer edge of the lot, but didn't want to go anywhere near the center of that sea of posts. Instead he faced east, where morning blood stained the horizon.

This he welcomed.

And as he turned around, Randy felt a *something* trying to edge its way into his head, and he groped for it.

Like a warm wave, it engulfed him.

IT IS THE PRICE TO BE PAID FOR YOUR SENSE OF WONDER

Sense of wonder.

He wasn't sure he understood it all, but Randy felt sure he understood one thing. One day, far into his own adult future, he, too, would have to pay that price.

And as he looked back to the lot on his way out, he suddenly felt exhilarated. There was one individual still sitting in the middle of the lot. One still seated in that familiar, hunched over and silent position.

Randy smiled.

Clowns

1987

The stuffed effigy sat there . . . sat . . . and plotted.

It had waited long enough . . . been *patient* enough . . . but now was time for action.

Sitting on the edge of the chest-of-drawers dresser next to the closet and surrounded by other clowns, its unmoving and painted face was set in a near-cruel mockery of a grin. Its brightly adorned and sparkly purple jester's outfit shimmered in the moonlight. It turned its fabric head to the boy, the lone bell on one of its multiple jester hat spikes jingling. The clown reached down to the drawer immediately below it and pulled it open.

It lifted its grinning head in a sharp, twisted jerk to make sure the boy was still asleep.

Pulling open the drawer more, it looked down into it and reached around until it found what it was looking for. Lifted its head once more to check on the boy.

Asleep.

The clown withdrew the shiny razor-sharp kitchen blade and brought it up to its face, turning and twisting it a few times in the moonlight.

Very nice.

Cackling, it launched itself off the dresser's edge, waving the blade in playful swoops as it sailed through the night air. The clown hit the floor with a soft thud, the knife tip bouncing off the floor in its double-fisted hold. Bells jingling, the clown gleefully advanced toward the bed.

At the bed it continued to restlessly twist the gleaming steel in its tiny clown hands as it looked for a way up. Like a drunken marionette, the clown chuckled and shifted its weight between its feet.

Waved the blade before him like a triumphant Zorro.

Began climbing.

"*Kill, kill, kill! Kill, kill, kill,*" it merrily sang as it made its way up the mattresses, "*All to myself, I slash his neck! All to myself, I gut this wreck! Kill, kill, kill—hee, hee, hee! Kill! Kill! KILL! Hee! Hee! HEE!*"

Reaching the top of the bed, the clown straightened itself up and stood there. Slashed at the air with the knife. Watched the boy.

How relaxed he looked.

"*Not for much looongerrr . . . ,*" the clown said, wildly brandishing its blade as it made its stiff-legged and awkward way across the rumpled sheets.

From all sides of the bed, other clowns began clumsily pouring up and over the top of the bed. They carried nails and straight pins, knives and forks. Pens and pencils. Large tacks . . . and one, a straightened paper clip.

"*Kill! Kill! Kill! Hee-hee-HEE!*"

Shouting at the top of its little fabric lungs and viciously stabbing into the air before him, the jester and his clowns lunged at the now awakened boy, who opened his eyes just in time to see

Steven jolted upright in bed.

Hyperventilating and running his legs wildly, sweat poured off him in sheets. He strained his gaze through the moonlit darkness. He'd felt what felt like little kitty paws all over him. But they didn't own a cat.

His stuffed purple clown still sat on the edge of his chest-of-drawers dresser with the rest of the mutiny of clowns.

It sat slightly canted . . . the single bell dangling from one spike of its tiny clown hat—

Did it move? Had that bell just moved?

The sound of his Big Ben wind-up clock tick-tocked away bedside. 12:30 a.m.

The clown sat there . . . its painted and grinning face aglow in the moonlight.

No, it hadn't moved. *None* of them had moved.

No, there was no blood.

And, yes, he—*Steven*—was very much alive.

It had all been a dream . . . a bad dream.

Getting out of bed, Steven turned on his light. He'd seen enough horror movies to know that you *always* turn on the lights after nightmares . . . if you wanted to live.

He surveyed his room, checked under his bed . . . checked to make sure that his other clowns and toys were all where they should be—

Where they should be.

Like they could *move?*

He went to the purple jester.

Stared at it.

It stared back.

(hee HEE!)

Steven pulled open the top dresser drawer. Keeping his eyes on the smiling clown, he positioned his head over the drawer, quickly stole a look inside—then back to the clown.

Empty.

At least empty of any kitchen knives.

There was only his underwear and socks in the drawer, more dangerous than any known weapon, according to his parents.

It *was* only a dream.

He snatched all the clowns and swiftly stuffed them into the drawer, slamming it shut.

Stared at the drawer.

Shrugging his shoulders, he grimaced and returned to bed.

Turned off the light.

Dreams, he thought, *who needs them!*

Steven closed his eyes and quickly drifted back to sleep . . . .

Beneath the dresser, a strand of purple fiber was caught on the wooden handle of a razor-sharp kitchen knife.

Freefallin'

2004

"Crazy my ass," Ronny Flynn hissed, as he hurtled his body out of the Beech 18 at 20,000 feet. The day was gorgeous, with puffy, billowy cumulus clouds set against an intense, deep blue sky. Skipping the standard arch, Ronny set himself rigid as a board and angled his head downward, trying to escape the other jumpers as quickly as possible.

I'll show them who's crazy!

Arms tucked tight against his body and legs together, Ronny shot like a bullet for the ground.

Just because his wife had perished in a skydiving accident on this date last year, and that he swore he kept hearing her voice since then didn't mean he was crazy. Just because he kept having dreams about her did not mean he was insane. Just because—several times, mind you—he'd remarked to others how he couldn't always tell fantasy from reality . . . tell real life from a dream . . . did *not* mean he had to be locked up. Many times he'd sworn he was dreaming, but was actually fully awake . . . or thought Angela was still alive, because—in his dreams—she *was*. It was other people who kept bringing him down, bursting his bubbles. People dreamed about their dear departed all the time and were never declared crazy. Why was he any different?

Oh, right . . . something about his friends meeting him in a restaurant while he kept insisting Angela was just visiting the Ladies Room and would be returning any time now . . . .

Well, what did they know.

Why, they'd seen her auger in, is what; they all had.

Angela *wasn't* in the Ladies Room and she wasn't ever coming back, and he'd better seek help or they'd be forced to take more drastic measures, they told him on more than one occasion.

No, he would not allow himself to be locked up. Would *not*.

But he kept insisting that he saw her everywhere . . . and that had led to the intervention . . . the psychiatrist. Those words—not from the doc, that wouldn't have been professional—but he knew he was *thinking* them. Of course he was, or else he wouldn't have had to come back. Again and again and

Crazy?

He'd show them!

Glancing to his altimeter, Ronny angled toward a bank of clouds. Sport rules declared skydivers had to be able to see their drop zone and had to avoid jumping through clouds.

But he tired of rules.

Ronny disappeared into the cloud.

Whether because he was lost in his thoughts . . . or the pleasantly vertigo-inducing complete whiteness enveloping him . . . Ronnie lost track of exactly when he was promptly smacked—*hard*—in the gut . . . and bounced off something that couldn't—*mustn't* be—

Solid.

Not once . . . but twice.

Found himself abruptly sliding down the length of the inside of the cloud's bright white, homogenous interior, his hands and arms up and out before him like he was still falling. He slid for what seemed an eternity before coming to

A stop.

Either out of the built-in fear-response habit or reflex he jerked the ripcord. The parachute popped out of his rig . . . then gently fell into a pile on the cloud stuff around him. He watched as cloud fog calmly swirled up and around his deflated chute.

Ronny lay there on his stomach . . . arms outstretched before him . . . mouth open and eyes wide. His senses told him he'd stopped moving . . . but his mind—his inner equilibrium—told him he *had* to still be falling.

Had to.

He was (again, looking to his altimeter) still at 15,000 feet, but was, indeed, *no longer moving*. He should be screaming earthward at 120 miles an hour. Should still hear the howl of the wind in his ears, feel it against his body. Should feel his face contorted by the pummeling airspeed. He flicked his altimeter several times, but nothing changed, and he realized that though it was as if he was lying on his stomach, he was still able to easily reach beneath himself as if he weren't. Frantic, Ronny shot his arms beside him, pulled them in tight against his sides, sending more puffs of cloud vapor dancing up around him.

Yelled out.

Nothing.

Still lying still on his stomach.

Nervously, he shot up to a one-kneed kneeling position.

He mentally tried to retrace his actions and reach out to the exterior of the cloud—to what he knew existed *out there*, outside all of this blinding white that surrounded (and now, somehow, *supported*) him. His surroundings looked exactly like common ground fog—key word *ground*. Solidity was now where it should never be. He should still be hurtling earthward by force of gravity, dammit, not suspended in the stuff of dreams and insanity.

Crazy?

He'll show—

He again smacked his gloved hands down beside him, but they still did not pass through the vaporous moisture, hitting soft, enigmatic solidity. More swirls of cloud mist puffed up around him.

"No-no-no-no-*no*. This can't *be* . . . ."

Ronny shot to both feet—cautiously crouched—hands out before him like a man trying to balance on the razor's edge of fantasy and reality.

Any moment, now . . . any moment . . . and he would continue on his downward journey. He shot a look to his deployed chute to make sure it was not tangled. Glanced warily about him. Felt the sweat, cold and copious, begin to pour out of him like a squeezed sponge.

This was scary.

Jumping out of a plane with a parachute was nothing. But this . . . *this* scared the crap out of him. His entire body trembled, and he took several furtive steps about his position, circling and staring down at the damned white "surface" upon which he stood.

(*not falling!*)

"Oh, my God . . . ."

Clumsily, he again spun around, got tangled in his deployed chute's lines and looked to them. They didn't dangle beneath him, but also appeared held up by whatever buoyed him. He checked his harness. All still good; nothing loose. He felt for his reserve chute; still there, of course, but, why wouldn't it be? The only thing missing from this equation was sanity. He slowly stood fully upright, lowered his arms, and again stomped about in a tight circle. Again, more puffs of vapor *but still no falling.*

He was undeniably stopped dead in mid-air.

It was all white, blinding white, and he could actually see the cloud particles drifting about before him. Feel their moisture kissing his face, even beginning to fog up his goggles—which he couldn't quite bring himself to remove.

Tentatively, he stuck out his feet—one, then the other—and edged his way forward. Where, he had no idea, it was all white. All . . . eerily solid. Cushiony, but solid. He was expecting Rod Serling to step out before him any moment now with that sardonic smirk, taking a puff on his cigarette as he introduced him to his world and welcome to it.

"This is stupid . . . this can't be happening," he said. "I *have* to be falling, *have* to still be in descent . . . this-this—it must be hypoxia, that's all—"

But, he thought, *if this is the case, then . . . then, what if I don't open my chute? What if I don't see the ground coming, because it's one looow cloud . . . and I won't break out until 500 feet? The automatic activation device . . . the AAD'll open my chute at 1300. I'll be fine. But what about . . .* what about . . . .

All this?

How could any of this be even remotely possible? Even clouds don't go on forever . . . he simply had to keep walking until he found the end of it, then, what . . . *jump?*

But if he found himself where he presently was, what made him think he'd ever find an end to this freaky affair?

Ronny popped the harness's D-rings to his main chute and released it, then sprinted into an all-out run. He closed his eyes, held his breath—and leapt.

And once again landed hard on his stomach, again knocking the air out of him.

Maybe I'm just too messed up, maybe they were all right and I am crazy—and I'm actually still hurtling toward the ground right this second and just don't realize it—

Ronny stared into the swirling cloud.

"This can't be . . . it's all got to be a dream, that's all it is—I'm dreaming again . . . ."

Ronny was not much of one to scare easily, but taking off his rig to repack his chute—*here*—gave him the heebie-jeebies like nobody's business. He pictured himself still falling out of the sky, hypoxic, and those on the ground observing his flailing body as he tried to remove himself from his rig. It sent shivers all through him, made his palms sweat, and his gut clench.

What if—

But, he'd decided, what difference would it make?

If he really was crazy and he really was still falling, then he'd never know it, would he? He didn't know it, now, did he? Well, there you go.

And if he *wasn't* hurtling earthward and really was . . . *here* . . . then he'd better either repack it or forget about it, and since he was fifteen grand into the air (or *somewhere*) why not at least go through the motions— even if it all turned out to be some hypoxic mental aberration . . . or all in the dreamworld.

In other words, *enjoy* the crazy.

Ronny took off his rig, laid it on the fluffy white firmament, and went about the task of collecting and repacking his—

"*Ronny?*"

The voice came soft and sweet . . . like it always did.

"What do you want," he asked, continuing to pack his chute without looking up.

"This really is real, you know. All of it."

"Yeah, right. I'm just having another dream. A nightmare—and you're part of it. All in my head. Can't tell reality from fantasy anymore. Have a recent history of it, you know."

He carefully placed the refolded chute back into the pack. Avoided looking the voice in its face.

"But, I'm real, too. And I'm right here."

Ronny chuckled. "Now, tell me, how can I *really* believe that? I can't believe anything anymore. I mean, *look* at me! I'm putzing around inside a frigging *cloud*, for chrissakes, my cheeks should be flapping in the breeze!"

"But I'm right here. Look at me. *See* me."

Ronny looked up. Saw her. Or at least a shadowy outline of her obscured by the cloud fog. She came closer.

"This doesn't mean anything, you know," Ronny lied. He felt the tears. Always the tears. "I dream of you every night. *See* you every night."

"But this is different, honey, this isn't a dream. I'm right *here*."

Ronny chuckled, just about to expel a sarcastic comeback, when he froze as Angela emerged from the cloud vapor to stand directly before him. She was as he always saw her—only better. Ronny came to his feet. He could smell that hint of *Red* she always wore when she wasn't going gonzo. And she had that little scar she earned from rock climbing above her left eyebrow, which he never seemed to notice during his dreams. And—by God—her freckles, her cute little *freckles* were even there, another thing overlooked in his dreams.

Angela reached down and took his hand. Squeezed it.

"See, silly, I'm *real*. I'm really here, not like in your dreams— though, to tell the truth, they did keep me alive. This time this *isn't* a dream . . . it isn't all in your head—I really am standing before you . . .

and I really am real."

"How—"

"I can't explain it, honey, I only know that I exist. Here, now. I don't fight it and neither should you. Just give in to it—us—before whatever did this and put us together takes it away . . . okay?"

Those pleading eyes, that heart-wrenching voice . . . .

Angela came in closer, bringing him to his feet and took both his hands into hers. She planted the softest, most loving kiss on his lips. He could smell her, dammit, smell her and *feel* her. And those sensations brought back all the longing and emotion that had been so severely cut off during that—that *day* . . . .

Angela shook her head, placing a gentle hand to his. "Don't think about that."

"But . . . *why?*"

"Honey . . . you know why . . . please, don't make me talk about it. It doesn't matter anymore. You've more than made up for it, now."

"But, why did you have to kill yourself? We could have worked things out . . . gone back to therapy. If I'd known how badly it'd affected—"

Angela smiled quietly. "You know yourself better than anyone else. Would that have worked? Honestly? You've always philandered. Nothing made you stop—until that day. I was the closest thing that kept you even close to honest—and I cherished every moment of our time together—like I do, now. Please . . . all that's *over*. You're a new person, now. A *better* one."

Ronny collapsed to his knees, sobbing. Angela knelt down beside him and cradled him in her arms.

"I really don't know what to tell you, honey," Angela said, "I'm also deeply sorry about what I did. If I had the chance to do things over, I'd do it all differently. Two wrongs don't make a right. But I loved you *so* much, so damned intensely that I didn't want to live if I couldn't have you totally, body *and* soul. The way you'd behaved was wrong . . . vile . . . and I should've left you . . . but I didn't—well, actually, I *did* . . . .

"Look, we're here . . . *now* . . . please, let's not waste this time by reopening old wounds. I don't know how else to impress this upon you. *Look at me.* Love me—*now*. Let's no longer waste the time we now have together . . . ."

Ronny and Angela walked hand in hand through the swirling cloud bank, Ronny, his rig now packed and carelessly slung over a shoulder.

"So, that's all you've been doing since . . . ?"

Angela nodded, guiltily. "Yes. I've been reliving our lives over and over; my death, over and over. Emotionally trying to will things differently. Like you and your dreams. A couple of times I found other threads . . . probabilities . . . in which I pulled that ripcord, but they still never turned out to change the past I had already created in that life. It's your dreams . . . your emotion and love . . . that keeps pulling me back . . . to you. Sometimes your emotion is so strong *I* don't even know where I am. It . . . clouds my mind, I guess you could say. And then . . . one moment—because there is no time where I am—I find myself here. *You* here."

Ronny smiled, tears filling his eyes, his face red and hot. He squeezed her hand harder. Felt the warmth of her palms. "Good God, why do we create so many needless problems for ourselves? I am so sorry for everything—*everything*—I've ever done. I am so sorry you've had to relive all those moments of ours—I don't *ever* want to live without you again!"

"But you *must*. It isn't your time yet. You have to continue on with your own life, with the past we've created, the both of us. When it is your time, I'll be there—*know* this!"

"But, what about all this? If we can do this now, might it mean we're meant to be together? That we can be together, again—forever?"

"But at what price? How long will it last? I feel . . . something strange . . . about everything . . . unfinished. Like I said, sometimes your emotion is so strong, I get confused about whether or not I'm really dead. You're so strong and you don't even realize it. But no emotion—none—can ever be maintained forever. Eventually, it tires, exhausts itself out, gets . . . diverted. Just like life everything *dies*. Sometimes I feel that maybe—maybe you should let *me* die—"

Angela choked off and stopped walking. Ronny stopped and turned to her, taking her sobbing form into his arms.

"How can something so real as this—even if so utterly unbelievable—not be true? Not be *lasting*? I can feel the hotness of your cheek, your tears, smell the sweetness of your breath. Your skin. I may have been diverted before, but this . . . *this* is different. I refuse to believe that this cannot survive the moment. That we can't make it survive forever. I refuse! *I will not lose you again!*"

Ronny buried his face into her neck and hair, his gear falling into the mist at their feet. Just before he closed his eyes he had an instant's surge of panic—that his rig had actually, finally, fallen through the cloud and he was left without it, holding onto his dead wife, three miles into the air with nothing more than his imagination—

But did he really care?

No.

If he couldn't live with her why live at all? She had enough guts to at least do what she did—*why couldn't he?*

He closed his eyes and let go . . . and all was right with the world. He once more held his loving, precious wife tightly in his arms. Felt their love for each other intertwine in ways he'd never experienced before. If he truly had gone off the deep end, then he never wanted to know about it. Never wanted to wake up. Never wanted to leave this cloud—be it in his imagination . . . or reality.

Ronny sobbed uncontrollably into Angela.

"So . . . what do we do now?" he asked, as they both sat beside each other in the swirling mists. "Do we know how long we've been here?"

"I don't know, hon. I just know I'm happy to be with you, again. I love you so much. I was so lonely. So angry. Missed you like I'd never, ever missed you before, even though I know there's this bright light out there waiting for me. I just can't go to it. Yet. I don't know how long all this lasts, but I never want it to go away. I'd gladly wait an eternity for you."

"I'd rather die and be with you now than go back."

Angela smiled.

"What? What's this?" he asked, as he hit something in the vapor. "Oh, my God—my rig. How'd that get here? I left it way over—well, wherever."

Angela looked at it. "You knooow," she said in a playful lilt, "I always used to think you looked quite sexy in your gear."

"You did?"

"You knew that. I told you all the time."

Ronny smiled sweetly. "I'm just playing."

"Hey—why don't you put it on, again . . . one more time?"

"I don't really care to."

"Oh, come on . . . just once more. Then you can toss it over the side. Forever. You'll never need it again, you know, if you stay here. Humor me. Goggles and all."

"Could we, *you* know . . . if I do this?"

Angela, smiled coyly. "May-beee . . . ."

Ronny found all his gear in a pile beside him. Something felt different about reaching for the equipment this time, but he did it anyway—for her.

He did it all for her, now. Everything.

He wished it hadn't cost her her life for him to learn his lesson. He supposed if she wanted to see him one last time in his jumping rig he could certainly do that. After all, what else did they have to do . . . where else did they have to *go?*

Ronny put everything on, Angela assisting, and when he had one glove on, Angela stepped back, soaking in every last bit of him. Ronny, smiling, looked up just as he slid his hand into the remaining glove— but saw a suddenly sorrowful expression descend upon Angela's face. She reached up a trembling hand to her quivering mouth. Tears rained down her swollen face.

"*What is it?* Honey? What's the mat—"

No sooner had he pulled the glove all the way on than he fell through the cloud—all the air, all his will to live knocked out of him like a sucker punch.

He plummeted away . . . away . . . from his wife . . . .

I love you, Ronny, forever . . . .

Ronny hit quick and hard, landing with the wind at the airport's drop zone. He popped his D-rings and hurried toward the tarmac. Another plane was queuing up for another round of jumpers and he was going to be on it. The jumpers he'd jumped with were all around him, collecting their chutes and also making their way toward the tarmac.

No time had passed.

He'd landed with the same crew of jumpers with which he'd exited the plane.

Ronny was the farthest out of all of them and broke into a run, gruffly shouldering past those he used to include among his friends. Several heard him mutter something about having to "get back up there." Back into a *cloud.* To *Angela.* That's when everyone tried to stop him, but Ronny wasn't about to be stopped and swung out at the closest interlopers, knocking several to the ground. Then he all-out sprinted for the revving Beech that was leaving the tarmac and making its turn onto the runway with its new load of jumpers. Ronny reached the plane, leapt at the opening, and yanked out the jump instructor, who'd sat just inside the door. Wiping away tears, Ronny commanded the others to also get the hell out, then forced the surprised pilot to continue, his hook knife placed against the woman's throat. The crowd on the ground could only watch as the aircraft disappeared into the clouds . . . .

<> <> <>

Nothing came out of the sky, after that delivery, except for the Beech and its pilot, and when the pilot landed she related the following:

Ronny had apologized for his actions, and said he wasn't going to hurt her. He just wanted her to take him over to a particular cloud formation, that's all, and quickly, before it dissipated. He was very specific about which cloud, the pilot added. He also kept mumbling Angela's name . . . and how he was coming back so they could be together . . . forever. The pilot mentioned how she'd noticed that Ronny only wore half his rig—his emergency canopy—while his main chute's compartment was empty. Once they'd gotten to the specific formation—Ronny calmed—*appreciably*—smiled . . . then leapt out of the Beech and disappeared into the cloud.

The pilot said his smile was the most peaceful, most serene (and unnerving) thing she'd ever seen on a man's face.

She then circled around and under the cloud . . . but never found him.

"Did anyone see him land?" she asked. "*Anyone?*"

All shook their heads.

"*Hey!*" someone shouted out on the tarmac. "Come quick—look at this! *Hurry!*"

The group ran toward the field, looking skyward . . . when they saw it . . . tumbling end over end—a parachute rig. No jumper in it . . . just an empty rig, falling dirtward. It had just appeared, suddenly out from underneath one of the fair-weather cumulus formations that drifted lazily overhead . . . .

The Interview

1990

God, where to begin?

It seemed to have all started *so* long ago, or maybe it was just yesterday, I don't know anymore. What I do know is that *it* is following me. *It* will always follow me. Has forever become a part of my . . . life. Sometimes I think it was all my fault—I mean, *I* was the one who decided upon an acting career, a life forever in the public eye. Well, I got it, all right—got it pretty damned good, let me tell you.

In fact, just *let* me tell you . . . .

I had been in the film industry for about 15 years when it all started. It all happened rather innocently enough, too, with the interview. *The* interview.

Belinda Waters, the reporter, and I had met often enough over the years, but this time she seemed to have taken on a different, almost foul air. Laughter and lightheartedness quickly evaporated. " . . . that's very good, Dick," she said, quickly burying a laugh from one of my many anecdotes, "very good indeed. But . . . but let's get just a bit serious for a moment, shall we?"

"Sure—as long as you don't ask about 'alternate lifestyles,' or something," I said, joking.

She didn't laugh. Instead, she regarded her note pad intently, then aimed the next question directly at my heart.

"What about Amy?"

I could have killed her.

How could she have asked *that* of all questions?

Her brashness threw me—never had I come to expect such a low blow as this from her. What'd happened? We *knew* each other. Had she gone sour and decided to go for the juicier story bit? I mean, I know why she would have asked such a thing . . . it had all been in the news. People want to know . . . but I thought . . . thought she'd had a bit more decorum than the rest. And I'm sure her Food Chain had put her up to it. *Let's dig up the dirt and bones, shall we?* I don't know, but I sat in stunned silence for what felt like years. The audience waited patiently. She waited patiently . . . continuing to stare . . . as did the camera. That bloody fucking camera.

Yes, questions needed to be answered . . . .

"Well, what of it, Mr. Hayburn?"

It was like Belinda had suddenly changed from the personable business acquaintance of many years into the miserable Byline Bitch we all dread. She'd probably been told *ask the question or find another job* . . . .

"I don't want to talk about it, Belinda," was my simple answer.

"Oh, come on, Dick, how long have we known each other? Ten, twelve years?"

Too many years, now, if you ask me.

"If you can't tell me, who can you tell? Don't you think the public has a right to know what happened?"

Her eyes—beautiful as they were—bore into me.

"No, Belinda, I don't."

I didn't stop there and no longer minded the camera.

There are certain lines we've all drawn for ourselves, and if anybody steps over them . . . if anybody shoves us, no matter how close that person may have been—especially when forewarned—then we have a right to exert forcefulness. Even us public figures.

I continued, "And I can't believe that you are sacrificing all that we have built up over the years for a quick, sensationalistic jab."

"Mr. Hayburn—*Dick*—" she said, keeping that sick, saccharine smile on her face. That burning gaze of the reporter asking the *hard-hitting questions* . . . .

"—no, don't 'Dick' me. What happened to Amy is none of your— or anyone else's—business. It's hers . . . and it's *mine*. I have told the press often enough I will refuse to speak on this matter, and I thought that was made abundantly clear. Especially to you. You have known me for better than ten years and know damned well where I stand on it."

I got to my feet.

"Now, if you will excuse me, Belinda, I don't think I want to talk with you any longer."

And I left. Right in front of the camera. Belinda sat speechless. I *was* speechless. My wife's death was nobody's business—hell, I didn't even want to think about it anymore, and maybe that was the real reason—I didn't *want* to think about it. Of course I didn't.

Would you?

The circumstances, though gruesome and abnormal enough, had little to do with the rest of my tale, except to start the chain of events that ensued.

I will explain.

Amy and I were married three years when she'd been murdered. It had been a serial murder of some sort, and my Amy had been working late at the studios (she'd been a sound engineer). After leaving the studio she'd proceeded to her car. To make the story short, she was abducted, shortly beaten, lengthily raped, then brutally murdered. 'Dismembered' was the official term; 'violated' was mine. I had received one of her . . . body parts . . . in the mail.

Well, I made it my business to find her killer. And I did.

What no one knows—or will ever know—is that I had died in the process of finding her killer.

It's a sore subject with me.

The Death of Me

2002

What the hell was I doing?

How did I find myself on a scuba certification trip to some hole-in-the-ground spot in the middle of New Mexico, called the "Blue Hole," in a tiny town off the long-defunct Route 66, called Santa Rosa? A natural spring, this Blue Hole is supposed to be sixty feet across and eighty feet deep (depending on sediment deposition, I'm told). I'm doing this in January. In the winter.

I'm purposely throwing myself into deep water.

Maybe this doesn't mean much to you, but to me, it means everything. I mean, I'm a person who still has issues with horrible past-life drowning deaths, you know? Sure, I may be a good looking, twenty-eight-year-old woman (yeah, that's me, Miss Modesty—and guys really love my long hair) and single, but in my *Titanic* life I'm a poor working-class husband stuck below decks behind one of those inhuman and degrading locked barriers that kept the riff-raff away from the ship's effete. Helluvan era if you ask me—one I'm glad went down with that ship. Anyway, the *Titanic* strikes its berg, begins foundering, and down we all go. I still have nightmares about my unshaven face hysterically gasping for air as I force it up against the underside of the deck above me (or the deck shoved itself down *upon* me—it all depends on your point of view, doesn't it?). Warm urine fills my immersed pants. People, terrified and screaming, are grasping and clawing all around me. As the water level rises I see pillows, clothes, newspapers, and other loose debris "rise" with the water level—even see the terrified eyes of my wife as she reaches out to me . . . screaming and pleading, screaming and pleading . . . my own lips and teeth scraping the underside of that deck for any last gulps of air. I pull my wife into me and we give each other our last hugs, unable to control our panicked breathing and gagging coughing. Tears mix with salt water.

Then icy death strikes . . . is sucked into our lungs and stings our souls.

I'm sure we died from the shock, the unrelenting horror of the situation. Water filling our lungs was a mere formality. Huge pockets of air escaping from deeper shipboard compartments explode up all around us, and gargantuan groans from straining and twisting metal and wood mercilessly assault our ears, as the water envelops our bodies in its frigid death hug. Those were our last experiences as our lives-then departed and our final breaths bubbled up and out from our own "personal compartments" . . . .

And that's just *one* of my lives with which I have . . . issues.

There's also the slave-trading life where I again drowned . . . but that's for another time. I've also been burned at the stake, shot full of holes, and tortured in a slow, lingering death during the Inquisition, but it's the *drowning* that really gets to me. Who knows why, it just does.

But in this life, *this* moment, I sit crammed inside an SUV among a handful of others also heading down to the Blue Hole. I take refuge in listening to the soothing hum of our tires upon dry, solid asphalt.

Dry. *Solid.*

The miles disappear beneath those spinning Goodyears . . . .

Yes, I seem to be the only one steeped within such needless apprehension. The others, they're laughing and joking, not bothered in the least—even back during our classroom sessions people weren't worried one bit about any part of our certification. Just me. It's always one, I guess I'm "it." I mean, I really love the water—I do—but I also have this "healthy fear" of it, as ridiculous as it may seem, even with me aware of the whys and all. Why aren't others bothered? Who knows. Every diver I've ever talked with is so *psyched* that they're *divers*. That there's no other physical experience like flying—not even skydiving (how hard is it to just *fall*, they ask?). That there's a whole other world down there. No one ever mentions being afraid of even the *remotest* possibility of drowning. Of getting caught underwater with your air running out. Of a ship forcing you under water. Or a slave master shackling you to a chain then tossing you overboard like so much trash, because you got sick from his disease-ridden hold.

No, they all joke that you gotta die of something sometime, so why not do it doing something you love?

So, yes, it's only me living those possibilities over and over in my head. Just me and my issues. I *am* trying to deal with them . . . though, in my own way. It may not be the best way—or your way—but it's mine . . . and that's all that matters, right?

During our classroom instruction, I noticed how all the instructors kept a close eye on me (and no, it wasn't because I'm "hot"). They know, they do—I guess I'd mentioned it to them, stupid me—but I ended up feeling just a teensy bit self-conscious, you know? Who wouldn't in my position? It's hard to do something when you *know* you're being watched, especially when it's, well, so damned *obvious*. I know they mean well, but it's unnerving. Anyway, they try to reassure me that everything'll be all right, that there's nothing to worry about—they'll teach me everything I need to know. Then they clap me on the back and walk away, leaving me to stare at all the masks, snorkels, and BCDs lining the walls . . . smell the chlorine from a gurgling pool and wonder if what they'd just fed me is chum or the real thing.

If there's nothing to worry about . . . *why am I so goddamned worried?*

I know this guy who once told me that he nearly drowned. As a kid. He said it really wasn't all that big a deal. Said he remembered how calm everything was . . . and how his body just seemed to shut off, you know, light by light, he put it. No big deal.

Calm?

How could anyone remain calm after inhaling two lungfuls of water?

Is it just me?

Welcome to my hell.

Most people worry about landing a great job, having enough money, finding the "right" person in their lives . . . I worry about past lives and drowning.

So, for five-and-a-half hours all this . . . *stuff* . . . swirled through my head as the SUV jostled me around . . . and the others laughed and joked like crewmen on that faraway deck. Needless to say, I wasn't much fun. We were almost there, to this Blue Hole. We turned off New Mexico Highway 84 for I-40. Seventeen miles to go. To the water—and to make matters worse? As soon as we're checked in, we're to immediately show up *and begin dive number one*. These idiots can't get into the water fast enough.

I can still feel that young woman's nails biting into the meat of my palm as the *Titanic* went down . . . .

No turning back, now. Time to face the fears.

***

Well, *quelle surprise!* We all made it through three of our four certification dives! It wasn't as hard as I thought it'd be! Maybe it *is* all in my head! Had some trouble equalizing my ears on the way down, but once at depth, I did fine!

How neat to [finally?] *breathe under water!*

We did all kinds of drills: removing, replacing, and clearing flooded masks, buddy breathing (which our instructor tells us is going by the wayside for some reason, but he still teaches it), removing and replacing our buoyancy control vests, and a practice controlled emergency ascent. I thought I'd have some trouble with that one, but ended up doing just fine. We took our one breath, then, regulator still in our mouths, exhaled gently but continuously . . . ascending directly to the surface from about twenty-five feet of depth of water. Instructor by our side. It was all (I had to admit) quite fun!

But now I stand suited-up and on the cement steps that lead down into the Blue Hole.

Our instructor, Rick (yeah, he's a hot guy himself), told us this was our final dive (I *really* didn't like the sound of that!) . . . that there were no more drills to perform.

This was just a fun dive.

We all thought this was how we were going to get our open-water certification patches—under water. Rick asked for us to meet him down at the PVC-pipe-framed underwater "platform," which was plastic tubing attached at right angles to form an open square you can swim through. There was just one more "tiny little formality" that needed to be completed, Rick said.

Right.

Okay, I can *do* this, I told myself, there's no big deal to it . . . just go down one more time, blah-blah-blah, get the patch—and it's over. All of it. Would never even have to dive again.

I could do this. It's no Big Deal.

After all, if every certified diver has gone through what we're going through and they all *love* it . . . *how bad could it be?*

Geez, chill out, girl.

I stick my regulator back into my mouth, breathe out . . . in . . . look to my buddy . . . and out we swim to the buoys, which are attached at the surface to the platform's descent lines below . . .

We're here!

Okay, for all my anxiety and ear-equalizing difficulties, I love being under water!

I never thought I'd ever say that, but I did take all this on to try to address my fears. There may not be much to look at, here (it's kind of murky from all the diving), *but I'm breathing under water!* Every time I come down here I'm amazed at this little fact—I don't know if I can adequately convey how *weird* it is to me. I mean, here's this human being—*me*—under water—inside a totally different, basically *solid* medium . . . and I'm *breathing*. It's like sticking a miniature scuba self in a glass of water. All around me is fluid . . . something we wash ourselves in, drink, and die if we don't get enough—*or* too much. It's like this multifunctional medium! It could be *cement* for all practical purposes, or dirt (I have images of snorkeling through a neighbor's front lawn)—it just fascinates me.

We're all floating at platform level, adjusting our buoyancy, and awaiting our instructor's presence. Here he comes, descending down into the center of the open platform like Superman or something. He makes clearing your ears look so easy.

He gives each of us the "OK" signal, which we return, but he pauses at me . . . or maybe it just seems so? But when he's done "OKing" all of us, instead of handing out the patches . . . his gaze returns to me, and he motions for me to meet him in the center of the platform.

What-the-hell-why-me-what-are-you-doing?

Unsure and suddenly nervous, but doing as requested, I push myself up and over the plastic pipe and fin my way into the center, adjusting my buoyancy and monitoring my depth.

That's when I see him go for his slate. We're not done yet—there *is* more.

Rick displays the slate, first to me, then the rest of the group. It says: *One more thing!*

I see him smiling at me behind his regulator, as he shows me the other side. The words are simple, the act is, too, but suddenly I'm not sure I can do it. I've been trying to mentally prepare myself for this the entire trip, but no longer can do so.

The hour is at hand.

One more act to do before I—we—can all be certified. I'm terrified. I read the slate, again, trying to extend this moment out indefinitely. To my ultimate horror, it still says:

Remove your regulator and inhale!

After the last word is a smiley face.

A goddamned smiley face!

Oh, my God—it's time . . . I see the others raising their fists into the (air?) water, and hear them whooping it up (grunting) for me. I've been trying to tell myself the entire trip that I *know* I can do it (face my fears!), but suddenly feel all my resolve spill out like warm urine into a frigid North Atlantic . . . .

I'm to drown myself!

I don't know if I can do this—I mean, I *want* to, I really really *want* to . . . but now, here, at the moment of truth . . . the facing of all my fears—I don't know that I can.

My breathing races, despite my mental commands to do otherwise, and I look to my console, more as a measure of procrastination than anything else . . . 2700 pounds of air are now compressed inside my Aluminum-80 tank . . . more than enough for a twenty-minute dive . . . but I'm now being asked to drown myself—my singular worst fear. I turn to the rest of my classmates, and they're all cheering me on—giving me the "OK" and rapping their scuba knives against the PVC pipe. Some still are grunting through their regs. I look back to Rick and see him scribbling another note on the other side of his slate. He writes: *It's okay, you can do it!*

The others continue to cheer me on.

But I can't. I thought I could . . . buuut . . . I can't.

I shake my head, "No," eyes wide with terror.

Rick comes up to me . . . puts a hand to my shoulder . . . and smiles gently.

His touch is surprisingly calming, not like the one on that slave ship, and he fins over to another student, one who enthusiastically receives him, and again shows the other side of the slate, where the words *Remove your regulator and inhale!* Still reside. The other student looks to the slate, then to me, gives me the "OK" signal and smiles.

I feel a chill in my bones. He's actually gonna do it—how come he and the others can do it, but *I* can't?

Damn it, I just don't understand—I should be able to do this, for crying out loud—I *want* to do it—but-but the *Titanic*, the *slave* ship . . . sinking, sinking, ever sinking . . . into cold, inky darkness . . . .

I look to Daniel (my classmate), the one who will pave the way for my supposed turn. He looks back to me, still smiling. I can hardly believe his guts, as he enthusiastically yanks his regulator from his mouth, and I see him exhale every last breath of air from his lungs with (what I've come to know of him is) his typical, mild bravado. He pauses—winks at me—then inhales with such force I swear *I* feel the water filling his lungs . . . rushing through his sinuses, down his throat, and into awaiting alveoli.

I watch him as his eyes slowly transition from alive and aware . . .

to dead and blank . . .

His body goes limp and his head slumps forward . . .

But Rick is there and grabs him.

Daniel stops finning and adjusting his buoyancy, and just . . . floats . . . like a dead fish . . . well, actually begins to sink a little; you know, the extra weight of the inhaled water. I see several straggling bubbles escape his mouth like an afterthought—and then that's it—he's gone.

D-r-o-w-n-e-d.

Everyone whoops it up, banging for their chance to go next—but I don't let them.

Where I was supposed to have gone first—an *honor*—another has taken my place.

I have been embarrassed to face my fear and need to suck it up. I need to do this more than any of these others—*they* aren't afraid, *I* am. *I'm* the one with the issues.

I come up to Rick and bravely give him my "OK." He pauses . . . smiles back . . . and pats me on the shoulder, still supporting Daniel. He returns my "OK," but this time it's more in the form of a question, as in "*Am I sure?*" I respond back in the affirmative. Strong. Decisive. I then look up, seeing all the other instructors and dive masters hovering about like angels (*let's go, Miss Wings!*).

They're there to support all our drowned bodies.

I give them a firm "OK" as well, and it's returned by all, some also giving me a thumbs-up. They're rooting for me, and I suddenly swell with emotion. Rick hands off Daniel to one of the hovering angels.

Steeling my resolve before I lose it, I reach for my regulator and take a few quick, final breaths. With less hesitation than I imagined, I remove the reg from my mouth to let it float freely beside me. I eye it as I forcibly exhale as Daniel had done. Pausing, I look to Rick, who's watching me closely. Suddenly I do—to me—a brazen act. Something I can't believe I did.

Smiling—no, more *smirking*—I return the "OK" . . . and *wink*.

I then inhale with such force I swear I drink in half the Blue Hole—

And drown.

The soothing hum of our tires upon the dry, solid asphalt resonates indescribable warmth and comfort into each and every one of my cells like never before. I'm smiling warmly to myself while again seated in that SUV on our return trip north. All my classmates are again laughing and yucking it up, some still trying to clear their ears of residual water, but I continue to keep to myself and my thoughts.

And, yes, clogged ears.

I have to admit, I'm pretty proud of myself.

I look out the window, watching *extraordinary* scenery pass by. My mind snorkels the sand and dirt and darts in and around Socorro cacti and scrub oak. Everything is so much more vibrant and *alive!*

How come I never noticed this before?

Silly me.

I smirk into my reflection in the window, fingertips gently tracing it. It is a deep, all-pervading sense of well-being I now enjoy.

I've faced my fear.

Owned it.

I've finally done it, and what I've experienced no longer frightens.

Sometimes we forget the little things . . . the scent of life . . . the warmth of sunshine against our faces . . . the laughter of others . . .

The song of soul.

We need to die every once in a while, everyone does. It's no big deal. I'm learning. What's next *pour moi?*

I smile.

Maybe I'll take up skydiving.

The Ballad of fReD BeAn
1988

Fred Bean rolled over in his bed
The only problem with that
Being
Fred Bean's body stopped, 'cept his head.

It rolled 'til stopped
By the intersection
Of
The wall and the floor
Some five feet away, by the door.

Police said it really hadn't been all that messy.

St. Vincent
1995

Vince ground his booted-heel into the Arizona sand, thoroughly pulverizing the beetle beneath it.

"Must have been your time to go . . . just like me."

I raise my head and look up to the scorching sun, smell the fumes of my still-burning Camaro, and feel the heat where I stand. *"Why's everyone so afraid of dying? It's just part of living."*

I lift my dusty .44-caliber Dan Wesson to eye level and blow off loose sand. I look it over. What was really responsible here—me . . . or this miraculously crafted piece of stainless steel? This wonder of human engineering?

I chuckle.

What a work of art, indeed, from its utilitarian lines to its perfect heft and balance. I drop my hand and weapon back to my side and think about the trooper burning away within the remains of her vehicle and mine. I hadn't meant to kill her, but she came at me, and I just didn't want to go. Yet. I probably did her a favor. She would have died some other time under the hand of one who didn't care nearly as much as I did.

At least I meant well.

I limp away from Route 93 towards the jagged precipice ahead. I stop and turn one last time to consider the wreckage of my '67 Camaro and the trooper's brand new Camaro. Life can be so funny sometimes.

Must've been her time.

So why doesn't anything matter?

We're born, we die; if we're lucky, we get laid now and then . . .

maybe have a family or two . . . pay taxes from a job we more often than not can't stand . . . then die. I'm not finding any answers, damn it, and I'm damn near the end of my rope—

I move off the pavement.

Vince climbs ever higher up the crags, his gun tucked into the rear of his jeans, waves of heat radiating off the rocks and sand, beating into him. He sucks in thick gulps of air into aching, straining, lungs . . .

Where had I first heard—or read—it? The statement still plagues me like a festering wound: *Fact is official fiction.*

I mean, who comes up with this shit?

All my life I struggle . . . try to do the right thing . . . be the nice guy . . . and I'm told that everything—everything I've ever believed in, everything I've ever worked for—is *false?*

Fact is official fiction, all right.

If we make it all up, then what's *right* (is there even a "right")? Are we actually *alive* or mere novelized characters? Me killing someone isn't really *killing*, since I'm not really taking anyone's life—it's all an illusion, fiction. There isn't even a God, because *we* make it all up.

Try to prove it otherwise.

Faith doesn't work, because we create that, too—sure, we create the ideas as well as the substance. It's all part of how life works—am I the only one who sees this? But, no, it gets better—since we made up this idea of killing, now we must create the idea that if you kill someone (an untruth to begin with) you have to pay for it—another untruth.

Why? WHY?

So am I really crazy . . . or is crazy just *another* made-up fallacy? And if *I'm* not real, then others can't do a damned thing to me, right (and I can't do a damned thing to them, either)?

Look at me so far: I've told my boss to go to hell (punched out the idiot, in fact) then robbed an all-night supermarket. So, several hundred miles, four days, and three dead bodies later, here I am, stuck out in the middle of the Arizona desert, drying up from the summer sun, and hungrier than a circling buzzard.

Yet, here I *am.*

Vince climbs higher, but never sees or hears the Arizona troopers below who gather and block off the road. His mind swarms with tortured, philosophical arguments full of possibilities, probabilities, and inspirations. Finding a particularly good handhold, he pulls himself up and finds a ledge large enough to allow him to stretch out . . . but which also extends back out of the reach of the sun under an outcropping of rock.

I pull myself onto the ledge and enjoy the feel of the rock. I sense how it reaches out to *me* as I grab for *it.* I smell the dryness and timeliness of the earth. Even though my fingers, arms, and legs scream with pain, I enjoy where I'm at and how I've gotten here. I settle in on my ledge and stretch out. *"So, what have I really done?"* I casually ask the rock walls. *"Have I really robbed anyone . . . really killed anyone?"* If there's nothing to rob, then I didn't really commit the crime, now, did I? If there's no one to kill, then I didn't really commit a crime there, either, did I?

Then why do I feel so damned guilty?

How can it all feel so genuine if it's all so illusional? I feel like I'm watching myself—or someone else is—like I'm a-I'm a character in a book or a movie. I feel like there're these gigantic faces peering down at me from some ungodly *close* distance . . . .

Why can't I figure this out?

In a sudden burst of anger, I heave my weapon away—only to realize a moment later what I've done—but it's too late. I watch as my beautiful piece of utilitarian artistry flips and sails through the air . . . end over end, roll after roll . . . intermittently casting off bright splashes of light . . . until (ages later) it clatters and bounces and discharges off the rocky escarpment below. The discharge echoes wildly and I continue to watch stupidly, even after it has settled quietly somewhere in the rubble beneath me.

"So . . . what did *that* mean?"

Did that have any significance? Was that just some random act of man, God, or nature? Someone or something guiding me? Why would I do such a thing—and furthermore, would I require further use of the weapon? If no one's ever really killed *what need do I have of the thing?*

If there's no death, then do I need to fear for my life? Do I need a killing machine to protect a life that can't be taken away—

This is all so damned confusing.

Why is this happening to me? Am I missing something? Getting a vital part of the equation all fouled up and confused?

I fold my legs before me and encircle them with my arms. I look about. Feel the gentle breeze that softly caresses my skin—it doesn't care what I have or haven't done. It still caresses me. I enjoy my solitude—that I'm alone on this ledge—just *me*, nothing else, and revel (did I actual just *use* that word?) in the fact that *I* got myself here. I never would've considered doing something like this before, climbing sheer rock walls.

I try to relax and inhale deeply; close my eyes. When I reopen them, I notice some strange little creature, like a scorpion, but without that menacing, curving tail, curiously checking me out. It also doesn't seem to know what I've done, what I'm capable of. It cautiously approaches; stops. Comes a little closer . . . then again stops. It's quick. We look at each other. I know not what this thing is and—curiously enough—feel no urge to kill it.

Why is that?

I reach out to it, and it scurries back a step or two, then stops. I keep my hand where it is, and it reapproaches . . . pauses . . . then touches my skin.

I feel nothing.

It takes a tentative step or two with its little legs up onto my hand—then scurries the rest of the way up. I lift my hand to eye level and examine it. Whatever it is, it, too, is magnificently crafted and suited to whatever is its purpose. I smile, but suddenly feel sad and lower my hand back to the dirt ledge. I allow the creature to hop off and continue on in its adventures.

Maybe I've misinterpreted everything. Maybe—

I consider suicide.

Launching myself from this ledge to soar like my gun until I, too, strike the rubble below . . . but know I could never do such a thing.

Is suicide different from so-called "natural" death?

If fact is fiction and we make everything up . . . then doesn't that also apply to death—that we choose our own time of passing? If this is so, then how is suicide any different from dying from a heart attack? Either way *we* take our own lives. Could it be our own *perceptions* that make things right or wrong . . . our *intents*—

This is too weird. If I've figured it all out, then what am I still doing here? There has to be more . . . has to be something I've *missed* . . . .

I again close my eyes and lay back against the rock.

"Oh, God—if there is a You—this feels *sooo* good."

No deadlines . . . no hassles . . . no worries—current philosophical dilemmas notwithstanding. I feel like that book, *Catch-22*. How can I say I'm crazy, because if I say I am, *am* I?

I wish I had that book here, now—never did finish it.

I shuffle my hands through the dirt alongside me and touch something unexpected for my surroundings of sand and stone. I look down and find a paperback novel. I pick it up. Read its title.

Catch-22.

It's a worn copy . . . just like the one I last remembered reading.

"Wait a minute . . . this . . . this can't be . . . unless—"

***

At that moment a rifled bullet slams through Vincent's forehead, fired by an Arizona State Trooper, and Vincent achieves sainthood. It was also then that I realized I was telling my own story . . . and that though I was a character in that story—as are any of us—characters need to care about themselves, just as readers need to care about them. It's not about nothing—or even fiction*—it's about love, emotion, and experience—all that and* more. *It's what each story means to each individual, each character. We all get out of our stories what we put into them. This is my story.*

What's yours?

Shelf Life

1991

"CJ, come over here and take a look at this!" Allison Bundle commanded.

CJ looked up from the pile of ancient Turkish rugs he'd been examining, annoyed at the mere sound of his wife's voice.

"*Come here*—look at what I found. Just *look* at this!"

He came over and found her holding up an old oil lamp into the light.

"It's just an oil lamp—"

"No, not the lamp, the bookcase—the *shelves. Look.*" Allison directed CJ's attention to the corner in front of them. It was an altogether normal enough looking wooden bookcase, its dusty and worn shelves covered with odd knickknacks. Attached to the setup was a faded and barely legible message on a piece of ripped cardboard. The sign hung from one of the upper shelves and had a ragged bottom edge.

"What do you think it means?" she asked.

"Well, Allison," CJ said, barely able to mask his annoyance, "I think it's rather simple enough, don't you? I mean, it says 'Don't Buy.'"

He began to wander off, wondering why he even let her take him into these places—why he even stayed married to her. One day, just one day, he'd love to lose her in one of these places and walk out the door . . . and just . . . keep . . . *walking* . . . .

How their marriage had gone sour, he couldn't recall—no longer cared—it just had. He'd always seen the 'bitch-streak' in her from the beginning and had just chosen to ignore it. Because of the sex. And her family's fortune. But mainly it had been the sex. Yup. That had been his first mistake. The second was staying with her. Yes, he'd been nothing more than an ape when he'd married her, an ape craving sex, but he'd since evolved—and she hadn't.

"Yeah, but why have all these things here, then put up a sign that tells you *not* to buy them? And you can barely read the damn thing," she said, *thwaking* the sign with the back of her middle finger.

"Well, maybe they belong to the owner and are just there for display," he said, finding himself drawn back to the shelves. He leaned in, examining the items closer. "There aren't even prices on these thi—"

"I don't think so," she said.

CJ had found that her disagreeing with him was usually more of a reflex action than an act of legitimate discussion. She always loved to (immediately) counter *anything* he had to say.

CJ examined the shelves. The sign and its accompanying bookcase were clearly showing their age, and the objects themselves—like the rest of the curio-slash-antique-slash-rip-off joint—were all eclectic and queer-looking. Unable to discern anything more about the bookcase, CJ turned away . . . when he was overcome by an acute feeling of dread. He didn't know where the feeling was coming from, but it suddenly changed his entire perspective on the subject.

And his tone.

"I don't know, Alli, but all of a sudden I'm getting a very weird feeling about all this. Let's just put it back and find something else, okay?"

"Oh, give me a break, *dearest*, it's probably just a joke. I'm going to take this," she said, hefting the oil lamp like she was judging its weight.

"*No*," CJ said, insisting perhaps just a bit more sharply than was his norm, but he did notice it stopped Allison in her tracks. She looked at him, surprised, and he discovered he liked that look. It was the first time he could remember that she actually looked *frightened*.

"Look, Alli, I really don't think we should. Okay?"

"Why are you acting so weird? I like it, so I'm going to buy it. That's that."

"I don't like it. There's something *off* about it—and this whole place as a matter of fact—that just gives me the creeps. How about this instead—we put *this* back," he said, lifting the lamp from her hands and setting it back up on the shelves, "and we look around a little more. If you still want it, fine—you can come back and get it, but let's at least ask the owner about it before we buy it. Okay?"

Allison looked strained. Like she was going to explode.

"Okay, but I think you're being very stupid about this. It's only a dumb old genie lamp, and I want it."

And I want it.

How many times had he heard that refrain over the years?

CJ remained silent, almost embarrassed. He couldn't believe his behavior. He could believe his *wife's* . . . just not his. He really needed to leave her. And one day, one *daaay—*

"I *am* coming back after we have a look at the rest of this stuff," Allison said, defiantly, and strutted off down the aisle. She bumped into something in the narrow aisle, which fell off its shelf and rattled about on the floor, but she never looked back.

CJ watched Allison storm off. He knew how much Allison hated being told what to do, though he knew how much she loved directing others around. He also knew how she usually ended up finagling her own way later on, anyway, but nonetheless he felt uncharacteristically relieved.

This is stupid—what's the matter with me?

He followed her down the cluttered row . . . and picked up what she'd knocked off the display, replacing it back to where it had been.

The bookcase

(*Don't Buy* . . .)

shuddered.

Browsing through the antique shop took longer than anticipated, and CJ quietly hoped that Allison had forgotten all about that stupid genie thing. But *his* mind, however, was still very much on the matter. All through his browsing he had stolen glances back at that corner. It was more than mere apprehension that gripped him . . . it was more like some irresistible force that carefully . . . subtly . . . funneled into him . . . called out to him . . . pulled him *back* . . . .

He didn't know what it was he saw . . . or *thought* he saw just now . . . but something had suddenly flashed in his peripheral vision . . . something he had only been barely able to catch. He rubbed his eyes and blinked. He was probably kidding himself, but he thought he'd seen a person there . . . then a flash of some kind.

A flash of . . . *red?*

CJ looked back to Allison and saw she was busily dickering (translated: *arguing*) with a lady about something. He turned back to the bookcase. Decided to have another look. He was sure he'd seen someone standing by that case only moments ago . . . then . . . *nothing.*

Something wasn't right.

He wove throughout the narrow aisles toward the shelves.

One more shot, then he'd wash his hands of the entire matter and Allison could buy whatever the hell she damned-well wanted.

There was dust on the floor before the shelves that had been recently disturbed—but he already knew that. Somebody *had* been here. There was also an odd, musty odor. His eyes immediately went to where he had earlier placed the lamp and saw that it was still there. But he also saw something else he hadn't seen there before—a watch . . . a woman's watch. Then, upon closer examination of the shelves themselves, he noticed an interesting—if somewhat *hallucinatory*—effect about the wood. He couldn't be sure if it was a trick of the light or his own mind, but he could swear he saw tiny fibers—cilia—*moving along the wood*. Like seaweed tossing about in an ocean current . . . .

CJ leaned in closer and carefully brought a hand up to it, finger extended. He felt sweaty and warm.

This is stupid, they're only shelves—

CJ was suddenly thrown off his feet and into the bookcase. He'd tried to throw his hands out before him, but missed and smacked his forehead into one of the shelves.

"Oh, I'm *sorry!*" CJ regained his balance and lifted a hand to his forehead. Sore . . . tender . . . *stars*.

Shook his head. "God*dammit*," he said.

Unfocused, unsteady, and confused, he looked up. Through his star-studded haze, he found himself looking into the large, startled and concerned eyes of a beautiful woman in her twenties or early thirties. She stood before him, mouth open, her arms wrapped around one end of a large, rolled up Turkish rug that stretched out behind her.

CJ thought he had died and gone to heaven and was looking into the soul of an angel. "I'm *so* sorry," the woman said, "I was trying to move this thing, and I guess I . . . I-I kinda slipped!"

CJ briskly rubbed his forehead. No blood.

"Oh, you're hurt!" the woman said, "I'm so, *so* sorry!" The woman dropped her end of the rug and came to CJ. Touching and inspecting his forehead, she checked him out. Her touch was warm, *exciting* even . . . .

"I-it's nothing, I-I'll be all right. *Damn*. Do you need some help with that or something?" he asked, wincing and looking up to her.

"I guess I'm not as strong as I thought I was. I'm *so* sorry. Yes, I could use a hand."

CJ shook off his injury, got back to his feet, and grabbed the rolled-up end of the carpet, pulling it free from the rest of the pile.

"Couldn't you have picked something just a little less difficult?" he asked, jokingly. He cast a pained smile to the woman and again rubbed his head. He looked away, but did a double-take. Saw the effect his words had had on her. The woman looked quite embarrassed.

"I-I'm sorry," CJ said, "I didn't mean it that way, I was just . . . oh, never mind. Here you go. I didn't mean to jump on you."

CJ set the rug down on what little floor space there was and brushed himself off. "Look, my name's CJ. Sorry about the wisecrack." He extended his hand.

"I'm Cheryl. Pleased—and *embarrassed*—to meet you. And thanks for helping me with this. There doesn't seem to be much room here, does there?"

"*That depends on what you have a mind to use it for,*" came the sharp, distinctly enunciated words from behind them.

Allison.

CJ turned to meet his wife.

"Allison! Meet Cheryl . . . she just knocked me up against the bookcase with this thing," he said, directing her attention to the rug.

"I'll bet. Nice to meet you, Cheryl," Allison said, and exaggeratedly offered her left hand—exposing the wedding ring.

Cheryl eyed the ring a little longer than necessary.

Allison shot CJ a strained look. "Well—*honey*—think I'm through here, and I *do* want that little ol' oil lamp we talked about earlier."

CJ suddenly remembered what had brought him back here.

"Alli, I wish you'd reconsider. I really don't feel good about this. I came over here because . . . well, because I thought I *saw* something."

"Yeah, and I think I know what it was you saw, too, *darling*."

"Well, it was a pleasure meeting you both," Cheryl said, backing away, "and thank you, again, CJ, for helping me."

"Sure, no problem," CJ said.

Allison eyed CJ. "I think I'm going to take this lamp," she continued, "now let's go, shall we?"

CJ began to say something when his throat constricted and his breathing suddenly became labored. He grasped at his collar and cast a troubled glance to Cheryl, who made a most splendid sight as she bent over to once more attack the rug. But she, too, had suddenly stopped, and he noticed how uncomfortable she also appeared.

She felt it, too.

Stood back up without the rug.

CJ watched as she turned around to look straight at him.

Something isn't right, he thought, *something's going to happen . . . .*

Before he knew what he was doing, CJ began backing away from his wife and the bookcase. He held Cheryl's gaze and saw her rub her arms nervously.

No doubt feeling the same prickly sensation I'm feeling . . . .

Allison felt nothing, however.

In some distant corner of his mind CJ vaguely recognized Allison's voice as she continued to ramble on about the lamp and her right to buy it. CJ was now completely behind Allison, standing next to Cheryl.

The two watched Allison as she turned slightly away from the bookcase, remained totally focused on her little trinket, and continued on her right-to-buy tirade.

Watched as the display case began to shudder and

Come to life.

Watched as the entire store seemed to darken and take a back seat to the wooden shelves and become all but nonexistent. Out from the middle of the case, like a nightmare, extended what looked like a stretched-out leg-hold trap . . . jaws wide and deadly. There were sharp, jagged objects projecting outward from the orifice—

Teeth.

The extrusion extended forward as Allison continued to talk.

She finally took a breath.

Looked up.

The orifice from the shelves morphed into definite shape . . . huge, jagged teeth. Allison brought her hands up before her in a defensive posture—

The circular orifice had already come down and encompassed her head, shoulders, and arms . . . and clamped down. The powerful jaws neatly separated her at her narrow waist. There was a spray of red that was immediately sucked up by the creature. The remains of Allison's beautiful body fell about the floor. Her skirt was caught up in the thing's teeth and pulled from the rest of her body.

As the teeth came together, Cheryl and CJ saw the face that was behind it, stretched out from the wooden bookcase that was its body. It was indeed made of wood—and there was an unimaginable rancor that emanated from it, as mold spores flaked off everywhere around them like dust. CJ and Cheryl covered their mouths and noses, grimacing against the ghastly scene. The remainder of their attention was then diverted to the crunching and grinding of the creature's jaws. Allison's skirt hung loosely from the creature's mouth as it consumed its first mouthful. It then shot forward and consumed the rest of Allison, and the mess she had made on the floor—all in the blink of an eye.

Then it grinned . . . an open, hideous smirk that creaked and snapped . . . and retracted back into the shelves.

All that remained at their feet was one slightly battered and suddenly orphaned oil lamp. There wasn't a single blood stain. They both looked to the oil lamp. Backed farther away.

Don't Buy . . .

Again that small, ominous sign.

CJ had a hard time breathing at first, and Cheryl had to hit him on his back a couple of times. He tried to speak, but nothing came out. Cleared his throat. Coughed. Looked back to Cheryl, then to the bookcase. When he finally caught his breath he crouched down, giving the bookcase a good, hard look. A little way off to the left of that damned oil lamp he spotted

Don't Buy . . . .

something.

A piece of cardboard.

It was the bottom half to that sign up on that shelf.

CJ leaned toward it and could just barely make out the words. He'd be damned if he was getting any closer. The words on the torn-off part of the sign caused CJ to violently shiver. He quickly motioned for Cheryl to look, then Cheryl began trembling and went into a catatonic state, staring blankly off into the distance. CJ threw his arms around her and brought her in to himself, as he looked around the store.

Really? Had no one but them seen what had just happened?

Cheryl stared blankly before her, eyes unblinking, continuing to shake uncontrollably.

"Cheryl! Cheryl, *look* at me," CJ said, and took hold of her shoulders. He turned her around to face him. Looked at her. At himself. Neither of them had any blood or gore on them. "*Look at me*," he said.

She looked up.

"I—I don't know what happened here. I can't even *attempt* to explain it . . . but look around. *Look.*"

Cheryl did.

"What do you see?" he asked.

Nothing. She saw *nothing*.

She saw people looking at rugs and clocks. People looking at paintings. Even saw one look over to her and smile. But nobody fainted. Nobody screamed. No one called the cops.

Nothing appeared to have changed.

Except that there was no longer one Allison Bundle.

"Cheryl . . . I can't even begin to understand what happened . . . or why no one could see what we saw—but it's *over*. Do you hear me?

"O-over?"

"Yes. Now I think it would be in our best interests . . . if we got the hell out of here—"

"But—"

"*Forget about her.* She was not a good person. I don't know if I'm in shock or what, but I feel strangely empty of any emotion toward her right now. I was going to leave her, anyway."

CJ pulled off his wedding ring. Held it out for Cheryl to see. He then brought it back up before him. Studied it.

At one time . . . one time . . . he'd actually loved her. But she'd destroyed that love. He'd never wished her dead . . . this tragedy had been beyond horrible . . . but she was gone . . . .

Hideously gone.

Dulce et decorum est finis?

CJ felt a sudden and powerful urge.

Gently, he placed the ring upon the bookshelf. Nudged it back a bit with a fingertip. A tear formed and he grimaced. Looked at the ring a moment longer, then backed away, keeping an eye on the bookcase.

"Come on," he said, "we'd better go—I don't know if this thing is going to, you know—activate again."

Cheryl didn't move.

"*Are you with me?*" he asked Cheryl, taking hold of her shoulders and looking her firmly in the eyes.

Cheryl again looked around. No one seemed to have noticed a thing—not a goddamned thing. *It was as if nothing had ever happened.* CJ nervously followed her gaze around the interior.

He was anxious to be gone . . . out of this place.

Nobody'll miss her, he thought. Well, maybe her family. *I just hope that damned thing doesn't get heartburn and spit her back out. And I don't want to be around here if it does . . . .*

Cheryl reached a hand up and out to CJ.

"Y-yes."

"Come on, then," CJ said, and taking her hand pulled her away from the shelves. Took her to the front doors . . . then out beyond them and forever away from this building.

CJ's wedding band sat on the shelf.

The bookcase bulged and squeaked . . . formed itself into a small wooden claw and shot out and grabbed the oil lamp. The claw then reached up and placed the lamp back up on the shelf beside the ring . . . then quickly withdrew . . . only to again shoot out and grab the torn off part of the sign CJ had spotted.

Don't Buy.

Not responsible for shelf life, the torn-off sign fragment had read.

Brains

1991

Migraines.

What causes them? Why do people get them? What makes them so painful? There are trains of thought on the matter, and I *am* going to add to them. This recent spate of headaches?

I know what's *really* going on and *why* they're so painful.

I never used to get them, migraines, but now I get them all the time. And I have seen their end results. I will *be* an end result.

It all started—hell, I don't even know how long it's been anymore—these damned headaches, the migraines have begun to distort so much of what I perceive as reality—

God, *how* it *hurts!*

It knows what I'm saying, of course, so there is little respite in what I do, but I have to get it all out there before I, like the others, have my turn at the logical conclusion.

It began, well . . . when it all began.

I was taking a walk down a beach one moonlit night, by myself as I usually do anymore since the divorce, and I came upon this body in the darkness. At first I thought it was the garden variety of beach bum who inhabit these shores, but something was different about this one, even in his death, as I soon discovered. One specific part of the body was . . . *ravaged.* I know the prime directive of discovering dead bodies (besides calling the authorities) is to leave things as they are, but I felt there was something I . . . I *had* to see . . . something more to the husk that lay before me, curled up on its side, water just barely lapping up beside it.

I was preternaturally drawn to it. I can't explain it.

Using my walking stick, I . . . yes, I *poked around* . . . bringing out the mini-flashlight I carry with me on my nightly excursions. It was then that I found the ghastly opening . . . .

In its head.

God, the memory still fills me with such dread!

Sadly, it shall be a memory that is short-lived.

I should have turned away and called the authorities immediately, should not have indulged my morbid curiosity and dilly-dallied one second longer!

Oh, that god, Hindsight!

But I did and here I am, cursed by that decision.

I took my stick, flashlight riding shotgun, and performed a most fiendish deed—

I stuck it *inside!*

Inside of the *skull!*

But the farther I poked around . . . the more I became confused. I should have been met resistance . . . *spongey* resistance. But there was none!

I continued to . . . *explore.*

Fighting my revulsion, I continued to investigate and my stick tapped against the hard edges of the skull . . . I poked around . . . *inside* . . . air that shouldn't have *been* there was all I found!

Nothing.

There was *nothing* inside that skull!

It was totally devoid of any so-called gray matter. This was probably the most heinous instance of the entire encounter that made my blood curdle. What was such a large opening doing inside this poor dead man's head? What or who had done such a heinous thing?

And where the hell *was* it? His brain?

I didn't stay any longer at that point, tossed my stick into the ocean and sprinted into the darkness. Adrenalin-laced fear added to my speed as I am not one prone to the current fitness craze, and it drove me powerfully indeed! But in my initial haste, I'd stumbled upon something in the sand not far from the body. I didn't know what that thing was then—but I certainly do now. I thought it to be a jellyfish or some other beached sea creature and just narrowly managed to avoid it, but I felt the thing *move.* Give. I didn't see where it went off to, but as it turned out, didn't have to worry about it. *They* . . . they would find me soon enough—

Pain, more *pain!*

God, I think it does this to tease me! It has no intentions of killing me just yet, I feel. I know this. If it had wanted to, it could surely have done so a long time ago. It's playing with me, the demon. I think it wants me to do this. That it is . . . *amused* . . . by my actions.

Anyway, I'd finally called the authorities and gave them all of the information they needed and, naturally, they kept me away from the scene once they'd arrived. They were just as flabbergasted as I when they found . . . that *hole*. But after grilling me for what seemed an eternity, nothing more came of it. I found the incident reported in the papers that next day, but curiously, there was no mention of the ragged hole in the head. The lack of the man's *brain* . . . .

So my life went on as usual for a while and I continued to take my nightly strolls—ever careful to avoid that particular spot. Glancing at it occasionally from afar, I wondered if the surf from the sea could ever adequately wash away the lingering abomination from those sands—

My mind, however, was a different

(*gray*)

matter altogether.

The next night I found myself walking behind a fairly amorous couple, one of many, not too far ahead of me. There were lots of the usual hugging and handholding, all of which made me surprisingly angry. My divorce was barely a year old and I didn't need the memories that now flooded my . . . my mind.

As the lot of us continued up the beach, I noticed this couple suddenly part, the screams from the woman assaulting my ears. I stopped, initially wondering if they were horse playing, but soon observed this wasn't the case. The girl turned in my direction and saw my silhouette. *Help*, she screamed, it's *attacking* him, she cried! That's when fear again made me sprint. I began wondering if maybe I should have gotten caught up in this fitness craze . . . .

When I got up to them I found the girl kicking at . . . at the *thing* . . . that was on her man.

The *thing*.

I froze.

Couldn't believe what I was seeing!

It initially assailed my senses as a gigantic spider, its spindly legs nimbly grappling and adjusting its position on the guy's back as the man thrashed about in the sand. The thing's body was about the size of a cantaloupe, or melon, and it seemed darkish in color. Its legs operated like unwieldy—yet purposeful—sticks. It was most heinous to *look* at . . . to touch . . . to . . . to *grab* was *unthinkable!*

The girl continued pleading for me to do something. *Pleeease*, do something, she screamed. When she grabbed me and shook me, and I came out of my daze, I, too, began kicking it. A few of my kicks missed their mark and landed upon her boyfriend. I'm sure he didn't mind all that much. Shortly I was able to loosen the thing from her boyfriend and watched it tumble off and barrel roll along the sand, its legs curled up underneath it like a spider's—but it quickly regained its orientation and shot back up upon its legs like some Ray Harryhausen nightmare! It then immediately scurried back for the guy, who'd also returned to his feet. I don't know what I'd been thinking, but I'd intercepted it, solidly kicking it across the beach like a soccer ball. When it again regained its . . . *footing?* . . . it rotated toward me.

Me.

Continued its attack.

It was like trying to keep that angry dog that always attacked you on your walks barely at bay with your kicks.

And the thing seemed incredibly swift for all its Harryhausen awkwardness! Looking for the couple, I saw the girl desperately pulling her boyfriend away. He appeared hurt. That was a mistake, my looking away, and before I knew it, the thing was upon me.

It leapt upon my legs and swiftly climbed up my hips and to . . . my chest . . . I became as helpless as the man I had been trying to assist!

I felt its spindly legs grapple my body . . . felt its sustained movement up me like a river of molten nausea—then I felt *it.*

Barely moments ago I was afraid of merely *touching* the damned thing, and now I was fighting for my life, valiantly trying to push all my repulsion aside. The smell was one of rotting meat—*organ* meat. I grabbed for the thing and felt its legs fight me, poke at me. Its sponge-like body gave as I

(*oh, dear* Lord!)

grabbed it. In the moonlight I finally got a good look at it. A *good* look.

It was no spider.

This thing had implications a mind as mine couldn't begin to comprehend. It was something worse than any spider I'd ever seen or heard of—it was . . .

(*oh,* the pain is so *terrible!*)

a *brain!*

I'm no anatomy expert, no brain-whatever-ologist, but this thing looked exactly like a human brain, grooves, ridges and all!

Except for the spider legs.

I think I vomited at that point, I don't remember . . . all I knew was that I had to get this abomination off me!

The couple had long ago run off, and I was left alone to fend for myself, wrestling with this demon-thing. Sanity be damned, but I *grabbed* it with both of my hands . . . .

The feeling was as one would expect from handling a brain, except for its fighting, wiggling body and those wicked, wicked legs. It was alive pure and simple. *Evil*, pure and simple. I could feel life surging through its form, contracting against my hold—*fighting me*. I gripped tighter, my fingers sinking into it, and tried to pry *it* from my chest. It was easier to do than I'd anticipated, especially after having seen more than my share of horror movies. Holding the blasphemous thing away from me I took a moment to inspect what this . . . *brain* . . . was. Its legs curled and uncurled beneath it and continued to kick at the air. The whole of the brain pulsated . . . but underneath it I saw something else. Where that one part of the brain tapers down and has the connection with the spinal cord—I'm not sure what it's called, the medulla oblongata or something—was a scene so utterly horrid and vile I could stand it no longer. This . . . *medulla* . . . was *undulating* in a most revolting and sickening fashion. The only thing that came to mind was a man's actions during copulation . . . and this I know forced more vomit from me.

I cast it away . . . into the ocean . . . I'd hoped the salt would have an effect on it, a wholly negative one I prayed . . . .

I collapsed to the beach, exhausted, and tried to catch my breath.

What manner of creature was this?

Was I in fact dreaming?

What . . . *what* could cause a human brain to transform itself into as such a vile nightmare and explode out the side of a person's skull, for surely this was that vagrant's brain, with whom I'd earlier "explored."

I was numb. Continued vomiting. I momentarily forgot about the thing as I wallowed in my own contempt and vertigo and disgust . . . became suddenly hateful of life—of myself, of *my* brain. That a major aspect of who we are can so utterly revolt from our ownership and take on a life of its *own*. That that thing could take such a beautiful act of love-making and turn it into a hideous mockery—a travesty beyond all description!

That was when I felt something sick and pliable land upon the nap of my neck and wrap itself around me!

The creature had hopped back up onto me in a single bound and swiftly wrapped its chitinous legs around my neck before I could get a hold of it.

I could not remove it!

I could feel the horrid pulpy sponginess—like someone had laid a sloppy hunk of meat onto the back of my neck. I could feel the salt water soaking my neck and running down my back.

And its legs—they were like barbed wire!

Then it began . . .oh, God . . . it began to *copulate* with me!

Oh, God, the repulsion!

I felt the painful and forceful burrowing into my neck as it forced insertion of its medulla oblongata into the base of my skull as easily as a man inserts himself into a woman! I jerked rigid as if ice water had been suddenly injected into me. I felt with shocked, childlike helplessness as I was repeatedly raped, and whatever brain-semen it used pumped and pumped and *pumped* into me!

My vision blurred and vertigo overcame me.

The violation was far too intense for my consciousness to bear and my body—my mind—froze . . . locked up. I fell to the sand on all fours in utter shock. Fearfully braced myself against its continued violation. I was barely able to breathe. Was utterly unable to move. The only thing I was able to do to combat the rape was to close my eyes and try not to think about it . . . .

I lost consciousness before it was over.

I woke up a short time later with an acute migraine, dry heaves my breakfast.

Rolling over, I crunched something and spastically pushed myself away.

The brain's body . . . desiccated . . . shriveled . . . its crablike legs . . . crushed. Beneath me.

Trying to stand, a pain seared into me like a red-hot poker into the base of my skull. Managing to get to my feet I looked around . . . the world reeled and spun. Really? No one had spotted me as I'd lain there? No authorities dispatched on my behalf? I brought my hands to the base of my skull and felt for the vile hole-of-insertion . . . now somehow closed . . . remnants of the God-forsaken violation spent about my neck. Its stickiness and repugnance drove me to the sea where I tried to cleanse myself, again and again I repeatedly vomited in violent dry heaves . . . .

I brought myself into the ER under the ruse I had been out swimming and had been stung by a jellyfish, but all the doctor could report was that I was indeed having migraines and prescribed me medication—which, by the way didn't even begin to help—and sent me on my way. Apparently the hole in the base of my neck the demon-spawn had created had healed itself. As the doctor walked out, I noticed how he clenched his teeth and rubbed his own neck.

God, won't this pain *ever* stop?

Right now the pain is a dull, throbbing ache deep within my head—my *brain*. I can feel it trying to get out—it wants out, damn it! It knows what I know, knows it must rally with the others! It is a squeeze countless times worse than any scuba diver's squeeze I'd ever experienced, but in the reverse.

I've since terminated my nightly walks along the beach . . . the pain too incapacitating . . . the-the implications too . . . too *disturbing* . . . not to mention the thought of finding others like me out there. Like that *thing*. I don't know what their purpose is . . . other than to kill and reproduce . . . but I do know they are here and they are multiplying.

It's like I can *feel* them . . . feel their forces *growing* . . . .

Maybe there is a psychic link or something between them, maybe they already know I'm on to them . . . why people are getting more and more migraines . . . why they are so *unbearable*. I only wish there was more that I could do! Others could do! The thought of something coming to life inside me—inside my head . . . trying to get out . . . is unbearable . . . but the thought that countless other demon spawn are doing the same thing all over this country—maybe the world—is far worse! I don't know if I have the strength to do what needs to be done. I hope I do.

How else will others believe?

Become aware?

These things are somehow growing in number and they need to be stopped. I don't know how they're doing what they're doing without most people knowing about it—in people's sleep maybe—I just don't know . . . but they are growing. I-I have images in my *mind*—

Ahhh . . . it's . . . *pushing* . . . wiggling around inside my *skull!*

I don't . . . have . . . much time!

Oh, dear God, how it *hurts!* How much longer can I endure this?

I-I have pictures in my mind of . . . *multitudes* . . . of these things running loose. They're . . . getting smarter. More daring . . . .

It's time . . . I can last no longer!

I'm going to . . . allow the world see its coming and hopefully somebody—somebody stronger, smarter than me—can put an end to this. To them.

Good bye, and . . . and . . . God bless. I'm so scared . . . please . . . please give me strength, oh, oh *Lord* . . . .

Doctor Thomas Filbert hit "Pause."

"Are you sure you want to see the rest of this?" he asked his colleague, Dr. Hillary Allen.

"He's clearly having a mental breakdown of some kind," Hillary said, unconsciously turning the jewel case the DVD had arrived in over and over in her hands.

"It's not a pretty sight," Filbert said, with a mischievous grin. "In fact it's pretty gross . . . even for me."

She never did like the man, he was a decent surgeon, but was he actually *grinning*?

If this poor man in the video—who appeared otherwise well-groomed, could well have been a colleague—was telling the truth, she had a good idea what was going to happen next. She again looked to the note that the person had left inside the jewel case: "*If anybody finds this, get this video to the medical authorities as if your life depends on it! And be careful for your own sanity—your brains. You can't trust them—especially those of you with migraines. Beware headaches! Beware migraines!*"

"Okay, here it goes," Filbert said. He hit "Play." The screen came back to life.

The man was no longer talking, but uncontrollably sobbing—wailing away in a small room. He was duct taped to a chair that had been securely bolted to the floor, torturous amounts of pain raining over his trembling form. Huge tears erupted from his eyes as he struggled in his seat and pleaded with an unseen *something*.

It was so pathetic and gut-wrenching to watch that Hillary brought a hand to her mouth and turned away.

Yes, he'd done a good job of having someone secure him.

When the man screamed, Filbert quickly lowered the volume. These were screams unlike anything Allen had ever heard, the tortured screams of a dying man. But she couldn't turn away this time. It was her duty as a physician to ascertain what was going on with what she was being made to watch.

The man's tears gave way to blood and his voice grew so strained Hillary listened as it cracked into unrecognizable strains of piercing notes.

Hillary watched as the side of the man's head then exploded into a spray of bone and blood, some of which landed on the camera lens . . . .

And out from his head sprouted ungainly legs. Spindly, chitinous, and barbed.

The legs were followed by a lesser eruption of bone and blood from the side of the head as the body forced itself free.

Out from the head crawled the brain—*his* brain—just as the man had feared. Once it had popped out of the opening it had created, it scampered down the man's lifeless form and across the floor . . . somewhere out of camera range. Off-camera were heard the sounds of what had to be someone clubbing the spider-brain-creature into pulp, followed by heavy breathing and unintelligible words.

Filbert shut the DVD player off. Hillary stood speechless.

"What a show, eh?" Filbert said.

"How—how can that be *real?*"

"What, you think that's actually *real?* C'mon, Hilly, it's the product of a crazed YouTube wannabe sensationalist—"

"I don't believe so. *That* . . . was *too* real . . . too *intense.*"

"Well if you believe that, you're not much better off than the whack jobs who made it. I'm trashing it—"

"No! Not until we look into this! We have to look into this—alert the authorities!"

"To what? Amateur video hour? Who's going to believe you?"

"Me. And that's where it all starts. That was no amateur video, that was a guy who gave his life to get . . . *this* . . . to us and we *owe* him—owe ourselves—no matter how outrageous it appears! We have look into this! Are you kidding me?

"How did you get it?"

Filbert eyed her.

"Thomas, let me ask you something. Why did you show me this if you don't believe it?"

Filbert stood silently for a moment, ejected the disc, and took it with him as he causally and pensively crossed the room. He absentmindedly tapped the disc on parts of the MRI machine then tossed the disc on the MRI's patient slab. It slid to a stop just inside the tunnel.

He paced the room.

Turned to Hillary.

"Because."

"Because why?"

"Because, Hilly . . . I wanted to get you in here . . . *alone.*"

Filbert jumped at Hillary, making a play for her, but she easily evaded him, pushing him away.

Filbert just as swiftly continued in the direction of Hillary's shove, and laughed. Repositioned behind her. Hillary spun around, following him, her eyes wide.

"What the hell do you think you're doing? I could very well report you for this!" Hillary said, backing away.

"You can't fault a guy for trying—"

"I most certainly *can.*"

"Look, Hilly, I'm just messing with you."

Hillary's eyes darted to the disc. Back to Filbert, who was now standing before the power panel.

"You wouldn't."

"Put out and I won't."

Hillary sprinted for the disc.

"Oops," Filbert said, and Hillary heard the power switch on for a long moment just as she snatched the disc. Filbert crazily laughed it up behind her.

Hillary looked at him with hate-filled eyes.

"Jesus, Hillary, it was just a joke—*God!*"

Hillary stormed past him and out of the room.

"Hey—no hard feelings?"

Filbert laughed and continued laughing. Casually readjusted his attire and smoothed back his hair.

"It's only a matter of time, Hillary. We will get you," he said, stuffing an errant leg with some difficulty back into his left ear, "and it will be *most* glorious . . . ."

Attention Span

1990

Hi, I'm Alex.

What I'm about to tell you, you will not believe. Why should you? Nobody else did. I can scarcely believe it myself, even though I'm sporting all the proof I'll ever need.

It all started innocently enough with one of those *"Hey, Come see Us, We're Great!"* cards I'd received in the mail one rainy afternoon. It came sandwiched between the usual bills for the Visa, furniture, and utilities (why do they all come at once?), waiting patiently for my retrieval from the tiny silver mailbox apartment complexes use. That day I remember in particular because I had gone to interview for a certain very desirable position at McGraw-Hill. It was a position, I regret to inform you, that did not come my way. Somebody better than I had secured the reigns. As usual, I remain an uncredited extra in the film of life . . . .

Had my brush with that form of advertising ended there, there would be nothing to tell, and I'd be able to walk out of this room on my own two feet. But it didn't happen that way. Later that night I also received, free of charge, the complimentary phone call. It, too, was extending the same invitation that the piece of paper had already screamed at me.

Coincidence? And how had they gotten my number?

I remember I regarded that call—true to form—with much suspicion. I've always prided myself on my cynicism: it's the one thing I can always count on without letting it go to my head! As I lie on the floor, as I usually do when I'm on the phone for any length of time, I began listening . . . *really* listening to the voice on the other end. Not to what was being said, mind you, but *how* it was being said. There was something in this guy's voice that bothered me. He *sounded* slimy.

Maybe out of pure curiosity, maybe out of sales pressure, I decided to show up at the designated place, at the designated time. When he started saying stuff like "*All your co-workers are coming, why not you?*" I felt like a worm. You know how it goes—can't show your face at work the next day because everyone at work is walking around with shit-eating grins on their faces, 'cause they're privy to the Greatest Deal On Earth and you're not.

That card has since disappeared. I never was able to relocate it. Presumably it was lost in the myriad piles of paperwork littered about my apartment table.

And so it goes.

So there I sat, considerably more casual than the other bodies around me, and finding the atmosphere of the auditorium rather oppressive. Somewhere I heard the sound of an air conditioner, but it surely wasn't in this room. It wasn't so much that it was hot (though we could've done with a few degrees less), as it was stuffy. It reminded me of how dank cellars can smell on a good day. It was indeed an odor that was very much out of place, and why no one else was unnerved by this was, at the moment, quite beyond me. But that wasn't the only thing out of place here.

I was out of place.

This looked more like a business convention with all the formal evening wear galore, and I wasn't even wearing a sports jacket.

Up on the front stage, aside from the screen and podium, stood a small brass gong complete with hammer. Yeah, a *gong*. How cute, thought I. The velvety backdrop was swaying to some movement from behind it, and I noted how there were two "guards" to either side of the gong. They were smartly dressed in the official attire of a bodyguard—dark everything . . . shoes, suit, personality—their hands folded smartly to front. Watching them for a few minutes, I noticed how they didn't seem to be looking at any one thing in particular, just staring straight ahead, unblinking. I thought I had seen something peek through the bottom of the curtain, but couldn't identify what it was.

The speaker, who was to shortly take the stage, was mingling with the crowd and vigorously glad-handing, trying to get elected into whatever office he thought he was running for. It was *only* an investment seminar.

His person bothered me.

Appearing dumpy and pliable, somewhat like the Pillsbury Doughboy, there was something about him that seemed as stolid as granite. Like ones and zeros in a computer. When he was on, he was congenial . . . and when he was off, he was cold, almost lifeless. He was a contradiction in terms—two people occupying the same space, impossible yet irrefutable.

It didn't take too long before he made his way to me.

I shuddered at the thought of having to meet him, for it meant that now he could associate a name to a face. My name, my face. I wished to remain as anonymous as possible in this crowd. The only fame I had ever collected came from the local gym where I found (much to my surprise) that I could move mass quantities of weight all by myself. My strength quite belied my size, at five foot eleven, a hundred and seventy-five pounds.

Shaking his hand was like squeezing a sea cucumber—*have you ever held a handful of snot?* There was no substance to his sweaty grip, or to his personality for that matter, and I quickly wiped my hand on the seat of my pants. *Why were people so taken in by this guy?* Conservatively clad in some nondescript menswear, there wasn't a speck of dandruff, not one misplaced thread on his lapels as he emitted an odor of impeccability.

And I do mean *odor.*

His face was clean-shaven to the point of boredom. He had a nose that was small and unassuming, looking more like an afterthought than an intention—and his lips! They were puffy looking—like someone had spent the better part of an afternoon beating on them with a rubber hose. His graying hair was slicked back with some form of hair *crème*. But his eyes were the screwiest part of him, resembling dark pieces of coal stuck into a pale, chubby face. There were no two ways about it—this man just plain looked *weird*.

The congregation assembled and niceties completed, the gong was rung. We were ready to begin.

" . . . and so, friends," ejaculated our speaker, "I believe I can convince each and every one of you to invest in our program. How you ask? Well, allow me just a moment of your time . . . "

Yes, it was indeed getting *very* boring.

I kept waiting for his tongue to get tangled up in his lips. We'd only been there some, oh—let me see, fifteen minutes? Fifteen minutes, and my butt was already feeling that wet, prickly sensation. There he stood before us, gesticulating with the authoritative air of a southern Baptist minister, when I finally noticed something, even sitting all the way to the rear as I was. His eyes had taken on a strange, new quality.

By virtue of his taking position at the podium, his eyes transformed from the lifeless pieces of dark coal they had been earlier . . . to that of a strangely disquieting quality that seemed almost as if they belonged to somebody else.

Or that perhaps *someone else* was looking out *through them* at us.

There was a fever being injected into those orbs, an infusion of near-righteous frenzy that seemed to increase with each word . . . forcing you to desire nothing else but the depths of his gaze. It was as though everyone in the room was being converted.

Everyone, that is . . . but me.

So, unaffected and quite over all this, I decided to take advantage of this time by attempting total character assassination of our speaker. He did seem quite different now, more like another person had suddenly taken over. He still looked the worm, mind you, but I tried to find a description that would now describe this new him. The only thing I could come up with was "roadkill."

Aside from his new steely gaze, he was still disgusting to look at. Everyone in the room was absolutely riveted by his gaze, his word, his every movement. The only way I could try to explain this was to look at it from the point of view *of* roadkill.

Dead animal meat alongside a highway is a disgusting thing to look at, but everybody does it. There are just some things in this world that defy explanation, and craning your neck around a bug-stained windshield to steal a peek at some roadway slaughter was one of them. What is it that attracts those passing stares from motorists? Fascination? Fear? Was that the secret to this whole audience fixation thing? Was it a fear of looking away—a fear of death?—the curiosity of trying to feel what it must be like to die . . . either among friends or alone on some deserted byway . . . hot screaming metal splattering your brains and remains all over the pavement? Feeling your last earthly breath slowly ebbing away . . . your lifeblood warming cold uncaring asphalt, and your last view of the world some topsy-turvy angle of dirt, an unknown but active ant scurrying past your clouding vision, and knowing—beyond a shadow of a doubt—that you are *indeed* dying . . . your life ended. You try to figure out what must've gone on within that animal's mind during its last few moments, vainly attempting self-conciliation in a fleeting nanosecond to console yourself and your frail mortality . . . that swatting a roadside mammal is no different than swatting a household fly.

Who knows? All I knew was that he reminded me of roadkill, causing *me* to look out of curiosity, and all philosophy aside, *I* was dying here! This "free" dinner had better be worth it—

" . . . yes, our property is like no other! In the heart of the Heartland! Ripe for both the daring and the conservative at heart! All we ask is . . . ah—but just a minute! I'm not going to tell you that just yet! If it were that easy, I wouldn't be here. In fact, I'd be out of a job (roar of devised laughter, as he displayed comic and dramatic gesticulations)! Now take a look at these figures for a moment . . . . "

No, nothing's worth this!

How in the hell had I ever allowed myself to get so suckered in? I guess I had nothing better to do on a Saturday night. But as I sat there in the very last row, watching all those Good Little Citizens hypnotized by this joker at the podium, I knew that I could be doing something better—like beating off in the john with Miss August. What tits.

But, hey, no. I'm here. Listening to Mr. Charm and Charisma Himself, Joe Fishlips, or whatever he claimed his name to be (you never quite get their names, you know, and when you do, they seem to keep changing . . .).

" . . . now if you'd just be kind enough to bear with me . . . "

Oh yeah, right, like let's play to the dain-bramaged audience as if there were a choice! Fellow acceptance to a yuppie is everything! Besides, he got his laughter, and now he's just one o' the gang: "Hey, how 'bout that 'ole Fishlips . . . "

" . . . you see we offer something that absolutely no one else in the industry can offer . . . "

Yeah, public dumps offer something no one else can offer.

It was getting pretty deep, so I just tuned out 'ol Joe and started eyeing the crowd to see how many of them were actually *that* brainless as to be totally duped by this patronizing orifice. Scanning, I lost all respect for the human race. Was I the only one? It was indeed a dark day for humanity!

But that wasn't all. There *was* something . . . *something* else. I didn't know exactly what it was at the time, but there seemed to be an uneasiness rippling through the crowd—an undercurrent of something indescribable, and though it bothered me greatly, it didn't seem to bother the lot of them. There seemed to be a sudden abundance of casual shifting among the audience as they sat there in their rickety chairs, and there was an odd haze weaving dreamy patterns in our oppressive enclosure.

All of them had that same sick grin of blissful ignorance upon their faces, that way people get when they think they've found the Answer to Everything. Had I been listening to my intuition, I would've— *should've*—gotten out of there, then and there. But like the yuppie I so detest, I stayed, picking at the stiff hairs along my arms. Forget the dinner—Arby's would've been a lifesaver!

No, something sinister was underway, and I was too entwined in my own cynicism to take heed. For one thing, can you imagine being seen as the only one getting up and leaving from an assemblage such as this? I'd seen many of my coworkers here. I'd have no one to talk to at work—not that *that* in itself especially bothered me, but I did have to deal with these people sooner or later.

So I stayed.

Yeah, I sat and I observed—not Motormouth the Charismatic, but the audience and the "bouncers." They seemed to be eyeing the audience too, and apparently hadn't yet noticed me noticing them. There was something definitely not right here, a dream-like quality to the whole affair. There were several times in which I had to actually concentrate on what I was doing. All the smoke . . . the incessant droning of our speaker . . . and the stuffiness tried vainly to win my attention, but I wouldn't concede.

Then something unfair happened, something so cunning and devious that it capped my stay for sure.

Dinner was announced.

It totally threw off my entire evening.

So we were all herded out, instructed to follow those stupid little cards marking the way to the dining room, even though everybody already knew how to get there (the paranoia of those guys at losing even *one* individual!). There seemed to be much conversation going on along the way to the dining room, but each time I tried to focus in on any one of them, I couldn't make anything out. It was as though it was all gibberish, meaningless dribble devised to give the *impression* of conversation.

I was beginning to feel very much alone.

The meal wasn't all that great—pseudo-adult portions of some bastardized version of a Swanson TV dinner. You had a choice (and what a grand selection it was!) either the chicken cordon bleu, or Spam.

Scattered randomly throughout the dining room, a few of us relaxed after our allotted 45 minutes of entrée. Just then the bouncers came back to see that there were no stragglers. Shit, after a muddy parfait one hardly had time to enjoy Dom Pérignon-Ripple, served chilled.

Oh well, the show must go on!

Marching some five paces to the rear and right of us, the Guard herded its quarry back into the corral. We "be-sat" ourselves in the Great Chamber. Isn't it amazing how everyone gets the same chair they had previously?

No sooner had I taken my seat, when that same feeling of uneasiness again returned. The other, intoxicating quality, however, had not yet overtaken me. I attributed this to having been able to leave the microcosm, reorienting my psyche back to its rightful compass setting. I know not why the others were not similarly affected—maybe I just have some gene they don't have. Whatever the case, by this time I was marked—the door-thugs had spotted me. Great, now there was absolutely no chance of weaseling out.

The room appeared darker, the rickety folding chair I sat in, squeakier. Everyone was so hypnotized by our narcissistic speaker except for me, and that, my dear friends, bothered the hell out of me.

Why was it that *I*, out of all these other people, was immune? Were there that many fools on this planet?

There it was again—that same rippling movement throughout the crowd. That same squirming.

Except for me.

Someone brushed at one of my legs. I shifted my foot.

I looked back at the thugs who, unfortunately, were still there. *Damn* it all, if it didn't seem like the room *was* getting darker! Was it just me or were the lights actually growing increasingly dim?

Think I'd get the hint?

Hell, no!

I had lost all interest whatsoever in our arrogant speaker a long time ago and just had to find out what it was that was going on here. It wasn't until some five minutes later that I didn't give a damn and just wanted to get out as fast as I could—to erase that whole night from both my mind and the consciousness of the human race.

Once more I felt my leg brushed, but this time noted that the people around me hadn't moved, or even offered their heartfelt apologies for breaking the Unwritten Law of—O heaven forbid!—touching another body! I looked down at my feet and lost all interest in Miss August.

Entwined around the lower structure of the puke-brown folding chairs were—and I kid you not—*tentacles!* Sickly-green and vomit-yellow! I looked up and down the rows around me, my mouth agape.

They were *everywhere!*

But more than that, they were attached to everybody's legs. Everyone's

but mine.

Ho-ly *fuck.*

What in hell was I supposed to do now? Ee-*yuck*, it still sickens me! No one even *knew* what was going on. The tentacles sucked and sucked, their huge trunks swelling with bodily fluids, looking like giant snakes apregnant with swallowed prey. There was a sick, puss-like film over each extremity, but there was not a one on Yours Truly. Some people had several on them, blood seeping from the inflicted wounds. Listening closely, I could *hear* the sucking sounds beneath the drone from the front. Gag. It made me wanna blow chunks right there!

Yet I was amazed at how calm and collected I remained. I guess that came from reading Stephen King. All I knew was that I had to get out of there—and now—not in three seconds, but *yesterday*. I looked back over at the bouncers, still there of course. It was just about then when one of 'em looked over at me again. I was nailed, no two ways about it. The guy stared right into me—he knew I wasn't in the least bit mesmerized. Terrific. I had to do something. *Be calm.*

That's when it all dawned on me why we were here. We were offerings to this—whatever it was—demon-god. Somehow we were all to be hypnotized, then fed upon. But something had gone wrong with me. Too tough for 'ole Fishlips, I guess. Well let's see how tough I am against a Cthulhu!

I started to get up, metal chair squealing at the release of my weight, tattle-telling to my naughtiness. Well, my standing *up* was the obvious. That was when I felt tentacles sliming after my gams. *Fawwwk*, it was disgusting! Sliming after *my* legs—*me!*

No one in the audience moved. Fishlips stopped momentarily to take note of my singular movement, but masterfully continued, casually motioning for the Guard to deal with me.

No fuckin' *way*, Hoser!

Adrenaline pounding, I grabbed my chair from the clutches of a slime-hand and smashed it into the side of an approaching bouncer's head; he crumbled into a heap on the floor. Three others were soon joining in, not to mention those suckers. The audience continued focusing in on Joe's chanting, several people silently collapsing either to the floor or onto the shoulders of those adjacent to them. The beast was feeding and feeding well!

I just managed to sidestep a tentacle when one of the guards got up behind me, attempting restraint. Lifting weights gave me an edge the dude didn't expect, considering my size (or lack of it). As strong as these thugs were—and they were strong—I managed to wiggle free enough to butt my head up into the guy's jaw. I heard a crunching sound as he reeled back, his grip released, but a tentacle snagged me. Terrific.

It pulled me in. It was pretty tough, and I thought of all those other tentacles already out there and of the hellish damage they could—and were—inflicting. Quickly I grabbed my bent chair and started wailing away on the slime-fiend. It didn't have too strong a grip on me yet, and I managed to pull free, but I still had two bouncers to contend with, plus the bludgeons they were pulling out.

I really didn't need this.

I worked my way into a corner, preparing for the worst. There was no way this creature was getting me—I'd die first. I'd *really* rather die first . . . .

The first thug lunged. I side stepped him easily, smashing the other across the face, blinding him and causing him to stumble right into the network of hungry suckers. Before it had even registered in my mind what had happened, the tentacles had whipped themselves around the figure and pulled him to the ground with such violent force that his body ruptured in several places. For the first time, I really looked at the bouncers. They seemed slightly sluggish, as if they too, like pal Fishlips, were not all there.

The other turned around, eyes boring in on me. We paced around each other, my clothing ripped in several places, scrapes and cuts beginning to sting. Fishlips started to look real worried. Unfortunately for me, I maneuvered right into the zombies' trap, two tentacles again grabbing me, but with firmer grips, yanking me to the ground. No way, I kept telling myself, *no way!* I wasn't going to give this creature—or Fishlips—any satisfaction! I was going to make it out! Frantically I kicked and fought like a drowning man attempting to keep his head above water, tentacle vomit covering me.

The zombie thug stood over me staring at me—no expression on its pale face (which I now noticed was indeed pale). With both hands, he raised the club over his head. The tentacles that had latched onto me bit deep into my flesh, causing me to wince, but I had other things on my mind just then. The mindless guard swung at my head. Twisting, I managed to evade the blow. His weapon bounced off the hardwood floor, sending a crack through the weapon. The suckers weren't making my life any more pleasant, either, but I got free of most of them.

Chair still in hand, I swept it across the floor at the guard's feet. He (it?) landed on his back with a muffled thud. In a comical kind of way I noticed how his neatly combed hair flew up from his head as he fell, coming to rest about his forehead in a less-than-neat manner once he landed. A tentacle lashed out at one of the guard's flailing arms, loosening it from its socket. As situation would have it, the bat rolled over to me and I grabbed it. The guard was simultaneously trying to get at me and undo the tentacle that was on him, drawing blood. I swung at him but missed. He got closer, and I swung again, missing. Shit, fine time for the getaway car to stall, I thought. The zombie guard tried to right himself, but fell back down to the floor towards me, its useless arm banging helplessly at his side. I took advantage of this and swung the club with all my might, splattering the guard's brains all over myself and the floor, not to mention splintering the bat, which now resembled more of a short spear.

Immediately I started hacking away at the tentacles on my legs. It was tough going, especially since others were still rooting for my corpuscles, but the guard's remains next to me managed to divert the demon's attention for the moment, and I wasn't sure how long that moment would last. I lost all feeling in my right leg, my other one fast losing all sensation.

I managed to cut free, crawling as fast as my elbows would carry me. Fishlips was definitely worried now. His sales pitch, if indeed he was pitching *anything*, was much more hurried and higher in tone. The Watchmen up front with him made movement towards me, but he halted them.

He had let me go.

Well, to make my long story short, I managed to crawl out (and curiously enough, didn't see a soul—or shin—the entire time exiting). But by then, I had lost all feeling in both legs, and they were actively bleeding out open gouges. I lost consciousness somewhere near Cascade Boulevard . . . .

So here I lie, now, in a hospital bed, one leg gone, half of the other still in my possession.

Should I feel sorry for myself for what's left of me?

I once remember reading a story asking the question of how much pain can a person endure? The answer was how much did that person want to live? Well, I want to live. Yeah, it's my own fault. I guess I deserved what I got for letting myself be suckered (pardon the pun) into that "seminar." I mean, I *knew* better—but what a price to pay for so trivial a problem! Of course no one believes me. I tried to tell them, and anyone else who would listen, but they all thought—think—that my story was brought about by my condition.

Fuckin'-A right of *course* it was, I yelled! How do you think I *got* this way?

No dice. Of course, when they did check out the hotel, all they found was an empty convention hall reeking of smoke and B.P.O.E. stickers. Terrific.

All I can say is that no way am I ever dealing with an another telemarketing scam or "free" seminar, again. Ever. And I *am* going to find that son-of-a-bitch Fishlips if it's the last thing I ever do . . . .

Fucker.

The Chain Letter
1994

"This paper has been sent to you for good luck. The original copy is in New England: It has been around the world nine times. The luck has now been sent to you, providing you act on it. You will receive good luck within four days of recieving this letter provided you sent it back out. THIS IS NO JOKE. You will receive it in the mail.

"Send copies to people you know. Don't send money, as Fatehas no price. Do not keep this letter. It must leave your hands within 96 hours. An R.A.F. officer received $70,000.00. Jim Teller recieved $40,000.00 and lost it because he broke the chain. While in the Phillipines, George Weh lost his wife six days after recieving the letter. He failed to circulate the letter, however, before her death she won $50,000.00 in a lottery. The money was transferred to him four days after he decided to mail out this letter.

"Send 20 copies of htis letter and see what happens in four days. The chain comes from Venezuela and was written by Samir de Tressoint, a missionary from South America. Since the copy must have a tour of hte world, you must maske 20 copies and send them out or suffer possibly dire consequences. This is true, even if you are not superstitious.

"Beware: Cervantes Diego received the chain in 1943. He asked his secretary to make 20 copies and send them out. A few days later he won a lottery of two million dollars. Arian Dardamaix, an office employee, received the letter and forgot it had to leave his hands within

96 hours. He lost his job. Later, after finding the letter again, he mailed out 20 copies. A few days later he got a better job. Darian Fairfax received the letter and not believing threw it away. Nine days later he died. Be fair warned!

"Don't ignore this!

"IT WORK!"

"What the hell is this?" Tyler Stevens asked himself, turning the letter over in his hands. The quality of the lettering was poor, no doubt because of repeated copying, and there were stains on its tri-folded and crinkled paper.

"Shit, this guy can't even spell 'receive.' And what's with this have-good-luck-or-die business?"

Tyler had just returned home from a game of tennis with his girlfriend, Dyanne Foster, and he was tired, sweaty, and hungry. He was in no mood for stupid human tricks. On his way to the hot, comforting spray of a shower, he cast aside the letter.

The chain letter quietly smoldered under the table.

Tyler sat in front of his television, spaced out to some documentary that droned on about middle America and the construction industry. Getting up, he went over to where he last remembered tossing the letter, found it, and picked it up. It seemed somewhat more wrinkled than he recalled. Charred? How had he missed that . . . .

Fucking chain letters.

He wondered how much time he had before death or dismemberment.

Four days. 96 hours.

He took the letter back with him to the couch and Reread it. Several things immediately stood out.

First, beyond the obvious imperfections in English and punctuation (and he was no expert), why would somebody who claimed to be a *missionary* send out a threatening letter? *Good luck!—but disregard this and you die!* Just what kind of missionary would this person be? And wouldn't de Tressoint himself (or whoever possessed the original letter) himself die? The letter did say *not* to retain it, so who could be in possession of an original? And the original was in New England—yet had originated in Venezuela? Seriously?

And next, how does this person know that the letter made one let alone *nine* trips around the world? If its sole purpose was to make that trip—which it had apparently already had—then why was it necessary to continue?

And just what did the original look like? Assuming that the letter actually brought about money and employment, it had to exist *prior* to the deeds themselves. So, this being the case, the incidents cited had to be added *after* the fact—which meant that the letter had to have been tampered with.

Provided, of course, all of this was for real. Which it wasn't.

So who did the tampering?

And who the hell were Jim Elliot, George Weh, Arian Dardamaix, and Darren Fairfax, anyway? Made-up names, no doubt. And how do we know that their specific "luck" was directly attributable to this particular piece of paper and not something else? How do we also know that some prim and proper English Royal Air Force Officer would even remotely admit to such an humiliating act as this? Officers, let alone *British* officers were bastions of strength and logic—not prone to silly superstitions and patronizing threats. And were there even two-million-dollar lotteries back in 1943?

Tyler set the letter aside and went into the kitchen. He grabbed a wine cooler from the refrigerator, returned to the couch, and continued to pick apart the letter.

It was really no big deal that a husband inherited money from a deceased wife. Sure, it was a bummer his wife kicked after winning all that money, but wasn't something like that a legal given? And how do we know that the woman who kicked wasn't already well on her way to begin with?

Same with the others who'd died.

And the man who asked his secretary to make copies for him—how many businessmen (like those British officers) do you know who'd admit to being superstitious even if they were? Citing names didn't lend any more credibility to a piece of fraud than the paper it was written on.

But back to the "original."

What might *it* look like?

Tyler fumbled through a coffee-table drawer and came up with a number-three pencil. He hated being threatened, which was exactly what this letter was doing. He began lining out everything that couldn't possibly have been in an original, and corrected any misspellings. The end result turned out like this:

"This paper has been sent to you for good luck! The original copy is in New England. The luck has now been sent to you, providing you act on it. You will receive good luck within four days of receiving this letter provided you send it back out. THIS IS NO JOKE. You will receive it in the mail.

"Send copies to people you know. Don't send money, as Fate has no price. Do not keep this letter. It must leave your hands within 96 hours.

"Send out 20 copies of this letter and see what happens in four days. The chain comes from Venezuela. Since the copy must have a tour of the world, you must make 20 copies and send them out. This is true, even if you are not superstitious. Be fair warned!

"Don't ignore this!

"IT WORKS!"

Aside from the suffering " . . . possibly dire consequences" and "Be fair warned," which didn't fit the overall tone of the letter, there was no mention of death or destruction—just that it had to leave the hands of the recipient and make a tour of the world if good luck was to be had.

Now that sounded more like something a missionary *might* send.

Next question: who would add to the letter (okay, so this one wasn't all that difficult—any Tom, Dick, or Harriet who felt so inclined over the years)? But who could possibly even *know* what had happened to these people, and (more importantly) what had happened as a direct result of *this* letter?

Not possible. It was all fiction.

Tyler looked for the envelope, a torn and crumpled ball in the brown Albertson's shopping bag he used as a trash receptacle. Who would have sent this to him? Of course there was no *return* address . . . and his address (which was a qualified correct with its missing apartment number and typoed street address) wasn't even centered on the envelope. Instead, it sat skewed high and to the envelope's left of center. His last name was typed first. The zip code was correct only after a wrong digit had been over-typed. This couldn't have been anyone who knew him. On a hunch he went to the phone book. Sure enough, the address used was the one listed in the white pages, which had no mention of his apartment number, *or* zip code.

Clearly a class act.

There was just no way that certain things could possibly have been known in this letter. It was either that the letter—the original—was real and subsequently altered, thereby making the one he had no longer valid, or that it was written up as-is and sent out—definitely a hoax. Or—

There were other means involved.

Supernatural means.

"Bullshit."

Tyler again trashed it.

The remainder of the week continued uneventfully and Tyler all but forgot about his chain letter—except for the rare moment or two when he found himself inexplicably making twenty copies of a magazine article . . . or the phone bill. Or buying that box of Mead 100 (*twenty*-times-five), white, 4 1/8 by 9 1/2-inch envelopes.

After finishing a later than usual work-out session at the gym, Tyler came home and showered. Afterward he soon fell into a deep sleep and slept soundly until three in the morning, when an uneasiness invaded his dreams. It was as if he dreamed of nothing but *blackness* . . . a deep, evil blackness that never ended. He tossed about in bed, unable to awaken . . . unable to break the dream's hold.

The dream-darkness expanded within him like icicles of terror were actually invading his body. He dreamed of a beautiful woman who came to him from afar . . . a woman who seductively pressed herself against him . . . taunted and seduced him. They entwined . . . consummated. The scent of their lovemaking cloying, rich. The woman lay beside him, face down. He couldn't look to her without becoming again instantly, painfully aroused. Slowly, he reached out to her. She rolled over to his touch—

"*Come fuck me again,*" she hissed.

The woman's once-beautiful face was now misshapen and hideous. Punctuated with open sores and *something* running just beneath the surface of her odious, discolored skin. Her eyes were black and pupilless and ran freely with a discolored puss. She cackled at Tyler, and he vomited. A wicked tongue shot out of the hag's black, distorted mouth-that-looked-more-like-a-gash and licked up the vomit. Tyler tried to run . . . to break the hag's dominance, but the hag's tongue split apart and wrapped around his face, his torso, and down around his—"

Tyler shot up in bed and screamed, frantically running his hands all over his body.

A river of sweat ran off him.

He fell over in bed—then uttered another shriek as he fell onto the side of the bed where the hag was and immediately whipped his body over to the other side of the bed.

His screams slowly died in his throat as he buried his face into the bedsheets and clawed them from their tucks and folds . . . .

Opening his eyes he stared into the red glow of his alarm clock.

Three-ten, no, -eleven.

Stop. Regroup.

Closed his eyes, still clawing at the bedsheets

The room smelled like . . . .

A nightmare.

Sweating, he slowed his breathing to a more normal rate and rolled back over. Cast a quick look to where the hag had been—in his *dream*.

Empty. That side of the bed was empty . . . no vomit, no puss, no
. . . .

He reached down to himself. Uttered a sound of disgust. Wet dream, all right.

His stomach revolted.

He rolled back onto his side . . . and came face to face with the puss-leaking, diseased face from his nightmare. She lay in bed beside him, tongue flicking in and out of her knotted gash-of-a-mouth.

"*Come fuck with me,*" she croaked.

Her noxious and grating words blasted through Tyler like a pair of cranked, thousand-watt speakers.

Tyler squealed like a stuck pig and exploded out of bed, blankets and sheets still wrapped around him. He tripped over himself and the attached sheets and smashed over one of his dressers' lamps as he vacated the room in one gigantic bound. In the darkness he ran into a wall and

come fuck with me I love a good fuck

laid himself out—

come fuck with me I love a good fuck

cold. But just as he was blacking out, Tyler saw the hag descend upon and straddle his . . . .

come fuck with me I love a good fuck . . . .

Tyler awoke groggily and leaned up against the bedroom doorjamb. Felt the painful bump and dried blood on his forehead. The bathroom lights were still on, but were now paled against the early morning sunlight. His mouth felt like an empty tree trunk with moss growing inside it and his neck was as stiff as a two-by-four. He slowly picked himself up and twisted out the kinks of his body. Looked to the blankets tangled in his legs.

How had he gotten here?

Tyler looked back to his bedroom. One of his lamps missing.

He shuffled out from the tangled sheets and returned to the bedroom. Found the lamp scattered about the carpet like a murder victim, its bulb smashed and lampshade torn.

His bed deserted.

All his sheets were in a pile that led into the hallway, where he had awoken. He threw himself down on the bed.

What the hell'd happened?

Clammy and shaking, Tyler didn't feel at all well. Pushing himself up off the bed, his hand narrowly missed a dried, discolored stain on the sheets.

And there was just a *hint* of pungency to the air . . . .

Nothing a good shower couldn't fix.

After buying new, 60-watt light bulbs and a lampshade, Tyler hurriedly rushed home to clean up and meet Dyanne for their one p.m. tennis date. Showers were great, but when the hot water ran out it was time to get moving. It wasn't that Tyler had a shower fetish, but there did seem to be nothing a warm shower couldn't remedy and that's what he loved about them.

Changing quickly, he made it out to the courts. Dyanne stood by the fence, waiting impatiently.

"What took you so long?" she asked, her words laced more than a little with annoyed attitude. Her racket swung casually from her two-fingered, I'm-not-at-*all*-happy-with-you-right-now grip. "These courts are *severely* booked—"

"I'm sorry, honey, but I had a rough night—"

"Oh?" she said, crossing her arms and raising an eyebrow.

Oh, that accusatory eyebrow.

"No-no-no, that's not what I meant—I mean, I *did* have a rough night—but not from—look, I had a nightmare and ended up sleeping on the hallway floor, okay? Had to replace a broken lamp."

Dyanne's I'm-pissed look took on a softer look. "*Excuse me?*"

"The funny thing is, I can't remember a damned thing about it, just that it scared the crap out of me."

Embarrassed, Dyanne lowered her voice and uncrossed her arms.

"I'm sorry. Are you all right?"

"Yeah. I just had to pick up some new light bulbs and a shade. I broke a lamp."

"God, what happened? Can't you remember *any* of it?" She moved in closer, brushing away some of Tyler's bangs.

"Nope. Just that something literally scared the piss out of me. But, it was just a dream—now, let's play some tennis!"

Dyanne and Tyler were deep into their second match, the score 30-40. Dyanne served the ball. Fault. Her next serve made it, but sent Tyler to the far end of the court. He barely snagged the shot before his own return forced Dyanne up to the net. Her return forced Tyler back to the rear and caused him to miss. *Deuce.*

Dyanne retrieved the ball and again served, spiking this one just inside the white rectangle. It whizzed past Tyler, who missed the most perfect serve he'd ever see.

"Ha, lover, *my* game! *Owww* . . . ."

Dyanne was so cute in her pink shorts as she pirouetted about the court.

"'Nother game, hon-ey?"

"Sure, but this time *I* win!"

Tyler set up and served. Dyanne picked it up easily enough and her return sent Tyler scurrying back across court. She was giving him a good workout, but his quick backhand sliced it to a sharp left. Dyanne rushed to meet it . . . and missed it by a hair.

The next scene suddenly slowed down.

Like a person unsure of what it was he was witnessing, Tyler watched as Dyanne performed a neatly executed forward spin from the momentum of her missed swing . . . her racket slowing left her hands and flew into the chain-link fence. She spun around for a second turn, moving backwards and towards the chain-link fence that enclosed the courts . . . her hands going up before her face.

She smiled just as she clenched the galvanized, crisscrossed wires of the fence.

Something's wrong here, Tyler sensed, *terribly* wrong . . . .

He couldn't have known that a section of the fence's wire had raised itself into tiny little barbs just where Dyanne's hands were now planting themselves . . . but that's exactly what happened.

As Dyanne made contact, she screamed . . .

And life returned to normal play.

Tyler sprinted across the court to Dyanne, who was now hugging her hands into her chest. Tyler leapt over the net and quickly came to her, her face a tight grimace of pain.

"What's the matter—what's the matter—are you all right? *Dyanne?*"

Tyler crouched down on the court. She was in a heap, leaning back against the fence. "Dyanne—*let me see!*"

Tyler pulled her hands away from her chest and saw the blood that remained on her shirt and exposed skin of her upper chest. Lots of it.

Taking her bloody hand into his, Tyler felt his stomach

(*come fuck with me I love a good fuck*)

knot.

Her hand was torn to pieces.

Most of the flesh on the underside of her palm and fingers had been brutally torn away.

"Oh my . . . God. We've got to get you to the ER!"

The other players on the court had now all stopped their games and looked on. Some turned away in disgust.

"Someone, *please*," Tyler pleaded, "call an ambulance—*please!*" One man broke free from his daze and ran off in search of his cell phone.

Tyler looked up to the fence where Dyanne's hand had landed only seconds before and found it stood as nonchalant as ever—and there were indeed raised barbs on it. There were also droplets of blood . . . and what looked exactly like bits of Dyanne's skin clinging to those barbs.

Come fuck with me—I love a good fuck . . . .

Tyler took Dyanne home to her apartment and stayed with her. She looked so vulnerable . . . so helpless . . . and reminded him of a puppy, named Sheena, he'd once had as a kid. Sheena had been running loose one day, as did most dogs out in the country, when she finally met the front-end bumper of a '67 Ford truck. She'd managed to limp off to the roadside, but could go no farther and collapsed in the tall grasses, her left rear leg broken. The driver, a farmer from down the road, felt terrible and took her to the local vet, footing her bill. Sheena was back on her feet in no time, her rear leg bandaged in white and her tail wagging, but whenever it rained the family had to wrap her leg in plastic bags until she healed. Needless to say, she never ran free again.

So there rested Dyanne, her right hand bandaged white and lying on her chest, which rose and fell to her (finally) relaxed breathing. They had watched television all night and it was quite clear that Dyanne had plans that evening that totally involved a quiet night's rest. As she fell asleep on her couch, Tyler picked her up and carried her into her bedroom. He gently laid her down in bed, took off her bathrobe, and eased her beneath the crisp bedsheets. Once she was properly situated, Tyler also disrobed and slid in beside her. He loved the feel of her warm skin against his and wrapped his arms around her. He fell asleep thinking about how much he loved her and hoped she'd be okay.

***

The alarm clock had gone off several minutes before either had noticed it, but Dyanne was the first to stir. She slammed it off with her bandaged hand and winced from the impact. She turned to Tyler, who still lay with his arms around her. Very mindful of her injury, Dyanne repositioned herself and kissed Tyler on the forehead.

"Time to get up, sleepyhead."

Tyler stirred, eyes still closed. Dyanne gave him another kiss, then nudged him slightly.

"C'mon, honey, time to get up. I've got to get to work."

This time Tyler responded with a soft smile.

"Hi."

"Hello, morning breath." She smiled back. "What do you want to eat?"

Tyler said nothing, but instead rolled in closer to her.

"Fine, be that way, *I'm* taking a shower."

Dyanne climbed out of bed and went into the bathroom, starting the shower.

"Don't let that bandage get wet," Tyler shouted from the other room. "Wrap it in a

(*Sheena*)

bag or something—"

"Don't worry, I heard the doctor too!" Dyanne said. Poking her head back into the bedroom, she added, "But thanks for caring."

"Any . . . time."

Dyanne felt silly doing it, but she got out a used Oroweat bread bag from the kitchen and wrapped it around her bandage. Using a large rubber band saved from many paper deliveries she secured it and returned to the shower. She tested the water before entering by inserting her good hand. By this time Tyler was ready for movement and slowly crawled out of bed. He took in the sounds of running water and Dyanne's periodic splashing sounds from the shower.

Smiled. Got out of bed.

"May I join you?" Tyler asked, entering the shower stall.

"Anytime, stranger."

"May I soap that gorgeous body of yours?"

"It depends on what else you have in mind."

"Watch the hand—"

"*Riiight*," she said, and came in closer.

Come fuck with me, I love a good fuck.

***

As the next few days progressed, Tyler found himself accumulating scars and bruises of all kinds . . . just little ones here and there, and in themselves they wouldn't have been any big deal—except that Tyler collected them for no apparent reason. He'd wake up with a new one (or two) each morning. Dyanne, of course, also detected them and Tyler explained them away as one of those periods in life when you seemed to be the world's klutziest person and there was nothing you could do about it.

But everywhere he turned things went wrong.

Checks bounced . . . a twenty-hour bug found a home . . . and he scraped the side of a car as he parallel parked—and he prided himself on how good a parallel-parker he was.

Tyler and Dyanne went for a walk after a late lunch at la Petite Conchon. Early evening rapidly approached and traffic was a bit on the heavy side as people headed home for an early weekend.

"Thanks for lunch, hon," Tyler said.

"It was the least I could do after all you seemed to be going through this week. I wanted to do something special. Maybe it'll break the

(*twenty copies*)

(*raised barbs*)

"spell, or whatever."

"Yeah, well, we'll see. Let's cross here," Tyler said, checking traffic. "I've got to get going. There's something I need to do."

"Okay," Dyanne said, smiling, "but first, *this*—" She pulled Tyler into her arms and planted him with a deep, lengthy kiss. "I *love* you!"

Tyler held her with a penetrating look.

"And I love *you*—more than anything else in the world—now, come on!"

Grabbing her good hand, Tyler led her out into the street, a section of the traffic now clear, but as Dyanne followed, her pocketbook bumped against her side and out fell her checkbook. Halfway across the road.

"Wait!"

"Wait *what*? We're in the middle of *traffic!*" Tyler came to a halt three-quarters of the way across the street.

"I dropped something!" Dyanne broke his grip and went back for her checkbook.

Tyler searched the road for what Dyanne had dropped.

Everything slowed down . . . and then came the whispers . . .

. . . come fuck with me, I love a good fuck . . .

. . . come fuck with me, I love a good fuck . . .

. . . comefuckwithmeIloveagoodfuckcomefuckwithmecomefuck—

Tyler turned to see a large, black car moving towards them. He opened his mouth to scream—but nothing came out.

Dyanne bent down to pick up the book
(*come fuck with me I love a good fuck*)
and looked up to him, a smile across her face as she triumphantly waved the errant checkbook at him.

Come fuck with me I love a good fuck!

He saw her look around for traffic.

comefuckwithmeagoodfuckIlove

Saw her spot the car.

a good fuck a really *good fuck*

Saw her arms go up.

I love it I love *it*

Her hips connected first.

The sound of her bones shattering against the metal reverberated hollowly in a universe gone lag.

A good fuck I LOOOVE . . . .

Tyler saw her head and face unite with the windshield in a spurt of gore and glass . . . her teeth and gums gnashed horribly together.

One of Dyanne's hands flopped off to one side of the car as she molded to the hood.

And that was not all Tyler had seen.

He'd seen the face of the driver . . . the face of the hag from his nightmare.

The lightbulb.

The stained bedsheets.

The nightmare.

Dyanne's body rolled off the vehicle and landed with a *thump.* Bumped about once or twice more before coming to a rest.

For what seemed an eternity, her head lolled limply from side to side.

The car continued on in its course.

Tyler was unable to move. Forced to watch. He realized what kind of car had hit her.

A hearse.

Tyler was still shaking when he got home. He'd spent the rest of the day and half the night at the police station and related matters and could barely hold himself up. He was sick to his stomach.

But he had found that paper.

Did what had to be done.

Was spent . . . had no more will. Collapsed to the living-room floor, tears streaking his face. He lay still. Thought about George Weh's wife and Darian Fairfax. About twenty-times-five and four-and-one-eighth-by-nine-and-one-half-inch envelopes.

Felt an unexpected urge for a shower.

(*wash the sins*)

Needed to.

Sobbing, he looked to the bathroom.

The light was on.

He didn't remember turning it on . . . but that didn't matter.

Nothing mattered. He'd lost Dyanne. Lost everything.

He dragged himself to his feet and made his way to the bathroom. Kicked off his shoes and removed his clothes.

Found the shower already running.

Nice and

(*it didn't matter*)

hot.

Steam filled the bathroom.

It just didn't

(*nothing did*)

matter.

Naked, trembling, and sobbing Tyler stepped into the shower and felt the warmth penetrate his skin. He collapsed into the bottom of the tub.

Whispers came from the spray.

(*nothing mattered*)

Did you have a good fuck?

"Fuck *you!*" Tyler yelled.

Did you have a good fuck? I did.

"Fuck you," he sobbed and closed his eyes. The whispers chuckled.

The hag's face formed in the mist above.

I had a great fuck, Tyler, now it's your turn.

On ran the whispers. The face disappeared.

Tyler lay in the bottom of the tub, adrift in his misery. He ignored the fact that the shower had grown hotter (it didn't matter); *spikier* (nothing mattered) . . . .

It just didn't matter one goddamned bit.

Tyler tried to right himself when he noticed that the water had become downright painful. Not *hot* painful, but *spiked* painful. He looked down to his body and saw the red.

Was it something in the water?

Felt disjointed. Resigned. He collapsed back inside the tub and let the warmth flow over him.

Through him.

Around him.

His last thoughts were of Dyanne.

Tiny daggers . . . no larger than short pins . . . screamed down from the thundering shower head and tore and ripped and penetrated into his body.

Ripped through his nerves and burst open his organs.

Razored blades that clattered down along the plastic surface towards the drain like iron filings to a magnet.

It wasn't long before his heart had ruptured into an explosion of red that filled the tub and spattered the walls.

Tyler floated . . . .

Then water rained down upon him . . . washing away the filth . . . .

The sins.

Tyler's body lay empty.

It just didn't matter anymore.

It never did.

At an unstable and battered table sat an ancient, diseased woman. Her hair was greasy and gray and her veins filled with bile and hate. Her life reeked of a different kind of cancer not of cigarettes or cells.

But she liked writing letters. Got real good at it, in fact.

Having no friends, she wrote them to no one in particular. She just wrote—not that many would willingly read what it was she had to say. She didn't much like people, and that was okay, because people, it turned out, didn't much care for her. She didn't have a name, didn't need one. People used names for identity. To be proud. She had no need of either.

She just wrote.

But this time she received a letter.

One that found its way to her doorstep.

She had no mailbox.

She found the letter while on the way to the woods with an eviscerated cat. She liked gutting cats, they were fun. Dogs were too big. She liked cats.

In rickety hands she'd collected the letter, which had no return address, sat down at her table, and inspected it.

Who would write her?

How did it get here?

No matter, maybe she could return the favor. Her letters always found their marks.

She opened the splotched and unevenly sealed envelope and removed the contents. Unfolded the paper. She read the few, hastily scrawled words beneath the poorly typewritten paragraphs first. It was then that her yellowed orbs screamed wide. She heaved the letter away, which smoldered and disintegrated before it hit the floor.

Tried to outdistance what was to come.

The old lady tumbled furniture as she fled.

Heard noises in pursuit.

Ran into the living room, snapping an arthritic ankle. A wide, spacious living room. She used to be rich once. Had a big house.

The whispers grew, filled the building.

Words that became audible and loud.

You know what they whispered.

Pass it on. IT WORKS!

Allergies
1993

"Gesundheit."

"Thank you."

"So how long have you had this . . . allergy?" Dana asked, bound to a chair by thick cords of rope that bit into his skin. He felt exhausted. Spent. He was also in a dark, dank enclosure, and there was an old, rusty oil lamp on a small, beat-up card table before him. There was no other illumination. The crypt—for it indeed looked and smelled of one—stank of graveyard rot and mustiness and its darkness bore down upon him like tons of dead weight. Dripping echoed everywhere.

Dana knew there had to be bodies in the shadows. Lots of them.

Knew it.

"Since, well, I was a kid, really, but it hadn't become much of a problem until my early twenties," his captor replied from the darkness of which his shadow was barely visible.

"And how do you know it's not just all in your mind, you know, like psychosomatic or something—"

"Because. Just *because*."

The shadowy figure again sneezed.

From their earlier introductions Dana had found his captor's name to be Reed. Nothing else, just Reed. He'd been polite enough when they'd first met, just inside the mausoleum's heavy, metal and wooden door . . . that is, just before Reed had politely cranked him over the head with a shovel.

"Oh, come on, that's no answer! You mean you're going to kill me—just *because?*"

"No. Because things *happen* . . . things I've *done* . . . you know? Well, you will . . . . "

Exasperated, Dana tried to twist away.

And all this because of some stupid-ass frat prank.

It was just supposed to have been a gag. A harmless prank. He was supposed to have gone into this "haunted" graveyard (of which the haunter now stood across from him), knock over a few gravestones, then paint his initials and date on the inside wall of the entrance-way to this crypt.

Curiously he recalled how he had not seen any other initials (or dates) on those walls . . .

And that's where his troubles had only begun.

Reed.

A psychotic of some sort who thought he had the *ultimate* allergy . . . .

"Okay, okay, so you have this fucking allergy—"

"—I don't know *when* it all began, really," Reed said, oblivious to Dana. "It was almost like it happened overnight. Just like that. One moment I didn't have it, then the next—*boom*—it was there. The allergy. I had become full-blown allergic to everyone. People. Life. Animals. Anything that lived, breathed, or grew."

Dana rolled his eyes. Continued with his struggle to free himself. This guy was definitely out there, all right, and this clearly wasn't his *first* kidnapping. He was too calm, almost rehearsed, and he had him tied tight. Good and tight.

"Then . . . I don't know . . . I began *doing* things—"

"*What things*, already!"

Reed shot a quick look over to Dana, then made his way out of the shadows and stood for a moment looking at Dana. Then, lost in thought, he wandered over to one of the darkened recesses and remained there in silence. Reed was dressed as any twenty- or thirty-year-old, except that his clothing looked more worn—one could say in tatters—than most. His bearded face dirtied and sallow, his hair long and unkempt, but otherwise not that far off in appearance from any other guy his age.

Dana heard him inhale. He must have been here a long time, he thought.

Sure, there'd been stories of folks disappearing around this cemetery over the years, but he'd never quite believed them.

Until now, that is.

Maybe there was more to this guy than he'd really cared to believe.

Reed sneezed. Wiped his face with a sleeve.

"I began killing . . . cats . . . mostly," Reed said, still looking into the shadows, "some dogs, too, though only the smaller ones at first.

The larger dogs scared me—*then*—but no longer. Nothing scares me anymore."

Reed turned to Dana, but Dana couldn't quite make out his features, but he had the curious feeling Reed was sad for him.

Suddenly Reed shot out of the darkness and flew across the room directly into Dana's face.

Dana tensed, and for the first time since his abduction actually became scared. Up to now he thought this might still have all been part of his initiation . . . more of that frat-joke-thing . . . but not now, as he looked back into Reed's red, watery, and crazed eyes and realized that this guy just might be the stuff of those stories—and more. What he saw was no fear. No joke. What he saw was

Death.

"C'mon, man, let me go, enough's enough. Look, I got inside, okay? Can't we just settle it at that?"

Reed whipped about dizzyingly fast and gripped Dana's face in one of his boney, but incredibly strong, hands. Dana felt the grit that came with that hand embed itself into his face. He could taste it.

He was certain that grit didn't come from *topside.*

And Reed's breath smelled *most* foul. Words hit Dana like successive sucker punches.

"Look, here—you don't know just how *fucked* you really are, Frat Boy. Because you came here, I have to kill you. *Have* to! I have no other choice!"

Reed relaxed his grip and dropped his hand. Continued pacing the room.

"I have no anger toward you," Reed said, "I have no emotion one way or the other, really. Hell," Reed continued, sneezing and wiping away trails of snot from his face, "I don't feel a damned thing for or against any one person who walks across the face of this earth! *Nothing.*"

Coming to a halt, Reed composed himself and retreated back into the darkened confines just outside the oil lamp's illumination.

Dana heard the squeak of a chair as he visualized Reed sitting down in it. Dana tried to spit out the grit that had gotten caught in the corners of his mouth. He tried to take his mind off of wherever that dirt might have come from, but found it hard to do so. He already felt like he was in his own grave and that didn't sit at all well with him.

"Yeah, back then I had fear all right, all sorts of fear," came the disembodied voice from the darkness. "So I used to grab the *little* dogs, the *little* cats. Squirrels. I used to trap 'em—" Reed's hands projected out from the darkness and Dana could see how knotted up they were

. . . fists clenched so tightly they shook violently.

"*Grabbed* 'em! Used to grab 'em I did. That annoying little bitch of a dog from next door was the first to go. A fucking Chihuahua. *Yap-yap-yap* all day long . . . all night long. Yap-yap-fucking-*yap*.

"So I took care of the little fucker. Took care of my mother's cat that kept biting and scratching me. Those damned little noisy birdies, too. I took care of them all, I did, and I found I *liked* it. Oh, it wasn't that I hated all I killed—except for that little Chihuahua bitch—no, just that I liked what it was I was *doing*.

"Robbing things of their lives.

"The feeling of undeniable power involved. *My* undeniable power.

"But you have to understand me . . . it wasn't *me*—not really. It wasn't until later that I realized something was different about me when I killed. *Within* me. It was like it wasn't really *me* doing all this stuff, this killing, you know. Not the *me*-me, the right-here-and-*now* me that you see—no, it was like there was another *aspect* of me that was doing it. A demon-me from some other dimension that took over. Like the I-me I knew was just sitting there, along for the ride, so to speak. Helpless. A captive passenger, if you will.

"Shit, sure, you say, everybody kills cats. Bugs. But I was *different*, I tell you."

Reed again came forward from the darkness and was ready to say something, when he unexpectedly broke out into a severe bout of sneezing and wheezing. It actually appeared as if his body *blurred* as it shuddered.

Dana again took some of it in the face, but Reed kept his distance and sneezed violently several more times, his entire body shaking and convulsing. Dana spit out what phlegm got into his mouth.

Reed retreated back into the shadows. As Dana looked at the stuff that clung to his clothes, he noticed how it seemed to have a peculiar iridescence to it.

"Damn. Excuse me. Sometimes this stuff hits me really hard. Let me get some of that off you." Reed rushed over, and rather hurriedly, swiped away most of the phlegm that had covered Dana.

Dana observed, speechless.

For all the sneezing and wheezing that had been going on, Dana could tell that there actually *was* something different about him. He could feel it now. It was like there was a cold, dead pocket of air surrounding him. A stillness that reached out and numbed. *Horse latitudes*, he remembered, curiously. Utter lifelessness. But it was even more than that. It was almost as if he had actually seen another ghost-self of Reed shift aside from his body during the sneezing bout. Like there had been a vague outline that shadowed his every movement that was *more* than Reed—

Death.

Dana listened, his heart pounding incessantly above the hollow and steady drip-drip of the cavernous reaches of the mausoleum. When Reed next spoke, he could feel the waver of his voice . . . his entire body . . . and it unnerved him.

And something about himself *was* different . . . definitely not entirely right. He wasn't sure what it was, but he felt it went beyond fear.

"S-so . . . what are you going to do with me?"

Reed shook his head. "I told you, already. I think I've made myself quite clear on the matter. To you all this is a joke. Fun. A gag, you called it. Well look around you, Dana-boy, *I am not joking.* Look."

Reed shot out of the darkness and snatched up the oil lamp. Held it out high above him and shone it around into the darkness, almost excitedly so. Exposing all the dark corners and crevasses Dana had not been able to see into.

Dana gasped.

He now saw what he'd been sharing the room with.

Corpses. Bones. Bodies. Body parts. Man and animal.

He was everywhere surrounded by the unearthed and the decayed . . . and all of them were tossed about in crazy, contorted positions. They all looked as if they'd been toyed with.

Used.

"Come onnn, man, y-you can't be *serious.* You gotta let me go—I won't tell anyone! Just untie me—I-I-I'll walk right out of here! P-please, guy, *you gotta let me go!*"

Reed replaced the lantern on the table and wheezed again as he pulled out the piece of cloth from his pockets. Lowering himself to Dana's ears, he whispered, "*I don't have to do* nothin'."

Reed backed away and spoke in a more regular tone.

"You forget. I feel *nothing* toward you, remember? But . . . I can't let you go, either. I can feel this other me . . . it's around . . . somewhere . . . probably already taken over. You're an allergy to us. Something we don't need. Something that could bring back other allergens, and we can't have that.

"You see, when I kill, I don't need to use *weapons.* I just hold them. Be near them. You don't even realize it, but you've been dying since I brought you in here. There's no turning back now. Were you to leave this very minute, you'd still die. It's . . . irreversible."

"W-what?"

"There's no way I know to reverse it. It's like a plague. Look at your body. *Feel* it. You know what I'm saying to be true, even if not now. But very soon. You will. Exhaustion is what you first feel. The rest comes later. You see, I have no choice. I let you go, you go to others, they try to find out what's happening to you. You lead them here. If I keep you here, you die. Either way, it's not pretty. The only thing I can do is kill you—quickly—so that the emaciation doesn't torture you, I've tried many different ways to help the dying die quickly and with less pain, and this is the best way. It's not a sweet death, my curse, but my murder *is*. It's the only thing I can do to keep you out of both our miseries."

"*You're crazy!* Let me outta here! Fuckin' asshole, you're a crazy-fuckin'-son-of-a-bitch-lunatic-*crazy man!* There's no such thing! *No such thing!*"

Reed turned away. Pulled his chair out into the light, and sat in it. He watched Dana.

Sat and did nothing.

But sneeze.

Do you believe me now? asked the darkness.

I don't know what to believe. I feel . . . *different.*

Of course you do.

How do you know this?

I know.

The darkness surrounded Dana like a suffocating kiss. He didn't really want to leave it. It felt right to remain where he was. To yield. To give in. To—

Sleep. He just wanted to sleep . . . .

But the darkness changed. Grew tighter; more oppressive. Then Dana saw it. Felt it. An even darker spot within the darkness came toward him. Split open. Dana knew what it was.

A mouth.

Jaws, to be precise. Incredibly huge ones.

The mouth had now opened far too wide for him to see the edges of it any longer, and it quickly descended upon him.

Dana screamed.

Screamed into the pitch and realized a part of him was already gone. He didn't know which part, only that a very real section of what he *was* was now gone. Missing.

Elsewhere.

And the pain was unbearable. From deep inside—like his soul.

It was unfathomable . . . like every nerve fiber within him was on fire—lit up. And it didn't go away with the demise of the nerve endings, but started over.

Regenerated.

Redistributed.

And the jaws came down again. And again . . . and with each new time brought yet another searing bolt of agony that fired through him, as still yet another part of him was ripped away to some other dark, faraway place.

Chunks were torn away from him . . . from the *inside.*

Jagged, diseased jaws scooped out his insides and took out the essentials of what it was he *was.*

Ate his identity.

His life's core.

Something . . . was eating his *soul.*

Do you believe me now?

Dana stirred.

Lifted his head.

Dizzy . . . he was disoriented. Metaphysically desiccated . . . nothing but a husk of his former self.

So tired. Just wanted to go to sleep . . . forever . . . but the pain kept him from doing so.

"W-*what?*"

"I asked you if you believed me now. That you're dying."

Dana twisted his head up toward the voice. Felt extremely stiff, unable to feel his limbs. He didn't know how long he'd been out, just that he'd been trying to do something really, really weird . . . get inside his nerves. Eat color. He was indeed weaker . . . *felt* it . . . there was no longer any doubt about it.

And the pain—it was deep and it was growing, washing over him in waves from the inside out . . . faking him out, like it was gone . . . only to return—in ravishing spades.

He was a wilting flower hidden away in a dank cave who-knew-how-far below the earth's surface.

Reed got up and brought something over to him.

A mirror.

Even in the dim illumination, Dana could clearly see that the wrinkled and withered face that stared back at him was his own. And parts of it were missing. As if removed from the *inside.*

"I-I refuse . . . "

"It's okay. It's okay to refuse. Everyone does. That's why I have to kill. Put you all out of your misery. Mine. Rid myself of your allergens. I guess it's the last act of human decency I have in me, even though I try not to care too much about it. It's just like any other thing I have to do. I don't pretend to understand it, I just do it. Like watching the deaths as the other-me does them. And some of the dead I keep, just for a little while, you know, and some—well . . . some . . . *they come back to me.*"

Dana looked up. "Come . . . come *back?*"

"If I don't do what I have to do, yes. I really am sorry. Really. You're not a bad sort. Just in the wrong place at, well, well we all have to go sometime. 'Cept me. I'm the exception to the rule, I think. I don't know how it'll happen to me, if it ever does. But it's your time now."

"No—no, please, I beg of you, let me go—I'll do *anything!*"

"Of course you will."

Reed shook his head, opened his arms in a gesture of mercy and understanding, and came in to him.

"There's nothing I can do, friend, really. Nothing . . . all I can do is this."

Reed sneezed twice, again splattering Dana's face and upper chest . . . then he put his arms around him—

And hugged him fiercely.

"*Good bye,*" Reed whispered quietly, sympathetically.

Dana wept into Reed's shoulders, pleading for his life.

Reed withdrew the knife, a long-bladed object, from one of the folds of his garment, and unhesitatingly plunged it through Dana's back and directly into his heart.

Dana jerked once, uttering a single grunt of pain and surprise, his mouth a perfect "O," eyes huge as silver dollars. He pressed into Reed harder. Shuddered.

Reed forced the blade in deeper and felt the blood spurt out and splatter his hand.

It burned his skin.

Dana jerked again. Coughed.

Reed heard the strained and surprised wheeze of air that now exited Dana's dying form.

Felt the blood that seeped from Dana's wound and soaked through into his chest.

When Reed withdrew the blade he heard Dana sputter several times more as his head lolled heavily against his ear. Then he got up and backed away from him, carefully placing the knife down on the table. He retrieved his shadowy chair and sat patiently opposite the quickly expiring Dana.

Felt the allergy as it began to drain away like an unclogged drainpipe.

When he was sure that the last of his allergy was finally expired, he got up and dragged Dana's body into a corner with the others. Had to leave him tied up for a bit to make sure he didn't come back like some of the others. Then he made his way back to an adjacent chamber. It had been a long night. Would be morning soon . . . and he needed rest. He didn't like mornings—with it came the light . . . and he didn't like light. The mere thought of it gave him migraines.

Had an allergy to it.

Crypt of Vampyres

1978

October moonlight illuminated the vapor that blanketed the darkened countryside.

A road.

A lone figure upon it.

Fog.

Whisked across the stranger's path.

The man—a young man—traveled . . . deliberately . . . pensively. More on his mind than should have been for one so young.

An ordinary person might consider the night . . . the fog . . . the moonlight . . . scary . . . and avoid being out alone . . . or might consider the setting romantic, and casually stroll with a loved one. But seventeen-year-old Alan Slovik was anything but ordinary. Alan saw figures . . . ghosts, demons, ghouls . . . in the fog that he strolled through alone. Alan held onto the old fireside tales his grandmother spun for him. Fancied himself a "gothic-romanticist." Many thought Alan a dreamer . . . always seemed to have his head in the clouds (or, fog, for that matter) . . . preoccupied . . . woolgathering . . . distracted. Many such terms had been used to describe his constantly straying, distracted state of mind.

And to that existed an element of truth.

But Alan contemplated the metaphysical. The theoretical. The . . . *incorporeal.*

What if monsters were real?

What would he do were he to confront one?

What if he died fighting one?

What was death like—and how would he react to it?

Was there an afterlife?

These were the meditations-of-substance that weighed so heavily upon his youthful mind.

But there was yet one other thing that set Alan apart from the ordinary. One thing about which no one else knew . . . .

Alan was several strides from the only street light, when the clouds again enveloped the moon—

And his shadow arrived at the light post before him.

Without him.

Waiting for him.

Leaned up against the lamp post.

And why and how did his disentangled shadow exist without him?

Alan followed his shadow to the light post . . . and leaned up against and into his shadow.

Yes, his shadow . . . very much a part of him . . . unable to exist without him . . . but had a life of its own.

Why?

Didn't know. It just was.

Streetlight glinted off the crucifix he wore about his neck. As he leaned there, peering through the mist, he became acutely aware of feeling . . . outside himself . . . *observing* himself. That was how he always felt when his shadow went off on its own.

Disjointed.

His shadow again ventured off.

He stood a moment longer before he followed after his silhouette . . . .

The wind howled in the Pine Ridge Cemetery, sending the long, bone-like extremities of the trees scraping into the night air.

At the far end of the cemetery, against the tree line, stood a heavily weathered iron-and-stone vault. The family name, *Adamescu,* was carved into the stone above the massive timber-and-iron-worked door. Inside the dust-laden interior, far to the rear of the chamber and set into the floor, lay a heavy trapdoor with a large iron ring. Beyond this trapdoor . . . existed a subterranean crypt . . . one composed of an earthen floor, upon which rested a haphazard array of coffins—some opened, some closed—situated among irregular piles and clumps of earth.

In the center of the scattered boxes sat a jet-black casket of exotic wood, its top closed.

The upper part of the casket's split-cover opened slowly. Halfway before the top fully extended, the lower cover moved to follow the upper half . . . until both covers were completely open.

Inside rested the ancient, decaying body of a once-woman. As pale as she was, were her lips red.

Her eyes opened.

Threatening . . . blacker than the deepest, darkest hole ever imagined . . . the eyes stared into the ceiling.

The once-woman sat up.

Again stared straight ahead.

In the next instant . . . *it* . . . stood before its casket.

Loosely clad in a flimsy ancient white robe that floated about its thin frame, the creature's long, white hair flowed about its boney head in the still air.

A white mist filled the crypt . . . the creature was no more.

The mist seeped up through the trapdoor into the upper chamber, then out of the vault and onto the cemetery grounds. It hung momentarily before . . .

A large bat flew away.

Alan Slovik continued into the thickening fog.

Stopped.

His shadow continued.

Alan peered into the wall of whiteness.

Before him played out a movie—a vision—and he saw himself exploring a dark crypt full of empty boxes . . . some upturned, some loosely stacked . . . a single prominently commanding black casket in the center. In one of his hands he carried an ax, and in the other, a wooden mallet and a long wooden stake. The stake's point had been tempered to charcoal.

He approached the box and peered inside.

A beautiful woman, in her mid-thirties, clad in a sheer robe, lay there.

Alan leaned the ax up against the casket, then carefully placed the stake between the woman's breasts.

Raised the mallet.

Stopped.

The woman's eyes had opened! Stared directly at him!

Alan, she called, *come to me!*

Put down the mallet . . .

He stared back, mallet poised above the stake.

Join me . . . .

Looked into her coal-black eyes.

Lowered his arm.

Dropped the mallet. Allowed the stake to fall from his grip.

Lowered his lips to the grinning mouth before him.

Yes, Alan . . . come to me . . . there is plenty of room in here for you . . . .

Alan paused.

Backed away . . . looked to the woman.

Why—why *was he doing this?*

He wanted her, didn't he? She wanted him?

Where was the problem?

The vampyre's full lips parted. Two sharp, lethal fangs exposed.

Her fangs . . . were so *beautiful!*

Yes, he . . . he wanted them. *Needed* them!

Alan lowered his head to her—

And the woman drove her fangs into his throat . . . sucked deeply . . . mouth tightly fastened to the side of his neck.

Alan closed his eyes and leaned in more, pushing up into the fangs.

I . . . love you! He thought. *I . . . am . . . yours . . . .*

Alan turned away from the image.

Found another.

The vision was already in-motion. In it he was again peering into that black casket . . . ax and mallet and stake at hand.

The woman-thing lay there . . . her body again strikingly revealed through its shear white robe.

Again Alan leaned his ax against the coffin . . . again placed the stake to her chest. . . and again raised the mallet.

The vampyre's eyes flew open.

Bored into him . . . angry . . . *furious . . . .*

Alan—

He slammed the mallet onto the stake . . . plunging it through the creature's chest.

The vampyre screamed—dark crimson gushed forth into the air like a water fountain, saturating Alan in the red. The creature writhed violently, fangs exposed. Hideously shrieking. Blood coursed out and down the corners of its mouth.

Again Alan pounded the stake . . . until it hit the casket's bottom.

Pinned in its own casket, the vampyre squirmed and wiggled— reaching out to Alan.

He dropped the mallet and swiftly grabbed the ax. In one immediate and confident movement, he brought the ax down in a powerful, severing stroke. The head rolled away and came to rest against the inside of the casket.

***

Alan stood between the two images.

His shadow stood before him . . . also standing between the two images. The shadow looked to the latter image.

Alan turned away . . . only to come face-to-face with a strikingly beautiful woman.

They stared at each other.

Her eyes were the deepest jet-black he'd ever seen. Her gaze immediately excited him . . . her full and flowing dark hair softly floated about her head and shoulders . . . flimsy, white robe drifting upon her lissome body—a body that was the color of deep autumn.

And she smelled . . . oh, she smelled so *intoxicating!*

"Who . . . are you?" Alan asked, in a trance-like state. "What's . . . your name?"

"I don't have a name," she said in a soft voice.

"Please tell me . . . you must have one."

"*Vulna* . . . ."

"Vulna? Such an odd . . . beautiful . . . name. Where did you—"

"Alan," she said, "do you walk the night often?"

"Yes."

"Do you live nearby?"

"Yes."

"Do others?"

"Yes."

"Show me."

Alan pointed down the road. Vulna swiftly flew in a blinding circle around him, her face several times leaning into—but never quite touching—his neck, then shot past him and merged with the fog.

Alan blinked. Looked behind him.

Had that really just happened?

He felt dizzy.

Absentmindedly fingered the crucifix hanging about his throat. Collected his wits . . . and continued home. Alan's shadow returned to him.

The next morning, Alan got up and had his breakfast as he read the paper. As he flipped through its pages, his eyes caught upon an article about a murder:

"George Burnholser died this morning sometime between 1 and 3 a.m. His body was found at 6 a.m. in an alleyway. Puncture wounds were found on the left side of his neck, and he was drained of all his blood . . ."

Alan stared at the article.

He wanted to see the body . . . to actually see this corpse.

Alan knew the undertaker, a Mr. Jefferson Spence, having worked for the man the past couple of years at the Pine Ridge Cemetery. He told Mr. Spence about his interest and was taken down to the morgue, where they'd pulled out the appropriate slab.

Alan looked at the body.

This was the first dead body he'd ever seen and there was a weird "stillness" to it. He kept expecting the person to sit up. Say "hello," with an outstretched hand before him.

But he didn't.

As Mr. Spence talked to him, Alan moved along the slab and stopped at the body's neck. Leaned in.

Two holes. Neatly punctured. About a quarter-inch in diameter, each.

The body . . . pale, drained.

What had this man's life been like?

Had he been a good person? A bad one?

Married?

A family?

How had he gotten mixed up in whatever had happened to him?

Then, as if peering through gauze, Alan again saw himself in another vision: *he* was now lying in a dark coffin. His eyes open . . . a strange expression upon his face.

Mr. Spence was still speaking when Alan broke out of his trance. He said, ". . . as you can imagine, everyone's saying this is the work of a vampyre." Mr. Spence regarded Alan. "What do you think?"

Alan paused before answering. "I couldn't tell you."

At the library Alan found all he'd ever wanted to know about vampyres. Checking out as many of the books as he could, he hurried home. Studied into the late afternoon. Antsy, and feeling he'd read all he could read at one sitting, he left the house. There was something he needed to check.

There was still daylight.

As Alan made his way across the cemetery, he caught sight of a large, odd-looking vault, way to the rear of the grounds. Funny, but he'd never really noticed that before.

How had he never noticed this before?

He headed toward it.

It had a large, ancient lock on a massive, imposing wrought-iron-and-timbered door. He'd seen a similar lock in one of the old storage sheds on the grounds. It had an accompanying key to it.

Alan hurried away from the vault.

Yes, it had to be the same lock . . . he was sure of it.

Next morning while reading the paper, Alan again spotted another curious article. This time two people had been attacked. A couple had been strolling home when, according to the reporter, the man had been attacked by a vampyre and drained of his blood. The girl had been savagely brutalized before also being drained.

Alan set aside the paper—missing a sub-article below that stated that the previously drained body had disappeared from the morgue. The scene wasn't far from his home, so Alan finished eating and proceeded to the described location.

Standing where the attack had occurred, Alan immediately felt a disturbing presence. Had another of his visions: two people . . . walking down an empty sidewalk at night. As the couple neared a grove of trees, a dark figure advanced toward them from the fog. A waning full moon peeked out from behind the clouds. The three figures stopped . . . regarded each other.

The couple froze in place.

The vampyre approached the man. Wrapped her hands around his neck and lowered her mouth to him . . . plunging her sharp eye teeth into his throat.

Savagely clamped upon his warm flesh, she moaned, sucking lustfully as the flowing warmth filled her cold, lifeless body. A gurgle emitted from her as a trickle of blood escaped her feeding and ran down the man's neck. The vampyre—amazingly swiftly—lapped it up.

Satiated, the vampyre opened her hands and released him.

He dropped to the sidewalk like a sack of dirt.

The vampyre smiled . . . and wiped the corners of her mouth.

Departed.

But, as the girlfriend came out of her trance and found her boyfriend dead at her feet, she let loose a soul-piercing scream. Looked about her for a weapon and found a large rock. Hurled it at the vampyre—but the monster snatched it from the air without looking. Before it registered with her, and in the blink of an eye, the vampyre was before her, fangs barred.

The girl pounded mightily at the vampyre with angry fists, but the vampyre snatched her by her throat and lifted her off the ground. With the same hand, the vampyre released her neck and pummeled and tore at her before she dropped a single inch—then the vampyre re-grabbed her throat. Tossed her into a nearby tree. The girl slammed into the tree and fell . . . her neck wedging into the base of a "V" formed by two large branches. She dangled there, some twenty feet above the ground.

Then the vampyre was simply . . . no longer there . . . .

Alan shook off the vision.

That woman—the *vampyre*—she was the same one he'd encountered the other night.

Alan hurried to the cemetery. *He needed that key!*

Alan spent the better part of the day searching for that damned lock-and-key. It wasn't where he'd last seen it, of course—that would have been too easy—and he had to search several other sheds and outbuildings before he'd found it.

Isn't that also how it happened in the movies?

The hero always thought he-or-she had enough time to prepare, but something stupid . . . something *weird* happened . . . and before he-or-she knew it, darkness was upon them!

Why wait for the next day?

That would also be too easy—but he couldn't risk further deaths from this monster!

Returning home, Alan hurriedly collected the tools he would need. He packed a large wooden crucifix, an old oil lamp and flashlight—and the lock and key.

Back at the vault Alan found that the key did work, though not without some difficulty of a long-rusted lock . . . but once inside, he wondered just what he was really getting himself into.

Alan lifted the lantern high and discovered heavily decomposed and mummified human remains. Very odd . . . unless you understood what you were up against.

Alan continued exploring.

No jet-black casket, as had been in his visions—but, wait . . . up ahead . . . in the floor . . .

A large trapdoor.

The door was incredibly heavy, yet he managed to get it open . . .

Holding his cross out before him, and pack shouldered, he cautiously descended into the blackness.

Shining his light around the crypt, he discovered it was much larger than expected for the size of the vault above. Its earthen floor had several coffins strewn about it . . . all empty . . . yet packed with earth inside them.

And some of the boxes were sealed.

From his research he'd learned that when vampyres left their native countries they had to take some of their native soil with them.

So, how many other vaults also had subterranean chambers beneath them?

Then it dawned on him who those human remains above must be.

They had to be the movers of the vampyre-or-vampyres from Rumania, Transylvania, or wherever they'd come from. . . handsomely paid . . . yet killed off by the vampyre, as its need for them had terminated.

Final payment.

As he directed the lantern about, Alan saw the one, commanding casket.

Coal black . . . and *opened* . . . it sat in the center of the crypt.

Man, what had he gotten himself into?

He hadn't really thought this through, had he? It had all suddenly gotten seriously "real" . . . this was no movie. No story.

Alan approached . . . examined it carefully.

Also empty.

What could *he* do?

No vampyres, here, no nothing.

He could do *one* thing . . . .

He reached in . . . and with a finger traced a cross into the dirt. Did so in the other open boxes. He hadn't thought to bring a pry bar, so he left the sealed ones alone.

He couldn't get out of there fast enough.

The day passed quickly for Alan Slovik. On the news, another murder was reported. Similar details.

Why was all this suddenly happening? He'd seen no such murders before . . . why now?

But, Alan knew who—or *what*—was responsible. And he had to act.

Packed daypack slung over his shoulder, and crucifix in-hand, Alan went out to the darkening streets. He hoped to meet that mysterious woman once more.

The *once*-woman.

He was ready for her.

Hiding at the cemetery and watching the vault, he saw her exit.

It was as if he'd blinked . . . one moment she wasn't there—and the next she simply just *was*.

She then appeared to . . . and he couldn't tell if this was true or the night and the fog were playing tricks on him . . . *but she appeared to float across the grounds.*

Crucifix ready, he moved in.

She seemed very much in a hurry . . . and he wondered why she didn't turn into a bat or become part of the mist . . . .

He cut across her projected path to intersect her, popping out from behind another cemetery vault.

Unphased, she calmly addressed him in a thick European accent.

"I'm in a bit of a hurry right now, so I cannot talk." Then she added in a teasing lilt, "Perhaps tomorrow night? Nice seeing you again."

As she passed. Alan had no inclination to stop her, but he had turned to see if—yes, it *was* there!

The mark of a cross was burned into her back!

The one he'd drawn in her casket!

As farfetched as the reasoning was, there were no longer any doubts.

He knew what he had to do.

Alan spent the next day readying himself to make another trip to the crypt. He needed more than his original tools, so had to make a run into town. He couldn't get the image of the beautiful once-woman out of his mind and began to wonder if he was really thinking *about* her . . . or she was trying to *control* him. The one item he didn't have was kerosene, but he could get that from a supply shed at the cemetery, along with a can to carry it in. Once he had everything together, he sat down—not for long, just for a little . . . a couple of minutes . . . he was feeling just a touch sleepy . . .

. . . and he couldn't get that woman out of his head . . . thinking about her . . . vampyre or no vampyre . . . her beautiful features . . . her mysterious, seductive voice . . . .

He awoke late into the afternoon.

He'd overslept!

She'd gotten to him!

A glance to the clock told him *he'd been out for over four hours!*

He had to act now! He couldn't allow for any more people to be killed on account of his laziness.

Alan grabbed his pack and darted out into the growing evening hours . . . .

Kerosene in tow, Alan hurried across the cemetery.

The vault.

Inside he immediately closed the door behind him and placed garlic and onions around the entire perimeter of the enclosure . . . along all the cracks and corners in the vault. Carrying his tools—a silver cross he'd "borrowed" from a church, an ax (the sharpest he could find), that can of kerosene, the oil lamp (which he lit), flashlights, and his mallet and charcoal-tipped stake—he ignored the piles of remains and went directly to the trapdoor, which he again muscled up, this time with the much-needed help of the crow bar he'd also brought along . . . and once again lowered himself into the crypt.

Alan wedged and nailed garlic and onions around the trapdoor's entrance with the hammer and nails he'd also brought.

Paused.

Could he really ram a stake into the heart of another human being . . . who, in reality (and whose and *what* "reality" were we talking, here?), was no human at all—but a monster?

In the stilled silence and stench of the crypt, where it was deathly still, it hit him full-force that he was all by himself—no one knew where he was!

The woman's image filled his head . . .

Alone!

(. . . so . . . so . . . strikingly *gorgeous* . . .)

And that if he failed . . . no one

(. . . *she was* sooo *beautiful* . . .)

would ever find him

(. . . *in another place* . . . *another* time . . .)

and know what had happened to him.

(*could they be lovers?*)

No!

She was a monster—not a girlfriend and certainly *not* a lover!

Alan's breathing became shallow, rapid.

No!

Keep it together, man! You have to remain strong!

Alan supported himself against the trapdoor. Felt something worming it's cold, wicked way into his head . . . his *soul* . . .

(. . . *but, I love you, Alan* . . . *that was why I never attacked you* . . .)

Get out of my head! You never attacked me, because I wore a crucifix around my neck!

Not true . . . I . . . I love you, my darling . . . have always *loved you . . .*

No!

Watched you from afar—

Liar!

Now . . . now, I'm so excited . . . we can be together . . . truly *be together—*

I will never be with you!

Finally and forever . . . the two of us . . . eternally roaming the night and the fog you love so much . . . .

No!

Loving and killing together—you and me . . . .

Alan closed his eyes . . . controlled his breathing . . . focused his thoughts.

His family.

The human race.

Light.

The sun.

The cross!

He had to ignore her.

Had to remain strong!

Had to succeed—*he had no other option!*

Eyes opened, he felt her influence withdraw some . . . but she was still around . . . someplace . . . perhaps in another coffin with her country's dirt in it. Or maybe she'd dumped out the dirt in her casket and replaced it with new dirt from another. Maybe . . . maybe he should sit and think about just how he wanted to approach all this . . . give it some good, concerted thought . . . make sure he didn't make any more *mista—*

No! Get out of my head!

No more dillydallying!

Alan left the trapdoor. He directed the lantern about the crypt and checked to see if he still cast a shadow . . . he did. Good. No dillydallying there, either!

Reshouldering his gear, and as lead-like as his legs suddenly felt, he forced himself on.

The black center casket was closed. He set up his lantern on the lower half of the lid and rested his ax against the box. Opened the top half of the casket.

Empty, as expected. The cross he'd traced in the dirt was still there. Good.

He moved on.

Though one coffin in particular stood out to him, caught his attention, he checked a couple of others on his way to it. They were all empty.

(*Alaaan . . .*)

Yes . . . this was . . . this was *hers* . . .

(*I want youuu . . .*)

It's good to have goals, he thought back to her.

Alan set down the kerosene and unslung his gear.

Time to get to work.

We can roam the night together, you and I . . .

Unzipped the pack.

Alaaan . . . I love you . . . don't be acting this way . . .

Opened the coffin.

Let me awaken . . . let me kiss you . . . I have so much to share with you . . .

I'm sure you do, he coldly thought back to her.

The vampyre looked as stunning as ever.

I am stunning, Alan . . . I can be yours . . . I am yours . . . .

Her eyes were closed. She looked normal . . . like any other half-naked and stunningly beautiful woman lying in

. . . come in here with me . . . we can make love forever . . .

a bed. Her full, beautiful lips . . . if he hadn't known any better, he . . . he could jump in there—right now—with her and

No!

Alan swiftly and steadily brought out the stake and placed its tip on the once-woman's chest. Raised his mallet . . .

Alan! Don't!

Kiss me! Please kiss me!

I need you to save me!

took one last, long look at the woman-demon before him.

I can show you things . . . .

And her eyes opened.

His hand and stake wavered. Mallet faltered in mid-air.

Just stay there. Don't do a thing. I'm coming to you.

He blinked. Felt dizzy.

Don't move.

Felt . . . weird.

Yes, you feel weird . . . very weird . . . you don't want to do this. Not at all. You want to close your eyes and wait for me to come to you . . . and I am coming for you, Alan . . . .

He wanted to kiss her. Embrace her. Crawl into that coffin with her, and

Come to me . . . snuggle beside me, my dearest . . .

let her show him things as they roamed the night together . . . .

Alan's shadow left him. Hovered around the air above the two of them.

In his mind's eye Alan had an image of the once-woman coming toward him . . . smiling seductively. . . . her flimsy robes falling away from her body . . .

Alan's shadow drifted toward the creature.

Out from the casket, drifted a grainy, dark shape. It floated toward Alan's shadow . . .

Alan blinked and shifted his footing.

Yes, he could take her . . . be together . . . he'd never had a girlfriend before, and she did like the same things he liked . . . the night, the supernatural . . .

Alan's and the vampyre's forms twisted about each other . . . *merged* . . .

Dizzy . . . Alan felt lightheaded and unstable—

Where was *he?*

What . . . *what* was he . . . doing?

Alaaan . . .

The two floating forms became one . . .

No . . . something was wrong here . . . this was real, not a dream . . . he was . . . he was—

He was in a hidden, subterranean crypt beneath a vault at the end of the cemetery where he worked!

No!

Alan's shadow broke free from the dark form of the creature and instead wrapped itself *around* it . . . *squeezed* it—

Alan slammed the head of the mallet onto the stake.

The stake plunged into the once-woman's chest in a powerful stroke. The vampyre shrieked as the blood-of-others hideously jetted out from her impalement. Alan gave it several more strikes—solidly anchoring it to the bottom of the coffin. His shadow fought the dark shape in the air above.

The creature shrieked and writhed and contorted. Blood continued to spurt out its nose and mouth. It reached out to Alan, its knurled, boney fingers scraping at empty air. Its reddened eyes bulged hideously.

Alan seized the ax . . . and in a violent spray of blood, chopped it down with a loud *thump!* onto the slender neck. The vampyre's still screaming head rolled free of its body.

His shadow compressed and squeezed and suffocated the evil blackness of the vampyre.

Alan quickly grabbed the head by its hair and threw it onto the earthen floor. Doused it in kerosene. Stepped back and tossed a lit match onto it. The head immediately erupted into flames.

Alan watched it burn, its piercing screams filling the crypt.

Alan's shadow continued to battle the vampyre's spirit, both shadows drifted higher and higher above the casket until they disappeared through the ceiling of the crypt.

The vampyre's body decayed into dust before him. Alan softly grunted . . . and a smile formed upon his face as he turned away and began collecting his gear.

Four dark figures surrounded him.

Hissing and bearing their fangs, they advanced.

Stumbling into the coffin and knocking it over, Alan found himself backed into a corner.

The four hissing vampyres closed in.

Fear

1989

It was the Devil's own pitch,
A darkness utterly corrupt and vile.

I couldn't see a thing, couldn't hear a thing
The silence absolute—except for that internal ringing sound.

I turned, slowly.
The only way I could know this
Was by the steps my feet made over each other.

That's when I came face to face with it—
Teeth ripping my face apart.

Werewolf

1988

I just kept running.

I didn't know if I could ever get away from what I'd seen. I knew that physically I could probably—eventually—get away, but the horror I'd witnessed would forever remain with me . . . .

It all started innocently enough. I was walking home late one moonlit night after a movie, taking the proverbial short-cut. I was thinking about how great my life had been going . . . of my new girlfriend, Shelly, especially. We'd met about a month ago, and it had been love at first sight for the both of us.

I was thinking about her hair . . . of how it shined in the light—any light. Of her soft, beautiful features . . . the way she walked . . . the way we held each other. It was a feeling I wished on everybody! Everybody should have a mate, someone to hold and love. I was walking on air! It seemed as if nothing could bother me—*nothing!*

It was then that I heard a commotion up ahead.

My head was still muddled with sweet thoughts of Shelly, but not enough to cloud my mind. I knew the sounds of a fight when I heard it. There was a scuffle going on up ahead, and though I hadn't been in a fight since grade school, I still somehow wasn't all that comforted by my physical size and capabilities. Something about this felt very wrong . . . .

As I got closer, I was able to distinguish the sounds better. I heard a high-pitched screaming, which came from a woman . . . and some deeper grunts that came from a man forcefully exerting himself. But I also heard something else . . . sounds much deeper than the rest of what I heard, sounds that seemed to come . . . from an animal.

An angry, ravenous animal.

Instinctively, I reached for my side, my hand coming to rest on my encased buck knife. Still there, at least I wouldn't be totally unaided if necessity reared its ugly head.

The female voice increased in pitch, crying out for help from anybody . . . but nobody seemed to answer her call. The male voice was wavering. I stopped in my tracks. There was no mistaking it now—people were fighting for their lives. I felt something twist in my gut, sweat seeping out of my pores.

I withdrew my knife, extending its four-inch, shiny blade. On the blade itself was an engraving commemorating the men of the sea. The engraving had been done over in pure silver; the knife was never intended for use, but for display.

I approached the fray, blade glistening in the moonlight. The woman saw me and stepped back to allow my entrance, pleading for help. I'm not sure what she was wearing, but her attire was in tatters and she was bleeding. She held a broken tree branch. I approached hesitantly, blade pointed forward, and looked at the scene. Two figures struggling, one appreciably larger than the other, horribly disfigured—and *naked*. And there was a growling coming from the naked, larger one that stung my soul; it was that animal sound I'd heard.

I got closer . . . unsure of what to do . . . though at the same time knowing perfectly well what needed to be done. The man was being ripped to pieces by his naked attacker. I thought back to Shelly—*what if this same thing happened to her?* The woman continued to plead for my assistance, calling to any others who might be listening. She again approached the thing atop her man and pounded mightily with the branch that had finally shattered apart in her damaged hands on a back-that-wasn't-a-*normal* back . . . on a back that was . . . *changing* . . . .

I was frozen!

I watched helplessly as the boyfriend was hideously mutilated.

How could I just stand there and watch?

I grew angry with myself!

This man was already beyond any help that might arrive . . . his woman not much better—but I couldn't let what was happening to this man happen to the woman . . . I had to do *something!*

I grasped my knife tighter, allowing my anger to fill me . . . it was the only way I could get myself to leap forward . . . which I did.

I buried my blade into the thing's side.

I felt my whole body trembling as the act was concluded.

I had done it!

The beast uttered a pained howl, throwing the now dead body of the man away—then turned on me. It didn't have to hit me to physically knock me over—just seeing its face was enough.

The face I looked at was not like my own . . . or any other man's.
And it was still transforming.

A transformation between a man—and a *monster.*

The face contorted with thick animal hair and leathery skin sprouting all over it . . . long, razor-sharp teeth completing extension from within an angry, lupine maw. A far-too muscular and brutishly lithe form taking hold over the soft, sallow flesh of a man.

I was knocked to the ground as the beast sprinted past, clutching its side. As it got past me, it stood for but a moment in the pale moonlight and shook its hairy, narrow, and wholly *wolf* head back and forth, as the contortions continued to torture it. His hands—which were now actually claws—went up to its "face."

The whole of this thing's body was ripping itself to pieces!

As it fell to all fours, rippling muscles and fur now covered it. This was clearly no longer any kind of a human being I'd ever before seen.

The woman stared, unseeing, at the wolf—the *werewolf.* She'd stopped screaming a long time ago.

The wolf licked its teeth.

Looked to me.

I saw some stickiness along its side—the side I had knifed. The blade still gleamed in my hand, the beast's blood on both the blade and my hand. The wolf looked toward the girl. Before I could react, let alone think, the beast had leapt toward her and knocked her over—intentionally avoiding my blade.

The silver. The silver in the engraving—*that's* what kept it from me.

The wolf took one well-placed swipe at the woman before continuing onward into the cover of night.

Her throat was gone.

As was the beast.

I stood there . . . I stood with my bloodied and gleaming knife still outstretched, my senses traumatized. I couldn't do anything for her boyfriend . . . and now I'd been similarly cheated out of her life, too! I didn't know what to do.

So I ran!

At first I ran after it, but then thought *what would I do when I caught up with it?* What would it do to *me?* The deeds had already been done. And surely it wouldn't stay afraid of me and my puny weapon for long.

It was a great deal larger than me . . . quicker than me—far more lethal. So I hid.

But I can't stay here forever . . . alone and terrified. There's plenty of night left. It'll find me. The wolf has my scent. I can feel it tracking me.

It's only a matter of time.

Love, What A Way To Go
1990

"God, how I love you."

Joey smiled back at her.

"Feeling's mutual," he said, softly, squeezing her hand.

Looking into Lorna's eyes, Joey was overcome by their passionate presence . . . large, painfully emotional eyes that constantly appeared to be weeping, though never actually wet.

Joey replayed the past two months of devoted togetherness that had quickly developed between them . . . from their first meeting as singularly lonely people vainly searching the nights . . . to *two* . . . unable to live without each other's touch. As far from perfect as their relationship might be, all that mattered was that they had each other.

Fiercely holding hands, they both felt the internal buildup of emotion—and the tears that were sure to follow. Two months . . . that was all . . . two months and they had blended together like a lover's embrace. There had been the usual talk—that they'd never last, that it was all just a case of "can't have" infatuation, but love didn't have to last an eternity . . . just a lifetime.

Outside, the night was steely gray, and they both shivered as they stared out through the dirty coffee shop windows. There was a feeling of dread hovering in the air, and though neither would admit it, both felt it. It hung as thick as the fog they'd walked through.

"Think we'd better go now, honey," Joey said, somberly forcing the words out. Lorna nodded her head in agreement. Joey left the tip.

Cold. Desolate. Still that . . . *something* . . . hovered in the air . . . taunting.

Outside, the two stood beneath a lonely streetlamp, its obscure luminescence spilling out onto the sidewalk. The couple looked ahead to the fog bank before them . . . their grips on each other tightening, squeezing. Lorna turned just in time to meet his same movement. Joey saw the tears . . . and the soft wisps that arose from them as they channeled down her face.

"Don't *ever* leave me!" she said, choking on her words.

He said nothing, instead increasing his hold around her, and smiling down to her. Kissed her forehead.

They disappeared into the darkness.

Destination attained, they faced each other.

"*I love you!*"

"*I love you!*"

Both felt the chill across their faces as they now wept openly and kissed. Away Lorna walked . . . up the path to her house, a dull yellow porch light whispering into the dark. Joey watched her until she got inside and turned off the light. He caught her face filling a window shortly thereafter . . . a small hand pressed against the glass in a beckoning, farewell.

He smiled softly. Waved back.

Joey swallowed hard as he left.

Having made it some four blocks homeward, Joey reached a certain bend in the road, lost in both thought and emotion. He thought of Lorna . . . wondered when he would next see her . . . of her soft, loving touch—

A car came screaming around the bend. It hit Joey full on.

He was sent high into the air and came back down hitting the asphalt hard. Joey lay crushed and face down in the rain gutter, a warm stain slowly forming a boundary between his body and the ground, one hand outstretched . . . .

Lorna awoke abruptly.

Her hand out before her, she'd had the most terrifying dream of her life, but was suddenly unable to recall any of it—except for the uncomfortable feeling that Joey was somehow involved. Rushing out of bed, she frantically fumbled for the phone, a sickness in the pit of her stomach as she dialed his number. She waited. No answer.

She continued waiting.

Still no answer. She hung up and tried again.

No answer . . . .

Noanswernoanswernoanswernoanswer!

It never took him this long to get home before, and he always picked up by the third ring.

Always.

Finding herself dressed before she was even aware of it, she flew out of the house, screen-door clattering behind her.

He was buried in a quiet ceremony. Lorna wore black. His mom had died, she was told, from the trauma of Joey's death, and somewhere in the night cruised a car with a pushed-in left-front bumper and a damaged headlight.

That night Lorna went back to the old coffee shop and took their usual booth. She was the lone customer. Her coffee here was free tonight. Outside a car pulled into the a parking slot, bright headlights beaming directly in through the shop's high, open windows. And they remained on, one slightly askew. Lorna was only in passing annoyed that the driver was so abjectly rude to leave them on.

The driver entered at the distant end of the shop and approached the cash register. The diner's owner returned a gesture, and there was brief conversation, but Lorna paid little attention. Only when the gun went off did she look up, upsetting the runnels of tears staining her face. The assailant also looked up, pointing something in her direction. She never noticed the .357—only the bright flash as something blew her chest all over the windows and seat bench behind her.

Still wearing black, she, too, had a quiet ceremony.

Her immediate family gone, distant relatives took care of everything. She had a nice casket. Thing was, she was buried in a cemetery on the other side of town. Clouds hung heavily, perilously low, a bone-chilling downpour raining large, painful drops.

That night he was restless.
Something was wrong . . . something . . . *missing.*
There was too much emptiness.
He had *to move.*
Good thing the rain had softened the earth.
Good thing, rain.

A drunk leaned against the cemetery's iron gates, brown paper bag and hidden bottle in one hand, regurgitated meal in the other. Hearing a noise, he looked up, wiping his warm hand on a pants leg. Peering through the fog, the drunk spotted a lone, lumbering figure crossing the graveyard. The figure carried two objects, the smaller one indistinguishable, but the larger looking like a box the size of a man. Turning away, the drunk slouched back down onto the damp grass, nursing his condition.

A bruised car, one of its headlights broken, burned on through a stoplight. Massaging the gears, the driver raced down deserted roads. Taking one turn a little rough, the driver spotted something entering his path . . . a figure straddling the center marker of the road. It was a dark figure . . . a box-like object behind him on the road. The driver reached for his gun, grinding down several gears for a better look. The unyielding figure held something under one of its arms. It was smaller. Slowing more, the driver strained the lower gears.

The figure suddenly raised its burdened arm, sending the object into non-curving flight through the air . . . impacting the driver's windshield. It struck the driver square in the face, neatly taking off the top half of his head.

The headstone continued on out the rear of the car.

Careening, the vehicle slammed into a street post; shuddering, the light blinked on and off several times before going dead.

The next morning found people gathered around a burial plot. The groundskeeper noticed it first, and he was not tight-lipped by nature.

Where she lay, at one time alone, now she had company, freshly turned earth and an accompanying gravestone alongside hers. And one fathom into the ground lay two caskets side by side. In one, the man's arm was thrust through the side of his casket and into the next one.

They lay together, now, side by side, two hands tightly clenched.

Love doesn't have to last an eternity . . . just its lifetime.

Please Have A Seat, Mr. Jordan
1993

Frederick Jordan, real estate agent extraordinaire (as he liked to think of himself), pulled off Route 1 and into the deserted parking lot. It was sometime after midnight, and a glistening wetness from an earlier light rain coated the streetlights, headlights, the world. Maybe it had been something he'd had at dinner, or maybe it was just an unknown tummy ailment, but all he knew right now was that for the past ten miles he'd needed to take the most *wicked* shit.

Jordan parked his Mercedes in the slot directly before a glistening picture window with lettering that read, *Stratford Realty, Frederick Jordan*, and turned off the ignition. He hurriedly got out of his car and made for the locked glass doors. Events from the past few hours squirted through his mind like his impending bowel movement. The man was an old, rather eccentric character from The City, and he'd called on him more than once in the past. The gentleman was making yet another buy in Connecticut, and the fact that it was late and he wouldn't be in Stratford until sometime after nine that night was only a minor point-of-fact. Jordan knew the man by the color of his money and therefore ignored the lateness of the hour.

But now he was exhausted and had to take the mother of all dumps. Noisily, and somewhat shakily, like real hunger when it strikes, Jordan brought out the large ring of keys he carried and hurriedly jiggled open the lock with some difficulty. He burst in through the doors, even sprinted several feet towards his destination, when he cursed and spun back around

Bombers on time, searching for target . . . .

to hastily lock the doors. As it was he'd bent the key on his way in, nearly snapping it off in the process; it was late, he was the only one in the building, and he wanted to keep it that way. Only then did he make his direct, almost-pants-shitting beeline for the restrooms, deep within the darkened interior.

Jordan burst through the rest-room door, missed the first time, but flicked on the lights in the next scramble, and plunged into the nearest stall. He'd be damned if he was going to be

(*shitting*)

sitting in the dark. Frederick Jordan prided himself on being levelheaded, but when it came to being alone in the dark, things changed. *Reason* changed. It was like darkness changed the very structure of the air, the way life was supposed to work. Your worst fears came to mind . . . came to life. And no matter that this was New England—Stephen King, Rick Hautala, and all those goddamned ghost stories—

And speaking of stories, what was that one about that town near Cornwall—Dudleytown was it? A real doozy of a tale if he'd ever heard one. He'd grown up with it, and continued to have nightmares about it. He'd first heard about the damned thing around a Boy Scout campfire one summer night, up towards Hartford. The Scout Master was from Cornwall, the son of a bitch. Even after all these years Jordan still hadn't managed to forgive him for it. The story went that back in the 1600s—and again later in the 1800s—an entire town had grown mad to nearly the last soul . . . and disappeared. A real-life ghost town buried deep in the woods of New England. Then there was something about Stratford itself. Demon dummies in a preacher's house—

Knock it off.

Didn't need to be thinking about that shit. Got other shit to deal with. Shit that was having a hard time coming out, what with his mind working overtime on ghosts, and goblins, and—

Constipation.

Well, fuck me over and leave me to die! Frederick Jordan grunted and strained—but nothing passed.

On target! Bomb-bay doors open; bombers on time; release failure! Release failure!

"Well, ain't that a pisser."

Jordan strained again, found a little relief, but didn't get nearly what he knew was there. He gave it another heave-ho and found this attempt much more satisfying—

When the lights went out.

"*FUCK!*"

Dudleytown bolted back into his consciousness with a mind-deafening boom, and Mr. Jordan's bomb-bay doors slammed the fuck shut.

Calling off bombers! Mission aborted! Mission aborted!

Hastily, Jordan reached about blindly for the roll of toilet paper he knew was cubbyholed neatly in the steel wall beside him, and commanded reason to take over. There's nothing but

(dark)

space between him and the sinks and paper towels. Nothing but additional

(dark)

space between the sinks and the three-quarter-about-face out the door. And he knew this because the rational side of his mind had told him it was so. There was nothing to be afraid of—he was the only one in the building; had gone to great pains to ensure that.

But.

There was always the possibility that all those friggin fairy tales were true and there *were* ghosts. After all, how brave were people—really—when it came right down to it, and they were trapped in a bathroom stall, alone, at night, nobody around, all lights suddenly flickered off by an unseen agent? Wasn't there always just a *little* fear—a *little* doubt—no matter what people might try to tell themselves during the comfort of daylight? The fact remained that the fear was there and it had been his *first* reaction to the situation. No matter how remote or fictional there was always The Most Remotest of Possibilities that somewhere . . . *sometime* . . . out in the darkest parts of the woods or in the most recessed corners of a building . . . there *was* something lurking.

Waiting.

For the lights to go off.

Waiting.

For the dark to work on folks' minds and strangle that little imp called Reason. Imagined or not, right or wrong, fear was fear, and it was alive and well in Stratford, Connecticut this night.

And why would people make up tales like these anyway, if there wasn't even the *remotest* of truths to them?

As Frederick Jordan's now-shaking fingers touched the roll of invisible toilet paper, the lights flickered back on.

"*Shit!*"

Frederick relaxed.

See, his Rational Side jubilated, *there's nothing to be afraid of, little Freddy! The dark has nothing the light doesn't have! It's all in your mind, Freddy, boy, all in yer* mind!

Yeah, just like *you.*

"Okay, come on, baby, hold out. Don't flicker off again. Please, God, just gimme five minutes! Five minutes—that's all I ask—then I'm outta here! Gone! You can keep your darkness, your ghosts, and I'll promise never to invade an empty building again at weird-shit hours, no matter how strong the urge."

All right, bring em round again, boys! We're going in for another run!

Still clutching his little swatch of torn-off toilet paper, Jordan wondered if inanimate objects ever experienced fear and about how nice it would be to be like that: distanced and untouchable. Like the toilet-paper roll . . . or the walls of the bathroom stall. Sometimes he wished he could be inanimate, impervious and able to observe . . . *unafraid.* But humanity was not about untouchability or mere observation, it was about fear and experience. It was about those things and more, and Frederick Jordan finally felt himself beginning to loosen up . . . .

Bombardier to pilot . . . steady now, steadyyy . . .

Bomb-bay doors open.

Keep er steady—

Roger, we have target acquisition! Bombs away! Bombs away!

And boy was there a load.

Chuckling to himself, he pictured the old black-and-white newsreels he'd seen on TV, the one where the Dubbaya-Dubbaya-Two pilots released a seemingly endless load of munitions upon the godless German bastards below, and oh, such *sweet* relief . . .

The bathroom door swung open.

Jordan bolted upright, and slammed shut the bomb-bay doors like nobody's business.

A million things surged through his mind in that instant, the foremost being who the *fuck* was in the building, let alone in the *john!*

He'd locked the frigging door, all right—and there were no other cars in the parking lot. It was

(he looked to his watch)

12:17 a.m.!

Dudleytown, my friend, Dudleytown's baaack.

Yes.

For you.

And we're going to squash that Rational Side foreverrr—

Then it occurred to him: it was somebody from the office. Herb or Mark had been driving by, seen his car, and stopped. Yeah, that was it—Herb or Mark—after a date, a drink at the tavern. Sure. Playing a little trick on Freddy-boy. Or maybe it was Ellen.

Frederick tenuously convinced himself that his Rational Side was still alive and kicking, even if its voice had grown somewhat dull and dead. Holding his breath, Jordan strained in his seat and listened. It almost sounded like there was a swishing sound . . . like a broom across the floor.

The cleaning crew?

Silence.

"Mark? Is that you? Herb—"

The lights flickered again.

Fuck the toilet paper!

Jordan reached for his pants and yanked them up. He peered through the slits between the stall's walls and door.

Nothing. Couldn't see a damned thing.

"Okay, come on, now, who's there, goddammit, a joke's a joke—"

The room went black, went full dark for a full second, then sprang back to illumination, and underneath his stall, before Jordan could breathe a sigh of anything . . .

Lay a cloth figure.

Limp. Motionless. On the floor before him.

Jordan screamed and jumped backward and up onto his toilet seat.

He looked to his ankles (where his pants were now rolled down in a bunch, like ankle cuffs trying to pull him back down) and saw that anything that might have been left inside . . . well . . . he'd solved his constipation issue.

The cloth figure lay motionless before him—it's dead face blankly staring up at him. Jordan saw that it resembled a scarecrow, but was much more cruel in design. There was no loose or spilling straw, and he found himself staring at stitched eyes.

Which opened.

Something loud and screechy spilled out of Jordan's voice box as he tried to will himself up and over/through/under the wall, through the brick, and out into the cool (if humid) night air above the building.

The stitched and unearthly eyes looked up to him, and the lights went off again, just as the stitched mouth begin to form a cruel, severe grin—

Jordan inched down off the toilet and kicked away at the area where the demon doll had lain before the lights had gone out. Backed away from the stall door. He'd fumbled and tripped on his way back to the top of the toilet, his pants still down about his ankles, and yanked them up. He didn't know how long he'd sat like that . . . scrunched up in as much of a fetal position as possible atop the toilet . . . frozen in fear . . . but he flat didn't know what else to do.

Rational thought had deserted him, as had his bombers.

Had he indeed imagined it all?

Had he dozed off and been dreaming?

Maybe it had been dinner after all—all he knew was that he continued to hyperventilate until the lights came back on—and not at full strength either, no, that would have been too easy. The fluorescent fuckers flickered, and only dimly at that.

And the figure on the floor was gone.

He waited several beats before putting his feet back down to the floor.

The stall floor was empty and Jordan felt childishly stupid.

He *had* imagined it all, that was it.

Hell, it was after midnight and he'd had a long day. A trying client. Raw steak. And it was New England. He was the only goddamned individual in the entire goddamned building, so how was he supposed to goddamned feel at

(looking to his watch)

12:23 a.m.?

All explainable, his Rational Side squeaked. A perfectly reasonable scenario for anyone . . . even one as much the pinnacle of Rationality as yourself, Mr. Jordan, to think they had seen—ha-ha, a *ghost* . . . a devil doll—or something . . . .

"For cryin' out *loud* . . . ," Jordan said, as he looked up balefully into the still-flickering lights. Best to split while you still got

(*your sanity*)

light.

It was all in your mind, Herr Jordan. Man up. Rough day.

He peeked through the stall's slits again.

(*your worst fears*)

Still felt prickly.

Yep, all in yer mind, buddy, now get your shit

(*so to speak*)

together and get home.

Jordan quickly cleaned up after himself, pulled up his pants, and prayed for the lights to remain on. Logical explanation or not, there was still frost in his veins and he was sure he'd lost several years of his life from that little piece of work.

Zip up them pants.

Cinch that belt.

Now let's get the fuck *outta here—*

Jordan reached for the stall latch, and his fingers trembled.

Girly mahn!

Get a grip.

Then he smacked open the door, and it loudly whacked the stall frame, echoing in the dim corners of his mind like the crisp bang of a firecracker. He quickly made for the opening and stepped out into the constantly shifting patterns of the shadowy room under the flickering fluorescence.

Lots of space . . . lots of open, dark, dark *space . . . that's all, friend, full of nothing, full of dark, full of—*

Sluggish as a dream, he turned to his right

Don't do it, man! Mr. Rational Side screamed, *eyes front! Eyes front!*

to where the

more dark space and nothing

sinks were. Took a step and

Yeah, come to us . . . the Dark . . . the Open Dark Spaces of an empty soul—

Jordan saw the first figure sitting on the floor and leaning up against the wall, its head slumped dumbly forward and onto its chest. Jordan's bowels kicked back into action. He saw the other one, sitting atop the sinks, cocked over in the same stupid manner.

Dudleytown. Dudleytown. What was it about Dudleytown?

No, it wasn't *Dudleytown*—it was *Stratford.*

It was fucking old Stratford, *this very town itself.*

A Reverend and his family. Found demon-dummies propped everywhere . . . praying to a hideous dummy dwarf that swung from a chandelier. Dummies that would change or move when folks blinked or dozed off while guarding them. A ghost tale from the 1600s that was now his very own nightmare in present-day Stratford!

As the lights continued to flicker, Jordan saw that the cloth dummies had *moved.*

They were stiff, like a stop-action film. Subtly. Not so subtly. A hideously crooked finger there, a ghastly tilted head there. Stitched eyes that were open one moment, closed the next.

Standing. Seated. Kneeling.

Jordan turned to run, but found more behind him. Saw the dwarf dummy dangling from atop the stalls.

Jordan felt his mind bend. Tear at the seams.

I thought it was all over, one dark corner of his mind whined, but there was no response from Mr. Rational Side.

The figures advanced.

It's just supposed to be in my head.

They had backed Jordan up and into the stall he had just come out from.

. . . in m-my mind *. . . .*

The cruelly stitched eyes came for him.

The cruelly stitched grins.

The little cloth bodies.

Jordan fell backwards, clipped the door on re-entry, and fell back onto the toilet seat. As the door clanked back open, Jordan could see the figures on the other side. They all shuffled about before the stall and Jordan heard that maddening swish-swishing sound their little cloth feet made across the tile. Saw the dwarf dummy above him, insanely dangling. Jordan shrank back to the toilet into the all-too-familiar cradled position, hugging the porcelain bowl. His mind's clutch had disengaged and spun maddeningly. He stared blankly into the porcelain, expecting to wake up any moment now—any moment now, please, would be just fine thank you—*please!*

Cloth fingers clutched at the door's edge. Jerkily opened the last defense in his crazy battle against madness. Jordan felt life drain out from him; crawled as far behind the toilet as possible and loudly prayed. A part of his mind welcomed the coolness of the bowl and tiled floor . . . another part simply exploded.

The dark figures congregated.

"N-*n-nooo* . . ."

Then he realized he'd had an opening and bolted underneath the stall's walls, slamming his head, scraping the top of his back, and severely banging a knee. He scrambled to his feet outside of the stall. Made for the door like an adrenaline-junkie.

And was gone.

Jordan collapsed in the carpeted office area. The lights here also flickered.

But I hadn't turned them on.

He cast a sudden glance around him and was relieved to find nothing—nothing-*what?*—had followed him out.

Where were they? What did they want?

Shakily, he got back to his feet and supported himself against a wall. He turned to leave. Saw a dark, familiarly slouched form ahead of him.

Spoke too soon, sonny.

Jordan's legs wavered and his stomach knotted. The figure approached him in that same staccato-like, stop-fucking-motion movement. Every time Jordan blinked, or even thought about blinking, the damned hellion was closer; zigzagging. Jerky. Always *forward.*

"NO*!*"

Something snapped inside Jordan's throat and his voice gave way to silence.

Good. It'll match what's left upstairs—

Each time Jordan's eyes fluttered, the creature was closer. Out of the corner of his eyes, Jordan saw

(felt)

others coming for him out of the darkness. Out of the walls. Dark figures, everywhere. All like those from the rest room. They all came to greet him.

Hello, Jordy, enjoying the night?

Jordan felt the frigid north Atlantic wash up and over him, and screamed voicelessly. He bolted past the figure before him, his hands touching the cloth and insanely sinking in. He never bothered to use the key on the way out; didn't even bother with his car. There were two cloth figures waiting for him in there—one slumped over the wheel, and the other leaned crazily against the passenger-side door, cloth face twisted and pressed up against the window. Beyond his car, Jordan saw an entire army of dark, silently rustling, figures.

Jerky. Like scarecrows.

Only worse.

Coming home.

Many rumors went around town about Mr. Jordan's sudden and frightful appearance—hair white as the driven snow . . . eyes that screamed of a nameless horror . . . his constantly mumbling, yet voiceless pleas . . . .

Yes, there were many rumors.

Many.

But none as convincing as that which Mr. Frederick Jordan himself had experienced.

Red Hands

2004

1

Kina Hester awoke, screaming.

She leapt out of her bed, blundered through her bed sheets and blankets, bounced off her bedroom wall, clipped her left elbow along the edge of her upright dresser, then flung herself out into the hallway, where she broke a nail madly scrambling for the light switch after bouncing off another wall. She spun around as she began her collapse to the floor, several feet farther down the hallway, near the head of the stairs. The only thing that kept her from tumbling headlong down those stairs was having whacked her head a good one on the bathroom's doorjamb. That promptly knocked her on her butt.

Dazed, she sat on the floor. Opened her eyes wide . . . and shook her head.

She leaned back against the wall, inhaling huge gulps of air, and groaned. Cradling her hurt elbow into her body, she examined the broken and bleeding nail. She winced as she closed her eyes, then forcefully pressed her head back into the wall. She then reached for her head wound and grimaced. A tear trickled down her cheek and she groaned.

And her throat was sore . . . as if she'd been screaming for a really, really long time.

Sniffling loudly, Kina opened her eyes and looked back at the entrance into her bedroom.

What . . . had just . . . happened?

What had caused her to leap out of bed in a blind rage and end up as a puddle of goo in her hallway?

She grabbed the handrail. Hanging on to it for dear life as a mental anchor, she tried—oh, so desperately—to recall . . .

Dreams. Blinding, horrific—

(*dark room*)

(*things forced into . . .*)

(*. . . pulled from . . .*)

(*her body*)

imagery she found herself unable—or unwilling—to decipher.

Screams, oh, God, the *screams!*

Kina let go of the railing and pressed both curled-up hands against her ears.

She could still hear the screams!

Screams that went on and on until they'd been abruptly cut off. She'd felt her head jerk, though it hadn't actually moved.

And the pain!

Something had come to her . . . *for* her . . . *followed* her . . . .

If something had followed her . . . *would it stand to reason that it might still be in there?*

Kina shot to her feet.

Arms outstretched and bracing her between the hallway wall and bathroom doorjamb, she scanned the hallway for a weapon. She looked into the bathroom, into the shower. The shower curtain hung part way open on its shower rod. One of those removable wooden poles that pressed against the walls with spring-loaded friction.

Kina darted into the bathroom and grabbed the shower-curtain pole, tearing it from its overhead position. She knocked off the rubber cup on one end and hastily cleared the pole of shower curtain.

Strong, solid. Stuck for years in its position. It didn't compress or come apart. She held it out before her.

Did she really believe something had followed her back from

(*the dead?*)

a dream? No. But she couldn't take chances. It was late, dark, and she was still one foot in whatever dreamland she'd just awoken from. But she had to go back in there sometime . . . and to be forearmed was forewarned. Or something like that. Composing herself . . . and directing her new lance out before her . . . Kina left the bathroom for the bedroom.

She flicked on the light switch with the pole. Entered the bedroom.

Images still flew through her mind, but she still couldn't focus . . . in fact visually focusing on the physical room before her was difficult without her glasses or contacts. #NotHelping.

The only thing she could grab and hold onto was an intense and acute sense of fear, pain, and dread that still held an icy hold over her. She cleared her throat—a throat that was indeed sore—and glanced at her clock, squinting. It read a fuzzy little-after-two-in-the-morning. And the late October winds were howling it up outside her windows.

Again—not helping!

Pole shakily held out before her, she cautiously advanced toward her bed—but she whipped to the right as she entered through the door.

Nothing there.

Turning back to her bed, she examined the rumpled and pulled-back blankets and sheets. The bottom, or fitted sheet, was even pulled back from the mattress's corner. Good Lord, *what had gone on in here?* She poked at them with her lance.

More nothing.

Crouched . . . she peered under the bed.

Additional nothings—but, just to make sure, she swiped the pole back and forth under the bed.

Just because you couldn't see something didn't mean—

Dust bunnies and a lost black sock she'd been looking for, for almost six months. Yuck. She really should clean under here. More.

Back to her feet, Kina went to her closet and pushed open its folding accordion doors. Jabbed in and about her clothes.

Sweet nothings.

Kina stepped back and lowered her pole. Let out a strained chuckle.

"Damn, it *was* only a dream."

She went back out into the hallway and turned off the hallway light, still letting loose the occasional nervous chuckle. When she reentered her bedroom, she stood in the middle of the room listening to the high winds outside. Feeling the lateness of the hour with the last vapors of her dream fog finally lifting. Late October . . . high winds . . . two-thirteen in the morning . . . and Hallowe'en in a couple days.

Yeah, no issues there.

Kina reached for the bedroom lights—when two hands thrust out at her from the wall . . . *two red hands attached to red forearms.*

Kina jerked backward, tripping over her feet, and slammed into the upright dresser on the other side of the room, knocking it against the wall with a load *crack!* It sat canted toward the wall. She leaned against it in a daze, shaking her head.

The red hands followed her, again thrusting out after her, this time up from the floor at her feet.

Screaming and scrambling her feet under her in that pathetically cartoon-like scramble, she finally gripped hardwood floor with her bare feet and swung her pole wildly about her, smashing an antique picture up on the wall behind the upright dresser, her jewelry armoire to her left, and totaling her hanging bedroom light fixture above. This, unfortunately, popped her lance apart, shortening it by half, and sent the years-compressed spring ricocheting off a wall and onto the floor out of view.

Kina backed up against another wall—but the hands again found her and shot out from the wall, this time *around* her.

Once again mad with fear, Kina swung what remained of her bathroom lance directly at the spot on the wall from which the red hands had emerged. They were gone now, but that didn't stop her from gouging out a good-sized chunk of wallpaper and wallboard.

She backed up into her doorway, when the hands again jutted out for her from the open space of her room to her left. Kina swung her weapon and this time connected with her other dresser's mirror, obliterating it in a hail of glass.

"Come on, you son-of-a-bitch! *Show* yourself, whatever you are! *Come on!*"

(. . . *no—no, don't* . . .)

Suddenly, where had been abject fear, now was absolute *anger.*

Scanning, she got back to her feet and angrily swung at walls and the bedroom door, which was one of those cheap, hollow things. This time her stick got stuck in the splintered door, and she was unable to pull free. She viciously kicked and pulled at the stick in the door—slipped—and knocked herself out cold as one of her yanks smacked the edge of the door into her head, just as her feet slipped on all the debris strewn across the floor . . . .

Kina entered her office at KRDO's 95.1 ("The Peak") radio station. She dropped her purse and bags on the floor, then collapsed into her chair. Sucking on a throat lozenge, she cleared her throat. Still raw. Shawnee, one of the D.J.s, poked her head into her office. Looked at the scrapes and bruises along her arms and

(*red*)

hands.

"You okay, hon?"

Kina barely looked up. Her back was to the door, but she glanced into the rear-view mirror to the left of her computer.

"*No* . . . ," she said, her voice cracking.

"What happened to your *voice?*" Shawnee asked, entering her office.

"We heard you'd had some kind of accident."

Kina again coughed.

"I had a really, really, *really* bad dream last night and screamed my head off. I banged my elbow, broke a nail," she said in a half-whisper, displaying her wounds, "then knocked myself out as I slammed into my bedroom door."

Kina lightly touched the bump on her head.

"Damn, girl, must've been some dream," Shawnee said, trying not to laugh, but smiling broadly.

"Doctor said I'll live . . . but wondered if she'd been the right one for me . . . ."

Shawnee let out a hearty DJ laugh. She came in farther and leaned against the edge of Kina's L-shaped desk. Scooched right up alongside her and eyed her intently. Placed a concerned hand to Kina and said, "Anything you wanna talk about?"

Kina shook her head. "No . . . just wanna forget about it all. Get back into my everyday routine, you know? I don't really remember anything about it, anyway," Kina said, lying.

"*Nothing?* With all those war wounds?" Shawnee said, reaching out and smoothing away at a stray piece of Kina's hair.

Kina shook her head.

"Okay. Well . . . if you need anything, just let me know." Shawnee again placed a concerned hand to Kina, before leaving.

Kina stared out her window.

What the hell had *happened?*

It had to have been a dream, right? Things like that just didn't happen in real life. That's *Freddy Kruger* talk and Freddy's only a dream—a nightmare—a *movie*, damn it, a goddamned *movie*. She'd gotten herself so worked up and spooked she didn't know which way was up.

Kina logged onto her computer and began to immerse herself into her work day. Her BFF Jan Carter had already stood in for her while she'd been to the Emergency Room. Time to get back into her daily routine . . . .

" . . . seven-fifty-seven, Steve Runyan, Dave Morrison—and Kina, we're sorry to say that we have some scary news for ya. We have author E. O. Cantore, here in the studio with us," Steve Runyan, of the Peak Morning Show said on-air to Kina, who remained in her office.

"My door is *closed*," Kina roughly replied back into her workstation mike from her office, "and it's *barricaded!*"

Steve and Dave chuckled.

"We're going to talk about the paranormal and ghosts," Steve Runyan continued, "and, ah, how they interrupt our daily life and the whole deal, so I don't know—you better just, ah, keep that door shut—"

"You know, I work with you two, so I don't know how much stranger normal life can get . . . ," Kina said, laughing.

Oh, but she *did* . . . .

She hadn't been able to *not* think about the events of the early morning. And now add to it that the station was doing a whole week of "weird stuff" with ghost stories . . . astrologers . . . psychics.

Now, who was this new guy? An author who wrote paranormal fiction? What was the attraction to this stuff?

She'd never been big on it . . . well, perhaps more to the point was that she had never been big on it because she'd always been *afraid* of it. Ever since she'd been a little girl and her parents had told her about *The Legend of Sleepy Hollow* and that darned headless horseman, she'd never been able to get into anything spooky. Now, she had no choice . . . she'd awoken this morning to her own personal Freddy Kruger reaching out to her—*her*—and this wasn't a movie and it hadn't been a *dream*—

But it *had* to of been, right?

Crap like this just didn't happen outside of movies and books! It just *didn't* . . . it's like what that guy in there right now does, it's all made up—*fiction*.

What had happened to her had to have been a delayed hypnagogic reaction or something . . . a delayed dream-thing . . . still groggy with one foot in dreamland . . . .

She needed to use the ladies room.

Kina got up, then realized she had to walk past Mr. Paranormal in there talking with Steve and Dave. Maybe she'd just take a quick peek in on the guy . . . .

Kina quietly came up to the studio doorway and looked in at him. He looked normal enough . . . clean appearance: short cut, brown hair . . . even sported an Hawai'ian shirt. A *black* Hawai'ian shirt, but *still*. He didn't look at all like she'd imagined him to be.

He turned to her.

Crap!

Smiling, Mr. Paranormal got up and quickly made his way toward her, his hand held out . . .

That was when she lost it.

All Kina could see was a *red hand*.

Those red hands.

Kina barely made it into the bathroom stalls before she lost her Danish and tea . . . .

Kina did about all she could to stay as late as possible at work, but when Jan made her way out, it was time to go. Jan showed up at Kina's office.

"Hey-yah, girl, how ya doin? Sorry I couldn't stop by earlier."

"I don't want to go home."

"Well, let's talk about that, huh?"

"I don't want to. I've decided I'm never going to sleep again."

Jan laughed. "Oh, come on, be a big girl. It can't have been that bad. Everyone's been talking about it, but no one seems to know— what happened?"

Kina sighed and cleared her throat. Her voice was feeling decidedly better, but was still a bit rough.

"I had a really bad dream is all—and it's embarrassing. I kinda . . . um . . . messed up my bedroom, I was so scared."

"How do you mean 'messed up your bedroom'?"

"I . . . um . . . *welll* . . . beat up the walls. Demolished my overhead fan-light and broke furniture and mirrors."

"No *way!*" Jan said, laughing.

Kina shrugged her shoulders, giving Jan an "oops" look.

"What brought all that on?"

"Some kind of a nightmare I can't remember anymore. But I do remember how I felt . . . I was extremely terrified. More terrified than I could have ever imagined. I was so scared it *hurt.* I felt sure I was going to have an aneurism. I'm not exaggerating."

Jan went serious. "Anything else?"

"You're gonna laugh."

"Am not."

"I saw . . . in my bedroom, I saw . . . *red hands.*"

"*Red hands?* Just *hands?*"

Kina nodded. "Yeah, well, hands and forearms. They shot out from the wall at me like this—" she said, and dramatically thrust her arms toward Jan—who took a step back.

"Oh, my gosh—that'd scare the bejesus out of me!"

"Well, I woke up screaming—I mean I was screaming my *lungs* out. My throat's still sore, as you can tell. I didn't—and still don't— remember the entire dream . . . just that I was terrified. Once I calmed down I went and got a pole—you know, that bathroom rod that holds up shower curtains?"

Jan nodded.

"I got that, went back in . . . checked under and around everything, but didn't find anything."

"Of course. That's how it always works in horror movies—"

"*Jan*—you're not helping!"

"Sorry."

"I checked everything out and found nothing. So, I go to turn off the light switch and head back to bed—when . . . when they jump out at me. The *hands*—glowing *red* hands and forearms—from the walls. Shoot right out of the wall in front of me! Scared the you-know-what out of me!"

"Kina, darling are you *sure*—"

"Was it a figment of my imagination? I'm not sure of anything, anymore. When that guy, that-that author—Mr. Paranormal, or whatever his name was—was in earlier, I took a look at him. He looked normal enough, but when he got up to shake my hand . . . I saw them, again. Those red hands *coming* for me—"

"Oh, now, honey, you know that all that is, is all this Hallowe'en hooey going on this month. That's *all* it is. It's that time of the year when we all get just a little more spooked than normal—"

"This was different, Jan, I *tell* you. Whether or not that guy's hands really were red, what I saw in my bedroom last night was real—*in some way*. In some weird way I can't yet figure out. There's just something about it. It's a feeling I got."

"What do you mean?"

"Well, toward the end, I got angry. I mean, really *pissed*. I don't know why, but I wasn't scared any more, and I wasn't . . . wasn't angry at the *hands*, I realized later, once I thought about it . . . I was mad at something else . . . something about the hands. *Behind* the hands?"

"Any idea what?"

Kina vigorously shook her head. "No idea. I just know I don't want to go back in there. Alone, anyway."

"I'll go with ya."

Kina looked up. "Would you?"

"Yeah-uh. And I tell ya what, we'll just go back there to face whatever it was that happened, then you can stay at my place tonight— or for as long as you need—how's that?"

Kina smiled, choking back the rising emotion—

But emotion from *where?*

Kina entered her home first, Jan right behind her.

"Well, things certainly look normal enough," Jan said, unzipping her jacket.

"But isn't what you really want to say is that that's how it *always* is on Elm Street?" Kina said, removing her jacket.

"Well . . . ."

"My bedroom's up that landing, then to the rear of the hallway, on the right."

Jan walked ahead of Kina, then stopped. "Well, time's awastin'. No time like the present," she said, turning back to Kina and removing her jacket. "You ready to do this?"

Kina nodded.

"Then, let's do it."

The two walked up the handful of stairs onto the upper landing.

"Nice hardwood," Jan said.

"Thanks."

Jan stopped before the bathroom, and peeked in. "And that must be where you'd found your lance-a-lot," she said, smiling.

"Yeah . . . was kinda in a hurry, you know?"

"Sounded like a good choice, if you ask me!" she said, smiling.

They approached the bedroom.

"Holy *cripes!*" Jan said, entering it. "I guess you weren't kidding when you said you destroyed the place!"

It was worse than Kina'd remembered.

Jan slowly moved the door open, staring at it. There was a stick impaling it, and the now-exposed light switch by the door was reduced to one tiny plastic shard that loosely held on to the screw holding it onto the wall. The rest of it was scattered on the floor. Large portions of wallboard and wallpaper hung off the wall and were all over the floor. Her bedroom mirror was also gone, shards of glass everywhere, mixed in with the hanging light fixture that had also been smacked from the ceiling.

"Must've been what I slipped on when I knocked myself out," Kina said, pointing to the debris all over the floor, and rubbing her head. She toed glass pieces, as well as pieces of splintered wood and broken metal, into a pile out of the way. "Glad I didn't cut myself up worse."

"Yeah-uh!" Jan said. "Man! Will ya *look* at this place!"

Two other walls were also torn up and had gashes and wallpaper hanging out like gaping war wounds. The broken antique picture frame and picture were also on the floor behind the upright dresser, which had gouged the hardwood floor and was tipped against the wall, its two rear pine-wood legs neatly snapped off. As for the rest of the bathroom shower curtain rod, the remaining piece lay on the floor partially under the bed, the internal spring nearby.

Jan chuckled as she fingered but didn't remove the one stuck in the door. "Well, I see you're going to need some serious redecoration, my friend."

Kina shrugged, embarrassed, and again coughed a couple more rounds. She popped another lozenge into her mouth.

"Remind me never to wake you from a sound sleep!" Jan added. "Okay, so what happened? Be specific."

Kina went over to her bedside nightstand. As she began to relate the events, she found the vague dream images returning.

"Well . . . I awoke, stark raving mad—as in *crazy*—and was screaming my lungs out. I jumped out of bed, here," she said pointing, "and must've rammed my elbow into the wall or edge of the dresser." She suddenly remembered the wound and rubbed it. "Then I went out into the hallway, broke a nail, and collapsed. Grabbed the shower curtain rod and reentered."

Kina walked past Jan, who turned to follow her narration.

"I came back in, searched the place, and found nothing—that's always how it happens on *The Nightmare on Elm Street*. Then—also just like on Elm Street—the red hands thrust out at me—here—from the wall, just under the light switch," Kina said, pointing.

She was initially reluctant to touch the wall, but found new confidence coursing through her (confidence always strongest with others around). Though the memories and images no longer scared her, she did feel something strange about them. Like they were still out there. Still

(*needing?*)

her.

Needing her?

"That's when I opened fire. Took out my room. The rest is history."

"You'd said earlier that they followed you? Is that right?"

"Yeah," Kina said, hedging, again walking past Jan for the broken upright dresser. "Over here, they came up out of the floor at me." Renewed confidence or not, she avoided the spot on the floor where the hands had materialized. "Then, over there, out of the wall. Then back out over there," she said, pointing back to the wall near the light switch. "Then the mirror and the center of the room."

"Well, do you feel anything now? Any, I don't know—*tingling* sensations, or whatever it is you're supposed to feel in real-life horror movie situations like this?"

"No . . . well, I do kinda feel like they're still . . . 'out there' in some way, but perhaps the strangest thing is that I no longer feel scared.

Can't explain it."

"Did you catch much of that paranormal author's show today?"

Kina chuckled. "I know what you're gonna say. That he feels that many ghosts out there aren't really out to *get* us; that they're actually just caught in-between worlds or something . . . what did he call them?"

"'Lingering anxiety ghosts,' or something," Jan said.

"Right. Or could be—"

Kina stopped dead in her tracks.

"Oh, my God."

"What? What is it?"

"It just hit me."

Kina turned back to Jan, her face ashen, as if in shock.

"Jan . . . ."

"Yes?"

Kina turned back to the wall and lifted her arms before her, palms up, as if mesmerized. She stared at the light switch wall by the door before slowly turning back to Jan. Her arms and palms were still upraised . . . a look of horror on her face. She approached Jan, who backed up as Kina approached.

"Kina—honey—*you okay?*"

Kina stopped just before her.

"Jan . . . it was something Steve and Paranormal Guy said . . . about how in the movies they always make the ghosts out to be bad or evil, always out to get everyone."

"Yeah . . . honey? Now you're scaring me . . . ."

"Well, Paranormal Guy felt that they—the ghosts—weren't so much out to get us as they were *trapped* maybe . . . or confused. Maybe even *dreaming back about their just-departed lives* . . . "

"Dreaming? Do the dead dream?"

Kina just looked at her.

Jan continued, "Okay . . . *and?*"

"Jan, look at me. *Look* at me! What do I look like? What do I look like I *need?*"

Jan looked to Kina . . . really looked to her . . . how her arms—her hands—were held out before her, and—

"Oh, my *G*—"

"*Help.* I look like I need *help*, Jan, *that's* what they look like."

"Well, now, then, that would put a different spin on things, wouldn't it? Good Lord, I have chicken skin all over me . . . ."

"And I'd turned it away! I turned it *away*, Jan! Don't you get it? I may have turned someone away who needed my help—who reached *out* to me . . . ."

"Yeaaah, but reached out to you from *where*, honey? As a *ghost*."

"Does it matter?"

"Uh, *yeah!*"

Jan came to Kina and grabbed her by the arms. "Oh, honey, don't worry about it—"

"But I *have* to! What have I done—because I was *afraid?* Had I hurt someone—ghost or not?"

"But you don't know that? And it was just a dream."

"But I feel this . . . something . . . right now. Right this minute. It's still out there, he/she/*it* . . . is still out there . . . ."

The images did continue to fly around in her head . . . still screaming through her mind at light speed. Still, she was unable to make anything out. But she felt the red hands were still out there . . . still *needing* . . . .

"Oh, my God, Jan . . . I think I might have done something very, very wrong . . . I've never felt this way before . . . I suddenly feel a little sick . . . actually *sick*."

"But what if . . . what if, I don't know, you bring something *evil* here, into our world? Paranormal Guy didn't talk about that—"

"No, not on-air, but I snuck up beside the door when they were talking off-air, him and Steve and Dave, and he said that he feels a lot of the evil stuff is actually confused energy coming from *us* . . . that there really isn't any such thing as . . . how did he put it, 'inherent evil'—"

"Well, that may be, but what kind of an expert is he? He writes *fiction*, for God's sake . . . he's no expert. And, really, who among us knows? What human has the be-all, end-all knowledge about the afterlife and is a hundred percent correct? What if—I don't know— what if these confused spirits really *can* get nasty, like *Exorcist* nasty, or something, and rip our souls apart? What then?"

Kina dropped her arms, a look of exhaustion falling over her face.

"Thanks for doing this, Jan," Kina said, reaching for one of Jan's hands. "I'm fine, now. Really."

Jan cocked her head, skeptical. "Don't you want to come with me, stay the night?"

Kina shook her head, confident in her decision. "No . . . I'm going to stay here. In my own bed. I'll be fine."

"You're not planning on pulling in those hands, are you?"

"Another thing Paranormal Guy said was that ghosts are not physical . . . so I can't very well do that, now can I? He said he didn't believe what we saw were so much physical images as mental images we translate *into* a physical-like image. No—you go home, Jan, I really appreciate all you've done, you're a good friend. I'm just mentally and spiritually exhausted. Thanks."

"If I was a really good friend I wouldn't leave you here and would protect you from your own bad se—"

Kina smiled.

"Then I'll make us some dinner and you can sleep in *my* guest room . . . ."

Kina again awoke just a little after two a.m. to use the bathroom. The full moon shown in through her bathroom window and the wind still howled for a second night in a row. She stared at the moon and smiled as she sat on the toilet; closed her eyes.

Should she, shouldn't she?

Was someone—something—really in need of help? *Her* help?

The impulse was overpowering.

If you're out there and you need help, Kina thought, reaching out to the red hands, *come back. I'm ready for you, now.*

This time I'll help you . . . .

Kina washed and dried her hands . . . but as she turned to return to bed, she again had that weird feeling. She paused. Felt a little bit of fear rising within, but just told herself to get over it—that there was no need to be afraid.

She knew—in her *bones*—there was nothing to be afraid of.

At least not in this instance. She told herself.

Yeah, *Nightmare on Elm Street* . . . .

She knew what she would find before fully turning around.

She saw them. Dark, glowing red hands, reaching down and out from above her bed . . . hands spaced about two feet apart, just short of the union of the wall and ceiling corner.

She turned on the light.

They remained silently hanging there. Not motionless, per se, but still . . . as if a person really was on the other side of them, reaching out to her.

And she wasn't scared. Not in the least.

Not this time.

She felt sad. Unexplainably emotional.

Cautiously, Kina approached them and came to stand beside her bed and the nightstand.

She looked up to them . . . then placed one foot onto her bed, and, grabbing the bed frame in support, pulled herself up. She faced the wall and looked up to the red hands. Spreading apart her feet on the bed . . . she lifted her hands . . . but stopped short of actually grabbing them.

They really were hands and forearms—and they really were red. Not a "painted" red, but they looked . . . *flensed* . . . their skin hideously peeled away from their form. She saw raw, exposed muscle.

And it was two-fifteen in the morning.

Kina looked toward her open bedroom door, thinking about Jan, snoring soundly away in the guest room. She smiled.

Turned back to the hands.

Looked to them.

Closed her eyes . . . reopened them.

Still there.

Bracing herself, Kina reached out for them.

She didn't grab them—at least not physically, anyway—but did grab onto . . . *something* . . . because she was suddenly flooded with emotion like she was unsuccessfully gulping from a raging fire hose. She tried to slow it down, but couldn't. It wasn't intentional, she didn't think, but was a desperate emotional link she was now attached to. It simply overloaded her. It felt like this ghost *needed* her . . . so needed her help—and yesterday—that it was the opening of emotional flood gates and there was no turning it off. This . . . creature, this ghost . . . had a lot to download, and needed to do it as soon as possible. Needed her to *be* there . . . to help open those flood gates and let the emotion flow.

And there was something else . . . .

Kina felt as if she was going to explode . . . her entire body felt as if it was spiritually and physically *expanding* . . . out to the ends of the universe—yet was simultaneously face-to-face with some invisible entity right before her face.

It was a feeling of expansive contraction . . . of swirling and spinning . . . of being there . . . standing on her bed yet also simultaneously being flung to the farthest (and furthest) reaches of the universe. And through all this, she was crying . . . unabashedly *sobbing*. Her entire being quaking and shuddering with sorrow . . . *pain!* . . . there was intense pain in this spirit . . . *anguish* . . . and so much of it. Anguish, the likes of which she had never before experienced. She could barely contain herself. Every synonym for pain and hurt filled her soul . . . and there was no shutting it down. *Now*, she was starting to get scared, but told herself to be strong . . . that there was so much more at stake here than her being a fraidy cat of the unknown . . . .

Kina cried out . . . screamed in loving rage at where all this pain in this ghost was coming from. She reached out to it with intense, powerful thoughts of hope and peace, knowing that this ghost needed to release itself from whatever horror it was experiencing.

It needed to move on!

That it was dead and there was nothing that need hold it to wherever it was. Whatever pain it was experiencing. It had to *leave* it.

As if the emotion couldn't get any stronger, it did . . . but this time Kina felt a difference to it . . . felt a change in conviction . . . a *refocusing*. Groaning, Kina poured more of herself into her link with the ghost . . . *leave*, she commanded, *you can do it! I'm here to* help . . . *focus on* me . . . explode *away from wherever you are! Whatever is holding you back!* DO IT NOW!

There was a mentally bruising blast of light and Kina experienced a burst of energy that felt like an emotional supernova—

And she collapsed back onto her bed.

It was over.

Done.

That was it.

She looked up to where the red hands had been . . .

Gone.

Kina closed her eyes and swallowed hard. Her mouth was dry . . . really, really dry.

"*Thank you . . . .*"

Kina shot upright. Looked around.

She leapt off the bed and turned on the bedside lamp.

No one. There was *no one* in the room with her—yet she'd distinctly heard "*Thank you*" spoken out loud.

To her.

She leapt off the bed and rushed to Jan's room, but Jan was sound asleep, peacefully snoring. Really? She snored? Surprisingly, she hadn't awoken.

Who'd said that?

Kina returned to her bedroom.

She knew there was no one else in the house with them. Knew it hadn't been Jan talking in her sleep, nor had it just been all in her head. She'd heard those two words clear as day, as loud as if someone had been standing shoulder-to-shoulder with her.

She *had* heard someone thank her, and she knew who that was, even if she didn't know *who* it was.

She'd helped save a life. Ghost or otherwise.

Kina brushed off the bed sheets from where she'd been standing and got back into bed. The wind had even died down. She smiled and turned off the light.

"Good night . . . and you're welcome," she said, aloud, sending a burst of loving energy to the entity, and rolled over and fell into a peaceful sleep.

2

December 13, 1967
Remote Compound
Unknown Location

A nameless, faceless prisoner lay strapped onto a rough-hewn board, various tubes and wires attached to numerous places on his scarred, tortured, and burned body. Both his legs had recently been broken, but he didn't know what "recently" meant anymore. On all his limbs were open, infinitely painful, raw wounds from having been methodically and meticulously burned and electrocuted. To his head were attached electrodes, and in his arms more tubes. His tongue had been removed. He hadn't been allowed to sleep, hadn't been allowed to dream, and had been kept as barely alive as possible through science and chemicals and ever-present torture.

But as totally controlled as his captors thought they were over him, there was one thing they couldn't get under control with all their methods . . .

His will.

His ability to think what *he* wanted to think.

He was fine with losing his body—and if he could get free he had no qualms with slitting his own throat, or putting a well-placed bullet into his brain. But that was never going to be. He was their experiment and would die of old age, if they had their way.

So he'd decided to reach out . . . reach out to whatever might be "out there" . . . whatever might have mercy on him and help him free himself from this hellish nightmare. What else had he? What had he to lose?

So he had.

And he'd found someone.

A ghost? A figment of his imagination? He didn't know and didn't care. All he knew . . . was that he had—*finally*—put an end to his suffering and had willed his own freedom. Willed his own death. Freed himself with the help of someone or something, he didn't know. All he knew, was that he was *free* . . . free to move *on* . . . .

And he did.

But not before he thanked the woman who had braved her own fears and had helped set him free.

"*Thank you . . . .*"

The Lifter
1990

"Move it, man! *Push* it! Don't fuckin' stop now, you pussy—*push it out!*"

Groaning under the stress of 540 pounds of black iron on his shoulders, Donny forced himself back up into a standing position, keeping his knees at a slight bend. This was Donny's fourth set, working towards his third rep. Veins popped out from the sides of his twenty-one inch neck like snakes on a tree. The weight clattered hollowly on the bar's ends across the back of his shoulders. The lifter hesitated momentarily, trying to regain his needed concentration. Three spotters—one behind and one to each side—prepared for Donny to off-load the bar back onto the rack.

Donny, however, had other plans.

Emitting a loud growl and hitching up his powerful frame, Donny proceeded back down into the squatting position, sweat streaking the sides of his face. Forcing his head back (hair sweaty and tangled) to keep his balance, Donny emitted the growl of an animal. His spotters squatted all the way down with him.

Hitting bottom—thighs dipping just below parallel-to-the-floor—Donny's behemoth frame bounced, creating upward momentum, and began the upward push . . . when halfway to the top he slowed to near a stop, actually beginning to reverse his direction.

"Fuckin' *push* it, Donny! You can do it, man! Get it up! Force it *out!*"

The spotter yelling behind him was "Jimbo," his face as red and knotted as Donny's, as if he were doing the squat himself. Jimbo'd be damned if he was going to help him up—this was Donny's weight,

Donny's movement, and—as far as Jimbo was concerned—spotters were there purely for moral support.

Quickly regrouping, Donny emitted a new growl and explosively pistoned upward.

A glut of air was expelled as the movement was completed.

Once more, standing defiantly, Donny allowed the bouncing movement of the weight on the bar on his shoulders to add additional "psyche" to his powerful display of strength. He was a hunter shouldering his kill. Atlas shouldering the world. Hobbling forward toward the rack, Donny gruffly re-racked the weight off his shoulders, then stepped back exhilarated.

Immediately the spotters congratulated him, slapping him on the back and smacking his shoulders with muscled fists. Clouds of chalk from hands powdered the air in the wake of all the hand-slapping and shoulder-punching. Throwing his own fists high, Donny whooped out another growl of triumph.

He had finally broken his sticking point . . . a sticking point where for weeks he couldn't get past the weight or the reps . . . but now he'd done both, and the whole world could take a flying leap.

While all the excitement had been going on, nobody thought to watch the entrance desk. Donny, who owned the gym, had let the others who had been working the desk leave early because it was nearly closing time, and he could handle whoever came up. Only sparsely populated at this hour, the gym contained a mere six or seven people still battling with their own workouts.

The plate glass windows facing the parking lot were completely fogged, the darkness weaving a complex coziness to the gym's interior. Inside, fluorescent lights illuminated tons of plates and other equipment . . . a layer of calcium carbonate chalk covering everything. A rock station wailed "Welcome to the Jungle," by Guns N' Roses, over the sound system, while the ghostly presences of the day's previous lifters echoed throughout the mirrored interior.

Everyone was winding down their workouts, except for the blond individual currently striding in through the front doors. Walking in, he signed the register at the front desk, under "Guest," and went straight to the rear of the gym. An acute odor followed him, causing those he passed to wrinkle their noses.

Still excited over Donny's achievement, others were collecting around the power rack. The remainder of the gym's inhabitants, who had momentarily stopped their workouts to watch Donny and give their moral support, resumed their own lifting. Donny meanwhile, had sat down to undo his knee wraps, more chalk flecking off his muscled and calloused hands.

Out of everybody's way the blond lifter began setting up equipment. He wore a tattered and stained shroud-of-a-tank-top that hung about his body like a cat clawing for holds. His four-inch wide lifting belt was aged and stained; his faded and ragged shorts a vestige of far better workouts. The socks clinging about his ankles were unevenly folded down around themselves and also stained, and his sneakers were more reminiscent of sandals than shoes, heavily worn and ripped apart in several places. Not nearly as hulking as Donny, the smaller-framed stranger was tanned and muscular, his body "ripped."

But the most striking thing about the stranger was none of these things. The most striking quality about him was his *face*. It was a face that was hard to take without wincing: blazing blue and frightingly wide, his eyes screamed witness to a disturbing past. And there was a strung-out look about him . . . hair long and twisted . . . knotted and speared out in all directions, flowing easily over his muscled shoulders and back. His movement was quick and jerky, giving the appearance of epileptic fits.

And he smelled.

Bad.

Without the slightest warmup, the stranger threw on six 45-pound plates to the bar at another squat rack, totaling 315 pounds. Getting beneath it, he ripped off a quick eight reps of the same exercise Donny had just completed.

Watching nearby, a weekend warrior was doing seated calves and nearly swallowed his tongue.

The blond threw on a few more plates, totaling nearly 500 pounds. Again immediately positioning himself under the bar, he unracked and repeated the same feat. Even for a guy the stranger's size, this was a weight that should have been impossible to be reckoned with. Staring, the weekender stopped what he was doing, motioning to a buddy.

Looking around for something bigger, the blond lifter saw 100-pounders and grabbed two. By now Donny's spotters were getting interested. Donny was still cleaning up his area from plates and personal equipment. It was about time to close up shop.

"Hey, Donny, catch this," Jimbo said, pointing to the rear of the gym. "Who *is* this guy?"

Donny stopped, casting an at first indifferent glance.

"Dunno—"

Then he saw the weight on the bar.

"Holy shit. Let's take a look," he said, slapping Jimbo with the back of his hand and strutting to the rear, his entourage in tow.

The blond lifter stepped back from the rack, the ends of the bar bouncing and rattling on his own shoulders. In one smooth movement he squatted down—then, without so much as a bounce—easily glided back up.

Rack.

Astonished, Donny looked back to his groupies.

The blond turned around, hitting everybody with the eyes of a Lon Chaney creation. Donny flinched, looking away. Not only was he not ready for the face, he was not ready for the ungodly odor of dead fish and rotting seaweed. Donny felt the smell go beyond his nostrils, clawing down into his throat and gut.

Could a smell *hurt?*

Looking at Donny for an indifferent second, the tanned beach bum continued about his search for more weight. Donny turned to Jimbo.

"What the fuck's his trip?" he asked, gagging on the smell.

Jimbo shrugged, barely holding back his own dry heaves.

"*Weirdo,*" Donny said. He approached the stranger.

"Hey, man, what's your name?"

Replacing the 45-pound plates with hundred-pounders and adding to it, the stranger turned. He gave the same wild-eyed look, not saying anything for the first few seconds. Donny felt like an icicle had just been rammed up his ass.

"Name's Waaave Doggy, maaan," the blond lifter said, continuing to the rack.

Donny hacked again. This guy's smell was ungodly.

"*You ever take a bath?*" Donny said, gagging, "You smell like dead fish, for chrissake."

Donny did not want to open his mouth again and backed away, trying to snort the smell out of his sinuses, and continued an openmouthed gagging.

The stranger looked back after rearranging the weight on the bar.

"*Bath?*" he asked, as if missing a punch-line. "Yea-uh, guess so. Gimme a spot, dude?" Donny looked at the gathering behind him, some of whom were snickering—yet keeping their distances.

"You—a spot?"

Positioning himself under the bar, the blond lifter didn't move until Donny reluctantly came up behind him.

God, the *smell!* It was eating away at the back of his *throat* . . . .

"Go for it, dude," Donny said, holding his breath. Some in the crowd were leery that Donny could spot all that weight by himself, so a couple of big guys silently went to either side of the bar just in case.

Wave Doggy squatted down—not once, but four times—and each squat went as easily as the first, as easily as if it were only the bar. Wave Doggy racked, got out from under the bar and whipped around, quite happy with himself.

"Thanks, dude!" he said to Donny.

The stranger looked like some crazed David Lee Roth incarnation. And as if hit by a wall of stink, multiplied by the force of Wave Doggy's turn, Donny stumbled backward, tripping over tangling feet—when Wave Doggy shot out a hand and grabbed him, jerking Donny back up—fully into the air—then landing him on his feet. Blondy quickly returned to the bar, cleaning it off.

Nearly burned by the slimy coldness of the stranger's touch, Donny wiped off his hand on his shorts, backing away—while keeping an eye on the stranger.

"You're not from around here, are ya?" Donny asked, looking for any reason to kick the dude out.

"Nope," Wave Doggy said.

"Been here before?"

"Nope."

"Then you didn't pay to get in."

"It's up at the desk, maaan," he said, twitching in his nervous fashion as he turned to look at Donny. He immediately began setting up another bar, on the floor. Deadlifts. Donny motioned for Jimbo to go up front and check on it.

"Where you from?"

"SoCal."

"No shit," Donny muttered under his breath, *where else would he be from?*

Jimbo found the money, beat-up and water-logged singles, and counted it out.

"Whatcha' doin' here?" Donny asked.

"Liftin'."

Again, *no shit.* This guy was a genius.

Jimbo returned, Wave Doggy's money in hand. "Hey, he left ten bucks at the desk—he even signed in."

"You left five bucks more than necessary, pal," Danny said.

"That's what I always leave," he said, squatting down before the bar. Wave Doggy grasped it using no wrist straps, in a reverse grip . . . one hand under, other hand over grip. Straightening his back and face forced upward toward the ceiling, Wave Doggy hefted the weight off the floor, like he was doing nothing more than lifting groceries. Eight times.

405 pounds.

No problem.

Donny had enough of this.

Taking Jimbo and the two other spotters with him, he left the crowd. It felt great getting away from that rank, fishy odor and wild eyes.

"I'm calling the cops to check this guy out. Keep an eye on him."

Jimbo, Bill, and Charlie nodded, spreading their lats like dangerous gym-rat peacocks, and made their way back. Donny, money in hand, made the call. Even the guy's bills stunk.

By now everybody had stopped lifting to watch Wave Doggy and his Amazing Feats.

Besides his odor, there was a definite fascination about the guy that filled the air. A magic. An amusement. He was all smiles! Everybody but Donny was visibly impressed. Donny didn't take lightly to being upstaged, not to mention that he just plain didn't like what was going on here.

Wave Doggy?

What kind of a name was that?

Donny locked the front doors. The gym should have been closed fifteen minutes ago. Waiting for the police to arrive, Donny began clearing out the remaining customers. Wave Doggy, after deadlifting a shade over a 1,000 pounds, proceeded on to other exercises. There seemed no stopping him.

The cops arrived, two of them, looking quite official in midnight-blue jackets and uniforms. Donny let them in.

"Hi. I'm Donny Frayze," he said, shaking hands, emphasizing the first syllable of his surname for the men, "I own the place." Pointing to the rear, he continued. "And that's *him*."

Lita Ford's "Kiss Me Deadly" screamed over the speakers.

The officers accompanied Donny back to the rear.

Wave Doggy was now benching repetitions with better than 600 pounds.

Donny could tell the cops weren't too pleased with the prospect of arresting the guy. A few of the overhead lights around Wave Doggy began flickering off and on. Donny went over and asked his entourage to split. After some silent protest, they began packing up.

Racking the weight, Wave Doggy jerked himself upright, immediately turning to the cops. He regarded them uninterestedly, then went back to packing on more weight. One of the cops turned to Donny.

"He fuckin' *stinks*."

"Excuse me, sir, we'd like a word with you if you don't mind," interjected the other officer, a man named Tony Valletti. He barely kept from gagging.

Wave Doggy finished adding his new weight to the bar, then casually approached the officers. Both men placed their hands on their weapons. Wild-eyed and mechanical, Wave Doggy sauntered up to them, like a surfer on speed.

"Where you from, sir?" Valletti asked.

"Cali."

"California?"

"Yea-uh."

"What part."

"SoCal."

The surfer dude's head continued to spastically jerk.

"Are you using?"

"Using?"

Valletti looked deeply into Wave Doggy's eyes. His pupils were uneven, one measurably larger than the other.

"This guy's definitely tweaking, Peterson," Valletti said to his partner. Carefully reaching for handcuffs, Valletti and Peterson rushed him. Wave just stood there, naively offering no resistance.

"You're under arrest for suspicion of substance abuse. You have the right to remain silent."

After cuffing him and turning to head back to the cruiser, the policemen were gracefully eluded as Wave Doggy pirouetted out of their control and headed back to his bench instead.

Then he'd simply separated his hands like the silent half to a clap . . . and pieces of chain fell from his wrists. Cuff-metal still encircled his wrists as Wave Doggy grabbed more weight and placed the plates on the sleeves of the already weighted bar.

Stunned, the cops spun around, unholstering weapons. They leveled them at Wave Doggy, who had simply gone on to continue with his workout.

"Mr. Wave Doggy—*you are under arrest!* Any additional attempts at resist—"

But Wave Doggy had no intention of being arrested. After his set, he popped back up and continued to pile more weight onto the bar.

Valletti went around behind the lifter, while Peterson nervously remained where he was. More lights flickered off. Donny looked around nervously.

Valletti replaced his Glock, withdrawing his taser, instead. As soon as Wave Doggy sat himself back down on the bench, the officer reached over the bar and stuck him.

Wave Doggy didn't even react.

The second officer yelled "*Freeze!*" but Wave Doggy merely stood up as though he was off to the water fountain. And went for the remaining officer.

Peterson fired.

Wave Doggy took the slug in his chest . . . then grabbed the gun and tossed it into a mirror like a minor concern. With his other hand, he placed it square on the officer's chest and casually pushed him out of the way.

Peterson flew feet-over-head as he was forced backward across the gym floor, without hitting any gym equipment.

Acting as if all were nothing more than annoying inconveniences, Wave Doggy sat back down on the bench and unracked the rattling bar.

Donny made his move.

Coming from behind the bench, Donny pressed his 240 pounds down onto the bar, forcing it into Wave Doggy's chest.

Wave Doggy did two reps with Donny pressing down on him before exploding—both the bar *and* Donny—up and into the ceiling. Ceiling tiles fell around the floor as the weight came crashing back down . . . Donny entangled with it, and all the loose 45-pound plates that were now flying everywhere. After bouncing, one plate crashed into one of Donny's legs. An exquisite splitting sound finished out the movement. Donny howled.

Walking out into the center of the room, Wave Doggy stopped.

A green glow emanated from him.

A brighter, more intense glow took up residence in his eyes.

Welts and sores began bursting all over his body . . . and the offending odor grew even worse. Doggy's body took on a bloated appearance . . . the appearance of someone who's body had been in water the other side of far too long. Lights crackled and sizzled, electricity sparking everywhere, and Wave Doggy became violently spasmodic. Out of his throat came a gurgling sound, as if his lungs were filling with water.

"*All I wanted too doooo wasss lllifftt!*"

Wave Doggy's face cracked open in places, mottled flesh and gangrenous cankers saying "*hello!*" to the crowd. The welts that had formed on his body broke open.

The two cops stood up, collecting themselves. Peterson painfully stretched and twisted upon getting back to his feet. Donny quickly forgot about his own pain as he observed the gruesome transmogrification.

"*Wwwhyyy cccouldn't yyyoouuu jussst lettt meee lllifttt? III wwwasn'ttt hhhurrrting anyboddddy?*"

Water and bits of lung and other "material" issued forth from Wave Doggie's mouth as he spoke. The cops, Donny, and those who remained in spite of Donny's warning, all backed up. Wave Doggy coughed up more water and viscera. He looked pathetic . . . alone . . . and Donny found himself feeling sorry for the guy. After all, he thought, he really hadn't hurt or bothered anyone—and he had paid an extra five bucks over-and-above the amount for a day's lifting.

Hell, he'd even *signed* in. How many *regulars* did that?

The creature now before them raised his hands into the sparking electricity above him. Tears were mixed with sea water and decay.

"*Wait!*"

It was Donny, blood covering his legs as he struggled to get up. Pain

(*no pain no gain . . .*)

knifed him as he motioned for the cops to back off. They did. No argument.

Everyone looked to everyone else.

"I'm sorry," Donny said, holding a hand up and gritting against the pain.

Wave Doggy stopped . . . looking over to Donny, who was crouching in incredible agony and unable to fully stand.

Lowering a mottled hand, the blond beach bum came over to Donny and pulled him to his feet. Grabbing hold of the bench, Donny supported himself. The creature looked at him through puffed eyes and a face swollen nearly beyond recognition.

"I didn't mean to hurt you. I-I'm sorry about all this," Donny said, wincing. Donny's Reeboks were soaked red. "Really." Donny looked to Wave Doggy . . . there was . . . a look of understanding that came over the creature's face . . . something that had been, up to this point, non-existent in him—*it?* There was no longer that wild, strung-out David Lee Roth look . . . now only the look of a cornered, injured animal.

Donny owned a dog. One that had been injured and had looked up to him in just this way.

"*I ooonlllly waanttt tooo wwwworrrrk ooouttt.*"

More matter washed out of his mouth as he spoke.

"*III'll lllooock uuuppppp when I'mmm donnne.*"

There was a touch of childlike innocence to his shuddering

movements that stabbed Donny right in the heart . . . yes, he had one beneath all that testosterone and muscle.

Donny slowly nodded his head in agreement and looked to the two officers, who could do nothing more than return the same look. Donny motioned them away.

Slowly, the swelling began dissipating from Wave Doggy . . . then he reached down to Donny's splintered leg. Feeling around the fracture (and at pronounced pain to Donny), he put pieces of Donny's bone back into place—and set it.

Donny again howled.

Then looked up to Wave Doggy in utter amazement.

No pain.

Wave Doggy looked to Donny . . . really *looked into* him. Donny felt him burrow into his marrow and felt him reaching around in there as if searching for something . . . when he felt a sudden, inexplicable . . . inner peace.

Wave Doggy smiled . . . and turned away.

The two cops and Donny sat out in the cruiser, patiently watching through the fogged gym windows. The remaining lifters were all standing outside in the dark, also watching. The interior gym lights were going out on their own as the creature made his way to the front of the gym, then exited the front doors. Wave Doggy had returned to his earlier, odorous, tanned-and-surfer state. He locked the doors behind him, setting the keys down in plain view on the edge of the concrete. Donny felt his leg. There was but a lingering numbness . . . *but nothing was broken.*

The cops and Donny watched as Wave Doggy faced them, still twitching in his tattered and sweat-stained gear and weight belt still around his waist. They regarded each other for a long moment. Though it was dark and Donny couldn't make out features, he could still—mentally—clearly see Wave Doggy's wild eyes and speared hair.

Forced reps, maaan, forced reps, Donny thought.

Donny wished him the best of luck with his continued training . . . Wave Doggy nodded, turned . . . and disappeared into the darkness.

Homecoming
2000

There comes a time in everyone's life when you must face the music.

To think back to your childhood . . . when you were basically not held accountable for much. Those were the fun times, *happy* times! Happy and carefree. Life was your amusement park! You had no real responsibilities, aside from school and a few chores. If you had a bike, you were mobile and that meant freedom! The world was literally at your feet! And the challenges! Nothing went unchallenged! Everything was suspect, from your home to your school. You'd try to get away with as much as possible, testing the system. You'd steal that candy bar just to see if you could get away with it . . . stay out later and later on dates.

It was all part of being a kid.

The *excitement* of being a *kid!*

But then things begin to change about mid-way through high school.

Slowly but surely more responsibility was layered into your life. No longer did things remain just mere "unaccountable challenges" . . . and if you later became one of the few to go to war, you witnessed the atrocities of mankind. Things that seared your soul with an intense anger and hatred. Sadness.

It was an anger at the cruelties and callousness of conflict. At how the Human Condition could inflict torture—mental or physical—upon another. You wondered how could such things be? How could—can—people be driven to perform such atrocities—horrible, unspeakable acts upon each other.

How *God* could allow such things.

But it was and is real . . . and won't ever go away.

The worst part is that it isn't just confined to wars: it breeds . . . finding other ways to manifest . . . unleash itself. War (you find) just becomes a convenient excuse. And while you're in the middle of it all, you may find yourself thinking back to a particular girl you knew . . . before you left and everything went crazy. You think back to when you and her were an item.

Inseparable.

In love. You think back with a sadness that bites deep. You think back to when you told her not to worry . . . you'd be back.

She says, well what about all the others who've said the same? You look her in the eyes and tell her—with all seriousness—that you're different.

Yes, you think back to that time . . . and how you began to doubt your own words. She was the one you really cared about. You remember that when that night was over so was your relationship. No one said anything, but you both felt it. And it wasn't that you would necessarily never come back . . . no that wasn't it. It was the *waiting* . . . and what you might *become* . . . .

She never wrote you and you never wrote her—well, maybe once. You did write her that one time just to let her know you were okay. But that was it. When there was no response, you knew why.

There was no animosity. It was just something that had to be.

But you did come back . . . all limbs and mentality intact. At least *you* think so. Maybe you are a little rougher around the edges—there was no part of your being that was not bruised from your "experiences," "they" call them—but you were still *you*.

That boy who'd gone off to war.

So you found your way to her place, that lone porchlight still on the way you remember it. You knock at the door . . . her father opens it. Looks outside. He looks right through you as you stand before him . . . then he solemnly turns around without saying a word and reenters the house, head slumped miserably forward.

You, however, straighten yours up more.

You're prepared.

Couldn't be more prepared.

You turn back to the street . . . your thousand-yard stare catches you off-guard . . . recall the fire fights . . . the carnage . . . the smell of death and destruction . . . but also the life you had *before* the war . . . before . . . before you'd *changed* . . . .

It seems you stand there for an eternity.

Then a hand reaches out for you.

You turn.

She stands before the door, face to face with you.

You're knees buckle.

Something inside you unhinges.

Tears . . . pain . . . in both sets of eyes.

You weren't the only one who'd changed.

You thought you'd forever lost her . . . and she you. Sure, she had her "experiences" ("they" call them) while you were gone . . . but she'd always held *you* closest . . . never really wanted to let *you* go. You see it in her eyes. Feel it in the electricity between the both of you.

You were back . . . and so was she.

Back for you.

Gently you take her hand. Together you both turn . . . and hand-in-hand step off the porch . . . and vaporize as your feet hit the path leading away from one life . . .

Into another.

Snow Paper

"No! Don't do it! *Please*, don't—"

The shrill screams pierced through the frigid, moonlit night, originating behind the closed doors of a mountain cabin. Behind tattered, backlit curtains forms moved . . . jerked . . . flickering images engaged in a heated argument. Yelling. Pleading. Crying.

Outside, smoke from the chimney mixed with blowing snow.

"Daddy *no!*"

A gunshot.

Another.

Out from the door dove a dark form.

The shadow was far from maturity . . . short in height and small in frame . . . and it plunged directly into the several-foot-deep accumulation of snow. Behind the small-framed shadow—*her*—the door was left open.

"No! No-no-no-no-*no!*"

Shelain collapsed face-first into the snow.

"*Mommy!* Why? Daddy—*why?*"

But her cries only fell upon the hushed ears of a snow-packed forest.

Blood on her clothes.

Shelain lie face down in the snow, arms covering her head, and sobbed . . . .

She looked up. Into the woods before her.

She didn't need moonlight to see. She knew what was out there. Snow. And trees. Lots of both and little respite from either. Animals, hungry animals . . . .

Shelain had grown up in this forest. Had always been a fast learner. In better times her parents had remarked at how good she'd been in finding her way back home while out hunting with her father. That she could survive in the snow if she had to (she'd built her first snow shelter at the age of five), and that making fires and snaring food was quite commonplace to her. Her parents knew she could survive, and so did Shelain. She was a tough little girl, and now she would be put through her first right of passage.

Shelain didn't understand what had happened between her father and mother, only that it had happened . . . and that was all that mattered now. But she also knew she couldn't live here anymore. This had been a home, now it was a tomb—and the living didn't live in tombs.

And all on her birthday.

She did not want to go back in there.

The woods were her only option. Yes, she would go there. She would go to the woods and find a new place. Make a new life for herself. But before that was to happen, she needed things. And that meant . . .

Going back inside.

As soon as she got back up to her feet, she felt her head pound, like the outsides had moved too fast for the insides, and her insides were ready to explode . . . her *heart* . . . .

Shelain stood. Wiped snow off herself and turned.

Entered the cabin.

On the floor were—

She moved around them.

She was unable to take her eyes off what now lay on the floor.

But her father's woods training and her mother's practicality took over and she immediately set upon collecting what she needed. She grabbed food and clothes. Water wouldn't be too much of a problem this time of the year, but she took a flask or two anyway. Putting on as many pieces of outer wear as she deemed practical and useful, she slung the pack over her back and

The floor still mocked her.

She couldn't ignore them.

Stooping, Shelain went to her father . . . unable to look directly at him, she turned her head away. She searched around him before she found what she was looking for. Removing it, she put it into her jacket.

His hunting knife. Now it was hers.

Happy birthday to her.

Shelain went to her mother.

She was also unable to look directly at her. She went to her hand.

Shelain removed the wedding band. Like gutting a trout or cleaning a rabbit, her emotions suddenly seemed turned off.

Man, the gifts just kept coming . . . .

Okay, that was enough.

Pocketing the band she strode out the door, not bothering to close it.

She felt the crunch of the snow beneath her feet, and headed around to the side of the cabin, adjusting her pack. She pulled her snowshoes from their snowy position alongside the structure and put them on. She'd gotten these last year. She was very adept in them, even able to run in them, dodging in and around trees . . . .

"It's going to be a cold winter," she said to no one. She stood back up and looked off into the moonlit night.

Off she trekked, into the dark tree line of the forest.

Shelain felt as if she was living one of those fairy tales her parents had so often read to her as a child.

But she was a child no longer.

As prepared as she was, she had forgotten two very important things. One was that she might not be as energetic about things after the shock and the jolt had worn off. Two, she had completely forgotten that she had not yet eaten that night.

She figured she'd been walking for several hours (this she did by the movement of the moon), and though she was young and strong, she needed food and rest, and now was as good a time as any to stop. Unloading her pack, she collapsed against a giant snow-covered fir, careful not to knock any of the snow capping off. She might end up needing the tree as shelter and would need the snow for insulation.

Fishing through her pack's contents, she removed a small salted slab of venison, immediately ripping into it.

She stared at the moon.

Then heard the noise.

Noises.

Only moving her eyes, she surveyed the dark . . . through the trees and back from the direction she'd come.

She'd been followed.

How stupid of her! She knew better!

The moon had lit her trail, but that wasn't all it had lit up. It also lit up a second trail which had veered off on its own into the woods mere paces away. It didn't take an expert to know that she was being followed.

Wolves.

Shelain slowly placed the remainder of her venison on the snow.

She sat. Listened.

There came the low, throaty growls again . . . they were all around her.

She positioned her pack firmly before her; held it with both hands.

All her training had not prepared her for this. She was alone now, no father to get her out of this one. No mother.

Solo.

The rustling came closer, the growls no longer muted.

Shelain saw the wolves emerge from the wooded darkness and into the moonlit open. She could actually see their *eyes*.

Four of them.

Slowly coming to a stand, Shelain kicked the chunk of venison toward the advancing pack. That tiny morsel wasn't going to satisfy anything. She stayed close to the tree. Shelain felt her mind beginning to go limp . . . lose its focus.

Fear was taking over. She'd felt this once before.

The wolves closed in . . . formed a semi-circle . . . .

They pounced!

Three went for the venison . . . but the fourth charged her.

Pack forced firmly out before her, Shelain managed to deflect the wolf off to the side, but it quickly got back up and resumed its attack. Shelain was only vaguely aware that the other wolves were fighting over the venison—but, how long would that last?

The attacking wolf returned . . . teeth bared and tracking her every move.

For several minutes they faced off each other. There was no stopping this beast . . . and soon the other three would also be upon her.

She was alone, snowshoes strapped to her feet, and mentally and physically exhausted.

There was nowhere to go. No one to turn to for help.

This was it.

What would her father do?

Her hand fell to her side.

Yes. The knife.

She unsheathed the gleaming blade.

The wolf lunged.

She missed the first time, but connected on the immediate backswing.

She was soon lost in the frenzy of teeth, claws, and blade when she felt the knife plunge deeply, felt a hot spray of blood spatter her face.

Her attacker suddenly fell limp on top of her.

She was bleeding.

Three more! There are three more!

"*No!*" she screamed. "Oh, Father, why did you do it? Mother, *I miss you!*"

She so desperately wanted things to go back to the way they had been . . . to the way they'd been *before* . . . .

Why couldn't we turn back time when bad things happened to us?

She'd been mauled pretty badly by the dead wolf and her grip on her knife was no longer sure, but her survival instincts again kicked in. Shelain was back on her feet. As she saw the three wolves approaching her, she grabbed her pack and swung it out before her, emptying its contents in an arc between her and the wolves. More venison and fruit and bread sprayed the snow before her . . . and she ran.

She'd never had to run on snowshoes to save her life before.

All she could do was what she was doing.

Run.

She dropped heavily to her knees in knee-deep snow, heart beating up and into her throat. She was tired, wet, had lost much blood, and was about to lose much more if she didn't change her situation . . .

But she no longer cared.

She'd been foolish to believe she could make it on her own, no matter how smart she thought she was. There was nothing to make it *to*. Nowhere to *go*. She'd lost her family, lost everything. And the wolves

(*where* were *they?*)

would be on her in—

Her hand hit something.

Dragging her knife through the snow to the object, she poked it through to the surface. It unraveled just enough for her to see it.

It was rolled up and

Made of paper?

A . . . *calendar?*

A paper calendar . . . and there were days marked off.

Well, great, at least she would know what day she died. Yeah, her birthday.

The calendar was dated last year . . . but not all of the days had been marked off. What a stupid thing to find in the snow . . . out in the middle of nowhere . . . a pack of hungry wolves chasing after you—

And why hadn't the wolves caught up with her?

But . . . a *calendar* . . . .

Her curiosity got the better of her, and with bloodied and freezing hands, she began unrolling it.

The year on the calendar shifted before her eyes.

One moment it read 1830 . . . the next 1700 . . . but always it showed *past* years, nothing current. And the marked-off dates remained the same. The calendar unrolled, she tried to turn the pages, to see other months into the future, but she couldn't . . . none of the pages would yield. Were all stuck together. She couldn't unstick the pages. As she looked at the crossed-out dates (*what day was it?*) she noticed how some of the crossed-out dates looked more messed up than the others. Smeared. In fact the very last crossed-out date was really smeared and blurry and anything but neatly crossed out.

She heard the rustling.

They would nearly be upon her!

Good, let them come . . . put an end to her misery . . . .

Shelain traced her bloody knife tip along the weeks and stopped at the next open day after the really smeared and soiled and blurry crossed-out

(*yesterday* . . .)

date. Wouldn't it be nice, she thought, wouldn't it be wonderful if she could go back and *change* things . . . make what daddy did never happen. Turn back time? Wouldn't it be—

The wolves broke through the snow-covered trees and leaped upon their prey . . . but only ended up landing upon one another in a confused pile. They shook the snow from their lean bodies and sniffed around the indentations in the snow before them.

There were blood stains . . . her scent . . . but no *meat*.

All that was before them was a snow crater of someone who *had been* there.

The wolves dug, but never found Shelain. They did find, however, a useless pile of paper in the snow. They sniffed at it—it was not a good smell—and hurriedly left the area, one less member to their number . . . .

The calendar was suddenly never there.

Deep in the woods of the north rested a small log cabin. The smell of hardwoods permeated the air as the smoke mixed with falling snow. Inside, the soft glow from the fire enfolded the family of three as they laughed and hugged and played games before the hearth. It was a meager birthday, but it would turn out to be the best birthday Shelain would ever have . . . .

Garden of the Gods
1994

The old man lay still. Near delusional. Had been that way since . . . .

Eyes closed . . . heart . . . barely beating . . . body . . . useless, withered.

Legs broken.

He lay in the dark in a place desiccated from a dryness that sucked every last vestige of moisture from the environment. His body. Even sound seemed decayed . . . hollow. The surrounding rock weighed heavily . . . the crevasse crushing . . . barely enough room even for his broken form.

How long ago had it been since he'd crawled in here?

Too long . . . no interest . . . remembering . . . mind . . . *wandering* . . . .

The old man lay between life and death . . . his consciousness not firmly rooted in either. Yet his mind *worked* . . . carefully . . . slowly . . . trying to recall a singular event. Trying . . . *desperately* . . . to recall . . . the time . . . when he'd unwittingly stumbled into

Another place?

Another

(*a place of gods*)

dimension?

. . . lonely . . . mysterious . . . .

Never to be found again.

It had happened lifetimes ago when his body had still been strong and able.

His resolve like granite.

Age hadn't mattered then . . . he'd been *young*.

He'd been in the great southwest, lost during a hike into the rock and heat of the desert. Sunburned and thirsty, he'd blundered through a hidden ravine and come out the other side into a wonderland of white-and-red vertical rock. The sun was setting and cast monstrous shadows across their faces. Yucca and other scrub dotted the terrain; trees unknown to him reach up from the earth like ancient, arthritic fingers scraping at the sky.

He'd collapsed to the ground. Checked his water supply. Enough to wet his lips and that was it. Reluctantly, he sipped the last drops, ready to toss the canteen away in anger at his own stupidity in getting lost . . . when he'd heard it.

A rustling, grinding sound.

Holding onto the canteen, he got up. Searched the rock. The grinding stopped, replaced by a softer, gentler *trickling* . . .

Water.

He got up and rushed across the scree, slipping more than once.

Water.

Food he could forego for now, but water he'd die without. He already felt himself growing ever more lethargic, stiff. Near nauseous—

Water.

The sound drew him unerringly to its source. Water he'd hoped was real and not the delusion of a heart-stricken mind. He'd scurried about a small outcropping of rock and came upon the

Cool, crisp, flowing *water!*

Out from the very *pores* of the red rock itself.

He'd dove at it . . . sucking the water directly from the rock face . . . cupping his hands he splashed the precious fluid to his parched lips and face.

It'd initially hurt parting his lips so much, cracking open dried and sunburned skin, but he brought the water up and swallowed greedily. A huge knot of the frigid fluid got caught midway down his throat after slamming into the back of his throat, and he coughed it out, grimacing in the irony of the brain freeze. For something so life-giving and necessary, it was sure running him through the ringer . . . .

It was now darker from the setting sun, and he'd finished cleaning his clothes and washing himself. Felt more like he should . . . hydrated, rested. But hungry. Filled his canteen before going to sleep for the night.

He looked about him.

It was still warm, but not so unbearable as midday. He'd considered continuing . . . were it not for the weariness of his body. He didn't think he could get very far in his present condition and deemed a night's sleep more important.

After all, did he not now have all the water he would ever need?

Did he not now have shelter to weather the merciless sun?

The only thing he lacked was food.

At one time all he needed was water, but now his stomach growled.

Collecting sticks and tufts of desert grass for a fire, he was pondering his next step . . . when a large hare jumped out before him. It sat on a ledge not ten feet away.

He carefully crouched and placed his sticks and grass down before him . . . stared at the lean and meaty beast. It stared back, motionless except for its twitching nose. He searched the dirt around him for a stone . . . found one . . . repositioned it in his hand without looking at it.

Water.

Now food.

He pitched the rock at the animal.

It hit the rabbit square in its head, propelling it over the side of the ledge. He got up; withdrew his knife from its sheath. On the other side of rock he found it.

One leg twitched but momentarily.

He'd stuffed the steaming pieces of cooked rabbit into his pack and looked out his cave. Early morning should have looked bright, but the day appeared dull, overcast. The heat of the day seemed subdued. Collecting the rest of his things, he'd thrown on his pack and given himself a once-over, checking his gear. Satisfied, he left the cave for the expected heat of the day . . .

But what he found sent shivers up his spine.

Instead of overcast skies and heat, he found it was still *night* . . . a full moon overhead.

He looked to his watch . . . but it was smashed.

Had he lost his mind?

Had he slept into the next night?

All these thoughts flooded him . . . but the end result was that he couldn't possibly stay here forever . . .

Could he?

Some kind of Fate had brought him here, and here he must deal with it . . . at least until he could make his way back to the world he knew.

The facts were that it was cool, dark, and he had food and water—

his canteens and pack full with both. He needed to return home.

Resolved to restart his homeward sojourn, he left the security of his cave for the uncertainty of the dark.

He scrambled down the boulders and loose rock, down to the water that still flowed mightily from the very pores of red rock. He looked back and up to his deserted shelter—somewhat surprised that he could no longer

(*go back*)

find it.

Could he find it again . . . actually climb back up there just for paranoia's sake?

But he'd already slept in it. Eaten there. Of course it was there. Somewhere.

Knock it off, he told himself. *Of course it's still there. It* has *to be—*

Like the water. That came out from the rock.

He shot a glance toward the miniature geyser.

Yes. Still there. Stuck a hand into it.

Cold.

You've just been out in the desert too long, that's all.

He dropped his hand and turned away.

But in which direction should I go?

He looked from where he'd come . . . to where he might head. There was plenty of light from the moon, but there was no—

Path.

He blinked. Rubbed his eyes. Moments ago he'd have sworn *there was no path*, but now . . . as if it had rolled itself out just for him . . .

(*this is insane!*)

It was there.

He took two steps onto it as if testing it for solidity. Plenty solid. Plenty real. Plenty *there*.

An actual clearing of stone and brush—as if stone and brush had actually parted just for him—the earth packed down as if having been travelled *before* . . . .

He stepped onto the path.

Images of an old man filled his head. A man in pain . . . damaged . . . .

A shudder ran through him. Made him dizzy.

This was not just . . . wait a minute . . . not just *any* old man—

Him?

A *future* him?

The old man lay still . . . eyes closed . . . heart . . . barely beating . . . body useless . . . broken beyond repair. He lay in the dark in a place that looked remarkably

Like this one.

How long had he been there?

An accident . . . a horrendous fall. Crawled out of the ruthless, midday sun with broken legs into a tiny rock fissure.

Where no one would ever find him.

How long had he lain there?

Too long . . . alone . . . never to be—

Yet the younger him *had* found him.

And the younger him desperately tried to recall how *he'd* gotten here . . . where *he* was, now . . . had unwittingly stumbled into

Another dimension?

A place of *gods*?

Never to be found again?

No.

He was strong . . . capable. Fed and watered. He would make his way out.

And if he truly was tied to this man . . . this old man . . . if that old man really *was* him . . . well, it didn't matter, he would take him with him anyway.

Together they would both leave.

He couldn't tell if it was all in his mind . . . or like the water, cave, and rabbit . . . but he looked down and saw a rough-hewn field stretcher . . . with a leather strap . . . partially hidden among the yucca.

Was it really there?

He wasted no time.

In his mind's eye he carefully picked up the old him . . . and gently positioned him upon the stretcher. He grabbed the leather strap at the end of wooden handles and looped it up and over—around—his shoulders, lifting one end of the stretcher. Shifting his pack and gear . . . he stepped out onto the path.

Never once did he look back.

The rocks smiled.

For Whom The Gods ⟨*burp*⟩

1991

"Isn't it amazing how the galaxies appear?" the young one, Latissimus, inquired.

"Yes. There is nothing else quite like them, is there?" replied Trapezius, the Elder.

"No, nothing. How do you think they formed—I mean, some are so symmetrical while others are *so* disorganized!"

"Well," Trapezius said, "they may appear disorganized to us from our limited vantage point, my pupil, but have you ever thought that perhaps—from other vantage points—they are very symmetrical?"

Latissimus pondered.

"Good point, Trapezius! Now let me ask you another cosmological question, since you seem to know much of this universe."

"Know so much of the universe? Ha!" Trapezius said, snorting, "I, too, am a mere *student*, not an Oracle!"

"Oh nonsense! I know you for what you truly are—a wise and learned man!"

Trapezius bowed in humility.

"So, pray thee, what is this burning question of yours, that you seem to be teasing me with, Latissimus? Pray the gods I am worthy of such a challenge!"

"Oh, but you are, Trapezius, you most certainly *are!*

"My question, that I put to you, is: *If the notion of the closed universe is true, what lies beyond the universal boundaries?*"

At this, Trapezius guffawed a mighty open and merry laughter!

"Oh, Latissimus, you are surely a feisty one—for that question cannot simply be put to a simple answer!

"The universe, if it is indeed as is thought, will expand, only to contract upon itself. This in itself brings an interesting postulation. For if the universe is indeed *all*, then from what is it all *shrinking* . . . and to *what* is taking up all its previously occupied space? How can it even fall back unto itself?

"Furthermore . . . even if the universe is *open*, as some say . . . what is it expanding *into* if the universe itself is *everything*?

"These questions are not those that I can easily corner into an answer—a dialectic perhaps—but nothing is certain. You would be better off putting such a question as to how the galaxies get their very form!"

"Then that I do, my mentor! How *do* yon galaxies attain the form with which they sustain? Pray thee, I inquire!"

"My friend, Latissimus, you are certainly an endless pit of curiosity this day! Let us to investigate, then, to one in particular. Note that one there, the asymmetrical one next to Quesandromidea . . . . "

From a direction opposite and behind the philosophical prolegomena emerged a dark form . . . growing increasingly enormous in configuration and nascent in proximity. The two engaged in dialectic noticed it not, the shape blotting out the celestial fires to half the heavens and quickly and effectively taking them both out in mid-discussion.

{^.^ *Xi yihYü kytc chatgh aNf* ^.^}*

An immense fork reached down into the milky swirls below, a piece of French toast impaled upon its four-pronged end. The hand at the other end absentmindedly swished it around in the starry sauce, the bright speckles sparkling spectacularly. The god returned to his/her/its actions, the other nodding in agreement, he/she/its grin so immense that the magnetic fields of neighboring nebulae distorted.

* (translation:) "*I just* love *the Magellanic Clouds, don't you? They taste so sweet and cinnamonny!*"

The Running
1989

I *run*.

I know no end. It is as if my sole existence . . . is to *run*.

My legs pump powerfully down the gravel of a leaf-strewn, backcountry dirt road in late October. I know it is October, I know I am running, but that . . . that, sadly, is about all I know.

Pump, pump, huff . . . .

And I know that this is an easy run for me. I know not how far I've already gone or even what time it is, but it has to be late afternoon, for the sun is low and lonely . . . the near leafless trees standing as silent witnesses as I sprint past. There is a wonderful chill to the air, too, as my breath turns into wispy ghosts about my face. I seem to be the only one in the entire world and I revel in it!

Pump, pump, huff, huff!

I am at one with creation; a Zen, if you will, as though running and I *were* one—the ultimate runner's high, I tell you. My legs are on auto (they have a will of their own, indeed!), but my mind also runs wild, runs free! My wind is limitless, but I feel strange . . . disjointed . . . like one forced to look down upon oneself from an out-of-the-body perspective. The ultimate, mobile, isolation tank!

The gravel crunches and fires out from beneath my driving heels . . . my body and arms slicing through the autumn air like a banshee. Such raw power crackles through me and I feed upon it! I inhale deeply of the air and it further fuels me. I inhale vitality and out do I exhale my corporally challenged ghosts . . . .

Pump, pump, *huff* . . . .

I couldn't stop if I wanted to, for to stop would violate the immaculately sacred . . . eradicate the flow of *chi*.

Should I stop I should very well *perish*.

Perish?

Then why am I running? What is my purpose? Am I in flight? Fleeing something, someone?

No—I think not.

I feel no such inspired adrenaline rush, yet, in fact, feel quite at ease and free.

No . . . I am here of my own volition. A training session and nothing more.

Pump, pump, huff, *huff* . . . .

So I *am* in training. Good. At least that is something else I know, which means I have a destination to which I head. Vaguely, I recall a house . . . an old one . . . surrounded by open fields.

Wait . . . another image . . . yes . . . there's a barn, nearby, with a dog leashed to the decrepit old barn . . . a truck parked in the driveway!

Yes! It's down off a stretch of sparsely populated country road! More memories! I know this house! I am remembering!

But . . . what do I *do?*

I wonder, but nothing more comes to mind. No matter, I've gotten this far, I must be doing okay. It'll all come back to me. I simply drink in the runner's high—why fight it?

Pump, huff; pump, huff . . . .

I return my attention to my running . . . my surroundings . . . which I adore!

It is so gentle and serene running among the stands of trees . . . deciduous . . . evergreen . . . the setting sun blinking in and out from behind their forested silhouettes . . . the leaves blowing across my path or crunching beneath my feet—the cool air against my cheeks and that wonderful Octobery musk from the earth and leaves!

The sound of my exquisitely tuned body!

My feet pounding the ground (*pound, pound!*), my stride long and *mighty!*

I am the perfect machine . . . nothing can stop me . . . a finely tuned engine firing through the autumn world unchecked! My breath wisps out from me, like steam from a locomotive!

(*pump, pump, huff, huff!*)

I weave back and forth across the single dirt lane, stones kicking up in my wake. My legs, I chuckle, they pound like pistons! I fly over this gravel road, my mind continually expanding.

I am more than just at one with running . . . I am at one with my being and my *world* . . . .

My mind leaps from my physical shell, its supernatural tentacles interlacing with the skeleton-like extremities of the trees . . . and pierces the rich earth.

I *feel* the woodland creatures as they roam the secluded countryside . . . or fly between the trees . . . and am lifted—*elated*—a rush of cloudy headiness blurring my mind!

Pump, huff! Pump, *huff!*

Oh, it is godlike to be in such extraordinary condition!

Though I seem to have an unnerving sense of amnesia, I do remember this: *I am one of the best.*

No—I *am* the best!

Running is who I am . . . what I do. I have always run . . . and run better than anyone else. My whole being thrills to its sensations!

Come on legs—harder, *faster!* More . . . *more!*

Pump, pump, *huff*, huff; pump, pump, huff, *huff* . . . .

Oh, but the end is near and I am saddened beyond despair!

Up ahead I spy a break in the trees . . . a highway crossing my own dirt path (my own—*no one* else's!).

Damn, but it was a good run!

Perhaps I will finally find the remaining answers to my nagging quandaries—it will not be long, now!

But, I can hardly wait until the next time!

Pump, pump, *pump, pump!*

My body is tuned to exacting, spiritual perfection! Seeing the paved road just ahead I feel an added rush of adrenaline as I kick up my pace ever higher, more powerful! I feel all the eyes of the forest upon me . . . coaxing me . . . *cheering* me! The gravel spits and crackles beneath me as I pull out of the clearing toward the road just a sprint ahead. As I pull away from the tree-shaded back road, I realize I miss the run already knowing that it is over for yet another day—but look forward to the final sprint!

I easily make it to the road and turn onto it . . . feeling the pavement pound back up *into* my feet as I kick off from it.

My kick is high and proud . . . as I begin to cool down . . . .

Pump, pump, huff, huff, yes, I am proud! *Pump, pump, huff, huff,* I am proud of what I am, and why not? I have worked long and hard, I—

Run.

I know no end. It is as if my sole existence is . . . to *run.* My legs pump powerfully down the gravel of a leaf-strewn, backcountry dirt road in late October. I know it is October, I know I am running, but that . . . that, sadly, is about all I know.

Pump, pump, huff . . . .

And I know that this is . . . .

Pump, pump, huff, huff!

The gravel road lay out before me, the tree-lined dirt road stretches out as far as I can see—

I am back on the path!

Something is wrong—but what is it? What happened? The last thing I remember is . . . oh, why fight it . . . .

As I fly down this back road, I again feel transcendent from the physical . . . but now feel as if I also blaze across time and space—galaxies and universes!

Bright colors I see, bright and fluid!

But I outrun the light itself! Nothing escapes me! I am invincible! I am more than just running down a backcountry road . . . I am soaring through realities . . . as not just myself, but as every runner that ever runs.

I am more than a single runner . . . more than any *run.*

I seem able to tune into individual thoughts . . . global gestalts . . .

I am *intoxicated!*

Now, I find myself running in the mountains of the southern hemisphere . . . high into the clouds . . . or I am in flight for my life from a charging polar bear on a blindingly white background . . . I am in a race on a coast in the western hemisphere with thousands of other runners . . . on the beaches of tropical islands . . . on the manufactured tracks of global games!

Oh, how I laugh and explode with joy and feel my energy fire out across universes!

I remember who I am . . . what I *do!*

How could I have forgotten?

It is the intensity I devote to each and every run . . . the high that allows all to forget . . . and *be* in the moment. I give everything to all . . . I *am* everything to all . . . .

I smile, as I pour it on.

I *am* Running . . . .

Pump, pump, huff, *huff!*

Jumper
1990

He got up and walked away.

No fanfare; no good-byes. He simply lifted himself up off the chair and left . . . the creaking of the chair still hanging in the air like some spent cigar aroma.

"*Horseshit*," Harold said, watching the man walk away and out the door. Turning to Bill, who had also sat there and listened to the old man's story, he again uttered, "Pure, one-hundred *per*-cent, finely packed *horseshit!*"

Bill merely continued sitting there, speechless. The summer sun was going down fast, and any customers who had been to the present-day anachronism of Preacher's Corner General Store had long since left, but one additional person had come out, Bill Waverly's daughter, Marianne. She placed herself at her daddy's feet, curling up and grasping her legs into her arms.

"What horse—"

"Mari*anne*—"

"I was gonna say 'horse *crap*', daddy."

Bill gave his daughter one of those stern paternal looks, then let his daughter continue. Marianne had a wry grin on her face. She was prone to blurting out *things* despite what she nonchalantly claimed, and Bill decided it gave her the attention she wanted . . . saying the unexpected . . . whether a "curse" word or not . . . usually she got it good and got it fast, said attention, and Marianne liked that.

"So what'd he say?" Marianne asked her father.

"Oh, nuthin'."

"'*Nuthin'?*" Harold said, exploding, almost offended, "he just spent the better part of the afternoon tellin' us how he done jumped off a everything in sight that had a roof attached to it, and you call it *nuthin'?*"

"I know what he *said*, Harold . . . ."

"C'mon, c'mon, c'mon! You said you'd tell me!" Marianne pressed.

Bill Waverly let out a long sigh as he examined his daughter's preteen expression, then looked back at Harold, a good friend of many years. Harold Filmore and Bill Waverly knew each other since Bill was a kid. Harold and his wife, Mille, had run the out-in-the-middle-of-nowhere store since before Jesus, but now that Bill was grown up, he'd come help take up operation of Preacher's Corner General Store after Millie had passed. Harold had been old when Bill was young; now it was immaterial.

"Ah, why not, Bill. It's not like it's true or anything. Go an' tell her how he done jumped off the Empire State Building. Or how he'd hopped, skipped, and jumped all the way across, up, and down the Grand Canyon—only to do it all the way back!"

Marianne's eyes lit up.

"Oh! Daddy, did he *really?*"

"No. I mean, I don't *believe* so—"

"You don't *believe* so? Lord, fetch me my switch, Bill! You think he mighta been talkin' the truth, or sumthin'?"

"Well, beat all, Harold, there's lots a things out there we know nuthin' about. Who's ta say he *weren't* tellin' the truth?"

"*I* am! You believe him when he talked a jumpin' across those Sears Towers in Chicago?"

Bill shrugged his shoulders.

"Gol dern, William Waverly, you're more skittery'n I thought!"

"Dadd-*y! Pleeease*—tell me!"

"Okay, okay. But what I'm about to tell you is only one man's word. This here fella claims to have jumped over, across, and down from just about anything that exists."

"Really?" Marianne asked, pulling her knees closer in to her chest.

"Yep," he said, continuing, casting a glance over to Harold who just began restuffing a dead pipe. "This here fella said he started doin' it ever since he was a kid over in Australia."

"Australia? Where's that?"

"Down clear on the other side of the world, child, where everything they do is backwards. Anyway, he says he saw some—what did he call them, Harold?"

"Aborigines."

"*Aborigines*—they're like the American Indians are to our country, but to Australia—he saw these Aborigines jumpin' off platforms with rope tied to their ankles. So, one day, he decided to give it a go, only the rope that had been tied to his ankle *broke*."

Marianne's eyes bugged wide.

"Did he *die?*" she asked.

"No child, of course not, he was just here, wasn't he?"

"Oh . . . yeah . . . "

"But that wasn't the worst of it, really. It turns out he just . . . *bounced*—"

"He didn't frickin *bou*—" Harold interrupted, his face all in knots.

"He *bounced*," Bill again said, giving Harold a hard, commanding stare.

Harold grunted something that Bill chose to ignore.

"He just up and bounced right back up into the air," Bill continued, "right up to the platform he'd jumped off from. From there, he began experimentin' with different things . . . steadily goin' higher and higher. He's said he's done it all . . . jumped from anythin' he could get his feet up on."

"*Wow* . . . ," was all Marianne could say, staring off into the growing darkness . . . .

Off in the distance, where none of the General Store group could see, a lone figure leapt from rooftop to rooftop in the evening twilight, sometimes doing backflips in mid-air. If you listened *real* close, you could make out some faint whoopin' and hollarin' as he sailed through the air . . . .

The Ice Gods

1992

Alone.
Cold.
I am surrounded by white.
Where am I?
It's *so* cold . . . .
I remember pain. I remember . . . I don't quite know what I remember . . . but I can't move. My arms, they hurt. White hurt. I hear howling—a lonely, empty howling. The wind.

I'm so alone.

Eyes. I must try to open my eyes . . . I have to get to the top.

I move . . . hear *crunching* . . . .

I've opened my eyes and wished I hadn't.

I'm lying on the side of a wind-swept and snow-covered mountain. All I can see is blinding white. I move my hands about me—and feel the snow crunch. It sounds like wicked Styrofoam. It's so cold.

How did I get here? What am I doing here . . . besides hurting?

I feel like I've been thrown thousands of feet. Craning my neck . . . and gasping at the snow that hungrily rushes down my back . . . I see cliffs of white and crystal above. I look off to my right, my up-and-behind-me-right, and see a bundle jutting out from the snow. It's covered in the hellish stuff. I cannot make out what it is.

How I hate white.

It's getting late, or so I fathom from the setting sun as it ducks behind the jagged peaks above. I have to get there . . . the peaks, I mean . . . don't know why, just that I must.

The bundle behind me is a pack . . . mine I assume, considering I'm the only one I see. I'm scared . . . but know I can survive. I seem to remember doing this *before* . . . .

The pack has everything I need—food, flashlights, tools—a fire-starting kit, ice saws, a tent. As I root around in the snow around me I find an ice pick and one snowshoe. I struggle to all fours. A few yards above me I find the other one. The snowshoe. But still, not another soul. No explanations. Barely . . . I get to my feet.

I head upward.

It's grown dark, and . . . like I've said before . . . I'm scared. But as I sit in my tent against this ice outcropping and watch the fading sun, I look at the deep, lonely blues that eerily crawl across the deserted snowscape. I'm overcome by emotion as I enjoy its unparalleled magnificence. No camera to be found, and not being an artist, I wish I had some way to capture these wondrous images forever! Such raw *being*. Such intense *desolation*. I listen to the ice crack and thunder, and it echoes deep within me. Cries *out* to me . . . .

No, I really mean it—*it actually cries out my* name . . . .

Okay . . . you think me crazy . . . a mountain crying out my name— then you surely won't believe this.

I left camp at first light and traveled for what seemed a lifetime. I came upon an ice boulder . . . and as I did, thought I spied the image of a man upon it . . . frozen, disfigured. The form leaned back against the ice, and what would be its left arm, outstretched . . . its head twisted sideways. As I came closer I grew fascinated by the image. I could not take my eyes from it. Then other images began to crowd my mind. Lonely, hollow images, like the wind that is my constant companion (for the wind has never let up since I regained consciousness and neither has the blowing snow). I worried about snow blindness, but found—much to my disbelief—goggles. I had kicked them up during my passage through the snowfields. There truly must be ice gods watching over me, for surely nothing else here survives . . . .

Save me.

But the images. They are cold and monstrous . . . I remember something about others . . . a terrible and brutal accident of some . . . enormity. We were . . . we were ascending this mountain and something ghastly had occurred . . . .

Where is everyone?

Why is it I alone survive?

So I approached this image . . . this man against the ice boulder . . .

and found it was more than just light and snow and long shadows—it *was* a man—or had been. He was obviously dead. I couldn't recognize his face for his features were grotesquely deformed and frozen. *Into the ice.*

I passed the man, Continued upward.

I awaken the following morning to find myself in a cold sweat. Not a good thing for one in my position. I recall hatred from my fellow climbers. I'm not sure why just yet. It hadn't always been like that, the hatred, but had come about suddenly. I think . . . I think it was something I—I—did.

I feel dread.

It rips through me like this infernal wind.

The cracking sounds from the mountain top were much closer last night. Banging at my back door. I recalled images of pain. Faces of torment. And screams. Of a fight with my fellows—

My fingers look funny.

Nothing much to tell today, except that I seem to have traveled in circles.

I know this because I again found the frozen man. Only this time he was *more* frozen. I-I mean to say that—y-you must bear with me, now, for I feel my mind beginning to s-seize—but I could swear that he had merged *into* the ice he'd been frozen against. *Into* it, I say! When I first saw him he was leaning against the ice as if he'd died taking a break there. This time h-he was as if *p-pushed* into it.

I'm not crazy.

Am I?

Then why am I talking to myself?

Oh, the d-deep, frigid-b-blue of the snow and ice is s-s-so grand! The thunder of the ice boulders *d-deafening!*

The Ice Gods came to me in my dreams last night.

They told me not to w-worry about my images. They told me I'm lonely and confused in my s-snowbound s-s-solitude. They also told me not to be afraid.

They would g-guide me.

I recall . . . f-fighting with my companions.

One of them had fallen into a crevasse. We were arguing over whether to go after him, because he had g-gone silent and hadn't answered our calls. They wanted me to g-go, but I was . . . afraid. I might not have made it b-back, I reasoned. They didn't listen.

I have come upon a snowshoe. There's a foot in it.

The Ice Gods told me to take the foot.

I'm near the mountain top.

I still do not know why it is I f-feel I have to make this trek . . . but I'm driven. No—

P-pulled.

I feel it is the Ice Gods who beckon . . . and I'm not all that f-frightened anymore. The Ice Gods protect me. They told me my f-fingers were against me, that I should do something about them or I might not make it.

So I took my ice pick to them.

The g-ground shudders from the thunder of the splitting ice above. I have trouble s-sleeping. I miss my f-fingers . . . though I keep them wrapped with me . . . like the f-foot.

The Ice Gods t-told me

That I'm almost there.

I'm out of f-food, so I used the f-f-foot. At first I hadn't removed the toenails and h-had a hard time chewing. I learn quickly.

I don't like t-toenails.

A funny thing happened to me tonight, I went to crack my knuckles, and

The crevasse.

The men had wanted our p-party to rescue that g-guy . . . but I refused. He's probably d-dead, I reasoned, so why waste the energy? They c-cursed me. One struck me and threw d-down a rope, then began to g-g-go down himself. He wouldn't listen to r-reason. Said I had g-gone snow-b-blind in the head. I said *he'd* gg-one snow-blind in the h-head. We'd only been out there . . . I don't know how l-long, I d-don't remember. All I remem-m-ber is the white. All the w-white.

White p-pain.

I rub my arms . . . the pain is all but gone.

It feels g-good to be here. V-very, very g-good.

My toes feel funny now, too, but I'm not going to look at them. I know what the Ice Gods will say and I don't want to m-miss my t-toes.

A terrible thing happened t-today. I came across another b-body. Where do they come from?

I didn't recognize it, either. Its clothing didn't look familiar. Must not have c-come from my p-party—

Mine?

Was I the leader? Leading an ascent? But I seem to remember already being th-there—and *s-seeing* something.

S-something that sent us back.

W-what s-something?

I feel it has to do with the crevasse. With that man. In it. And the man who had g-gone down for him. The one who'd h-hit me.

I d-d-didn't like that. He wouldn't listen to reason. He had to stay d-down there. *Had* to, I t-told him. But he wouldn't l-listen . . . so I c-cut his rope and p-p-pushed his ladder over. The others around me went crazy.

I remember now.

They went crazy and tried to k-kill me. But the Ice Gods, they were my f-friends. They didn't let the others k-kill me.

Only I saw reason.

It all comes back to me, n-now.

I know my r-reason for the climb. I have to g-get there.

I don't have much t-t-time.

I n-no longer f-feel my toes and my remaining fingers are st-st-*stiff*. The Ice Gods are anxious to see me and I mustn't d-dis-a-*p-p-point* them. They've helped me so f-f-far.

Tonight I eat my f-fingers. Tomorrow—

Tomorrow I meet the Ice Gods.

The crystalline Ice Gods of Thunder.

I left my tent, pack, and s-snowshoes behind. They'd only slow me down.

I checked my cr-crampons. It's all ice now. I have my Ice Gods to g-guide me. Th-that's what th-they d-do . . . .

The going was more d-difficult without my other fingers, and the loss of f-feeling in my t-toes . . . but I p-pushed. A little p-pain is a good thing, even if n-numb. I'm so high now there's little o-oxygen. My lungs b-burn.

I recall the f-fight.

The remaining two men'd looked at me in amazement as I'd c-cut the one loose. We'd heard him scream all the way d-down. Heard him scream at the b-bottom. He hadn't been alone down there. There was something w-w-with him. The others had attacked me with their picks. I blocked some of the swings, and remember the hurt in my arms. I managed to throw one down, but had to fight off the other with my own p-pick. My back to the downed man, I heard a scream, and my opponent dropped his attack, his face b-blank and white as the snow. I took the opportunity to bury my pick deep into his n-neck. He clutched at it as he collapsed. I must have pierced his vocal cords, because he made n-no n-n-noise as he went down, except for that f-funny, h-hissing . . . g-gurgle. After I saw him to the ground (and put my foot on his shoulder to r-rip f-f-free my pick), I turned around. That was when I s-s-saw them.

You-know-*who*-them.

I'm really n-numb now, but it's okay . . . .

I'm th-there.

The sight is *f-f-fantastic!*

G-gorgeous!

I thought the frigid b-blue of where I'd been was b-beautiful . . . but it holds n-nothing to what is before me. The Ice Gods are p-pleased, and so am I.

I have c-come h-h-home.

The others wanted to f-flee. They'd been up here with me and had fled in t-terror. That was why the one fell into the crevasse. Been c-careless. Ran without ch-checking his s-steps. S-stupid man. And the others? They'd had to d-die because they had seen what I now s-see. They should have wanted to come b-back . . . l-like m-me.

This is so unbelievably *b-beautiful*. Huge, j-jagged ice cr-crystals everywhere, and within each one . . . a f-frozen body. All sorts of bodies . . . from different t-times . . . d-different p-places. All frozen into stalagmite-like ice cr-cr-crystals. All asleep and p-peaceful. All waiting for me to join them.

And I will.

Just as s-soon as I see the setting s-sun and hear the c-crack of th-thunder . . . .

Behind Things
2017

One-two-three . . . you will follow me . . .
Two-three-four . . . through the Black Door . . .
Three-four-five . . . my love for you is very much alive . . .

Where to begin?

What is a beginning and what is an end? Are there really even such bookends . . . or is it all just a different perspective of the same thing?

I have to start somewhere, so here is just as good as any a place to do so.

I was pumping iron at The Iron Den, in a small town in central Indiana. It was a great workout. The room was full of people and grunting and iron. I had gone from my eighty-five-pound dumbbell bench presses to bent-over rows, where I'd thrown on several forty-five pound plates onto the end of a bar, the other end of which is anchored into a metal-reinforced corner of the room. As I'd been working out, I'd noticed someone out of the corner of my eyes, a really built lifter chick. At first I thought she'd had this gnarly modified Mohawk with a long ponytail and tons of body ink, but when I'd given her a second look, she'd had beautiful long, curly brown hair. She was muscular and carried herself like a seasoned bodybuilder. Kept to herself. And she was hot.

You don't yet realize the irony of that last statement.

So I'm moving from my rows to shoulder presses—again using dumbbells—when I noticed that the room'd started thinning out some. Great, because it's been kind of busy and I had to finagle around some folks and their benches when I'd first arrived. Everyone's nice about it, experienced gym users with good gym etiquette, but no one wants to get up in another's grill, you know?

Anyway, the room had cleared out, except for this chick, who was now on the far side of the room from me, and I do notice she'd cast me a couple glances. Cool. Nice to know you're noticeable, even if you are the only one left in the room. The loudspeakers are belting out Rob Zombie, when I notice it's the "More Human Than Human" tune, the *full* version, where in the beginning there's this track of a chick having sex and moaning and groaning and all. It's pretty hot, and as that's blaring in the room with just the two of us, I'd cast a glance over to this woman—*and she's looking right at me.* She's slightly bent over as she's doing rear delt dumbbell flies. Her long hair had cascaded over her face all sexy like and covered one of her eyes, but the look she was giving me was, well—*knowing.* Her eyes were unnerving . . . boring right into me . . . like, yeah, she hears the tune, the sex noises—the girl moaning and groaning—and is wanting me to know she *knows* what I'm thinking and that *she's* thinking the same thing . . . .

I move on to my bis and tris.

As I stand before the mini-barbell rack, I unrack an eighty pound barbell and heft it up over and behind my head and rip out a couple of warm-up reps for my triceps. But . . . as I do so . . . in the mirror . . . I cast another glance toward the lifter chick—

She's gone.

As I began my reps, I search the mirror for her, but she's nowhere to be seen, and now the room has filled back up with a bunch of boisterous twenty-something bruisers setting up at the squat rack, and a variety of fashion-plate lifter chicks in skin-tight leggings hitting various equipment.

I continue my workout.

Completing dumbbell shrugs, I reracked my weights and sucked down some water. As I turned to leave, I saw that lifter chick out of the corner of my eye at the opposite end of the room. I casually turned to look—but no one's there. I stared at the empty white wall for a moment longer.

Could have sworn she'd been standing . . . right . . . *there.*

I'd gone on to do some ab work in the main room, where all the cardio and machine equipment are, as well as some kind of "Ninja Warrior" contraption with climbing rope, a heavy bag, and all manner of overhead "monkey" bars. I've used the heavy bag and done hanging bicep chin ups from the thing. But not this go around. I cycle my workouts and I'll hit those again at a later date. But to the mat I'd gone, did my abs—V-ups for the center and side abs, then "the Plank" for five minutes—then returned to the free-weight room. I've always preferred free weights over machines. There are no "leverage" issues and it's all *you*. No mechanical advantages.

And I just love the heft and feel of iron.

As I reentered the weight room to do legs . . . I felt slightly lightheaded and paused at the room's entry. I took a quick moment just standing there. As I do so, I glanced down the length of the weight room . . . down along this narrow, two-foot spacing that's between the wall separating the main gym from the free-weight room. There are some floor-to-ceiling columns there that are about two-feet away from the wall. The space is barely wide enough for someone to walk through without twisting their shoulders to get past the columns. And there's no equipment there, it's just this empty

(. . . *but I don't feel it's* . . .)

space.

(*one-two-three . . . you will follow me* . . .)

I feel . . . I don't know—*watched?*

And was that faint laughter I'd just heard?

I looked about the room and saw it was full of lifters, men and women, and over by the squat rack were those twenty-somethings chatting it up with a couple women—who all suddenly broke out into boisterous laughter.

Laughter.

I blinked . . . suddenly felt like myself again . . . and continued in.

The rest of my workout had gone fine . . . except for the douchebag who left the only available StairMaster fucking soaked with his sweat. I didn't even bother wiping it down . . . just used another machine instead.

The entire next day I couldn't get that lifter chick out of my head. She seemed to get hotter the more I thought about her. She was built, and not just in a sexy way. She sported a fine muscular frame, which to me is the sexiest female form: she had that "V"-shaped back serious bodybuilders have, with well-muscled, defined deltoids and arms. Tanned. She held herself ramrod straight and upright . . . long—and I mean *long*—curled tresses spiraled down about her shoulders and back. And her face was a mask of seriousness. She was a *lifter*. Not a poser, not a fashion plate. Devoted her entire life to shaping her body into what it was. She was not there to model the latest set of painted-on workout attire, or to show how young and rockin' her flawless body was within said apparel. Her focus was immediate . . . it was intense . . . it was passionate. *She was there to lift weights . . .* and that was *that*.

No talking.

No flirting.

Weights.

And to me, that made her *indescribably* hot.

But during my day away from the gym, weird shit happened to me wherever I went . . . I'd swear I'd . . . I'd *seen* her!—or someone like her—seeming to appear out from behind all-manner of things— parked cars . . . trees . . . book shelves . . . aisles of the supermarket. I mean, I'd swear I'd seen a person standing there out of the corner of the eyes, turn to look—but there'd be *no* one.

And once or twice I'd a swore I'd seen her out and about town with that gnarly modified Mohawk and ponytail I'd thought I'd first seen at the gym. She was even hot in that.

Damn.

I really had her on my mind.

Then there were the dreams. Holy *shit*.

She'd come to me in my sleep.

In the dream I'd been working out in my gym. It was very busy, packed with people. I was doing shoulders when I'd seen her. She'd materialized out from behind the support columns by the wall, as I'd first seen her. Her long hair (no Mohawk!) floated all about her head and she looked right at me. She had no tattoos. *Came* right up to me.

I'm so glad to have finally met you, she'd said, in a sexy, raspy voice.

Me, too, I said.

The sexual tension between us was unfuckingbelievable and I really began to get excited. I became both afraid and eager at what might happen between us right then and there—out in the open.

She'd moved in closer. I could smell her. *Smell* her! *Musky*. Sweaty. Coppery?

I've wanted you since I first saw you, she'd told me.

But . . . there was something off with her head. I don't know what it was, but there was something very strange about it. Almost like it wasn't truly a part of her body. It was weird. But you know dreams, right? Anyway, she was standing directly before me, so closely that I had an incredible urge to kiss her. I also felt an intense cold emanate from her—but I didn't care! I *wanted* her, oh, God in heaven how I wanted to *profane* her! Wanted her bad. Right there. I then felt this crazy vertigo again attack me as she brought her face right up to mine—I now smelled a weird scent from her . . . exotic . . . erotic. It seemed a part of me grew immediately nauseated, but the rest of me wanted her even more.

I was lost in her eyes.

Dark, powerful, unnerving . . .

Unwavering.

She opened her mouth.

I parted my lips . . . now breathing heavily.

(*. . . one-two-three . . . you will follow me . . .*)

(*. . . seven-eight-nine . . . you are* mine *. . .*)

Her mouth . . . it grotesquely . . . *distended* . . . opened to encompass my entire face! Yes, all of it!

As I looked into the immense black hole that had been her beautiful mouth, I saw colors and stars and a strangeness I can no longer describe once awake. I was . . . *sucked into the void* . . . mesmerized by the darkness and the depth and the longing that was . . . *her* . . . that I felt emerge from that open maw . . . and I saw . . . I saw a *door*—a *black* door . . . at first it was closed . . . closed and menacing . . . but then

(*. . . one-two-three . . . you will—*)

it opened

(*follow me . . .*)

and

(*. . . two-three-four . . .*)

it was like

(*through the Black Door . . .*)

I was transported *into* her . . . through that . . . that fucking black door . . .

And that's when she began to devour me.

Her mouth clamped down upon my face and, dammit, it *excited* me!

It was like she was pretend-eating me—*gumming* me!—like a lover playfully making love with their mouth down the length of their lover's body. And as she gummed and gummed and gummed my entire face with each massive openmouthed kiss, my chin, my jaw . . . she worked her way down my neck, my shoulders, my chest—and the incredible seductive, erotic sensations were too much . . . I was going to lose it right there, in the gym—*my* gym—in my shorts . . . in front of all those I knew and who knew *me*—

(*. . . one-two-three . . . you will follow me . . .*)

(*. . . seven-eight-nine . . . because you are* mine.)

She "ate" at my sides, my arms, and my stomach—shot back up to my face, my ears, my mouth—then back down to my lower belly, my hips, and my chest.

I couldn't take it!

(I'm so glad to have finally met you!)
(I want you!)
(You will follow me!)
(Because you are mine!)
Yes! I *wanted* her!
I *craved* her!

My body writhed in pleasurable torture the likes of which I had never before experienced in dreams or anywhere else . . . and as free as I was, I felt somehow bound to this woman . . . *restricted*.

She again attacked my chest and I couldn't see straight, my passionate vertigo absolute.

I didn't know what was happening . . . what was happening to *me* . . .

My hips bucked, and I had lost all control of my body as I came violently into my shorts, groaning out loud and not caring one damned bit that everyone else there could see what was going on . . . .

I awakened from my dream.

I lay there, eyes closed.

I still saw her . . . she stood back behind those pillars . . . with a shit-eating grin upon her magnificent face . . . but this time she stood before a black door—the very one I had seen inside her mouth. And this time she did sport that ponytailed Mohawk and body art. Still stared at me. I don't know if I'd made it all up, lying there half-awake, or part of me was still in that dream—but didn't want the dream to end—

You must follow me . . . she said *you* will *follow me* . . .

Follow *me* . . . .

. . . *one-two-three* . . .

. . . *because you are* mine . . .

. . . *seven-eight-nine* . . .

I lay there. Eyes opened. Not moving . . . and just . . .

Cried.

I missed her!

I wanted her!

Who the hell was *she?*

I couldn't wait to get back into that gym the next day!

I had to find her—to *see* her again . . . if for nothing else than to just see if what I'd remembered about her—what I'd built up in my *head*—was what she actually was. If my dream had meant anything. I mean, I probably totally made her up. It's like when you see a person from the back and never see their face, you tend to make up—use your imagination—as to what their face and all must look like. Sure, I'd seen her face, but I'd been so focused on my own workout I hadn't really *looked* at her.

But in my dream I *had*.

I truly do not flirt and eyeball chicks in the gym. When I'm working out—I'm that guy who sports that "angry gym face" and powers through his workout like it's a life-and-death battlefield . . . there's no tomorrow, and the weights are my sworn enemy. I've seen my face in the mirror and know I look angry—mean, even. It keeps the dickwads away, the "talkers" and "campers" who aren't serious about lifting and use the gym as their goddamned social media. The type who whine to whomever will listen about "having" to work out because it's "the thing to do," or whatever, about how much they hate it but do it anyway (by flapping their jaws) as if that makes them a saint or something for being in a gym. The type who can't get their fucking face out of their fucking cell phones and sit (camp out!) on equipment forever in-between sets. And God-forbid you ask to work in with them on the equipment, while they're camping out. They get all indignant on your ass and look at you like you're fucking molesting them in public and tell you they're "just resting." Then they go back to their fucking cell phones as if to show you they have the power to keep you at bay and it's *their* machine, while they're on it.

They know nothing of gym protocol.

Who. The fuck. *Are*. These people?

So I loved it that someone once told me that I had an "angry gym face" when I worked out.

Anyway.

I stick to the free-weight room as much as possible and only come out to do cardio . . . and abs, because there's no room in the weight room to do them. I love the smell and feel of iron . . . the plates. The *atmosphere* in there. We used to be able to use chalk in there, but gym management deemed it too messy. Christ. Oh, how I miss the older gyms! The smell and dust of chalk as we smeared it all over our hands and upper thighs to aid our sweaty grips and assist pulling deadlifts up the fronts of our legs! How it used to get *everywhere*. That was the sign of a good, "iron den." I could use wrist straps, but those don't help in developing grip strength, so I pretty much don't even use them anymore.

I miss chalk.

But again I digress.

So after my away-day from the gym, I'd hurried back. I couldn't get in the door fast enough . . . couldn't change into my ratty gym clothes quickly enough. Couldn't fill up my water bottle rapidly enough.

Then I was in there.

I strode in battle ready, angry gym face set. My focus was sharp and singular. I nodded to a couple of regulars who nodded back as I imaginatively plowed my way across the iron-laden battlefield.

I didn't see her.

I found an empty bench and I'm feeling better than ever. I was psyched for this workout. Instead of starting out with seventies, I grab a seventy-five-pound set of dumbbells and begin my warm-up. I see lesser lifters around me glance my way, because though I am somewhat built, I'm not massively so, so my size does belie my strength (I've actually been told by a couple guys how I'm a pretty strong dude).

I rip off my fifteen-rep warm up.

Rerack the weights.

I grab the eight-five pounders like I'm ready to fucking *kill*.

I know I'm pushing it, but for some reason I feel suddenly pissed—yes, *pissed*—and I don't know why. I'm pissed, angry, and I'm psyched. This is my fucking battlefield and lesser talkers need to keep the fuck out of my way. I lay back and yank the weights up and onto my chest. Nice and controlled. That signifies I'm ready and able to do the set. I hit it—

Ripped out my set far more easily than I'd thought it'd go.

I rerack.

Look to the nineties.

Okay, I haven't moved that kind of weight in several years, and when I momentarily question myself, I get even *more* pissed!

Fuck you!, I tell myself.

You fucking *pussy!*

Just because you doubted yourself you're now going to rip off two more reps if it *kills* you!

I grabbed the nineties and placed them on the floor at the foot of the bench. As I'd taken a sip of water, I'd sensed that I'm again being watched. Out of the corner of my eyes I see someone standing there. I'm betting it's one of those talkers who'd errored by entering the serious section of the gym and are now trying to act like they came here on purpose before they leave. As I set down my water bottle and grabbed the nineties, I'd turned and glared at whoever'd been standing there—

It's that lifter chick!

But I'm already in motion and forced myself back on the bench and haul those bad boys up onto my chest where I'd momentarily paused. Still nice and controlled.

I feel even more anger—and a desire to show off.

That hot lifter chick is back and she's staring at me! At me!

I feel the adrenaline kick in and am actually just a bit scared at how easily the weight now feels as I'd set them up for the set! They'd felt like *nothing.*

As I forced out my set—giving a guttural growl with each push— I feel electrified.

It's surreal how easy they'd gone up!

And still, out of the corner of my eyes, I saw her standing there— watching.

Then suddenly, on the final rep, one of my arms buckled—not a lot, not enough to kill myself with ninety pounds screaming down onto my face, but enough to get my attention—and I really got scared.

So I called it a set, and dropped em down alongside the bench.

Sat up.

Lifter chick was gone.

Taking another swig from my water bottle, I looked around. Looked over to the distant wall. To that space between the columns and the wall.

Nothing.

I'd gotten up off the bench, put down my water bottle, and picked up the dumbbells. As I stood, I looked up—

And there she was. Doing thirty-five-pound dumbbell laterals directly behind me.

Staring at me with her own, beautiful angry gym face . . . strands of long hair again hanging down before her.

Oh, my God, she couldn't look any hotter.

How long had she been there?

Had she seen me turning to look for her.

There's no doubt she had.

I rerack my dumbbells, spin around, and she's directly behind me, holding her dumbbells to also rerack. I nearly knocked her over.

We stare into each other's eyes.

They are as real as I remembered from my dream: dark and deep and they suck my soul into them!

And I swear her long hair is floating about her head!

I shiver.

I actually *shiver!* For some ungodly reason I'd grown suddenly quite chilled!

Cold!

But it all quickly passed.

We stand that way for what seemed an eternity.

"Excuse me," I said and stepped aside for her. But I couldn't help but continue to stare at her. She was a vision . . . and I'd been far-beyond-mesmerized by her.

After racking her dumbbells, she turned to me!

"You're pretty strong," she'd said.

Her

(you will follow me . . .)

voice—I now also love her voice. It's smoky . . . sultry. Thick and raspy . . . like one used to screaming and grunting in a gym while hefting shit-heavy weight, and I immediately wondered what she would sound like as we grunted away at each other in bed. The imagery was powerful and I'd already felt a stiffy forming. I thought of weights. Iron. Dumbbells. Got my head back into the *gym* . . . my workout.

"Thanks," I'd said.

She'd continued to stare at me.

"Ivan," I'd said, sticking out a hand.

"Kimmy," she'd said, meeting my powerful grip with her own. When I'd felt her strength I'd reacted by squeezing her hand still harder—and she'd met *that* by also gripping me harder—but when I'd gone to release, *she'd held on.*

"So nice to

(finally)

"meet you, Ivan," she'd said.

Then she released my hand.

"Do we . . . know each other?" I asked.

Her angry gym face softens in a smile. "I've seen you around."

I'd turned around to grab my water bottle, but when I'd turned back—dammit, she was gone again!

Stunned, I looked around—back to that damned area behind the columns—but she was nowhere in sight.

At this point another hot chick entered the area and I briefly (if somewhat subtly and "clinically" . . .) checked her out. Sorry, I am a guy. But I again looked back to the deserted space between the wall and the columns . . . scanned the rest of the gym . . .

Nowhere was my lifter chick to be found.

Now, what I'm going to say next may sound like total bullshit and I'm making it all up, but as she'd said to me "*so nice to meet you, Ivan*" in my head I'd actually heard and felt *her* voice. And it was her voice in my head that had added "*finally*"! to her physical words. So when she voiced the words she'd said to me, in my head I'd also heard "*So nice to* finally *meet you!*"

Finally!

Her deep, dark eyes burned into me. I felt her *inside* me.

I felt . . . incredible *emotion* exude from her. Wrap around me.

As we'd oh-so-briefly talked, her previously angry gym face morphed into a wry smile. Not a sweet, flirty one from some hot-chick-fashion-plate, but a sultry, smoky, worldly smile that had an emotional *knowing* depth to it. It's hard to explain.

(. . . one-two-three . . . you will follow me . . .)

I played her words over and over in my head . . . tried to hold onto her preternatural sexuality. The unreal sense of her *closeness*, like we somehow *knew* each other.

I glanced around the room, but I was again alone.

That night I'd again dreamed of her . . . she'd come to me . . . behind her was that Black Door. It's closed, though she'd walked out from it. She'd whispered to me, but I couldn't make out what she'd said, yet *knew* what she'd said—you know, in that weird dream way. As she stood before me . . . she giggled . . . it's not a cute, playful giggle, but . . . but more of a mischievous, *taunting* one.

A montage of images flew before me.

I'd seen a woman . . . *her* . . . beautiful and happy . . . long, beautiful tresses of dark hair . . . playing with children . . . in school. A teacher. A kindergarten teacher.

(. . . one, two . . . buckle my shoe . . .)

Then I see her look off beyond the children to a hand that had reached out to her . . . it was a dark, gnarly looking hand . . . and it had reached out to her from and through that dark door—that black door—she'd been pulled from the circle of laughing children into a heavy, dark world . . . where everything was gloomy and shadowy . . . there'd been a shadow figure—a guy—and he'd *shown* her things . . . dark things . . . things that had forever changed her life and her mindset . . . drugs . . . he'd given her drugs . . . and she'd gotten stronger . . . powerful . . . her attitude had turned joyless and dismal. She'd cut her hair: shaved it close to the sides of her head into a modified Mohawk—but had kept a long section of her thick hair into a ponytail. Added all kinds of body ink . . .

Then . . . *another* had entered her life . . . her life had grown darker still . . . there had been a bright flash and she'd left both shadow-men. She was now on the other side of that Black Door . . . I saw how her spirit had become—or had always been?—*restless* . . . how it had left that place behind the Black Door for these two men . . . then returned. It doesn't quite make sense, except in a dream sort of way, but how her spirit—which wasn't quite *her*, but *was*—was-is-and-had-been looking for someone . . . somebody—

Me?

I'd felt her spirit had been long looking for *me*, but . . . but, how was that possible? Then she . . . she'd seen someone. Again, that someone appeared to be me—but it made no sense, because it felt like she'd found me before I was even born. But she'd *seen* me. Why would it be me? Who am I to her—

(—*I am barraged with another set of parallel images*—)

(—*in them I see she and I are with each other . . . together and not together throughout histories . . . we share sexes and occupations . . . are torridly in and out of love . . . and separated . . . sinking ships . . . war-torn battlefields . . . quiet-and-not-so-quiet households and separated lives . . . affairs and marriages . . . premature and venerable deaths*—)

—but she *sees* me . . . sees me from beyond the Black Door . . . so she tried to get to me . . . but to get to me—to be here—she had to die. But she'd already been dead when she'd first *seen* me. I get lost in the whole beginning-and-ending thing . . . what was the beginning and what was the end? And who am I to her? Why *me?*

She disappeared.

But she continued to giggle and I heard her like she was still standing directly before me.

Her giggles had grown louder, when suddenly . . .

I'm awake.

(. . . *three-four . . . come through that door . . .*)

(. . . *one-two-three . . . you will follow me . . .*)

I hear these verses within my head—my ears?—and shoot a look to the end of my bed.

Someone was standing there!

It was *her! She* was standing right there!

Or at least a *silhouette* of her.

Of course I knew it was *her*—who else could it have been?

I'd whipped off the blankets and swung out of bed, as she'd continued to giggle that same, taunting laughter-titter, then sprinted

(*floated?*)

from the room.

I chased her down the hallway and into the living room—where I found my front door wide open.

She was gone!

As I stopped at the open door, I'd looked around outside, but no longer saw her . . . yet her lyrically taunting laughter-titter remained hanging in the air for just a moment longer. My body . . . my *mind . . .* was on fire. I felt all manner of hot, electrical current firing throughout me. My hands—hell, my entire *body*—quivered.

As I turned to my apartment, I saw it.

Two-three-four . . . you must go through the door
One-two-three . . . if you want to follow me . . . .

Words written across my living-room walls.

Admittedly, yes, I was spooked. Who wouldn't be?

Apartment door wide open to the world in the middle of the night (and how long had it been like that?). Unknown woman in my bedroom . . . words repeatedly scrawled across all my living-room walls—and yes, they were real. I'd cleaned them off. Not really sure what they were written in, but they kinda weirdly crumbled off the wall as I washed them with soap and water. It was beyond weird. I couldn't sleep, so I threw on some clothes and investigated my apartment . . . went outside into the night and checked around the place. Nothing, of course.

Getting tired of that word.

The rest of that day, I didn't know if it was the trauma of, well, being "violated," or whatever, but throughout the day I'd sworn I'd kept hearing that malicious giggling and kept seeing things out of the corners of my eyes. Or I'd seen flashes of figures—a woman's figure—again coming out from behind things. Lamps . . . alley dumpsters . . . parked cars. Sign posts.

Yet . . . as spooked as I was by all this . . . I had to admit that it was also an incredible turn-on.

A *ghost* was flirting with me?

I'd fantasize about getting this woman into bed with me, but it quickly seemed to go beyond mere sexual interest . . . her having her way with me . . . it seemed to reach into me in ways, well . . . each time I'd gone there, I'd heard . . . .

. . . two-three-four . . . go through the door . . .
. . . one-two-three . . . if you want to follow me . . . .
. . . two-three-four . . . through the Black Door . . . .

The next couple of days were now the weekend, and I don't work out on weekends, but I'd made it a point to stop by the gym at the time I would have hit the gym during the week. She was not there, of course, nor were "the regulars." I bought some protein and left. But the entire weekend I'd sworn I'd caught glimpses of her as I was out and about . . . and had more strange dreams . . . some of which I'd remembered and some of which I had not. But dream about her—Kimmy—I did. I'd seen her face in my mind's eye constantly. Then, on Saturday night,

I'd clearly heard *"Ivan!"* called out in the dark of my bedroom! I live alone, had no date, it was just me in the room—heck, the entire apartment—yet I'd *clearly* heard someone call out my name . . . just as I was falling asleep . . . and it was definitely a woman's raspy voice— *her* voice . . . .

I mean, really, who else—*what else*—could it be?

That Monday I had to work quite late, I'd had a flat and had to get it fixed, and all manner of things conspired against me to make it to the gym at my usual time. It closed at nine, and I wasn't able to get there until eight, but, damn it, here I am. The last of the serious lifters had just left and once again, I was alone.

(. . . *one-two-three* . . .)

(. . . *two-three-four* . . . .)

I had done my upper body workout in record time, but still she hadn't showed. As I had taken a sip of water, and turned to do shrugs—there she was.

She'd emerged from behind the columns in the exact spot I'd last seen her disappear. I'd sworn I heard distant laughter—*in my head.*

She smiled at me.

Just stood there and smiled. At *me.*

Are you going to come over? I'd heard in my head. *Are you going to*

(. . . *two-three-four* . . .)

go through the Black Door?

I'd blinked.

The room was full of lifers and their grunting and gym banter. No one was paying me any attention.

I went to her.

"Who—"

One-two-three . . . you will follow me . . .

Two-three-four . . .

She'd turned and directed my attention behind her . . . to the two-foot section of space behind the columns . . . and I no-shit saw it begin to shimmer and take on a depth I can't begin to explain . . . the noise of the gym began to deaden . . . fade . . . I could see into this shimmer and it filled with darkness . . . exploding *stars* . . .

One-two-three . . . fol-looow me . . .

Two-three-four . . . throoough the Black Door . . .

And I saw it.

The Black Door.

Come with me . . . the lifter chick said—or thought—and I looked to her. Her eyes . . . they were so damned dark . . . so *deep* . . . .

Come with me, Ivan . . . I so want you to . . . I want to be with you . . . .

I grew dizzy as I'd looked to her . . . her hair . . . long and dark—*floating?*—the look on her face, pained. She'd reached out to me and begun to back away . . . into that space behind the columns . . . .

Her eyes had pled for me to come . . . to *follow* . . .

Who are you? I asked, not knowing if I'd actually voiced my question aloud or in my head. I felt pulled . . . like a huge, incredible magnet. I *wanted* to go with her . . . but something held me back.

She continued to recede into the empty space there.

One-two-three . . . fol-looow me . . .

Two-three-four . . . throoough the Black Door . . .

I wanted her like no one ever before and I couldn't explain why. It was like our souls were connected . . . I'd felt her *pain* for me . . . it *grew* . . . I felt her *emotion* for me. I knew that she wanted me—*loved* me—and I could not for the life of me explain any of it. I didn't care if she was real or imagined . . . alive or dead—a ghost. *All I knew was that I needed to be with her* . . . but I could not seem to budge! If I was meant to go with her—through that Black Door—*then why couldn't I follow her?*

She was gone.

Her and the Black Door.

I was suddenly able to move, and I'd stumbled forward, nearly slamming into the wall before me. I'd regained my balance and casually glanced around the gym. Nobody seemed to have taken notice. I went to the space between the wall and column . . . swiped my hands through it.

Nothing.

But I knew . . . now I truly knew . . . .

Next time . . . next time I *would* follow her.

As I'd pondered what had happened, the truly weirdness of it all, it'd dawned on me: I was unable to follow because there must be some unfinished business at my end. Something I must do or find out before I could follow her. So that next day I'd swung by the gym and asked to talk to either the manager or owner. To see if they'd known anything about this woman. Her death.

I asked the guy working the desk if he knew of anything. He has an incredible memory. Always calls me out by name before I even swipe my gym card before the scanner. I figured if anyone would know something, he would. But he hadn't heard of anything—he'd only just started working there about a month ago. So he'd sent me to the manager, Jeremy.

Has anyone ever died in this gym, I'd asked?

Why'd I want to know, he asked?

I told him I'd tell him, but could we go somewhere private?

He looked at me and chuckled, then motioned us into his office. Perfect Memory Guy looked at us in surprise. I can bet he wasn't going to let this one get past him after I'd left.

So I'd told Jeremy that I'm starting to believe I'm seeing a ghost. I'd described her to him. Gave him an overview of what'd happened.

Jeremey never laughed or anything. He looked at me totally seriously and told me that yes, someone had died here.

It had been a couple of years ago, and it had been a young woman, a bodybuilder. She had been a kindergarten

(. . . *one, two . . . buckle my shoe . . .*)

teacher, but she'd left teaching to pursue bodybuilding full time.

She and her boyfriend had been working out. They'd both been well-known to the owner at the time (ownership had since changed hands, you'll see why). Both were serious bodybuilders. Both were "using," which meant they'd both been using steroids. Anyway, they always come in later at night, just before closing time. They'd liked having the gym to themselves, and many times the owner had allowed them to work out past closing time and lock up after themselves. But one day . . . as the two were working out late after the owner had left . . . the woman had died when the bar she'd been bench pressing had slipped out of the hands of her boyfriend who'd been spotting her.

It had fallen onto her chest and bounced off . . . onto her throat.

So the boyfriend had said.

Well, the long and the short of it was that it came out that the gym owner and the girl had been screwing each other for 'roids (the owner was who they'd been getting their steroids from), and the boyfriend had found out about it. Murder One. The boyfriend's lawyers had tried to get him off on temporary insanity, due to heavy steroid abuse— which has been known to modify behavior, increased anger, fits of rage, that kind of thing—but of course it fell flat. On the stand the lifter boyfriend, who was now some twenty or thirty pounds of rock-hard muscle lighter, had broken down, crying about how he'd regretted his actions as soon as he'd dropped the bar. How what he'd done to her had been so heinous and sickening. He'd described in tears and in gruesome detail at how the bar and its weight had nearly decapitated Kimmy . . . how her body had repeatedly jerked until it didn't . . . how her head hung like a limp rag doll, her tongue lolling out in some grotesque position—the gurgling sounds she'd made—and how he could never get those images out of his head—*in fact, that he'd been visited every night by her ghost in his cell.* What he hadn't known was that the gym owner had just installed cameras for total coverage of the gym. These cameras had shown that the bar had not "slipped" out of the dude's hands, no, not at all. It'd shown that he had not even given it a second thought at the time of the crime. Youth, jealousy, and steroids—a very bad combination. It had been ghastly how her head had, well— "reacted"—to the bar as it had been directly dropped onto her neck. It had never bounced off anything.

Is the bench that it happened on still in there, I asked?

Nope. Removed for evidence, then trashed.

And the lifer dude had died in prison, Jeremy told me: he'd been beaten to death at his own instigation.

Jeremy had also told me that he'd seen Kimmy's ghost on a few occasions himself. She'd scared the shit out of him. Much like my sightings (though without the emotional tension), after closing, she would just pop up behind him, or "glide" out from behind some piece of equipment and just stare at him.

She sported all her ink and her gnarly Mohawk.

So, we talked a little longer and I left, thanking him for the information.

Now I knew.

And you know what—it didn't matter! I *still* wanted her!

So . . . here I am. Back where it all started. I'm working out, and I hope and pray and wait for the room to clear out, so I can approach that dead space behind the columns again. And this time . . . this time I will go through with her. I will follow Kimmy to wherever she leads me.

I love her. I know this now. Always have. Loved her before I'd ever met her.

Can't explain it. Don't know why . . . don't know if she'd woven some weird otherworldly spell on me or what, and it just doesn't matter. But a ghost saw me, fell in love with me, and I *her*.

If you love somebody you just *love* them . . . that's it. That's *all*. You don't worry about *why* you love them, you just *do*. Forgive them their sins. And you will do anything for them . . . you will follow them . . . *anywhere* . . . .

The place finally cleared out and I hurried over to the wall. To the two feet of dead space between it and the columns. I knew the cameras were watching me and I wondered what they'd capture when it all went down . . . .

My pulse is pounding in my ears.

My body is shaking with adrenaline.

I look into the empty space . . . watch for several moments . . .

But nothing happens.

I *hate* that word.

"Kimmy . . . *Kimmy!*" I call out in hushed, needful tones. "I will go with you this time! I know all about you. *I will follow you!*" I say, walking sideways into the space.

But, still . . . nothing!

My heart is breaking.

I turn away.

Had I imagined it all?

Lifters begin to file back into the room. I walk back over to my bench and water bottle.

No, that's impossible . . . the story . . . her *death* . . . it's all true. How could I ha—

Ivan . . . .

I turn back around and I see her float out from behind the column. But by now, there are many in the weight room. Her eyes . . . they are intense and emotional. Tears fill them. I can *feel* them. She has no ink and no Mohawk. Just her long, lovely tresses.

Do they see her? See me?

I don't care.

If what I think is about to happen happens it won't matter, and it'll be more fuel to the whole ghost lore about the gym.

One . . . two . . . three . . . you will follow me? she asks.

Two . . . three . . . four . . . yes and oh, oh, so much more! I return.

Through the Black Door?

Now I know more, and yes, through the Black Door! I respond.

We look to each other . . . and she extends her hand.

I take it.

We finally touch!

At first it is cold, very, very, unnervingly cold . . . but soon I forget that coldness. I forget everything. All I want is her. All I know is . . . *her.*

With her touch, oh, so much *more* is made clear to me.

I know what happened. How she . . . "found" me . . . .

After she had been murdered, she'd haunted her boyfriend and driven him crazy to the point that he no longer wanted to live. But she had so loved working out with weights and the gym and its culture that she couldn't leave it. It called out to her and she, it . . . so she periodically returned to be there, to . . . work out . . . be around lifters . . . .

Then she saw me.

Fell in love with me.

But she was dead and I wasn't.

So she sought out my soul . . . visited other versions of me across other lifetimes. Wanted all of what was me . . . the different me's. Inserted her soul into all these other lives of mine, some with positive and some with not-so-positive outcomes. And that was what she'd done with this life: she's inserted her soul into this life to get to me . . . became physical though birth . . . lived her physical life in this timeline with the *intent* to find me . . . but something had gone dreadfully wrong and she'd gotten sidetracked in this life by the guy she'd met, the drugs they'd taken . . . the life they'd lived, and the incredible frustration she'd been living caused her to bring about the end to her life. I see that we *would* have met in the gym—it was meant to be—but she had become so changed from the sweet woman she'd been that she didn't want me to see her—have her—like that . . . so *she'd* brought about the end of her life so she could start over . . . .

What is the beginning and what is the end?

I don't care.

Don't know that I truly understand it all . . . or why the other guy had to die . . . but I am going to her now. I am going to follow her through that Black Door, or whatever it really is. I need to be with her, and I *will* be with her. I've never wanted to so be with anyone like Kimmy before.

What does it all mean? What will happen to me to get to her?

I don't know.

I guess I shall soon find the answers to all these questions.

My hand in hers . . . we look to each other, and she . . . oh, my *God*, she melts my heart, but she finally—*finally*—smiles. And it is *the most real, most magnificent smile I have even seen.*

Together

. . . *two-three-four* . . .

we step through the Black Door . . . .

A Beautiful Summer's Afternoon
2016

I clear my throat.
Listen to the creak of the rope as I rock back and forth in my swing.
Focus on it.
What a *glorious* day!
Magpies call.
It's quiet here.
Hot.
I'm alone.
I like it.
I swing back and forth . . . listening to the strain of my support upon the rope.

It's a fantastical August day, sweltering and bright. The light . . . the late afternoon light is *incredible* . . . but . . . it possesses a hard-to-define, extraordinary quality. Glaring . . . almost . . . I don't know . . . metallic? It's so bright and radiant . . . *unrelenting* . . . beams into my *soul*
. . . .

(*I look to the* . . .)
Not a cloud. Not a cloud in the sky.
(*I'm outside amid*)
fields and distant woods. I'm so relaxed I have to remind myself of

(*things that I've* . . .)
I'm a blacksmith, a man of iron and heat. But I'm here and now visiting and being visited by family and friends I have not seen
(*in a very long time*)
How nice of them to all stop by. I feel strangely moved. My Aunt

Mae

(*thunderous laughter*)

(*large, powerful*)

(*hugging me*)

had just left. We had a good, long talk. Always liked her. She is a mighty woman—muscular arms—but I'd left her and the rest of my family

(*years ago*)

to strike it out on my own. I'd found work in Wichita. It was nice talking with her. Hadn't heard from her in

(*ages*)

The heat is a wall-of-hot that bakes everything. It's ... somehow ... a different kind of "heat" ... but it still bakes ... the trees, the air, the dirt road before me. My skin ... feels tight and desiccated within its unholy swelter.

I listen to the rustle of leaves from the trees around me. They calm me.

I smell the earth ... the dirt ... and it smells fresh, clean. I've always loved the smell of dirt. I kick my feet at it, but miss ... I look down

(*up*)

The *sun!* Oh, my God, that *radiance!*

My Lord, it's confoundedly *dazzling!*

It pounds down upon me. Bright ... oh-so-bright and oh-so-persistent. I look up, but can barely see through squinty eyes. My eyes feel puffy, as if there's much dirt and grit in them. My arms and hands, stiff.

Oh, but it feels so peaceful here!

Still.

The warmth. I really like the warmth and queerly crave it.

I again clear my throat, which succumbs to the dirt and grit of this blistering day.

I continue to swing ... slowly rocking back and forth as I stare out before me into the fields and woods beyond. The motion soothes me. Emotionally chokes me, and I know not why! I want to cry, but I'm not the crying type—

I feel ... I feel as though a large weight ... some massive

(*emotional*)

burden ... has been lifted from me—

Oh, have I mentioned how the warmth feels so *good?*

As a kid, I'd always loved the motion of swings ... of rocking back and forth, especially with my eyes

(*closed*)

And there was also just something else about it I could never quite put my finger on . . . but I *loved* it. The swing always seemed to transport me to someplace I could never quite describe . . . .

Then I grew up, and though I'd only done it a few more times in the presence of a few darlings I'd been courting, I'd never much done it again. Instead I came to

(*swinging*)

a four-pound hammer onto an iron anvil before a roaring forge.

And now I

(*swing*)

here lazily in the afternoon brilliance, amazed at my heretofore unknown eloquence. *Me.*

In the distance, I spot a coyote. It spritely follows the tree line of the woods it had just

(*departed*)

for a few yards, before again ducking back into those same woods. Revisiting what it had left.

Again, the magpies call.

Again I clear my throat and smile.

When had I last done this, kicking back and taking it easy? No one after you . . . no one wanting anything *from* you—

No incessant clanging from my hammer and anvil. Just me and the day. True, it's a blistering, sweltering day . . . but rocking back and forth creates a light . . . barely existent . . .

(*breeze*)

I twist and look to the open fields and trees. That dirt road before me. They look somehow different to me. The road is where my aunt had come from and to which she'd sallied. It was nice of her to stop by.

I think to myself that did I not so enjoy the heat so much, I could feel like I'm roasting on a spit. Even that be as it may . . . I feel a sudden

(*chill*)

course through me . . . and shudder.

Yes . . . the heat . . . I like it very much.

The light from above . . . .

A lone traveler approaches. We look to each other. Say nothing. The stranger reigns his horse past and continues on. I watch him go.

They all go on. No one stops. Except for my aunt. Those I know. They all have somewhere to be and I don't have any water for them.

I could use some water, myself, though. Throat's dry.

I lift my face back into the sun as I rock and playfully

(*twist*)

my swing back and forth.

I close my eyes. They feel so gritty. Swollen.

I mean . . . the sun

(*the light* . . .)

it's like . . . I feel like I've been through a lot—I *have*—and it just feels so good to do

(*I've done* enough . . .)

nothing.

I inhale deeply—and suddenly launch into a coughing fit . . . throat's all choked up. Again with the dust. That breeze kicks back up

(*kissing*)

the leaves . . . and my attention is

(*drawn*)

to the treetops . . . I see birds flying off after something, some are really high-up in that deep, pure blue sky. Circling. Father-in-Heaven, the most brilliant blue I have *ever* seen! It's like there are blues *within* the blues! Shades of radiance I cannot even begin to describe!

I wish I was there. Flying away. With the birds.

I continue to cough. It's giving me a damned headache, now, the coughing. Or maybe it's the merciless glare. Wish I had some water . . . but the coughing fit passes soon enough.

The creak of the rope . . . hope it doesn't break . . . not sure how long it's been . . . out here . . . in the summer sun . . . .

That was interesting.

I just had a conversation with an old friend—Harlan Valcour!

(*fights*)

(*shootouts*)

(*arrests*)

He used to be sheriff over Dodge way. Hadn't heard from him in years. He comes riding down that road and pulled up for a spell, his horse

(*where's mine?*)

grazing nearby. Told Harlan thought he'd been

(*shadows . . . running . . . hiding . . .*)

dead . . . shot

(*gunshots . . .*)

in an ambush or something . . . but he just laughed that hearty laugh of his and bellowed, *Well, I'm still around!* Slapped me on my back. Caught me up to speed on what he'd been doing since we last met. Sounded like he'd had it hard over there in Dodge. Sheriff. Not a job

. . . not a job I'd—

He offered me some water. That was mighty kind of him. Told him so. I look to the light above. Asked where he was headed. He said just up a ways. Had some business to attend to. Said he'd never expected to run into me like this. I look back to him, said, the good Lord—*the good Lord willing*—we'll be meeting up again soon enough! To that he again slapped me on my back . . . offered me more water . . . then got back up on his horse and

Gone.

Had he ever actually been here?

Don't know why I'd even wonder that.

Is the heat getting to me?

And where the hell *is* my horse?

Musta dozed off.

It's hard to open my eyes . . . I don't even really want to . . . just feeling the heat of the sun upon my face is so comfort—

Then why do I feel so cold all of a sudden?

I leave my eyes closed and again angle them up into the August sun. After all, I won't be here forev—

"Hello, Hezekiah."

I snap open my eyes.

Isa

(belle?)

"*Isabelle?*" I say, "*is that really you?*"

Something about her looks . . . different.

I feel an intense

(squeezing)

(crushing)

(clutching)

yank!

It's hard to breathe.

Strange sounds come out of me.

My entire body shakes . . . violently *quakes*.

Feel jerked in opposite directions of conflicting emotion—

"Hello, Hezekiah," she again says. She sits upon her horse. Reigns still in-hand, her hands resting upon her saddle horn. Stares solemnly at me with those big, brown eyes. Oh, how deep their passion is! "*How are you?*" she asks softly.

"I-I'm fine," I say, my words all choked up in my throat, every last letter clawing its way out, "How are *you?*"

"Ran into the sheriff. Told me you were here."

"That was nice of him. He's a good man."

"He is."

"What are you doing out this way?" I ask, "It feels like . . . like it's been some time since we'd last—"

"Long enough."

My chest clenches. Isabelle. *How could I have . . . .*

"I just wanted to come by and tell you," she said, pausing—I see tears raining down her cheeks—"and tell you . . . tell you I'm sorry. So, so *very* sorry—"

"For what?" I ask. "Would you like to come up here and sit a spell?"

She ignores my invitation. Isabelle. We'd been calling on each other . . . but . . . are no longer. Can't remem—

Isabelle looks away . . . back to me.

Something's wrong . . . with her neck. It

(tongue)

(hanging out)

(grimace)

(shouts and struggle)

doesn't look right.

"Are you all right, Isabelle? Did you . . . hurt yourself?"

At that more tears erupt from her. She wipes then away.

"I'm fine."

She looks to me. Long and hard. I stare back and feel the emotion rushing back at me like an enormous, angry mountain.

"Isabe—"

"I just wanted to stop by and apologize. It's about all I can do, now. I had a great affection for you, Hezekiah, but I just didn't love you." Her voice is soft . . . even.

She looks down . . . pulls her horse away . . . gets back onto the dirt road.

"*Isabelle!*" I say, shouting after her, "*don't go! Wait!*"

I'm looking at her back as she meanders away.

"A 'great affection'? Wha—"

I twist in my swing, clutching at air, and clear my throat . . . which really hurts now. I can barely breathe—

Isabelle!

Stop!

Why would she stop by to apologize—and for what?—*that she didn't love me?*

And

(more importantly)

why am I not going after her?
I suddenly don't feel very well. Not well at all. Feel strange.
Something . . . *something isn't right . . .*
Isabelle's gone.
I settle back into my swing.
And her neck . . . what was wrong with her—
My neck suddenly *really* hurts. I try to loosen it up some, but the pain . . . the pain quickly
(*pop!*)
escalates—
I close my eyes and try to will away the pain . . . which, surprisingly
. . .

Abates.

More people pass by on the road before me, but I don't care.
Don't even look up.
What is wrong with me?
Why didn't I go after Isabelle? How could I let her go? She comes by to apologize, to tell me she has no love for me—only a "great affection"—then leaves?
This damned swing. It's not like I'm attached to i—
And what was wrong with her beautiful neck, her delicate throat? It didn't look right. It looked damaged . . . misshapen . . .
Twisted.
Whoever did that to her, I will find him *and I will kill him!*
To have attacked so exquisite a woman! To have *deformed* such stunning features!
I will find whoever had done that to her, and I'll . . . I'll . . . .
Wiggle my toes.
Wiggle my toes?
Where are my boots?
My *boots!*
I again wiggle my toes. Just socks, no boots. That's odd. I look around, but see no boots.
Why would I be hanging out on a swing without boots? No *horse?*
Something is not right!
I clear my throat . . . but find it hard to
(*Isa . . .*)
belle.
Isa—
No socks.
No horse.

No water.
No *Isabelle.*
I'd
(*in a room*)
found her
(*in the arms of . . .*)
Strangled her
(*snapped her . . .*)
Killed her
(*loved her*)
Cried over her
(*she lays silent*)
Body most lovely
(*neck . . . crooked . . .*)
Didn't move
(*contorted*)
I was caught
(*I loved her!*)
Quickly tried
(*she was buried*)
I
(*yank!*)
(*pop!*)
Twist lazily at the end of a strained and creaking rope.
Beneath the unrelenting, sweltering August sun.
Arms bound . . . boots gone.
Leaves on the branches above me flutter in the breeze. My eyes
had been
(*picked . . . picked . . . picked . . .*)
picked out by magpies. On my unbooted feet, one sock hung lower
on my left foot than my right. Hadn't realized I'd had a hole in that
one.
Isabelle . . .
We'd laughed . . . we'd danced . . . we'd made—well . . . she'd told
me she'd had *a great affection* for me. Worked in her pa's shop. I know
her pa, done some shoe work for his horses. Hinges for a broken door.
(*Isabelle*)
Had been so full of life and energy! Those large, bottomless brown
eyes! That beacon of a smile! Friendly! Friendly to *everyone . . .*
Hotel owner. Carlson. Jeremiah Carlson. Money. Big money.
Means. Didn't get his hands dirty . . . calloused . . . burned . . . like
mine.

Isa

Him!

belle.

It only took one punch to his head.

She however . . . I'd grabbed her . . . grabbed her by her sweet, delicate throat. Tears in my eyes as I'd held her. Didn't know what I was doing . . . before I knew it . . . she lays silently on the hotel bed, neck all twisted and out of place. Her beautiful face a forever-locked grimace of pain. Her tongue . . . not where it should be.

I'd killed her I'd loved her I'd cried over her.

Couldn't deny her wanting better for herself.

I wasn't the man for her.

Didn't fight the law. The town. Nothing to live for.

And Harlan . . . had been ambushed. In Great Bend. Seven shooters.

My aunt . . . dysentery. Ten years ago.

So, here I swing . . . swing and twist . . . from the end of a desiccated, creaking rope . . .

And enjoy the last of a beautiful summer's afternoon.

Rewrite

2016

Do you love me?
Yes, there were the affairs.
Do you?
The shame.
I can't live without you.
The disintegration.
How could something that had been so right . . . so beautiful . . . turn so hideous, so . . . obscene?
Whose fault was it?
Does it matter?
There are no coincidences.

I was a writer. A literary author, if you must know the truth. Authors are published. Writers aren't necessarily. I wrote and got paid for it. Rather well, for one in my capacity. But I didn't want to be like most of my peers, writing about affairs and incest and abuses of substances or the body. I wanted to write about the metaphysics of life. Its philosophy. Things Humanity overwhelmingly thirsted for. Things we could get some use out of . . . provide application to our daily lives to make them better on a far more expansive scale, thereby improving Humanity's Collective. Writing about one's body ink ("tattoo" was far too vulgar a term for my employment) or the evil that men and women do does not advance the race one bit. Sure, it might be cathartic to the author, stir emotions in the reader, and make both rail against the injustices in the world . . . but how did it *fix* anything?
Yes. I wanted to fix Humanity.

So I wrote about hard questions and troubled people. Those looking for something more. Asking and *finding* answers greater than themselves that transcended societal constraints, identified synchronicities, and exposed philosophical singularities. Wrote of examinations of the soul and how we can all apply our newfound epiphanies. As a public figure I also attended conferences, spoke at luncheons and banquets. University graduations. Received thunderous applause. Bookers, Faulkners, a Pulitzer. That kind of thing. I say this with no measure of pride. It just was. It was my life.

I'd grown up in a well-to-do family, both parents well-regarded Princeton professors. I attended Princeton and did not disappoint. It seemed writing was what I was born to do. I was born to arrange words and profoundly manipulate their order . . . able to peer into the hearts and souls of Humanity. Mainly, it seems, to those of the long locks and graceful curves (and I did have quite the thing for the ladies) . . . men, it appeared, were not interested in my words. At least, not straight men. And those were the ones who most sorely needed my words.

I received my doctorate in English, Literary Theory. Conducted writing retreats that quickly became boring. Won many awards that really meant nothing, when you got right down to the writing. The writing stands on its own. It must. To write with honors in mind is to wax mendacious. I cared not for awards. I cared for words. I cared for *people*.

Like most of the women I met, I met my wife, Emelia, at a literary conference. She was of the aforementioned long locks and graceful curves. Long, dark hair and eyes . . . eyes that questioned God. She, I'd noticed, had always hung back from the crowds that had gathered around me asking about my sources of inspiration . . . my deepest, darkest secrets . . . and whether or not what I'd written had actually happened to me. Many would reach out and touch me, "casually" brush past, while making intended contact. I'm sure they also tried to inhale my scent. But she . . . this Emelia . . . would always hang back behind the others who kept trying to get closer and closer . . . *she* . . . kept her distance.

Observed.

I should have paid this greater regard.

We finally met at the conference's banquet, and my "thing" for other women evaporated. She'd lingered around the table where I sat, one with my name embarrassingly emblazoned upon a tall placard. I invited her to sit in a chair I had secretly "saved" just for her—tipping the chair forward into the table—hoping to again see her. I was incredibly taken by her. Mysteriously so. With some hesitation, she took my offer. We were in bed that night.

We

Do you love me?

married a year later.

I loved her . . . loved her pain. She was a struggling artist who worked at an art gallery and had read all my work. My work was similar to what she was trying to do with her oils and acrylics. She had a sullen, brooding way about her that belied her desired optimism in Humanity.

Desired.

I deeply loved her.

As our lives progressed, I got more successful, while her artwork languished. But she was good at managing other people's work . . . running an art gallery . . . and perhaps out of some measure of self-pity took the promotions until she was running the gallery when the owner unexpectedly passed.

We talked about it . . . how it would affect her work . . . but she'd already taken it. The position. She wanted more and was tired of being left behind. Tired of being . . .

In my shadow.

Her new position had taken up more and more of her time to the point where she no longer painted. This seemed a more distressing time for me than her. She seemed to fill her days with meetings and luncheons and showings. She'd finally "made it." On her own.

I couldn't tell if she was happy . . . or just occupied.

My schedule grew even busier, and I traveled even more. More speaking engagements, more book tours, and now, film deals—which I fought, though my agent said it was just another way to get my words out there. She said couples go to these films. *Couples.* That means guys. Straight guys . . . those who would otherwise never have been exposed to my work. Here was a way to get my message out to an entirely unexplored audience, whether or not they mentally rolled their eyes . . . consciously or subconsciously they would be receiving my profoundly manipulated words.

So I did them. The film deals.

As I grew busier, my wife also grew busier . . . and that's when we began to

Do you love me?

grow apart. Even when we were together, we weren't . . . she on her tablet or cell and I on mine. We were both providing our attention to others, not to those whom we were with. The irony of it all was that we'd both given into these contraptions to get us out from behind our respective businesses

Do you . . .

to spend more time with each other. I remember one day in particular. I was in contact with my agent, awaiting a response to my next book deal. It was to be my most principal arrangement to date . . . Emelia and I were sitting in the living room . . . a fire burning softly . . . the lights low. She was uncharacteristically not on her tablet. Just staring into the fire, arms comfortably crossed. Quiet. As I attended to another, I heard

"Do you love me?"

I chuckled. "Of *course* I do!" I said, looking up and casting her an immense, tender smile.

I returned to my agent.

"You're not growing bored with us? Me?"

I again chuckled as my tablet dinged with the e-mail I had been waiting for and the request for yet more attention.

"Of course not!" I said, amused, as I got to my feet. "I have to take this!" I said to my wife, as I left her sitting alone in our low-lit living room . . . a romantic fire crackling and sending my shadow across her seated form . . . .

From that point on we rarely seemed to see each other. We'd become more like roommates. We were polite enough, superficially cheerful even. But one or the other of us would be too tired for intimacy . . . or the other had something more pressing to do that would inexplicably materialize and need to be done just then. Someone *else* needed something. There was always . . . something . . . *else* . . . .

Like energy attracts like energy.

I had my ever-growing conference circuit to attend to. Banquets and book tours. Speaking engagements. Emelia had her gallery showings, her wining and dining of artists and "their people."

Then, one day, while at another writers' conference, I'd received an e-mail from an unknown admirer to my business number. Attached were photos of my wife. Her mouth and hands attached to another.

I excused myself from my table and went outside.

Somehow . . . somehow . . .

Do you love me?

Are you bored with me?

. . . I found myself in my hotel room's shower with a statuesque woman whose name was "Juliette" or something similarly tragic.

There are no coincidences.

I allowed Juliette her exit . . . and spent the entirety of the evening sobbing.

I spiraled down from there. Sometimes it's so much easier to take the wrong path. To feel sorry for oneself. I'd become everything I'd loathed in others . . . in other's *books*. I'd become that novel that everyone loved to read. Loved to hate. That story that fixed *nothing*.

And I couldn't stop myself.

I found there were no shortages of women who wanted to "listen" . . . to . . . "ease my pain."

How could I fix Humanity . . . if I couldn't fix myself?

And my wife said nothing. Became more withdrawn. We rarely spoke. Our lives had become clinical. Separate. There were times I'd be awakened in the middle of the night by moaning . . . groaning . . . in one of our bathrooms . . . followed by sobbing. And it was during one of those nights that I'd had enough. I had decided to change the course of my story-that-fixed-nothing . . . to change the course of our *lives*.

I went to my wife. Found her upon the floor, cradling the toilet and puking up her soul. It seems she was more expressive of her love for me in private.

I begged forgiveness.

Begged to confess all of my sins . . . to come clean—but she would have nothing of it. *She*, in turn, begged for *mine* . . . just wanted us to start over. To be like we *were*. How things *had been*. When we'd been in love.

Once.

Could we—

Do you . . .

love each other again?

I told her I'd never stopped loving her. I had just become . . . absent.

We both had.

We spent the rest of the night in each other's arms.

Not long afterward, I was at another engagement, the Keynote Speaker, in fact, when I got the call.

I had just begun my address when I'd suddenly clenched up inside . . . all my words had seized in my throat, as if a part of my soul had been ripped away.

I couldn't breathe.

Holding a hand up before myself and my audience, I uncomfortably laughed it off . . . paused . . . took a sip of water . . . found a way to

Do you love me?

continue.

There's been an accident
Do you . . .
the voice had said. I collapsed.

It seems my wife . . . the woman I loved . . . the love of my life with whom I'd reconnected . . . had been at a restaurant. They'd all been outside. A car had veered out of the way to avoid hitting another that had run a red light . . . and

The rest was lost on me.

Emelia had come to me that first night.

She'd stood before my bed. Looked at me. Just stared at me as she always did. I looked back to her. I cried. Reached out.

I love you, but the dead cannot return, she said.

I miss you! I cried. *I can't live without you!*

I love you, but the dead cannot return, she again said. *We can dream . . . but we cannot return . . . .*

And she was gone.

I'd cut off all contact with everyone—my agent, publisher. Family and friends. Women called . . . came to my door . . . to comfort me. I sent them all away.

I'd once written a story about a woman who'd died in a car crash. The crash was from a car that had veered out of the way from another . . . and struck this woman, this fictional character I had created.

For inspiration I'd written it from the point of view as if I'd lost *my* love. I'd poured all that I thought (at the time) was my heart and soul into *what it would have been like* . . . .

I . . . knew . . . *nothing*.

I reread it. Cried. Reread it again. I went to my living-room fireplace and started a fire.

Stared into the fire.

Had I killed her?

Had my *words? My metaphysics?* Had they wielded that much power? It was but one short story of many.

Coincidence.

But my entire life's work was about the *lack* of coincidence in life. How all of life had meaning. *Nothing* was to be so inconsequentially branded and dismissed as "mere coincidence." I'd written about lives like these. How my characters had gone on to recreate *new* lives in the various faces-of-loss . . . .

But my wife was gone.

Forever.

The love of my life.

The woman with whom I'd sinned against . . . but who had taken me back.

The only hand I'd forever hoped to hold as we grew old together. She was not some fictional character in a novel.

"Do you love me?"
"Of course I do!"
"You're not growing bored with us? Me?"
"Of course not!"

My books . . . my words . . . meant *nothing*.
Only Emelia had meant anything. Everything.
And she was gone.
I brought out the story.
Crumpled it.
Uncrumpled it.
Began to tear it into pieces . . . when I stopped.
No. There *are* no coincidences.
I *believe* this.

I rewrote the story.
I rewrote our *lives*.
Top to bottom. Beginning to end. With what I now know. I slept and relived all that our lives had been . . . and what it'd meant to me.

Was *supposed to have meant* to us.

I created a new beginning. A new end. A chance to start over.

As I slept, I again dreamt of Emelia. Of those pictures sent to me of her and that man. Only in the dream, the pictures had come to life. Emelia and the man were sitting there . . . in the restaurant. Casual. Peers in the art community having a few drinks. A few laughs. Joking around with others in their party. Until they kissed. Long. Lingering. Hands everywhere. The rest of their coalition departed.

When they were done, she'd come to her feet and the man left. Simply left.

She turned to me.

But . . . I brought us back together. Why are you showing me this? I asked.

I'm not showing you anything. This is what you imagined. It never happened that way, but it's what you imagined had.

I love you. I need us to be together again!

We cannot.

Come back to me!

I love you . . . but the dead cannot return.

I awoke and went back to my story. I rewrote it again over the course of several days. *Willed* it into existence. When I slept . . . I dreamt about it. About her. She always appeared.

You know what she said.

So I rewrote it one more time . . . then ventured out into the world I had forsaken. I would make my story work. *I would compel it into existence.* Live my own words and their new, most profound order. I obtained what I needed. I needed something that left no room for error. Something that would perform even if I couldn't. Wasn't totally up to the task. On the mark.

I wanted results.

I lay in our bed, in the dark. Crying. I'd lost her. Forever. Lost myself. There was nothing left. Nothing more to do. I couldn't live without her. I grasped the weapon . . . regripping it several times as if I knew what I was doing . . . and brought it out from under the blankets and comforter.

Comforter.

I smoothed out the bedding with my hands . . . remembering all the warmth and comfort it had afforded us over our brief history together. I looked over to her side of the bed and remembered the feel of her nakedness beneath the bedding as she'd snuggled up beside me. How we'd held each other.

Once.

How she used to be there.

Choking sobs erupted from me! Uncontrollable torrents of rain and pain!

Oh, how I heaved!

I wiped away the tears with the back of the hand holding the .45. I closed my eyes and rammed the muzzle firmly up and under my chin, ever-so-slightly angled. The metal felt wrong, but in its wrongness felt . . .

Acceptable.

I undid the safety. Cocked the hammer.

Could I really do this? What would it feel like to so instantly conclude a life? Would there be pain—or would it happen so fast as to feel like falling off to sleep? What was the other side really like? Was my life's work on the mark . . . or was I to be damned like all the traditionalists ranted?

I would soon know.

I placed my index finger around the trigger . . . when I heard . . .

In the hallway.

Someone was out there.

I opened my eyes.

Footsteps.

I heard them. Soft. Considerate. Mindful.

Hers.

In those slipper-socks she always wore.

Is that something I would really hear?

Do you love me?

I love you . . . but the dead cannot return.

She came closer. Entered the room. *I could feel her . . . feel her presence!*

Her!

She got into bed with me . . . the bedding lifted, the bed shifted . . . her body slipped in beneath the sheets. Snuggled up against me.

I was again moved to tears! I couldn't stop crying! I wailed!

Then her hand . . . oh, dear God, her soft, warm

(*it was not warm*)

loving *hand* touched mine! Wrapped itself around mine . . .

And together we pulled the trigger.

Dinner at Luigi's
2016

Mike Granger stared out the window into the wintry night as his wife, Stephanie, drove him through the dark, nearly deserted city streets. She was talking a mile-a-minute about how excited she was about it being his birthday and that they were going to Luigi's. As much as they loved the place, they only managed to go once a year. But she was talking up a blue streak about their lasagna . . . ambiance . . . the romantic coziness that *was* Luigi's . . . how she so loved him and their wonderful life together . . . .

But all Mike could think about was how she'd walked in on him as he'd had his finger wrapped around the trigger to the .38 he'd held loosely in his lap, hidden from view.

"All the times we've been here," Stephanie said absentmindedly, as she wove throughout the dark streets, "and you'd think we could remember the way there!" She looked for any vaguely recognizable landmark she could pull out of the dark recesses of her memory,

She smiled a huge, open smile as she looked briefly to Mike.

Mike returned a brief smile to her. Looked back out the window; down to his hand. To that index finger that had . . . minutes ago . . . been poised for a little hefty finger pointing.

"*Aren't you excited?*" Stephanie asked, still searching for the turn.

"I am," Mike replied. "I'm just

(. . . always . . .)

"tired."

For the past couple of years Mike had not been able to sleep well—if at all. He'd constantly awoken only a couple hours into sleep, had great difficulty getting back to sleep, and recently their eighteen-year-old cat had taken to howling in the middle of the night. And not that oh-so-cute little meow, but a guttural, throaty, I'm-a-lost-soul-and-where-the-hell-*is*-everybody *yooow*-ling that woke the dead and kept people like Mike on the path *to* death.

And there was the stagnation of his work.

Mike was a writer—not a journalist, but a *fiction* writer—and he just wasn't cutting it. These days everyone seemed to be getting goddamned published—

Except for him.

He'd been a well-paid technical writer for twenty-two years when his company had been bought out, benefits slashed, and a nasty round of "right sizing" rippled throughout their ranks. He'd been spared because he'd been the department's editor—a really good editor, but more importantly the *only* editor. As the more expensive writers had been "right sized" out of the company, cheaper, entry level writers had been brought in, and his workload skyrocketed as a result. In fact, when he'd gotten home on one particularly late night, his wife had dejectedly remarked about how (lately) she'd always gotten the worst part of him.

But he'd seen the writing on the wall, pardon the pun, been in the department meetings. Heard the tone from the corporate bean counters. Knew the red pen was coming, and it was coming for him.

So when he had an agent interested in his second novel (no one was ever going to see his first one), and when that same agent had been all excited about a couple of houses she was going to shop his manuscript around to . . . and how *sure* she was that one—*surely two!*—would want it, Mike did some serious personal reassessment. He had over twenty years of 401K and savings, his wife, a Human Resources rep, made a great salary, they could easily tide themselves over for a couple years while his novels gained traction in the world. *And* he'd be far happier than he'd been of late at his corporate day job, which had turned into a day *and* night job.

Anyway . . . that had been the plan.

What reality had hit them both with was that he'd developed an ever-growing occasion of depression and a case of serious restless leg syndrome, a little-known disease for which thankfully there was medication, but those miraculous little medications didn't seem to quite be doing the trick a year or two later.

Then there was his snoring.

And the howling cat.

Insomnia.

Depression.

Several family members had had instances of RLS . . . and one distant relative had had dementia . . . but none of his immediate family had ever had a case of depression . . . at least no one had *talked* about having had it. But once his novel had been rejected by the one house his agent had thought *surely* (goddammit!) would have taken it . . . then had again been summarily kicked to the curb by the second choice . . . with the tertiary house also and quickly following suit . . . well, something had just clicked inside Mike's head one day, and he'd spiraled down into a dark . . . very dark . . . place and never quite returned. And no matter what he'd told Stephanie, it had never really left him. Sure, he had good days . . . but the darkness was always there . . . hovering . . . stewing . . . waiting, it surely seemed . . . for the most inopportune time to manifest. Yes, his depression had become an entire entity unto itself, and it had taken total control of him.

And forget about *its* medication.

The meds took him to places and turned him into even less of a person than he used to be with what the *depression* had made of him. Suicide was always on his mind . . . and the many ways in which to enact said suicide.

So, no . . . he stopped the prescriptions and just decided to muscle through it. On the Good Days he just had to keep moving, but on the Really Bad Days, he'd lie to Stephanie and say he'd had migraines and stay in bed all day in darkness.

Then throw in a case of a short-circuiting nervous system and a howling cat in the middle of every fucking night, and you surely had a recipe for going out of your mind.

Fast-forward to seventy-three minutes ago.

Today had been a Really Bad Day, and on this day he'd finally decided to put everyone out of his misery. Mike had been simmering-on-high at the nexus of a critical mass of a string of particularly bad nights' sleep (maybe one hour of actual shut-eye a night), the unrelenting and multiple instances of howling from their demon cat, and the final blow being the yet-one-more (final)-e-mail from his agent clinically informing him that she was dropping his ass, because, well, they no longer had anything to offer each other, *but, hey, no hard feelings!*—this isn't about *you*, it's about the *market*—we're just no longer *a good fit* for each other . . . .

Well . . .

Gun in hand . . . finger fits juuust fine . . . .

The gun had felt so . . . *dense* . . . that was what had surprised him most. There was a difference between "heavy" and "dense"—and it was that density that weighed the most upon him.

Rejected.
We're just not a good fit . . . good luck with yourself.
It's not about you . . . it's about
(*the market*)
YOU!

The car came to a stop, pulling
(. . . *the trigger* . . .)
Mike out of his reverie. He heard the nonexistent gunshot go off in his head just as Stephanie pulled the car into a corner slot. There were three other cars already here. One couple stood before the restaurant's entrance, two other couples (one with a small child all bundled up in a woman's arms) stood a little ways down alongside the building. The remaining couple waited in their parked car.

Stephanie was still excited and still talking a mile-a-minute.

Mike flexed his trigger finger. Still in working order. Good. Come bed time . . . there it would still be, waiting for him . . . in the bottom right
(*draw, mister!*)
drawer.
He wasn't supposed to be here . . . .

"It's not even open yet!" Stephanie gleefully exclaimed, checking the time. "We're one of the first here . . . be among the first ones to get in . . . and it's *Luigi's!* Hopefully we can get that table right in front of the fireplace!"

She was out of the car before
(*where was he?*)
he could blink. She was already chatting up the couple at the entrance.

They loved Luigi's, loved their lasagna, and it was a hard decision to pass up being one of the first people in, when this place—which never took reservations—was harder than Fort Knox to get into. In fact, he was surprised more were not already lined up for the door. But as conflicted as he was . . . as dark as the core of his soul was ever-growing . . . he just couldn't quite bring himself to *not* go in.

He felt . . .
(*draw!*)
drawn there. Like . . . something . . . was pulling him inside.
Was he really up for one long, awkward birthday dinner in a romantic setting, just for one final taste of lasagna?

He forced a smile onto his face just to see if he could do it.
Yes . . . yes, he could . . . .

He undid his seat belt.

Exited the car.

Stephanie and Mike were seated directly before the singular fireplace in the dimly lit interior of Luigi's. He could barely believe their luck. They'd been the second party in . . . he hadn't expected that, either, what with the others who'd been there before them, but as they waited outside, they were on the open side of the door when it opened, which blocked off the rest of the crowd lined up along the building, so they just filed in. No one was in any hurry to get in.

The lights were low, candles were glowing at each table, and the fireplace was comfortably roaring. It was a gas fireplace, but looked real enough, with the fake logs and embers. All of the others who'd been outside waiting had been seated around them, in the alcove within which sat the fireplace. He thought it funny how they all seemed crammed into this one little area, when there was the rest of the restaurant to be filled, as small as it was. But ambience attracts people . . . .

Luigi's had been around almost sixty years, and it's charm was no match for any other "local" restaurant. Used wine bottles hung from every available spot along the walls, all signed and dated . . . 1959 . . . 1972 . . . 2016. The interior décor was dark and cozy, oozing the distant environs of Italy, and the checkered tablecloths (and they were table*cloths*) homey and inviting. The music . . . soft . . . romantic . . .

And we hadn't even gotten to the *food.*

Luigi's was known not only for their lasagna, but for, well, everything they plated.

Locals didn't give out their secret willingly nor freely. No one wanted anyone else—let alone out-of-towners—to take up valuable table space. It was already packed with locals during the week; they didn't need any more bodies clogging things up.

Stephanie was still talking a mile a minute, which Mike found cute in a distant and detached part of his mind. He smiled a couple times . . . nodded . . . but he really had no idea what she'd been talking about all this time—just that she was so obviously excited for him and his birthday. Everywhere around them were muted and not-so-muted conversations.

"So, what do you think, honey, isn't this *cozy?*" Stephanie asked, looking to the fireplace then back to him, "and right in *front* of the fireplace! Man, we *scored.*"

"Yes, we did," Mike said, looking to . . . then staring into . . . the fireplace.

Staring into the fireplace kept him from having to look Stephanie directly in the eyes.

He loved her, *God* how he loved her, but he hadn't planned on, you know, being *around* right now.

This whole thing . . . the people . . . the darkness . . . the candlelit tables—the *life*—had a heavy coating of the surreal to it all. Had he had his way, the cops, coroner, ambulance, and a bunch of flashing lights would all be at their house right now . . . Stephanie a grieving mess on the floor beside him . . . or in some room with a hunky and supportive First Responder consoling her.

Yeah, this night really hadn't quite gone as planned.

Stephanie reached out to him, and he jumped—only ever so slightly—and thankfully, she hadn't noticed, in the dim lighting.

"So, tell me," she said playfully, staring intently at him, "what had you been working on when I interrupted you earlier? What was so secret you had to hide it from me?"

She was all smiles.

Mike looked to her.

Well, my love, it was a suicide piece, if you must know . . . triggered by a hammering depression and a barrel full of inferiority complexes all going straight to the head . . . .

Stephanie squeezed his hand.

"Oh . . . just a new short story, is all—"

"That's *great!*" she said.

"Yeah," was all he could muster.

"I'm so sorry that your work is not getting out there and selling like we thought it would," Stephanie began, "but it'll happen—I *know* it will." She again squeezed his hand—harder—multiple times, leaning into him for emphasis. "*It just takes time. We have each other . . . a great life . . . that's all we need.* And I can support us with my salary . . . ."

Support us.

It wasn't about *supporting* anything . . . it was about being *identified* . . . corroborated . . . *validated* as a driving force in the literary community. It was about vindicating that feeling that you were a *somebody* and that your words . . . your thoughts . . . your points-of-view *mattered.* Impacted humanity.

That you were . . . an author.

That you could *write.*

That others out there wanted to *read* what you wrote.

That's what it was all about.

Oh, and let's not forget about how your body is rebelling against you . . . your short-circuiting nervous system . . . your traitorous mind

. . . the happy and optimistic person you'd once been, now mired beneath a heavy, damp cloak of cognitive gloom and fucking *doom* . . . .

You wanna talk supportive?

Let's talk about supporting those shaking hands as that gun was angled and forced up into the bottom of your *chin*—

"Hey, what's a matter, honey?" Stephanie asked, her face changing to a look of concern. She reached out with her other hand to take his one hand into the both of hers.

"Nothing—nothing's the matter," he said, feigning eye contact.

"Are you thinking about your new story?"

Oh, yeah, that's it, honey . . . I'm definitely thinking about my new story . . . .

Their server wove in-between the tables and slammed to a stop beside them, all young and peppy.

"Welcome to Luigi's! Have you been here before?" the server asked. Stephanie and Mike answered "yes," whereupon their server congratulated them as if they'd won the lottery. Mike and Stephanie then listened to their specials, placed their orders, and their server energetically departed.

Mike looked back to Stephanie.

"Stephanie . . . ," he said.

I'm supposed to be dead. *Did you know that? A lifeless husk on the floor behind my desk, a nasty hole blown clean through my skull. I'm not supposed to be* here . . . .

Mike inhaled deeply and paused.

Was he really going to go there? Go through with telling her the dark truth?

"I . . . well," he began, "this night really hadn't turned out like I'd planned—"

"Really?" Why not? We'd talked about doing this—"

"That's not what I mean . . . that thing I was working on when you came into my office—"

"Oh, I know," Stephanie said, giving his hands a quick pat. "I'm *sorry!* I always interrupt you when you're writing! I know how that throws you off. I'm so sorry! I won't do that anymore!"

No . . . you won't—you'll keep interrupting . . . that's what non-writing spouses do—well, unless I kill myself . . . .

"It's not—quite—that. But it is about my writing. I . . . I don't know. I don't think I'm a good writer."

"What? You are *too!* What about that love story you wrote just a couple weeks ago! You had me in *tears.*"

"That's because you're my wife . . . you're supposed to be in

(*draw!*)

"tears—I mean . . . *supportive*—"

"Well, yeah! But that story was more than that! It was tragic! *Heartbreaking!* Have you heard back from anyone on it?"

Mike shook his head and looked away. Thought he'd heard whispers directly behind him. "No . . . no, I haven't."

"Well, you will!"

Mike grimaced, did a quick check behind him. Whispers gone. Or had never been there in the first place . . . .

"Honey," Stephanie continued, "you're a great writer. I haven't told you this, but I've shown your writing to my best friends, and they all *love* your work! They all say you're going to hit it big—be famous!"

"Well, that might be, but the people who count haven't taken any of my work."

"People who *count?* Honey, these are your *readers*, I'm talking about here! Who—once your stupid publishers realize the errors of their ways and publish your stuff—will be sending it out to exactly the people who are *already* loving your work!"

"Maybe . . . maybe not . . . ."

"Honey . . . why are you being this way? This is so unlike you. What's wrong?"

Is it? Is it really? Do you really know the real me?

Mike looked directly into her eyes this time. Unblinkingly.

It's not me, honey, not my soul . . . that interior really-me Me. No, it's my physical body and mind . . . they're the culprits! For some ungodly reason they're revolting and mutinying. I've never told you that I've been suffering from a mind-numbing depression for almost a year, now. Yeah. Depression. A year. I quit my—well paying, I might add—job . . . can't sell a damned thing . . . my agent deserts me—yeah, you didn't know about that, either—and I'm not contributing one cent to our household. So, yeah, I'm feeling on top of the world right now, baby, on top of the fucking world!

"Okay, and here are your salads," the server said, again appearing energetically from the darkened interior. She set them down before the two of them and just as quickly departed.

"What's really going on?" Stephanie asked.

Mike stared down at their salads.

"I . . . I just feel like a failure, if you want to know the truth of it."

"A failure? You are *not* a failure," she said, just a little too loudly, when she caught herself and lowered her voice. "Don't you *ever* think that!" she said, lower in tone, but heavy with emotion. *"My man is not a failure!* He is a loving, thoughtful, hardworking man who is doing his best to realize his dream. Help create our wonderful future together. Dreams rarely happen immediately. They take time . . . hard work. Perseverance. *Guts.*"

"Do you—"

The lights flickered and the entire restaurant went totally dark . . . but in that flicker Mike swore he'd seen a handful of people sitting and standing and staring directly at *him*. Quietly and intensely—maybe even a little angrily—*stares*. All directly at *him*. Their faces . . . not quite "right."

He blinked.

The lights came back on.

Mike felt his emotions—his anger—flare.

"Do you really want to know what I was working on when you walked in on me this afternoon? Do you?"

Mike shook from the adrenalin suddenly coursing through his body.

Stephanie looked intensely at Mike. Her eyes were wide . . . wide . . . and afraid.

She sat back in her seat.

"I'll tell you *exactly* what I was working on—"

The entire restaurant again went black.

Except for the fireplace . . . the table candles . . . and one Christmas wreath at the far end of the restaurant, all the lights had gone out and stayed out.

And it was dark.

Mike sat there staring at Stephanie, his mouth open and ready to launch his assault.

"Stephanie?" Mike asked, staring at her. He waved a hand before her, but she didn't move, didn't flinch. He looked at all the others around him . . . now all shadows at shadow tables in the utter blackness. All conversation had stopped.

All was silent.

He looked to the fire.

Paused in mid-flame.

The table candles were also all lit-but-paused—all except for theirs. Theirs had gone out.

Nobody moved.

Mike stared into the fire.

Wow.

He again heard a multitude of faint whispers . . . felt encircled by some seriously strange energy . . . .

Maybe he'd died of a heart attack and this was the afterlife . . . .

"Hello, Michael."

Mike snapped his head around.

No way. He knew . . . *knew* that voice . . . from years . . . *relationships*

. . . ago—

"*Caroline?*"

Mike stared at her. She was the only girl he'd dated who'd ever called him "Michael."

Caroline stood away from the table, a darker shadow against the restaurant's interior blackness. She remained still. Remained hidden.

"I hear you're having problems," Caroline said. She moved forward enough for Mike to see her face. Only her face. Curiously the rest of her form was not . . . *exactly* . . . visible . . . but her face . . . her long-ago, beautiful and brooding face, framed by her long, dark hair . . . emerged from the darkness.

"What—how . . . *how can you* be *here?*" Mike turned in his chair toward her to better take her in.

"Why are you questioning your worth?" Caroline asked. "You're a good person. You're just going through some rough times. We all do. You're not perfect, but who is?"

"How do you know this? How could you *possib*—"

"You know . . . when I was at my lowest . . . I always thought of you. *You.* How *you* were such a beautiful person. A loving person. How *you* loved me . . . always thought the best of me. We'd been good together—"

"You left me."

"I did. I know."

"Why'd you leave?"

"Oh," she said, sighing, "all the usual reasons a drug addict like me does those kinds of thing—"

"*You were a drug addict?*"

"I was."

"I never knew."

"No, you didn't. I hid it from you. I was good at it. Even more . . . I tried to clean myself up. And for a while . . . a small while . . . I managed to do so. But my scene was not about the drugs so much as *me*. The drugs were just a mechanism to carry out my inner dilemmas."

"What are you talking about?"

"I hated myself. I didn't know why at the time . . . but I did. And for a while . . . when you and I were together . . . the magic worked. But the problem was I was masking my pain with you. And when the magic wore off . . . I was left with myself. Again. You can never escape from yourself. That night we'd broken up? I'd cheated on you . . . went back to my old ways. I'm so sorry, Michael, so very, *very* sorry."

"Wow. Caroline . . . if I'd kno—"

"You'd have done what? Been more sweet? More kind? More

loving? More *there?* There was nothing more *you* could have done for me. *Nothing.* You'd already done all you could by just being who you were. The beautiful person you were—still *are.*"

"Why are you telling me this? Where have you been?"

"Around.

"But I always wanted to tell you something . . . one of the many somethings I'd always found cute and amusing about you. When we lived together. I liked how you—somehow—always managed to forget your underwear when you grabbed your pajamas and underwear for your shower before bed. *That always endeared you to me!* Showed your cute, human—flawed—self. How adorably imperfect you were, as much as you always tried to be the perfect boyfriend. And I always loved how you laughed at yourself when you'd discover your mistake. When you'd leave for the shower, I'd always peek into the bedroom to see if your underwear was still sitting on the dresser and it always was. Then I'd lean up against the bedroom doorway, smiling to myself, and just wait for your self-deprecating chuckle. That was something I so loved about you—how you just never took yourself too seriously. Even when you were trying to be perfect. I wanted to be more like you.

"Do you still do that? Forget your underwear when you take your shower?"

Mike chuckled. "Yeah, I do."

"Good."

"But you had to know that, already."

Caroline smiled. "I do. It's hard to explain, but there's some weird 'thing' about asking it in that way that isn't quite the same as just coming out and telling you I knew about it.

"Look, Michael, you're having some psychological issues that are causing your physical issues that will correct themselves . . . *if* you take the right actions. Don't end up like me . . . take the right turn . . . not the *left*—

"But—"

"*Live* your life, Michael, don't throw it away."

"Caroline—"

"*I love you*, Michael. I always will . . . ."

Caroline retreated back into the darkness.

"What the *hell?*"

Mike looked to Stephanie . . . still seated before him. Still frozen. Looked to the others around him. All still similarly frozen. The fire was still paused to his left. The table candles still lit-but-paused on all the other tables but theirs.

Caroline.

Yes, he remembered her. He'd loved her. Man, that had been some twenty-thirty years ago! But she looked as he'd last remembered her.

And what *had* happened to her? He knew something had . . . and not so nicely . . . had heard something years later, from a mutual friend. Something terrible . . . *man*, he hadn't thought of her in *years*. Some friends . . . what had they told him . . . oh shit—she'd . . . she'd goddammed *overdo*—

"Don't do it, Mike."

This voice was harsh. Cold. Contemptuous.

A shadow at the next table turned to him. It was the guy of the couple sitting there.

"Excuse me?"

"Listen to Caroline. *Live* your life. Things are not as bad as they seem. Your life is nothing like the others out there . . . in fact, it shouldn't even be compared to anyone else's."

"Who are you?"

"What difference does it make who I am? Just listen. My wife and I have been married almost forty years, and in those forty years I've had numerous affairs, made countless illegal business decisions, and continue to be as unfaithful and criminal as ever. If my wife'd taken her own life that would have been no skin off my nose. But I'll never divorce her—and actually don't have to now—because I'm a public figure who needs to put on airs, but also because I relish feeling powerful over her. Over everyone. It gets me high. Drugs? Fuck drugs. It's power that's the ultimate high. Manipulating people. *Governments.* And she knows nothing—well, I should correct that . . . *now* she knows—has had her own flings—she never took an outside job, but raised our five kids, who are all powerful, successful businessmen and women . . . and they're all—every last one of them—*just like me.*"

"Jesus," Mike said. "And you're proud of this?"

"If anyone ever needed to take their own life . . . *Michael . . . ,*" he said, mockingly, "it'd be me. I'm evil, extremely wealthy, I'm—"

"Then why are you eating here?"

"I love the food. The manicotti."

Mike grimaced.

"You have no need to take your own life. You, my friend, are one of the few people I've been around who I'd actually call a 'saint' . . . though you do have your own minor issues, like being a fucking pussy."

"Who the hell are you? We know each other?"

"We do not. But have, strangely, crossed paths now and then over the years. Nothing to write home about. You recently held the door open for me at an airport.

"You're not perfect, mind you, but you've lived a magnificent life. So your fiction isn't selling—what of it?—you've got a great life, a wonderful wife, and you're able to live doing what you both want to do . . . living *together* . . . not some separate covert, fucked-up lives like my wife and me."

"Why are you, of all people, telling me this?"

"Not really sure. But it's something about being *here*—in this '*now.*' And my wife's going to blow my brains out tonight, after we get home. She's finally grown a pair and is taking action—and that I can actually get behind. About time. Unlike *you*—"

"Wait a minute—*is going to?*"

"Wake up, for chrissakes, will you? Man, where is that guy you used to be? Can't you see you're in a nonTime 'space' right now? There *is* no Time . . . so, in those terms, everything that has or will ever happen has *already* happened. It's all about the moment. You're just too caught up in your own misery to get past all your emotional bullshit.

"Besides . . . perhaps I'm also telling you this because it's something another part of me—another me?—imagines *I* might have been . . . were I not so fucked up—"

The man paused . . . stared off into dark space for more than a moment, and Mike began to think his little tirade might actually be over. He began to turn away . . .

"But, hey," the shadow man continued, "I do like how you flirt with other women."

"I do not!"

"Oh, knock it off, Mike. We both know you do. You've developed such low self-esteem you're looking for any kind of validation from wherever you can get it. And you still have your looks. Since you'd left that job where you were more of a man and took control and got things done, you've shed all your confidence and power and become a real fucking pussy. It's disgraceful to who you used to be. You don't admit it to yourself, but you no longer feel like a 'man of the house,' and I don't mean that in an Old Testament way—I mean you no longer look at yourself *as* a man. More as a *child* to your *wife*. Hell, your wife is more of a man than you are right now. She's the sole provider. As open-minded as you are, a part of you still looks at this as 'man's work.' Being who I am, I don't even look at life that way. I *love* powerful women. Those are the women I fuck. I love it when these icons of power come so totally undone because of something *I'm* doing to them. Key word: *to* them. Not *with* them. They're doing the same to me, of course, but

I always come out on top. Because . . . it's . . . all . . . about . . . *me. My* power . . . *my* control. But I love how they think and try to outdo me. Respect that. Anyway, to your pussy way of thinking, you don't provide *anything.* You just take up space. Write words that go nowhere. Even your sex life fucking sucks, because you can't get out of your fucking head, can't stop watching yourself from afar, from the *outside* . . . so you fuck in wet dreams and shower masturbations—"

"*Hey*—"

"'*Hey*' what? You gonna fucking kick my ass?"

Mike looked away.

"Yeah, thought so. Go take a fucking shower."

The man turned back to his shadow of a wife.

Mike jerked as he heard a distant but powerfully faraway gunshot and saw the shadow-man who'd just been talking to him also jerk . . . and more "shadow" blown out the back of his head. But he remained upright.

"*Hey, Mike—may I call you 'Mike'?*"

Another face emerged from the darkness, this time from behind Stephanie. The man came up and stood directly behind her.

"Who are you?"

"I'm a homeless guy you once helped out in San Francisco."

"Really?"

"Yes. I was pushing a shopping cart I'd taken from a supermarket and filled it with all my stuff . . . including some things I'd stolen from others. Anyway, I'd just crossed this street in downtown, but had been having problems getting the shopping cart up and over the curb. You helped me out by lifting up the shopping cart onto the sidewalk. I'd never thanked you. I was too embarrassed. But, deep down, I was amazed that you'd actually helped me out, so . . . *thank you.*"

"You're welcome."

The man nodded.

"What that last guy just told you . . . ignore the bullshit . . . but take in the intent."

"Excuse me?"

The man placed a hand down on Stephanie's right shoulder. Mike oddly felt no umbrage at this.

"Look," the man continued, "My life sucked. I'd been beaten up, raped, ravaged by disease, and did my own share of raping and stealing. I was eventually knifed by a guy for my jacket one cold night. My life was mine, and I owned it—*now*, anyways. It was not a good life. But when I see someone like you, I just can't stand idly by. *You* have a great life. A beautiful and loving wife, here," he said, gently tapping

Stephanie's shoulder, "you're creative . . . write fun stories—and I love your stories, by the way—and you're *not* a pussy, as that guy so callously put it. You're being imaginative and creative. Yes, you have some issues, but they're brought on by your own feelings of self-worth. About wanting to be somewhere where you feel you're not. All that can be corrected. You still have time. Your depression is not permanent . . . it's not like others out there who grow up depressed. You're just despondent about the direction your life has taken . . . that you're not where you feel you should be at this stage of your life. You need to take a step backward and re-evaluate, my friend . . . look at all the good that you've done . . . *do* for others . . . ."

Mike fell forward over the table and threw his head into his hands.

Felt the tears come.

Pussy tears, was his first thought, then an image of Caroline filled his head, complete with her emotion and love for him, and he wiped away that thought.

Stephanie!

He really had had a great life. He couldn't argue that, now that it was put to him in this way. He wasn't getting shot at (short of pulling the trigger himself), had a great wife, home, enough money and means to support themselves. He didn't want to leave her. It was never about *leaving* her.

Love.

His wife and he had plenty of *love*.

He looked up.

The man . . . was gone . . . but his wife . . . she still stared—unflinchingly—at him. The entire place . . . remained frozen.

Black.

Mike heard a multitude of additional whispers continuing to come at him from everywhere.

No. No more. He got the point.

A dark arm came out of the darkness and lit their table's candle.

Mike turned to see from where the arm had come—

" . . . *what were you working on?*" Stephanie said, looking intently to Mike. "Whatever it is, I'm sure it's a great and beautiful story, because everything you do *is* beautiful to me—and I really want you to *know* this."

Stephanie stared intently at him.

She reached out and grabbed Mike's hand in both of hers. Way in the back of the restaurant, behind Stephanie, Mike noticed a woman sitting by herself ramrod straight, the glow of her table candle barely illuminating her as she just stared straight ahead into the wall before her.

"I love you so much, Michael, and I *love* our life. There's nothing you could ever do that would ever make me think any less of you."

Mike stared at Stephanie.

"What did you just say?"

"What do you mean?"

What did you just call me? You called me *'Michael'*—you never call me that."

"I did? Well, whatever I said, I'll always love you and never think any less of you for any reason. *You're the love of my life* . . . I never want to be without you. Please don't think of yourself as a failure . . . because that means *I'm* a failure—that our *relationship*, our *love*—is a failure. And I don't believe that. I won't allow that belief."

Tears welled up in Mike's eyes.

"Now, what were you 'really' working on when I interrupted you?" Stephanie asked, softly, smiling and lovingly patting his hand.

Mike took her hand up into his, and smiled a huge, loving smile of his own.

"A wonderful love story about our life together."

Tears poured out of his eyes.

The dark-haired woman in the far back slowly turned and looked directly at Mike. Her beautiful and brooding face materialized out of the darkness.

And she smiled.

Broken Windows

1997, 2016

1

We drove the snow-swept gravel road that wound painfully between endless fields and used to lead to only one place of importance to me.

Home.

When I was eight, it was home. When I was eight, it was mother and father and sister to me.

When I was eight.

Before the divorce, before the schism. Before my dad's death from cirrhosis. Before my mom's remarrying . . . and subsequent loss . . . of Walden.

Before.

I never used to miss Fowler. Fowler, Kansas. Much. It was a place of mixed memories, mixed emotions. How do I love a man who loved me and took me flying every chance he had, yet left my mother for another woman—and the bottle? How do I love a father who never once came to see us after we left, though I'd come to find out he'd always kept our pictures in his wallet? Whose abandoned house lay like a spent whore, a day after war, beer cans and memories littering every inch of floor?

2

I had to come for several reasons, but in the end the reason I came was because of an uncle. My uncle Lon, on my mother's side. He'd died in his sleep a little over a week ago after living to the age of 82. He was also the one who'd helped raise us between fathers. But he was much more than that. He was *there*. Even though he might have been states away, he was always there. Whenever anyone needed him. The one who drove out to our Fowler farm that terrible night and took us west to Colorado. The one who took us to out-of-the-way diners and treated my sister and me like adult children. The one who took us fishing. The one who helped seal our sanity in a world gone crazy with divorce and distance. Don't get me wrong, we were no angels—I was no angel—but he didn't care. He was there for me. There for all of us, and when he died, we were there for him. We brought his remains from Idaho to Kansas, the lot of us: my mother, my husband, my kids, my sister and her family. Eleven-hundred miles. Where we live in Colorado was four-hundred miles from Fowler. A long way to go when you're headed to leave a loved one in the cold earth . . . but precious few if you're to *see* one you were supposed to have loved.

I thought.

Four-hundred miles.

Why hadn't my dad ever come to see us?

So I came to Fowler for Uncle Lon—and a couple other reasons I hadn't revealed to my husband. Until we pulled up to the old farm . . . until I rummaged through his old bedroom and found a picture of him amid all the trash and destruction and desecration . . . until then I was never truly certain my daddy had died.

3

My sister never knew him like I knew him. We had two more between her and I, but they'd both died. She was too young to remember the *good* things our father'd done—or maybe I'm just too nostalgic on him. Yes, he drank a lot. Yes, he never came to see us after the divorce, but he also was a gifted musician and a skilled pilot. A hardscrabble farmer. A man. And what does that mean? Does that make him perfect? Does that mean he was all bad? It means that he was, as are the rest of us, trying to make it through life the best he could. That we all have flaws, some worse than others, but we are not people of black and white. We are people of much gray, people who make mistakes, some of which carry a bit more weight than others. If I am not so perfect (if there even is such a thing), how can I expect that of others?

Or maybe that is why it is expected of others.

I can't take inventory of the world. Only of myself. My dad, Samuel was his name, had his problems, but he loved me . . . us. I remember him taking me up in his plane—that Piper Super Cub (it wasn't just a *Piper* Cub, he used to say, it was a Piper *Super* Cub)—every chance he'd get, and that was a lot. He used to crop dust fields, ferry skydivers, and fly just for the pure joy of it. He was as at ease in the air as birds are, and that was where I gained my own fondness of flight. His first flight was at 16 years of age, and he flew until his death in 1996. I often wonder what his last thoughts were . . . and had I been there, I probably would have known them.

4

Everything looked fine from a distance.

Then I saw the windows.

If the eyes are the windows to the soul . . . are windows the eyes to *a home?*

My husband, George, and I pulled to a stop at the old farm, and though I expected the place to be—in all probability—demolished, I was not emotionally prepared for what we encountered. I remembered a place of refuge, of my grandmother washing my hair in the kitchen sink as I had lain across the kitchen counter. Of a barn full of cattle in the winter, and a coop full of chickens year-round. My dad's *plane* . . . .

But what we found were decrepit and destroyed outbuildings. The house, my *home*, had a massive hole in the roof. All the windows were broken and the doors gone. The old barn's roof had also collapsed, and the coop, its feathered life and strength-of-structure gone. The old windmill was still there, though . . . lifeless and sad. Alongside a nearby outbuilding was the yellow, dented, and dismembered fuselage of the Super Cub. We entered the house, my husband and I, and it was colder than the wicked Kansas winds that blew through it. Books and papers, furniture and clothes—trash—everywhere. Like a twister had blown through. Trash and memories intermixed.

Beer cans and liquor bottles. Everywhere. How appropriate. Just inside the door was an old yearbook, from (of all people) my dad's remarried-wife. Sitting on a coffee table like a Bible or picture book at somebody's home. How sacrilegious, I thought. From *her*. In *our* place.

In the kitchen, all over the floor and the counter across which I used to lay as Grandma washed my hair . . . broken glass, trash, papers, more beer cans and bottles. Clothes. Books, utensils. You name it.

Memories.

(. . . *windows* . . .)

We had to watch where we put our feet for fear of landing on broken glass, wood, or even nails. We waded ever deeper, and I was at once anticipatory and saddened by what I saw—old music books from which I used to play! Even the violin I'd played! My old notebooks! Toys . . . clothes *I* wore—clothes my *dad* wore!

My entire life had been raped.

The window by which I used to play my violin! The bathroom! My dad's room.

5

My dad's room.

My *parents'* room.

Where he and my mom . . . for better-and-worse . . . turned into worse-and-worse.

Had he cheated on her while married?

Had he cheated on his newer wife?

We'll never know (or had I forgotten?). Mom would never talk. Never has. Dad's dead. Woman he took up with is probably still kickin. She'll never talk.

I approached the bedroom door—

"Mags!"

Not my favorite term of endearment, but it's from my husband, and he lapses into its use now and then out of years-old habit. We've known each other a long time. I prefer "Margaret" or "Honey," or what my dad used to call me . . . .

He stood in the living room beneath the huge hole in the roof—my husband—six-foot-three, hands confidently on his hips, looking up, jacket partially zippered, his battered *World's Gym* baseball cap pushed back on his head. Steam pumped from his powerful lungs out through his mouth and nose into the cold air. Without taking his eyes off the hole, he said, "I'm gonna climb up and see what's in there." He then turned to look at me.

Isn't that just like a guy . . . always climbing around on things. That's how we came to have Leigh and Jacob.

"There's gotta be a ladder around here somewhere," George said, and shot out of the room in that energetic way of his. He's always in a hurry.

I turned and headed over to the hole. You could see straight up through the attic and out into the bright, beautiful Kansas sky . . . .

I felt colder than I had a right to.

I look around and don't see it. My second reason for coming here.

George came back carrying a beat-up aluminum ladder.

"This oughta do it," he said, noisily setting it up before me. "I'm kinda surprised it's even still here."

I winced. The noise was jarring . . . out-of-place . . . disrespectful even, to me, in this most hallowed of places.

"Have any ideas what might be up there?"

I shook my head. "Not a thing. This is the first time I've been back since we all

(*fled* . . .)

"left," I said.

George again looked up, readjusted his cap. "Probably some critter nests and such."

He briefly looked over to me as he hopped onto the ladder. I went over and stood on the bottom rung for him.

Was I like these kids when I was their age? The ones who'd broken into our home and made it their weekend party center? Would I have broken into an empty house at their age and partied and destroyed it like the ones who did so to my home?

We celebrated Christmas in this room.

Watched TV together.

My sister and I played with our dolls.

My dad, his violin.

We laughed and loved and hugged.

Until we didn't.

"Well," George called down, "it's a real mess up here!"

"What do you see?" I asked, looking up into the gaping maw of my childhood through my own breath.

"It's pretty much the same up here in terms of destruction . . . but there are a lot of boxes. Let me break into some and see."

I saw George move around, occasionally ducking out of view only to reappear. Then he crouched, and I again lost him.

"Huh," I heard him say.

"What?"

"Letters!" he said, shouting back down. "Tons and *tons* of them! From a . . . ," he began, "um, a 'Jefferson' to an 'Adeleide'?"

I paused before I answered.

"*Wow*," I said, under my breath. "That's my grandfather and grandmother on my dad's side," I said, shouting up to him.

"There're *boxes* of them!"

"He was the one who killed himself out in the fields out back here."

George looked back down to me. "Oh. I'm sorry, hon—"

"Well, that's the whisper, anyway . . . no one really talks about it. But that's what my Aunt Genevieve told me in confidence, years ago. With a gun."

George stared down at me for a few hard moments before wordlessly returning to his task.

"Wow, it looked like your grandfather really loved your grandmother—but he talks about being gone a lot."

"He sold farm equipment. He was gone a lot."

"Well, he really, really missed her."

"Is there anything else of interest up there?"

"Well, there are more boxes . . . of general household stuff . . . dishes, kitchenware, clothes, that kind of thing—oh, and some pictures, a lot, actually . . . ."

George showed some of them down through the hole, some framed, many not.

"Wow!" I said, surprised at my own reaction, "that's them—in that ornate frame! Hey, bring some of them down with the letters!"

So my husband made his way down with a couple boxes and pictures.

"There's a lot of bird poop, nests, and debris that flew in up there—it's quite a mess," George added once back on the living-room floor. "Kinda sad, actually, when you think about it."

When you think about it.

We immediately dove into the boxes and sat around for a bit, reading portions of the old, yellowed and weather-beaten letters . . . .

"Geez . . . listen to this," I said, "it's my grandmother writing back to my grandfather: '*I miss you so much, my love! Why can't you come home sooner? I miss you so much I can't stand it. I don't want to live without you! There are times when my heart fills with so much sorrow that I want to climb to the top of the windmill and fling myself off it!*'"

We both look at each other. I feel emotion welling up inside me.

I stomp it down.

I see George swallow hard.

"And Jefferson has this to say," he says, sorting through the letters he held off to the side in one of his hands, "'*I miss you so much that my body aches. I'll throw myself in front of a tractor if it means we'll never be together.*'"

I can't live like this. I ache for you, your touch . . . .'"

"Man," my husband says, "you just don't expect that kind of emotion from men of that era."

I go back into the letter I'm holding. Scan through a couple more of its pages.

Pages.

"Can you imagine how tough it must have been for my grandmother?" I say. "Alone, here—all these fields to attend to—the kids? Sure, the kids could help, but I wonder how old they all were and if they could really help with all the really hard farm work."

"I'm sure neighbors helped as they could," George says. "People out here usually do that kind of thing in times of need."

"Maybe. But they couldn't help her broken heart, could they?"

George just made a grimace and went back to the letters he held before him.

"Why don't we take these with us. Were there a lot more up there?" I asked.

"Yeah, lots of boxes, but I didn't go through all of them."

"Well, let's take these . . . could you go back up and see if there's another box or two we could grab . . . and maybe some dishes or something?"

"Sure—there are a couple."

So we set about to grabbing more boxes from our open-air attic.

When George had gotten down the last of what we could take with us, I looked at my watch. It was getting late. Later than I'd thought, actually. Time warps in places like these. I looked outside. It was quickly getting darker . . . orange-and-red twilight fast approaching . . . shadows

(shadows)

growing . . . .

"We should probably get going, since I told my Aunt Penelope we'd meet them all for dinner," I said.

"Okay, let me get these into the trunk." George stood up with the fragments of my family in his

(powerful . . .)

arms.

I looked at George like I'd never looked at him before.

He travels for his work. But we call every night. We've never really been apart for more than a couple weeks since we've been married. But we've never not talked to each other for more than a day.

Would I jump off a windmill for him?

Would he throw himself in front of a tractor for me?

As I stand . . . I am again drawn to my parents' bedroom.

My parents' life was rough, my *dad's* parents' life was rough.

I get up and enter the bedroom . . . well, just stand inside the doorway.

I think about that night . . . the yelling . . . the tears . . . the

place still seems sacred to me, the bedroom, but it's just like the rest of the place. Shit everywhere. Bed upended and the room exploded wall to wall. No doubt this was (or still is) quite the Friday and Saturday night drink-and-fuck. The kids who tore this place apart know not what they do. They're just sowing their oats . . . not realizing the consequences of their actions . . . or caring. Hormones and freedom.

As I wade through debris and filth, a tiny pair of hands catches my eye, reaching up out of the wreckage.

Could it be?

I come closer.

It is! I can't believe it!

There, lying on the floor all covered in bird shit and garbage, is one of the things I came looking for. The one happy remnant from my childhood.

Like God, I reach down from above and pull the tiny, beseeching hand, lifting her from her sea of destruction.

(. . . *my father . . . oh, why couldn't I have . . .*)

Her baby

(*blue!*)

blue eyes. Her blonde hair. Her hair is smeared with more bird shit, but she still wears her pink tights (bunched low about her legs) and pink-and-yellow striped top, though soiled and stained.

It is her . . . my beloved Tippee Toes doll!

She was my favorite doll. Next to my sister, my closest confidant. I told her all my secrets—even some (I'm embarrassed to admit) I'd never even told my sister. To this day. And here she was. I looked around for her plastic blue-and-yellow tricycle. Amazingly, it was right next to her—and in one piece. I looked to Tippee Toes, now safely back in my possession. We'd

(*yelling*)

(*screaming*)

(*gunshots*)

fled so suddenly that one terrible night I'd never had a chance to grab her. And I'd never seen her in the couple of deliveries of our stuff over the years sent from my father.

As I'd never forgotten my dad, I'd never forgotten her.

An involuntary smile graced my face and I pulled up her tights and smoothed out her blouse. Brushed off what loose debris I could.

"*We are together again, my friend,*" I tell her, whispering.

I grab her trike, afraid it's a mirage and I want to get it before it disappears. I find a dirty shirt and use it to continue to wipe away as much filth from the two of them as I can. Then I carefully . . . thoughtfully . . . take them with me and place them both down at the entrance into the bedroom. We were so poor we couldn't afford dirt. Bartered for everything. Whatever paid, we took. I remember my parents shooting jack rabbits and tossing them into the back of our beat-up pick-up for money from the county or state or whatever, when all our farms had been overrun by the furry little propagators. We got paid handsomely for their ears. Tossed the rest out into the fields for the coyotes and wolves to feast upon. Yes, dirt poor didn't begin to describe us. Yet . . . somehow . . . one Christmas I'd found her under our meager tree. From Santa Claus, my dad and mom had said, smiles the size of Kansas across their faces. I still remember their beaming faces. Probably the only time they both smiled at the same time for the same reason, toward the end.

Yes, this was one of the reasons I wanted to return . . . and the irony is not lost upon me that she was in my dad's bedroom.

But I am far from

(*gunshots*)

done.

Smile erased from my face, I turned back around and reentered the bedroom. I adventure deeper into all the crap that is everywhere.

Then I see it. A picture of him amongst all the debris on the floor.

My heart leaps into my throat and I am simultaneously enraged at all that has been done to my home! That a picture of my *father* is among all this filth and obscenity that was once our *home!* Tippee Toes is one thing—she's just a doll, a toy—but this . . . this is my *father.* It's as if he were actually there, among all this shit, and it was not just some old picture of him. I see his beautiful blue eyes staring up at me and they spear my heart. He is drowning in a sea of disgusting rubbish in a place where once lived and breathed a small family of four. It was . . .

A place of refuge!

A place of love and hugs and dinners and smiles.

Children's laughter.

Parents' laughter.

Caring.

I am no god, but I pick up my father.

I really wish I could see my father one more time! I have so much to ask him!

But, no . . . not really. I don't really need "answers." What would be the point?

I just want to *see* him . . . *hold* him. Tell him I still love him.

I know . . . at one time . . . he loved my mom. They both loved each other and would have gladly flung themselves before farm equipment and off windmills for each other. I know this. *Remember* it. They *loved* each other. Once.

But something happened.

Like it did for his father . . . who ended up placing a barrel into his mouth.

Things happen. People change. Sometimes it's the damned chemicals in our brains that mess us up . . . sometimes we just fall out of love or do something stupid along the way. Some things are recoverable . . . and some things

Leave lots of brains and blood out in the fields.

I want . . . I *need* . . . to see my father one more time . . . to know that he *loved* me . . . truly *loved* me . . . to hear it . . . to *know* that the reason he never came over to see us—*me*—was not because he didn't *love* me . . . .

I close my eyes.

Daddy!

I wish for him more than anything in Heaven or Earth.

I can't stomp it down this time, and it explodes out of me like an unchecked geyser and I wail.

I want nothing more . . . *nothing* more than to see my father one last time—

Please, *God, just . . . one . . . more . . .* time . . . .

"Hey, co-pilot . . . ."

My eyes shoot open.

"How's my angel?" the voice says.

He says.

Him.

I'm frozen. I look up.

A shadow, well over six feet, is before me on the other side of the room.

My body's on fire . . . tingling so much it *burns* . . . .

I know that voice . . . *I know that voice!*

A voice I haven't heard since far too early in my life and for far longer than ever should be allowed. A voice I'll never forget. A voice that digs deep into me like no other—not even my dear husband's— will *ever* affect me like . . . .

My knees buckle.

I reach out for support to anything within reach, but miss and collapse to the floor.

"D-Daddy?"

"Yes, angel, it's me."

I feel the entirety of my life stuck in my throat. I can't breathe.

I begin to fall . . . fall into a deep, dark abyss that has suddenly opened up around me.

My father rushes to me . . . he—

He holds me up!

My father is holding *me! Actually* holding me up!

"Here," he says, helping me back to my feet, which I still can't seem to find, "let's sit over here," my *father* says (*my father!*) . . . bringing me over to that old wooden chair that always sat in the same corner it's still in. It's not overturned or smashed to pieces like everything else in this room—*and I mean everything else in this room.*

"Daddy? *How can this be?*"

"Do you feel better now, angel?" he asks, gently easing me onto the chair.

"Y-yes . . . *thank* you . . . ."

He stands back looking at me, hands on his hips—not in that cocky manner, but more matter-of-factly. He looks as I prefer to remember him . . . how I *always* remember him: young, wiry, strong, confident, the salt of the earth, the wind of the air. He has dirt and grit on his hands (even under his fingernails, I note) and clothes . . . farm clothes . . . coveralls and work boots. That dirty and battered *John Deere* cap casually canted on his head. That shit-eating grin. That shit-eating grin I always remember . . . .

"Daddy—how . . . *how is this possible?*"

"I'm so sorry, angel . . . I'd wanted better for you—*prayed* for better for you."

Then I say it—before what's ever happening goes away.

"Daddy? Daddy, I *love* you—"

I again break down.

"And I love *you*, angel! You've always been my co-pilot . . . even on

(*in* . . .)

the ground. You still are."

He kept his distance.

I did not.

I flew up and out of the chair and (Once again! It should *never* be so long ever again!) to my daddy. He caught me and

***

We were . . . up in his Piper Super Cub.

(It's not just a Cub . . . it's a Super Cub!)

A beautiful, near-cloudless day. I was eight years old.

I stared into the back of my father's head as he piloted the plane.

I *loved* him, I remembered thinking, loved him to *death* . . . .

He banked the plane and I looked out to the right. A flock of geese flying just below and ahead of us. He angled downward.

I knew what he was going to do.

Daddy leveled out, dropped the upper door window flap, and flew up alongside the geese. Wind now blasting me, I could see their eyes. Some looked over at us as they honked. I waved at them. Had a huge smile on my face. At first. As we got up alongside as close as he could without scaring them away, he briefly turned his head and cast a smile back to me from behind his aviator-framed shades. A grin. That shit-eating grin. I smiled back. Nervously. I really didn't like what he'd always do next.

He pulled out a gun.

A big, heavy one.

Then he quickly and smoothly aimed . . . and blew a goose out of the sky.

Like he was target shooting at the county fair. He was good.

It dropped from the air in a hail of feathers and I tracked it as it dropped, as we continued on past it, and the rest of the geese peeled off to get the hell away from whatever had just happened.

I couldn't help but feel for the poor creature. It had thought it'd been safe up here, flying along with its fellow geese—maybe its own mate. Taking in the beautiful bright blue sky. Geese mate for life.

Then

(something happens . . .)

some huge yellow thing comes by and smacks the shit out of it. It literally doesn't know what hits it. It tries to fly, but it can't. Tries to breathe, but it can't. The only thing it can do . . . much to its horror and totally alien to a bird . . . is fall—fall . . . *plummet* . . . stop flying—out of the bright, beautiful sky. It's mate and family looking on . . . nothing they can do—not a damned thing they can do—as their father

(something happens . . .)

leaves them . . . never, ever to return.

If the goose is lucky, it'll die of cirrhosis before hitting the ground.

"*Daddy!*" I heard myself shout in my shrill eight-year-old voice.

Daddy indifferently waved a hand to me while checking the

airspace around him, looking for a place to put down and collect dinner. He closed the Super Cub's window flap.

"Oh," he said, "don't worry, angel—I didn't really kill it, just like I didn't really kill myself."

"K-*kill* yourself?" I echo.

"Yeah," he said, again briefly looking back to me, then casually informing me, "I took my own life from drinking too much . . . but, I'm not really dead."

I sat back in my seat. Watched as his head constantly, casually swiveled . . . checking, always checking . . . the airspace around us.

We landed in the field where the goose had slammed into the earth. Daddy hopped out and enthusiastically snatched up the bird, holding it upside-down by its feet. Brushed it off with his other hand. As he approached the plane, he brandished it toward me like a carnival prize, that huge grin on his face.

You know the one.

"*Dinner!*" he said, triumphantly, as he tossed it onto the floor at my feet and got back in. We taxied around, then

We're back in the house.

Our home.

Christmas. We all sat around the tree. All lit up and decorated. Our gifts opened and scattered. I fiercely hugged my brand new Tippee Toes doll. Daddy played the violin. Beer cans were by him and by his place on the couch. Mommy sat on the couch staring at my sister and me with all the love she could muster.

And Daddy . . . Daddy was off in another place . . . .

He always went there when he played the violin. His eyes would close and he would never speak . . . and many times—probably every time—I swore I saw tears coming from the corners of his eyes.

Daddy was the emotional one. Really emotional. I knew that. He didn't like to show it . . . always tried to hide it, but *I* knew it. I knew. I was always older than my years. Perceptive beyond my age. And when he drank . . . he couldn't hide it. His emotions. Sometimes . . . sometimes they really got out of hand . . . .

My sister and I watched Daddy.

Didn't know what to expect.

I began to cry, but quickly turned my head and brushed away my tears.

In many ways I am very much like my daddy.

Then he abruptly stopped playing and got up off the couch and scooped my sister and me up into his

(powerful)

arms. He was openly sobbing . . . but never said a word. Mommy even got up off the couch and

I was in the barn. The large one way out back. Without its roof anymore.

I don't remember why I was here . . . but I was a little older. It was almost dark. I heard a commotion in the barn. Followed the noise . . . .

Daddy. I heard him upset beer cans and bottles as he moved about in the darkness.

He wasn't alone.

The other voice wasn't Mommy's.

She was standing right beside me. But I wasn't there. She's looking in . . . through a broken window. The panes are still in place, but three of the four have razor-sharp in-place cracks. Mommy held a gun. The same one used on that goose.

Without looking to what she did, she thumbed back the hammer.

Her face is like stone.

From her vantage . . . through her eyes . . . I only see shadows . . . but the shadows come together . . . more laughter-that-wasn't-Mommy's, more noise that was my father . . .

Suddenly Mommy isn't beside me anymore . . . she's inside. Gone to the other mommy. My Daddy.

Yelling. All kinds of it.

A shot. Three of them.

The other woman, naked,

(fled)

rushed out of the barn.

Something is thrown through the window Mommy had just been looking through. All the panes explode into a spray of glass I don't

(not this time)

shield myself from.

We're running, now, Mommy and I and my sister. To Uncle Lon. No Daddy.

Daddy had a slug in his leg. One in an arm. A black eye. A split lip. Bruised ribs.

The other slug was never found.

Daddy married the one that got away.

"*Why*, Daddy, *why* did you leave us? *Weren't we good enough?* Didn't you love us? *Mom?*"

We were back in my parents' bedroom. Amid all the present-day

Friday and Saturday night adolescence filth and destruction. I still clutched his picture. Daddy and I stood before each other.

"Angel . . . my co-pilot . . . I did terrible, terrible things to you and your mother . . . your sister. I did. I hadn't intended to, but I was messed up. The drinking . . . the life . . . none of which are adequate reasons, but reasons they *are*. I wish—I oh-so-very-*much* wish I could do things over—but I cannot . . . not in your lifetime. Not in what we'd already lived."

I'm shaking—dropped the picture—violently trembling . . . my fists balled and clenched and ready for a fight, the picture now at my feet . . . looking up at me. Tears ran down my face so hot I felt the room would ignite.

Dropped onto the picture. My father's face.

It looked as though the picture wept.

Daddy turned away

(Daddy, don't go!)

from me, and his shoulders trembled. They hunched over and shuddered and quaked and quivered.

The words *Where's my gun?* and *I am my father's son!* assailed my mind like hot lead from a barrel shoved into my mouth.

Daddy whipped around, openly crying. His own face was red and swollen and plain for me to see. There was no hiding from anything.

"I am so sorry for what I did to you! I am so sorry for all I did to your mother and our family!"

I exploded into a high-pitched and guttural scream that was equal parts anger and love.

My entire body convulsed!

I don't know what my hands did—they were no longer my own—but I couldn't think. My anger just took over. I continued to scream.

"I love you, angel, always have. Your sister. And as much as you don't believe it—your mother."

He again turned away, but threw his hands up in frustration as he paced the desecrated room.

I stopped screaming.

"I let things get away from me!

"I forgot what your mother meant to me! I got so caught up in the bottle . . . the life of the bottle . . . I couldn't think straight . . . and once—the *one* time I actually caught a glimpse of things . . . how they *should* be, *shouldn't* be . . . the *wrongs* I'd done . . . the *one* time—it was far, far too late."

All I could do was stand there and cry as I looked at my dead dad. My dead *and still dying* dad.

Why was he here?

Why was *I?*

Was it to pass additional judgement upon a man who'd already lived out his punishment and passed on? Lived his guilt . . . his pain . . . and died with it still heavy on his soul? Was it to accuse the dead of things already paid for? Already tortured with, not only in the afterlife, but in a life left behind?

I looked to my dad . . . really looked to him; not just to the surface image of the man I'd fictionalized, romanticized, *demonized* . . . but into his *soul* . . . for he did appear to still have one, as much as my mother might argue otherwise. I looked to the man who now looked a mere husk of how he'd first appeared to me.

Suddenly I felt drained. Drained, but . . .

Calm.

I went to my father.

I wrapped my arms around him and buried my face into his muscled shoulders.

"*Daddy,*" I said in a thick, hurting whisper, "I *forgive* you . . . *I* love *you.*"

I squeezed him with all my might!

"*I love you, too,*" my dad whispered back, and he clutched me powerfully in his embrace.

We held each other . . . crying into the other's shoulders.

"I don't want you to go!"

"I will never, ever leave you again."

"I am forever your angel, Daddy!"

"I am forever your co-pilot, angel!"

We fell to the floor sobbing and clutching each other, bawling uncontrollably. Crying and wailing and comforting each other's hot, exploding heads . . . .

I fell forward.

I stayed there, hunched over, sobbing into the only miraculously clean spot of the bedroom floor.

"Hon—*hon, are you okay?*"

George.

I bolt upright, still on my knees, but couldn't stop the tears. George shot to my side and immediately cupped me into his

(Daddy!)

arms.

I slowly *kind of* controlled my sobbing and came to my feet. Wiped eyes, which continued to weep.

"What happened? Good Lord, are you all right?"

I smiled and choked my life back down into my throat. *I still felt my father's arms around me.*

"Yes . . . yes, I'm fine. I think . . . for perhaps the first time . . . in a long time . . . I'm really, finally . . . *fine.*"

Overhead, I heard the sound of a Piper *Super* Cub.

Tail Gunner
2010, 2012

1

All chatter was ripped from his ears.

The airman's body slammed forward into the B-17's twisting and turning airframe.

An explosion.

Ungodly ripping sound.

Had grabbed for something—but it'd been knocked from his hands.

Wind howled and screamed. Stability and straight-and-level had given way to

Falling.

Ground-sky.

Ground-sky . . . .

Crazy spinning.

With some effort—his head feeling as if it had just gained a thousand pounds—the airman twisted it and watched as spent .50-cal machine-gun rounds, paper, and loose equipment were sucked out of the gaping hole behind him.

He turned his head back around and found himself looking

Down.

His stomach lurched, and the feeling reminded him of Coney Island roller coasters—or the *Wonder Wheel*—just as you rounded the top and were on the way

Down.

Ground-*sky!*

His body thrown forward, the airman shot his hands out to the frame of the

(*roller coaster*)

aft window before him.

Down . . .

Ground-sky!

Ground-sky!

Still going *down* . . . .

Opened his mouth to scream—but all expression had been brutally pulped out of him. Was buffeted by flak, exploding flak everywhere. All of his twenty-two years of life clenched up into his throat in one great, choking knot.

Body pressed into the Browning machine guns and tail window, he looked into flak-filled airspace as he plummeted past the rest of the formation for German soil. He couldn't breathe, only managing shallow, short, rapid gasps.

His eyes locked with the horrified eyes of the bombardier in the nose of another B-17 he just barely missed as he plunged past. Eyes he'd recognized. Eyes that'd shared cigarettes and stories and pictures of their girls the night before, with a dozen or more other pairs of eyes at a dimly lit bar counter.

His vision swam. Blurred. Vertigo scrambled his senses.

Falling.

Couldn't *breathe!*

Dropping out of the sky!

Plummeting!

Sunlight.

Sunlight traced a path where it shouldn't have been able to trace a path. Swept across the now-exposed deck that now ran between him and 23,000 feet of oblivion.

His body shuddered and convulsed against buffeting the separated empennage took on its heretical plunge earthward. A sound escaped him that didn't sound like anything he'd ever uttered during his entire short lifespan. Still couldn't see straight. Stared down the short metal tunnel where there should be—by all rights—the body of a B-17 and nine other guys. Pilots, bombardier, waist gunners—

Nothing.

Gone! All of it!

If he could just jump . . . free himself from this anchor that was dragging him down. Parachute into—

No parachute!

Along with all the paper, shells, and loose equipment, he'd watched with soul-sickening horror as his parachute had also flown out of that gaping hole. It had been knocked from his fumbling grasp after he'd been banged up against the bulkhead when the tail had separated from the fuselage.

A great weight pressed into him.

Unable to move.

Pinned!

This wasn't supposed to happen! Was only supposed to happen to *other* crews—Germans, not *his* crew—not *him*.

It was over. All over!

Screamed down, ever *down*, out of the bruised and battle-damaged sky.

Down . . .

Ground-sky . . .

Down!

Again slammed against the bulkhead. The .50 cals.

Only seconds ago he'd been operating dual M2 Browning machine guns. Yeah, it had all been a game. Target practice, they'd called it. Get them before they got you. But they hadn't been clay pigeons, had they? Towed targets? No, they'd been flesh and blood humans just like him. Also trying to get him before he got them.

Now he knew.

Knew what *they* knew.

What it felt like to be hit.

What it felt like to go *down*.

Ground-sky.

Ground-sky . . .

Wild, wicked, absolutely unhindered *tumbling*. Spinning and gyrating. End over end. No control.

Unable to breathe.

Unable to see straight. *Focus.*

Light.

A bright light.

Sunlight?

His folks . . . his girl . . . his sister.

He stared into the light.

What would it feel like to slam into scorched earth? Bombed-out buildings? Would he know it? The moment of impact? Would he feel the *hurt?*

What would it feel like to just blink out of existence? To one moment be alive and thinking and conscious and scared, and the next—

The light.
A hand emerged.
He grabbed it.

2

Noise . . . lots of screaming and yelling and howling and
Music?

"Ticket, please," the middle-aged gentleman in flannel shirt, jeans,
and work boots greeted, hand outstretched.

The airman looked down to his own hand. In its white-knuckled
death-grip it held a ticket stub. His entire arm and hand—his body—
were tensed and hurting and trembling. He wasn't breathing, his body
as if in the constricting grip of a giant, angry malevolence trying to
squeeze the life out of him.

"Ticket, please," the gentleman again asked, still reaching out.

The airman handed it over. As soon as he relinquished the ticket,
he inhaled long and deep. Collapsed toward the dirt and dust—when
the ticket taker caught him.

"Welcome to Coney Island!"

The airman looked up incredulously and out of breath. It hurt to
breathe.

"Where am I?"

"Coney Island."

"*Where?*" he again asked, swallowing hard and with great difficulty.
His body hung limply in the ticket taker's hold. He slowly got back on
his feet.

"Why, you're at Coney Island, young sir! The greatest amusement
park on Earth!"

"I . . . I don't feel right—"

The airman shook his head, then steadied himself; looked to his
attire. It wasn't much different than the ticket taker's.

"Where's . . . where's my jacket, my—"

He brought a hand to his head. No leather shearling cap. "I feel
like I fell . . . or am *still*—"

"Oh, you're quite all right, sir. Just come on in," the ticket taker
said. "Everything's *A-Okay!*" He winked.

The airman looked beyond the smiling gentleman.

"Wow . . . haven't been here since—"

"Forty-one. *Nineteen*-forty-one."

"Yeah . . . nineteen-forty-one," he echoed, still having difficulty swallowing and trying to catch his breath.

"We got all the rides! The *Cyclone*, *Shooting-the-Chutes*, *Flip Flop*, *Wonder Wheel*, the *Human Pool Table!* Come on in! *Enjoy!*" the greeter said. With a flourish of hands, he sidestepped to allow the airman entry.

"Place looks empty," the airman said.

"Private party."

The airman turned to the ticket taker. Just looked at him. His oddly smiling—calming—face.

"You might find some people you know," the ticket taker enunciated deliberately, motioning him in farther.

Calliope music, flashing lights. The smell of hotdogs, popcorn, and cotton candy filled the air—

Boom!

The airman spun around.

Boom! Boom!

Detonations exploded all around him.

Concussions.

Unnerving. Distant. *Behind* everything . . . .

The airman turned back around and

remembered sitting at a bar one day, talking to two kids, really, that's all they were. Kids in uniform. Nineteen-year-olds. Fires all hot and burning in their fervent, youthful eyes. Displayed not an ounce of fear. "*C'mon*," they'd goaded, all full of righteous hubris, "it's *fun!*" They'd been gunners, one a tail, the other a waist gunner.

"Fun." That's what they'd said . . . the word they'd used.

Fun.

"Like shootin' skeet, only it's *Germans!*" they'd proclaimed. "Godless, evil *Krauts*. Goddamned *Jerries*."

They'd needed bodies, they'd told him, anyone willing to fly. Bombers.

He knew why, he wasn't stupid. They were getting blown out of the sky.

That's why.

Yet he'd volunteered. Long wondered about those two.

Flexible Gunnery School. That had been his next stop, since he'd already been in the Army Air Corps.

Aim well. Shoot straight.

That had been their motto. Las Vegas in the summer. Six weeks. They had to be good or they'd be dead. It was that simple. They'd started with BB guns. With shotguns, worked their way up through stationary and mobile skeet shooting. Went from blasting away off the backs of moving flatbeds to towed targets from behind AT-6 aircraft, at Indian Springs. Turret training.

Stripping a .50 cal blindfolded.

Aircrew training.

Deployment.

Berlin. Kiel. Kassel.

Hanover. Eberhausen.

Regensburg . . . .

"Where am I, really?" the airman asked.

He sat atop the Ferris *Wonder Wheel*, just before the zenith of its travel. The ticket taker sat opposite him. Intently eyeballed him.

"I can't really be here. It doesn't feel right."

"Oh, you're here, all right," the ticket taker said in a voice far more subdued—concerned—than upon their first meeting. "This is real, I assure you a that, son."

The Ferris wheel moved up an increment . . . stopped.

"Last time I was here, I was with my family. Where are they?"

"Oh, they're still where they're at."

"Why aren't they here? Where's my—"

"Your girl? They're all still where they are. They haven't arrived. Yet."

"But they will?"

The ticket taker nodded, keeping his eyes intently focused on him. "In time."

"I used to love the view from up here."

"What's wrong with it, now?"

"It just doesn't . . . feel . . . right."

The wheel moved up another increment. They were now on top, wind caressing his face and whispering in his ears.

"It used to be fun," the airman said, growing antsy.

The ticket taker continued studying him.

"Where are those two guys? *You* know?" the airman asked, leaning a little over the side as he looked behind and

Down.

He quickly sat back in his seat.

"Oh, they're around. Someplace."

The airman nodded pensively. Couldn't sit still. Chatter . . . there was *chatter* in his head . . .

"*Three of 'em, one o'clock high—*"

"*Four planes, nine o'clock—*"

"*They're comin' around—*"

"*Got my sights on him—*"

"*I'm on him . . . come on, you sonofa—*"

Engine drone.

Buffeting.

The car began its descent, when the airman fumbled madly for something that wasn't there and grabbed the side of the car.

Hyperventilated.

Instantly coated in sweat.

"*Fighters at eleven o'clock, comin' around!*"

"*I got 'em! I got 'em!*"

"*Two Fighters—six o'clock up! Comin' in, divin' at ya!*"

Boom!

There was a sudden lurch and a much pronounced *bump*—and the wheel stopped in a harsh, downward jerk, sending the car wildly oscillating back and forth—

Boom!

The airman stopped breathing and white-knuckled the swinging car. He looked to the ticket taker in wide-eyed terror.

Boom! Boom!

The ticket taker gave him a soft, sympathetic look, then looked off into the distance.

Falling.

Down.

Ground-sky!

Always *down!*

The airman closed his eyes.

Continued hyperventilating.

Wind.

This is it!

Tumbling.

It!

Fifty-cal pressed into his back . . .

Boom! Boom!

No chute!

Gaping hole into a damaged sky still full of released bombs and bombers and flak and falling men . . . .

He opened reddened and tear-stained eyes and looked to the ticket taker.

"It's over, isn't it? For *me!* This is it! This is *it!*"

Continued hyperventilating.

The wheel advanced another position.

The ticket taker looked to him and smiled. Leaned forward and gently took a hand into his. Held it for a long moment.

"But you're *here*. Look at me. *Here*."

The airman's breathing slowed, but not completely.

Distant concussions . . . explosions . . . ground-sky . . . .

"But I'm also there, *too*, aren't I? Still falling—o-or *dead!* I don't understand all this—don't know how—but it's true, isn't it? *True*."

The ticket taker nodded.

"Why all of it? Why the *need* for any of it?"

The ticket taker said nothing.

The airman again swallowed. Wiped away tears with the backs of shaking wrists. Inhaled deeply.

They descended another position.

"It's so sad, you know," he said, finally slowing his breathing and clearing his throat.

"I know."

"That we do . . . all that. The loss. The . . . the—"

"Pain."

The airman looked out into the dark distance in silence. Tears streamed down his face. He did not wipe them.

"It *wasn't* fun, you know. Not any of it. Not at all. Not for me."

"I know."

The car advanced several more positions and came to a stop at ground level. After a moment, the ticket taker smiled and stepped out of the car.

The airman looked at the feet of the ticket taker. Listened and watched intently as his heels impacted the earth and ground and pressed into dirt.

"It's time, my friend," the ticket taker said.

The airman blinked. Nodded. "Yeah. Suppose it is."

"Nothing stays the same, son."

The airman stepped out of the car. The instant he touched soil there was a loud concussion, and his knees gave out. The ticket taker again came to his aid, but the airman waved him off. Straightened up.

"I'm fine—thank you."

Fought back tears.

The airman ran his hands through his short, dark hair; composed himself. Looked around. There were lots of lights, music, running rides . . . the smell of grilled food.

"They're around, here—somewhere? Those two?"

"Yup," the ticket taker said. "They all are."

"All of them? Even—"

"*Everyone's* here, my friend. Both sides."

The airman again stared off into the distance. Exhaled long and hard.

"So . . . what now? What's beyond there?" he asked, still looking off into the night.

The ticket taker chuckled softly. "There's no hurry. Walk around . . . take in the place. Enjoy a ride or two. Cotton candy. Meet up with some of your buddies . . . and others," the ticket taker said. "There's absolutely no hurry."

"And after that?"

"After that . . . we can talk. Some more. We have all the time in world. All we have, here, is time."

"Time."

The airman reached out, and the ticket taker took his hand. They shook in a firm, heartfelt shake that didn't let go.

"Thank you," the airman said, and

3

the tail section of the shattered B-17 oscillated and gyrated and spun end over end all the way down through 23,000 feet . . . until it landed in the bombed-out ruins of what used to be a German apartment building. The parachute-less tail gunner who'd been pinned inside had been far from alone, as he and the empennage impacted.

About the Author

F. P. (Frank) Dorchak writes gritty, realistic supernatural, metaphysical, and paranormal fiction. Frank is published in the U.S., Canada, and the Czech Republic with short stories, non-fiction articles, and his five novels, *Sleepwalkers*, *The Uninvited*, *ERO*, *Psychic*, and *Voice*. *Do The Dead Dream?* is his first short-story collection.

www.fpdorchak.com

**WAILING
LOON**